The Progeny of Angels

ZRSIOFOUR
KING OF THE MERS

Book 2

Barbara Dean

All characters in this publication are fictitious and any resemblance to real people, alive or dead, is purely coincidental.

First published in the United Kingdom in 2012
by Newpole Books

ISBN Hardback 978-0-9572470-1-7
ISBN Paperback 978-0-9572470-0-0

Produced by
The Choir Press, Gloucester

Contents

Prologue		3
Chapter 1	Lia Returns to the Causeway	9
Chapter 2	Haydes and Kiron	14
Chapter 3	Deron and Mariana Debarc-Major	19
Chapter 4	Dorri Perkins	24
Chapter 5	The Underground Sites – Code Name ESCAPE	28
Chapter 6	The Holocaust	36
Chapter 7	Unlocking the Code	39
Chapter 8	The Planetary Forces	47
Chapter 9	The Snowstorm	51
Chapter 10	The Gift of 'Enzyme Fire'	56
Chapter 11	Zrsiofour – King of the Mer People	58
Chapter 12	Mikell Lang	61
Chapter 13	Subterrania – The Mastermind Explorer	63
Chapter 14	The Challenges Begin	66
Chapter 15	Senithe – Custodian of Subterrania	71
Chapter 16	Odelia and Glashadou's Vigil	74
Chapter 17	The Longest Day	78
Chapter 18	Initiation by Fire	86
Chapter 19	Getting Started	94
Chapter 20	Master Raphiel	101
Chapter 21	The University of the Third Eye	105
Chapter 22	The Other-worlds	109
Chapter 23	The New Masters	121
Chapter 24	The City of Parables	126
Chapter 25	Capricorn – Queen of Winter	133
Chapter 26	Mary	142
Chapter 27	The Lightworkers	145

Chapter 28	Aquarius	149
Chapter 29	Uluru Mountain	155
Chapter 30	The Twelve Celestial Spirals	163
Chapter 31	The City of Five Pathways	170
Chapter 32	Madagascar – Makot	180
Chapter 33	The White Unicorn	184
Chapter 34	The Prophecy	188
Chapter 35	Belsize Creek	193
Chapter 36	The Beginning of the Final Days – Pisces	198
Chapter 37	The Crystalline Kingdom	206
Chapter 38	The Mer Infant	213
Chapter 39	The Healing	221
Chapter 40	Aries – Progeny of Mars	225
Chapter 41	The Assault on the Cradling	228
Chapter 42	The Void of Zero Energy	235
Chapter 43	Mikell Returns to Belsize Creek	239
Chapter 44	The Teachings of the Ancients	244
Chapter 45	The Invisible Cloak of Dictatorship	249
Chapter 46	The Chosen Ones	253
Chapter 47	The Tennessee Water Shed	257
Chapter 48	The Light of Hafnium – Taurus	263
Chapter 49	The Healing Mers – Gods of the Universe	270
Chapter 50	Taurus	275
Chapter 51	Rebecca	281
Chapter 52	Gemini	287
Chapter 53	Lazuli	293
Chapter 54	The Grand Master's Plan	299
Chapter 55	The Binary World	303
Chapter 56	Thomas	311
Chapter 57	The City of Boreal	315
Chapter 58	The Final Challenge	319
Chapter 59	Destiny – Ormus' Gift to the World	326

The tsunami that ends mankind's fifth civilisation will travel across the globe, taking all in its wake. There will be those who are swept along on the buoyancy of its joyful surge; there will be those who cough and splutter, clinging to hope as they desperately struggle to stay alive, and there will be those who lie beneath its mighty strength, stilled and lifeless within its power.

The Otom: may they be reawakened to the vision of their destiny to experience all there is to know.

Prologue

Throughout the world at the beginning of the twenty-first century, billions of people were becoming ill with a pathogenic illness that attacked the respiratory system. The disease gradually softened the ten anterior ribs and enlarged the capacity of the lungs. The change in the afflicted made breathing difficult and produced the same symptoms as chronic asthma. The illness was blamed on global warming and the consequent rise of atmospheric pollution, and the diseases carried by infected insects. Worldwide, medical research institutions struggled to find a cure for yet another life-threatening disease. In mankind's modern history, nothing of this nature was known to medical science.

The reactivation of ten molecules of deoxyribonucleic acid, DNA, had stimulated an unknown physical condition in man: an awakening of the genetic code inherent in the first organisms to exist within the Earth's oceans, genes that had lain dormant in man from the beginning of time. Many people had already died, their bodies unable to endure the transmutation, but for those who survived, it was to be their deliverance. These people were called the lightworkers – healers, philosophers: those that believed in the coming of a new age upon Earth, an age that was to begin after the destructive forces that were soon to be released upon the world. Within the laboured chest cavity of mankind, ten supple aquatic spines were growing, behind the redundant anterior thoracic ribs, to increase the lungs' capacity for inspiration. The new lung buds that were forming, which were mistaken for cancerous growths, were capable of filtering oxygen from water when necessary. Mankind was taking a step backward to its period of amphibiousness.

The lightworkers were preparing to adapt to a future life in the oceanic world of the Mers. They believed in the future events that their dreams brought them: a global holocaust and a journey to a world below the oceans, where they would begin a new life. Many moved away from the cities to live in coastal areas, believing this to be where the migration would take place. Those that remained inland took work that required diving skills, or skills in water sports, in order to acclimatise their changing bodies to long periods under water. Across the globe, the resettlement of thousands of families was seen as a good thing, a boost for the countries' economies, as house prices spiralled due to the demand for change.

A new way of life had opened up in Lia's country of origin, England, where major changes were taking place. Many British scientists and engineers living abroad had returned home to work on two British science projects: the Mars space travel project and a major farming development that they hoped would boost England's food supply for the burgeoning masses. The return of the scientists had been seen as a natural development, rather than a sign of serious shortages in the food chain. Most were disillusioned with working abroad, and, with a new government calling upon their skills, they had returned home.

Under these influences, Britain had divorced itself from Europe, which by then had become a self-elected sovereignty. With the government deciding to go it alone, Britain stood unaided, divorced from Europe, to do battle for her trading ground.

While these changes were causing unease among the British population, below the oceans another decision was causing misgivings among the oceanic people, the Mers. The Mers were to receive among them a nation of people towards whom they had deep misgivings. It was a matter of mistrust, concerning mankind's lack of respect for all things living, which the Mer race had seen much evidence of in the ocean world above them.

Under the Pacific Ocean, deep beneath the Marianas Trench, rose the gateway to the Mer world. Nearby, upon a vast plateau, stood the City of Memories, a city three hundred and sixty miles in diameter that had been lost to mankind in a time of his misrule. On the surrounding flatlands, acres of pyramid-shaped buildings stood inverted upon their apexes. These multi level pyramidal greenhouses, made of quartz crystal, were producing the food needed to support the lightworkers, the Otom. The multi-level rows of vegetation thrived in abundance, the colours, shape and textures created to encourage the human appetite. The vegetation was anchored in beds of crystal particles, which formed thousands of conical poles spiralling upward to the top of each inverted pyramid, while the point of each pyramid was anchored deep below the ocean bed. The buildings rose eerily from the seabed, their square, flat tops echoing the watery reflections of a high-rise metropolis beneath flood waters.

The design had been copied from one in progress on land worldwide, the CROP project. The CROP project's aim was to return millions of acres of agricultural land, on all continents, back to forestry, in order to reinstate the planet's natural climate. Future records would show that the radical changes within food production had come too late to stabilise the surface of the planet. The plan, however, had worked admirably below the oceans, where the Mers were using pyramidal farming to support the humans who were entering their world known as the one tribe of man, the Otom.

The Otom would have to embrace hardship from all sides to survive the changes in their way of living. They would need an unwavering faith in a future beyond the watery sanctuary that was to be their home for forty-five years. Changes to their diet would mean the absence of wheat, oats and similar grains that would not survive the future growing conditions below the Earth or upon land after the holocaust. The Otom would not be allowed to kill the ocean dwellers for a source of protein food. They were to live in peace among the Mers – a race of beings half-man and half-fish – and all ocean dwellers within the world's oceans.

The main source of protein for the Otom would be latvie, a vegetable-based food eaten by the Mers. Latvie was harvested from the tree roots of the vast ocean forests; it was a cone-shaped source of protein that had the taste and texture of red meat.

A few years before the holocaust, the weather patterns worldwide became uniformly tropical, as the ice masses of the North and South Poles thawed significantly. The result was heavy rainfalls that continued for weeks on end, regardless of the season. After that, severe gales would follow, combined with periods of extreme heat. By this nature, the oceans became warmer, and the new species of vegetation that would sustain the Otom flourished. The acres of inverted pyramids contained a humid atmospheric condition, which was kept constant by the volcanic magma that continually poured onto the ocean floor from the surrounding volcanic ridges.

The weather changes were catastrophic for all species on land, and many appeared lost to the Earth forever. As heavy rain poured from the heavens year after year, to be followed by extreme heat, the world's food crops dwindled and the Earth's forests began to rot, making atmospheric conditions worse. The crops failed on most continents at the same time, causing another hardship to overwhelm mankind.

Next to assail mankind was a plague of insects, similar to woodworm but able to survive in any climate. They began to breed rapidly on all continents. The microscopic insects invaded all inert wood, including the building timber used in towns and cities across all continents. Under these conditions, the world's civilisations began to deteriorate rapidly.

These were not the only problems that troubled mankind's daily life. Governments worldwide continued to suppress the public with fast-track legislation that fuelled the growing instability, especially among the young. Throughout the world morality had become tribal, with aggression towards outsiders malevolent and ever increasing. Territorial fighting and fatal wounding were an everyday occurrence. In England, a social war was raging out of control, as violent mobs turned on frightened law-abiding communities to kill and steal from them in order to survive. For the first time in decades, neighbours stood by each other against rebellious mobs of all ages that smashed their way into homes to steal and maim. Street lookouts were posted to raise the alarm, and everyone – men, women and children – came out to protect a home under attack. England had become a nation of small communities that did not welcome strangers. Racism and resentment vanished, as good neighbours and trusted friends were accepted regardless of colour or creed.

The news most days included the Middle East war. Iran, with the help of her ally, Russia, had overthrown the democratic government in Iraq, forcing the long-standing British and American forces out. The British government publicly avoided the gravity of the situation, as they prepared to put into action their covert plan, code name ESCAPE.

Beneath all major cities and surrounding open land, secret underground sites were ready, sites which had been built to withstand an atomic war. Places were surreptitiously allocated to those selected to survive: the influential, high-ranking, and those most needed for the survival of mankind. Access to these zones was simply, but cleverly, concealed beneath the sprawling concrete jungles of stations, walkways, large shopping malls, underground car parks, and airports – anywhere the government had allowed large areas of land to be covered, areas where the presence of people with large amounts of shopping or holiday luggage would be usual.

Within the national network of public walkways were sign-coded corridors that could be entered by any person recognised by their DNA imaging.

The corridors' strangely subdued lighting did not attract passers-by but, in fact, deterred them from approaching. Because of this, those entering the corridors could disappear undetected, which would enable any evacuation to proceed like clockwork. The nation's public had no idea that the places built for their recreation had such a sinister secondary purpose. Those of the human race who were to be secretly evacuated beneath the unseeing public eye were the privileged few that would survive, while ninety percent of the world's population was to perish.

The wealthiest and most influential had gathered for decades beneath the banner of 'world humanity', while, in truth, they were brought together to discuss the plan for a minority of mankind to survive World War Three. Meanwhile, the world's public and lesser statesmen believed they were discussing the guiding principles for world food production, peace, and the survival of mankind in entirety. Beneath the surface of every continent lay a network of tunnels that led to the main sites, underground cities able to support five thousand people and maintain their survival for fifty years.

Chapter 1

Lia Returns to the Causeway

Lia's deftness of mind and psychic awareness had become very evident within a few years of her birth as a human. These gifts were inherited from another world, where Lia had existed as an elder of a race of non-physical life forms that had experienced millions of life spans, and which now existed in the one world of the ninth universe, Holocene. As Lia grew to adulthood, the blossoming potential of the Holocene wisdom was encouraged, moulded and sharpened, by those about her, preparing her for the time when she would become a leader, a primary elder of the last of mankind, the Otom.

As Lia stepped ashore onto the Cornish earth that had once flourished with vegetation, a flash of lightning echoed above her. A memory from the past flashed before her: when she had been a child, Ormus had appeared in the light of a storm, reminiscent of tonight. Lia had woken from a fitful sleep to see a shadowy figure flickering across the window, the shadow reminiscent of a curtain billowing in the night air; she had felt unafraid and had fallen asleep again. Ormus had reappeared later in her life as a friend of her father, one who was to become her mentor, shaping her for a future role as a leader of the 'chosen ones', the Otom. Within a year of their meeting, her Holocene wisdom and future role were established, and Ormus had returned to his world, Holocene, just a few years before the world's impending holocaust. She had recalled the childhood memory once before, a year before the holocaust, that being the time for the 'chosen ones' to begin their migration to the world of the Mers. Was the reoccurrence of that memory a positive sign now that the Otom were returning to the Earth's surface? Lia pondered on whether the preparation was complete and immediately felt misgivings about such an important decision. 'The answers will come,' she murmured positively; 'they always do with time.'

'Best get along, Lia. Did you hear me? We must get inside the Causeway perimeter.' Edward, Lia's husband, spoke with some urgency. It was dangerous to loiter out in the open, as on the rocky beach beyond them stood a group of young adult Cunmen. The Cunmen stood watching them silently, their forms gaunt and faces pallid, their skin translucent and scarred by a world wasted with radiation, which they had miraculously been born into. They began to pick up stones and throw them, one hitting Edward on the shoulder; he moved in front of Lia to protect her, while taking hold of her arm and hurrying her towards the security gate within the cliff face. The oarsman jumped from the boat onto the ledge and ran towards Lia and Edward, leaving the unmanned boat to the mercy of the turbulent water. The boat groaned as it smashed against the rocky cove. Edward shouted to him, ordering him back to the boat. The perimeter gates were opening and the guards were hurrying towards them; within seconds they would be safe inside and the oarsman would be out in the cove, and out of danger. During this moment of alarm, Edward had not noticed Lia falter.

Safely inside the gates, Lia stood still for a moment and lifted her hand to her head. Feeling a trickle of moisture, she held out her hands to see a covering of blood. She felt shaken; not at their aggression but at her own. She had felt no fear, none at all. While out there, she had wanted to run towards them and lash out at them, to beat and flail them, to rid the Earth of them forever, in order to banish their evilness. Children, barely young adults; she had wanted to hurt them. How could she evoke such feelings after all these years? The adrenaline that had pumped through her body was making her feel sick, spreading its forgotten poison into her system in overload. How would the Otom deal with the merciless people that roamed the Earth still killing each other? Would they feel fear or would they feel the archaic urge to act with equal violence? Lia shivered; what was the point in saving a chosen few if they would react with equal force to any violence from the Cunmen? It was then that Lia called out to Hafnium, God of Universe Four.

'Hear my declaration, Hafnium. I make this promise to you: I will embrace death before choosing that my people take another life.'

Within the confined space of the stairway leading up to the Causeway – Lia's home before the holocaust – time stood still. A light surrounded Lia, gathering her spirit into the universe, drawing her unto the chequerboard of challenges where Ormus, her departed mentor, and Chiron, master of the challenges, waited for her.

As Lia appeared beside them she recalled her first sight of Chiron, when she had been a young woman. Ormus had warned her to heed her words, as in a playful mood she had asked, 'And the one with the purple onion upon his head, who is he?' Ormus had answered her curtly, 'Lia, that is Chiron, master of the challenges. You must begin to take his presence seriously, for he abides within your dreams, and his teachings are important to the challenges of your physical consciousness and should not be ignored.' A dark-skinned divinity stood before her, his head dressed in a purple turban edged with gold, his body swathed in a white robe with an indigo loose cloth that spiralled from his shoulder to his feet. Silver rays spun around his silhouette like shooting comets brightening a darkened sky.

Lia no longer felt the urge to laugh at his timeless apparition; she had grown older and much wiser, and during that time, Chiron had shown her the seriousness of his challenges. As Lia faced Chiron, she could see beyond him a myriad of stars through which the Milky Way spun its dazzling strata of magical timelessness.

Chiron advised her, 'Lia, it is time to make your peace with mankind.'

Lia looked into the fathomless blueness of Ormus' eyes, and, taking courage from the wisdom she saw there, she began with a voice that was strong and sincere, 'We, the council of elders, have brought the Otom through many years of change, and with Hafnium's guidance we will prepare them for the next challenge. But if the Otom are asked to make war, if they are to kill again, I will not be part of it. Another way to contain the Cunmen must be found, if the Otom people are to live in peace upon the earth again.'

'And what will you do, Lia, if Hafnium denies you this request?' Ormus' expression was one of amusement mixed with irony. Lia, the defiant young woman of the past, stood challenging the universe again.

'I will remain beneath the oceans in the world of the Mers, until my physical death occurs. The younger generations are those that will lead our people to another home in the galaxy. My time on Earth is coming to a close, and that will be my wish.'

The journey beyond Earth that Lia spoke of was to take place some fifty years into the future: a journey she would not be part of. Her part was now, making sure that the Otom were free of aggression. Free of the will to do evil. Lia's voice trailed away and she finished brokenly, 'To be free of the desire that I have felt … free of the impulse to cause harm. And it is my solemn vow to Hafnium that I will not return to the taking of life as a way of bringing about the Otom's return to the surface.'

The silence that followed seemed endless to Lia as Ormus took hold of her hand briefly and then released it. He was saying goodbye. Light began to encircle Lia as a strong and comforting voice that she had often heard before echoed around her.

'Thy will be done, Lia; I, Hafnium, have spoken. Lead your people upon the earth again, and have faith that even though you prepare for battle, I will deny it at the last. From today, lead the one tribe of man, known as the Otom, to the Earth's surface with faith, for that is their name and their challenge to be.'

Edward, concerned about Lia's injury, placed his arm around her shoulders while calling her back to him. 'Lia, Lia.'

Lia smiled. 'I'm fine. Really, it is nothing. You go on to your meeting, Edward. I will see you at home, later. I'm so looking forward to seeing the boys,' she added brightly.

Edward gave her a comforting squeeze. 'Have Dorri take a look at your head. I'll see you after I have inspected the new community housing.'

Edward set off with an accompanying military squad to inspect the results of his plans. He had gone a long way in his early lifetime from an hotelier's son to a well-respected architect. Edward had left university to succeed; his work was of an unusually high standard, and he had immediately become involved in the architecture of the oceanic farms for the future migration. During this time Lia and Edward had married quietly, shortly afterwards to become the doting parents of an infant son. When the holocaust happened three years later and they migrated to the oceans, they also had a newly born daughter, Carlen.

Chapter 2

Haydes and Kiron

The boys sat talking on a rocky embankment at the bottom of the garden, the backdrop of sea and sky merging as one grey image. Haydes and Kiron were waiting for Lia, their grandmother, to arrive. Dorri, the housekeeper, a woman well equipped to deal with two teenagers, watched them constantly from the kitchen window. The boys wanted to be outside in the open while she preferred them under her feet, which would allow her to feel more relaxed; while Lia's grandsons were in her charge she was determined nothing would go wrong.

Haydes sat talking to his brother. 'Their destiny was guided by the law of the stars, their actions resolute enough for the "chosen ones" to survive. The human race had reached a point of no return. The experience of the opposite of love in all aspects having been transcended, there was no choice other than to extract those to survive before the final aggression was unleashed.' Haydes finished his dramatic recital, remembered word for word from the library of historical events.

'What aggression?' asked Kiron, knowing little of the truth about his ancestors' history upon the Earth's surface, the age of accessing this knowledge being sixteen, an age that he had yet to arrive at.

'Mankind's aggression, the final violent act of the primeval malevolent Earthman, now called the Cunmen by the elders of our race. They are the Earthmen that remained spiritually untouched by the coming of the Holocenes, the "wise ones". Our ancestors are Holocene and Earthman merged as one.'

Kiron's eyes widened as he felt a flutter of fear, an emotion he knew little of.

Haydes continued, 'Over the ages, the Cunmen fought back for control of their species, for global supremacy. During the final years, the age of sophisticated mob rule, the Earthmen that survived the cull – which took place after the union of the Holocene travellers with the Earth women, selected to begin the new race of mankind – abducted some of these females, and a new race of Cunmen emerged with the intelligence of the Holocene and the dominant killing instinct of the Earthman, combined. With those attributes they ruled the Earth.'

Kiron, who was listening attentively to his brother Haydes, asked, 'How do you know all of this?' He was now feeling uneasy about sitting in the open.

'Because in this last year, I have seen the evil force of the Cunmen when I dream, and now the visions come during the day when I'm awake.' Haydes continued, 'I have seen far more in my dreams than is taught us in the classroom. I see the death and destruction; it is terrifying, but it was also inevitable.' Haydes rubbed his forehead irritably, wanting to unburden some of his heavy thoughts. 'Our race is returning to the surface, where we will learn the truth of our past. We must conquer our fear of the surviving Cunmen in order that we can live here upon the Earth's surface, as did our ancestors.'

Kiron asked his brother to tell him more about the past that he had no part of. He was terrified, yet enthralled by Haydes' dreams, dreams that he had shared with him since being brought to the Earth's surface from the world below the oceans.

The brothers were fourteen and seventeen years old, Haydes being the elder. They sat deep in conversation in the garden of their grandmother's home, which had been rebuilt in the original style of forty-five years past. The Causeway stood safe within a military perimeter upon the Cornish coast of England, which the boys were privileged visitors to in the year 45AA.

Haydes continued, 'The streets and prisons were overflowing with criminals, and much of the Earth's surface was laid bare by another kind of criminal, the world's powerful leaders and land owners. They controlled the unsuspecting masses with addictive chemical substances that they administered through the food and main water supplies. This subdued communities where disorder was breaking out, turning nations on all continents into submissive drug addicts.'

Kiron wheezed, his heart pumping fit to burst, his brother's words terrifying him. The elders' decision to keep this knowledge from all children below the age of sixteen had been wise, and they requested of those coming into this knowledge not to burden those younger with its content. Haydes was breaking the rules.

'Before the holocaust began in the east,' he continued, 'a chain of events was tearing the Earth apart. The masses were starving as the earth yielded fewer crops: grain that was further reduced by those in power who stockpiled the meagre harvests. Mankind continued turning upon each other. Across the globe, mankind mutilated, plundered and killed, destroying all forms of life in their search for food. The violence and bloodshed continued until the first atomic warhead was detonated, which caused a chain reaction around the world. The holy leaders of Iran had wanted the world to end, and so they released atomic warheads to all four points of the world. Those who had lived their lives consciously aware of the evil about them had prepared for the prophesied migration, and are our surviving elders today.' Haydes glanced at his brother, suddenly aware of his broken promise and the consequences.

Kiron was now in a state of trauma and Haydes began to panic. 'It's going to be fine, Kiron. I told you because we are safe. Gran Lia would never bring us here if we were in danger.' Haydes held his breath, praying that Kiron would calm down and start breathing properly.

Kiron began to calm down, his breathing becoming normal. 'Tell me what happened after that. Tell me.'

Haydes was unsure but his brother's insistence made him continue. 'After the third world war, the holocaust, our race migrated to the valleys below the oceans, where we were born. It was 37AA before the all clear was given, and those chosen to explore the surface of the Earth were sent above. Their task was to find land for future habitation, and they were sent to explore areas where they could begin to build communities for more of the Otom to follow. Twelve sites were to be chosen in varying regions around the world, each one chosen for the signs of renewed vegetation, and hopefully wildlife, although the latter has yet to be sited. At the time of the migration, Hafnium, the grand master of Universe Four, assured our elders that all wildlife species would survive the holocaust. Mankind had driven most of the animal species to extinction but they have survived within Hafnium's infinite web of life. Our governing council of elders in the City of Memories decided upon the twelve sites to be used for the migration, these sites being less populated by communities of the surviving Cunmen. It is 45AA and a significant point in our race's history that will be remembered as the first great event in Otom history.' Haydes expected questions from Kiron but there were none.

Kiron sat looking out at the bleak grey ocean. *It's so much more beautiful and exciting beneath the sea than above it, and I can always return there ...* With these comforting thoughts he dismissed his brother's revelations.

Dorri called the boys from the kitchen, 'Come along, you two, your breakfast is ready and your grandmother is due any moment now. I want your breakfast finished, your rooms tidy, and you two clean and shipshape when she arrives.'

Haydes got up immediately and started to walk towards the kitchen. No disagreeing today, he liked being with his grandmother; life was less predictable and often an adventure. Kiron was thinking much the same thing, as he stepped quickly in line with his brother, although he mostly liked his life to be consistent and without the unsettling revelations that he had just experienced.

'Let's ask Gran Lia if we can go with the military squad up on the guards' mount, then we can see what's beyond the perimeter wall.'

'Sure thing, Bruv,' Haydes answered light-heartedly, relieved that his younger brother appeared to have dismissed their conversation from his mind.

The two boys began to race each other down the long sloping garden towards the kitchen: a large brick extension that ran the length of the back of the house. Causeway cottage and the military perimeter that burgeoned out around it stood back from the towering cliff edge that formed a sheltered cove below.

The Causeway was the perfect place to begin a new community because of the escape route to the cove below by means of a natural stairway inside the cliff-face, which was entered from a rock edifice at the bottom of the garden. In the cove below, the concealed entrance was a metre above the large flat ledge that jutted out over the ocean, the entrance barred by a heavy gate that was guarded at all times.

Chapter 3

Deron and Mariana Debarc-Major

Deron and Mariana Debarc-Major were part of a team pioneering the return of the Otom to the Earth's surface. Their work took them back and forth between the Mer world, their home, and the newly established community sites which encompassed the Earth's barren continents. Both Deron and his wife, Mariana, were involved in the repatriation, thereby allowing their children, Haydes and Kiron, privileged visits to the surface. Deron and Mariana were happy about the arrangement, particularly as his mother, Lia, and Dorri were taking care of them in their absence.

Deron, a marine biologist, was primarily responsible for the Otom's food supplies that were produced upon the ocean plateau surrounding the City of Memories. In the last few years, Deron's work had shifted to the Philippines to work on a coastal farming project essential to the repatriation. The project had been running smoothly, well enough to allow him a few days with his family at the Causeway, and then Deron had received a phone call which had recalled him to the site after an attempted sabotage by local Cunmen.

Mariana was busy working alongside Deron's father on the sites of the new communities, the boys having been left in Dorri's care.

The society that Deron and Mariana had grown up in was a just system for all. Each person, after reaching adulthood at the age of eighteen, was awarded points for their contribution to the community, which related to the time and effort that were contributed, whatever their ability. There was still a need for those who could advise and lead, but the intellect of the individual was no longer a means of attaining unfair rights. The Otom community had learned long ago that the social pyramid system had never worked fairly in past societies, bringing only conflict and destruction. The Otom worked collectively to advance their knowledge while discovering mankind's true level of intelligence, and his destiny. Having witnessed the power of the creator's infinite genius during the holocaust, they understood that wealth was a meaningless goal and that a society could share and enjoy as a whole.

The social order was fair and all were well provided for, each person doing the work they were best suited to do. Even the temptation to take from others was denied because the system, which gave points of credit for the time laboured and not its distinction, was unique to the individual. A sense of self prevailed among the Otom; even though they lacked their natural habitat, the earth, sun and sky, they suffered the resulting health problems with a common solace. They merged congenially with the new world's inhabitants, the Mers, who had welcomed them and sustained them, helping them to settle into their new and strange environment, which eventually had become home.

The Mer world was a wondrous place for the growing child, Deron, and had been his home from the age of three years. He would spend his days playing in the ocean, safe among the Otom divers and the Mers, and his nights dreaming of travelling to the planet Mars, optimism and a sense of self being his strengths.

The psychic ability of the Otom children was finely tuned, their dreams taking them far beyond the Earth to other planets in Universe Four. The accounts of their nightly space travel were confirmed by the documented history of mankind, which they would not access until the age of eighteen. They learned the skills of diving and farming while growing to adulthood in a world where irrational fear was unknown to them.

The Otom held the belief that fear of the unknown had entered human life when mankind was lifted above the animal kingdom. The phenomenon of 'word' had planted in the minds of men the ability to believe in that which he could not see, touch, smell or hear but sense, fear. For the creature, man, fear was an intuitive reaction to the circumstance about him. The introduction of word conveyed belief in a dark and unreal world, another dimension of good versus evil that when spoken was accepted as factual in the minds of men. It was the imaginary world of fear that the Otom wanted to supplant. Their destiny had brought them confinement beneath the oceans in the world of the Mers, there to focus and advance their psychic abilities in order to banish all falsehood. The scientific knowledge and engineering skills from the old world remained with the Otom, ready to advance them in the future, but all other aspects of that civilisation lay hidden in the manuals of word.

At the time of the migration there had been a need for skilled divers to help the Mers harvest food from the pyramidal greenhouses that surrounded the City of Memories. The multi-level rows of vegetation thrived in abundance, the colours, shape and texture created to encourage the human appetite. The vegetation was anchored in beds of crystal particles that formed thousands of conical poles spiralling upwards to the top of each inverted pyramid, the point of each pyramid being anchored deep below the ocean rock bed.

The Otom's home in the City of Memories stood eerily upon a vast plateau, white and pristine within its dark watery environment, a city three hundred and sixty miles in diameter surrounded by acres of the pyramid-shaped greenhouses.

In the years that followed Deron's childhood, he became an accomplished diver, diving to extreme depths without life supporting equipment, his lungs accustomed to expanding and decreasing way beyond their normal size.

The Mers taught the newcomers their diving skills and supported them until they were able to harvest food for themselves. The Otom men, women and children quickly grew accustomed to deep water diving, each one eager to adapt, work and learn in the new environment. The Mer people quickly lost their unease with the Otom and very soon, their skills became the skills of man. Human children played in the deep ocean with the mermaid young and they became as one family.

At the beginning it was hard for the humans to adapt. Their cravings for a diet of land-grown foods, the drug-infused water supplies they had unknowingly consumed, were not easy to abandon. But good fortune often comes wrapped in ill fortune; they did not have the temptation of *choice*. Latvie was the main source of protein for them, which they harvested from the vast ocean forests with the help of their Mer companions: deep valley forests that, until the Otom's coming, mankind had never seen. All age groups went to hunt and gather the cone-shaped protein, which grew among the tree roots. Gathering the food, latvie, was a time of celebration that everyone loved. The food rich in protein had supplanted the Otom's craving for meat by the time one cycle of an Earth year was past. Forty-five years on, the Otom's nature had changed beyond recognition, and they would recoil at the memory of food eaten by early twenty-first century mankind.

Deron helped to provide a continuous supply in the food chain for the city's population, and to root out any trouble that might impede its continuity. The call that morning had come from the marine division who were responsible for repairing biological damage to the new food beds along the coasts of the world's oceans. Deron had been planning a weekend at the Causeway with his mother and family. He had just arrived when his two sons and Dorri came running from the house to tell him of the call. With the call completed, Deron said his goodbyes and left the Causeway; he was on his way to the Philippines to root out those responsible for another attack on the Pacific coral beds.

Without the continued growth of the coral beds, the re-habitation of the Earth's surface would have to be postponed. The life-giving beds were generating oxygen towards the surface, where the supply was still thin and toxic from the poisons unleashed in the holocaust. Almost two thirds of the oxygen-giving plants and trees had died, leaving the Earth's surface virtually uninhabitable. But the preceding ten years had brought severe and continuous atmospheric storms that had cleared ninety percent of the radiation from the earth, which had been seen as a miracle by both the Cunmen and the Otom.

The Otom, emerging onto the surface of the planet, were now faced with another danger, the Cunmen, those who wanted to destroy any chance of them returning to the surface. The Cunmen, the last of the primordial Earthmen from the beginning of time, were set on a massacre ...

Deron had said goodbye to the boys, leaving Dorri to explain to his mother why he would not be returning to the Causeway for the family gathering.

Chapter 4.

Dorri Perkins

Lia had met Dorri Perkins shortly after the death of her father, sister, brother-in-law and infant niece, all having died in a car accident. Lia had moved to Cornwall after the tragedy to live in her father's cottage, the Causeway, and with the help of her father's friend, Raphiel, she had set up a charitable retreat for children with assumed behavioural and learning difficulties. The holiday retreat was run by the 'lightworkers', those who were to migrate to the world of the Mers. With the money left from her late father's estate, Lia was able to purchase a small farm to support the carers, teachers and therapists who cared for the patients, who were mostly children. By the fifth year, the farm was an unbelievable success and Lia, now married to Edward, had given birth to their first child, the infant boy having been safely delivered by the local midwife, Dorri Perkins.

Much had changed in the time since Ormus' and then, later, her family's passing. Once again a time of critical tension challenged peace in the Middle East with the Palestinians cut off from the world because of their threats to eradicate Israel. The situation, however, was just a smoke screen for a more important happening. The British and American military had cut off the border between Iran and Iraq after it was proven that Iran was supplying the weapons which threatened another civil war and mass murder of Iraqi civilians. In the United Kingdom, DNA, retina and fingerprint identification came into force to eradicate the threat of terrorist attacks. The time had come to close the farm and move the community below the oceans. At this time Lia was heavily pregnant again.

The last day: Lia lay resting peacefully after the birth of her second child, a girl, Carlen. Outside she could hear screaming and shouting as windows were smashed in the town just a mile or so away. The crowds of frightened people were on the rampage as the first atomic explosion had rocked the world, lighting up the evening sky as bright as a summer's day and then very quickly turning it to a cloudy dusk.

Dorri Perkins, the attending midwife, trembled as she washed the newly born infant. Alone in the world, Dorri, the result of an unwanted pregnancy, had not married. She had seen too much neglect in the children's home where she had spent her childhood. Cruelty forced upon the innocent by those who were supposed to have cared for and protected them. Her childhood had left her without trust, an emotion Dorri had ceased to recognise at a very young age. She had been born in the far north of England, and as an adult, she had wandered gradually down south as her nursing career in midwifery had blossomed.

Hours earlier, on her way from the farm to attend Lia, Dorri had been chased in the street; her arm was still bleeding from the attack and the wound needed stitches, but she knew it would have to wait. Dorri could hear Lia comforting her young son, Deron, who was just three years of age.

'Don't look so frightened, darling, it's going to be all right. We will be leaving very soon now that your sister has arrived, I promise. Don't be frightened of the noise outside.'

Dorri felt the pain of never having had such a love of her own. She watched Lia draw her son up in her arms, trembling at what might happen to them as fear overwhelmed her. Dorri, startled by the ringing of the phone, moved to the door to listen.

Edward, Lia's husband, was speaking. 'Yes, we are ready and have one other cargo, a healthy girl. Fine, we will be ready for you.' Edward put the phone down and shouted up to her, 'Nurse Dorri, can you carry the bag I have packed for the baby plus your own, and put on the black coat beside it? It will be a short journey.'

Before Dorri was able to answer there was a knock on the back door.

Edward went to the stairs, then called back to her, 'Now, Dorri, hurry!'

A moment later Dorri heard heavy footsteps on the stairway and two men entered the bedroom. Without a word they began preparing Lia for the journey, wrapping her in a dark blanket and strapping her into a chair with Deron in her arms. Quickly they carried her downstairs with Dorri following. Edward, having wrapped the baby in a dark blanket, took one last look at the room where both of his children had been born and then hurried downstairs. Now all were cloaked and ready for their journey. Without a word the men led them out of the cottage and down the garden to the stairwell within the cliff face.

Lia took one last look at the world she would not see again until she was entering the last phase of her life.

Dorri moved swiftly down the steps to the cove, her injury having ceased to hurt while her mind was filled with fear.

Once all were onboard, the boat pulled silently away from the ledge and headed for the funnel of light upon the horizon. All began to concentrate on the light centred upon them. Lia held Deron tightly, knowing that her resurrection would be his. The light became a swirling mass within the ocean of her mind, and then nothingness. The mob that had entered the Causeway watched from the cliff top as the boat disappeared beneath a swirling void within the pitch-dark water …

The following day, as predicted, an earthquake swallowed up fifty miles of the open channel between the French and English coasts. The Channel Tunnel split in half as the resulting tidal wave surged down both sides of the English Channel, causing countless deaths along the coast and inland. To the west of Cornwall where the Atlantic fault line passed along the ocean bed, molten lava erupted across the valley floor, which as it cooled added some five hundred miles of land to the west coast of England.

A robin nesting in the main dome of the Eden project

quietened as the first tremble shuddered in the ground below. Outside the wildlife began to run, hopelessly panicked by what had made them jittery for days. The quake lasted for a few minutes, and then silence was followed by the roar of water that surged down the sleeve of the channel towards the west to meet the land rising in the Atlantic. The robin fluttered its wings in terror as the dome began to dismantle, and then a way up and out into the beyond appeared, out into the grey flakes of falling ash that were covering the world. A strong current caressed and carried him, the robin disappearing through the eye of the storm to a world of safety beyond the Earth.

As Dorri journeyed in her unconsciousness, she was aware of her companions' presence and could hear one of Raphiel's teachings, which made her feel safe. *With each new spark of consciousness awakened, so the Universe grows in size and expands. To life within, the Universe appears to have drifted further apart, when in fact, the Universe has become richer in consciousness from the experience.*

Dorri observed mankind's transformation opening up upon the Earth. Those who lay dying looked up to see a dome of rainbow colours encircling the Earth and a white light spiralling to its summit. This was their pathway to the worlds beyond physical death, while the surviving Cunmen began a new life in their underground sites.

Dorri's vision moved on five years. The radioactive fallout had not affected the Cunmen while they remained sealed in their underground sites, but they had the knowledge to leave the Earth and enter space, and were impatient to do so. They opened their sites to restart the space project and were quickly polluted by the radiation that seeped stealthily through the broken entry seals. Dorri watched as further into the future the Cunmen's intelligence changed to insanity from their exposure to radiation poisoning. Then she saw another glimpse of the future; it was as if the world were tumbling … moving its position in space.

Chapter 5

The Underground Sites – Code Name ESCAPE

The sound of footsteps on the shingle path announced Lia's arrival at the Causeway. The two boys, on hearing voices below their bedroom, rushed downstairs, landing in a sprawl of arms and legs in the hallway. Laughing and fighting, the boys fought their way to the front door, both trying to reach it first. They could hear their grandmother thanking her escort, before approaching the door to ring the bell. Dorri, having heard Lia arrive followed by the commotion outside in the hallway, opened the kitchen door.

One word to the boys was enough. 'Up!' she said resolutely.

The order rang out like a bolt of thunder, as the boys appeared to be dragged to a standing position with the command. Dorri moved towards the front door and opened it; Lia stepped in, her gaze surveying the boys with amusement before she turned to Dorri to greet her warmly.

'Dorri, it's lovely to be home again.'

'Aye, my dear,' Dorri answered, 'it is that.'

The two women embraced briefly, aware of the boys who now waited in obedient silence for an acknowledgement. This would not come from their grandmother but from the woman who took charge of their lives in the absence of their parents and grandparents. Lia would never step into Dorri's place of authority; she had too much respect for Dorri's commitment to the responsibility placed with her. Dorri turned to the boys.

'Well, come and greet your grandmother, where are your manners?'

The boys rushed forward with a sigh of relief; they knew by the tone of Dorri's Scottish brogue that she had forgiven the incident moments before and that there would be no comeback. Dorri was not always so tolerant with the boys when it came to discipline, a quality that the boys' parents respected, together with her capacity to love and her protectiveness towards them.

Amid the news of Deron's call to duty, the four spilled into the kitchen. Lia slipped her coat off, grateful for the warmth coming from the kitchen range and the wonderful smell of food that was cooking in the huge new oven. Kiron took his grandmother's coat while Haydes rushed around laying four places at the large kitchen table.

'Would you like a cup of hot tea before we eat, my dear?'

'Yes please, Dorri, it's been a long journey and I do feel tired.'

Not adept at showing outward compassion, Dorri carried on talking. 'The military are still acquisitioning the local underground sites. They say some are as big as fourteen acres, and built to support those that would be useful in rebuilding another world empire beyond a disaster.' Dorri's statement was spoken with a definite down tone. 'Came too fast though, the end that is; most of them didn't have a chance of survival. Word has it that these sites beneath ground level are being found on all continents, even those that were thought to be third-world continents, Lia. It takes some understanding where the money came from, or the know-how to achieve such an undertaking.'

Lia knew exactly who had built the third-world network of underground sites and filled them with supplies that could sustain five thousand people for as many as fifty years or more.

'They were not built for the populations of the third-world continents, Dorri, but for the Chinese. Especially the sites built beneath the African continent. China, as you know, had become a wasteland before the holocaust because of the pollution in the air and the damming and redirecting of China's rivers, especially the longest, the Yangtze, which was destroyed in the early earthquakes leaving the land about arid. After that, only the high ground and the region of Tibet were thought fit for human habitation. Our military have the locations of these sites, of which many are still closed.'

'Where did they get that information?' Dorri asked.

'The information on where the world's sites are situated was secured by a lightworker who worked as a high-level minister in the European government before the migration. The records, so far, have been found to be accurate. Tibet has three such sites, which is possibly the reason why China always refused Tibet self-rule. All governments at that time used the covert exercise code-named ESCAPE to safeguard against any disasters. They built thousands of underground sites across the globe that would each support five thousand of their people for fifty years or more, the plan being that as one was depleted they could move on to the next in the hope that they would survive until the Earth's surface was safe to be inhabited again. In the short time that the military have been searching for the underground sites, they have found no less than five hundred intact, which they believe contain every utility needed to maintain our communities for the fifty-plus years our race remains here upon the Earth.'

Dorri chose not to acknowledge this information. She planned to see her days out at the Causeway. 'They say the one beneath the Wiltshire plains is more than fourteen acres in size. The packaging on the supplies that arrive for the house, along with that lovely big stove,' Dorri nodded towards the new oven, 'they must have come from Wiltshire because they have the same series of numbers stamped upon them, preceded by WILT, as does everything else that arrives here at the moment. That's where the tea, sugar and dried milk came from.' Dorri's eyes glistened, and taking a deep breath she puffed out her chest to hide her feelings. 'Things are going to get back to normal, you'll see,' she ended.

Lia's wandering mind came back to Dorri. 'Yes, Dorri,' Lia replied, hoping it was the right response. 'The good news is that apart from the sites that were occupied at the time of the holocaust, only one of the locked sites has been found vandalised by the Cunmen. The site is near the Mexican border. It is bigger than the Wiltshire site, about one hundred and fifty acres. Apparently, the Cunmen from the European and Asian continents are migrating towards this point. I am told that access to all levels of the site has been difficult for them as they do not have the codes. A party of military scouts have come across large amounts of discarded packaging and products. They know what was on each level, and have been able to estimate what the Cunmen have accessed.'

Again, Dorri showed little interest in the affairs beyond the Causeway. 'Well, it's nice to be cooking food on a proper stove again,' she answered, while ignoring Lia's mention of the Cunmen.

Dorri had responded to the Cunmen in exactly the same way as Lia when confronted by them, and afterwards had felt the same remorse.

'I'm sure it is, Dorri, and it's good to be on land again,' Lia replied soothingly.

Lia turned back to thinking of her son, Deron, who was at this moment travelling through the void to another possibly dangerous assignment. She drifted back to her first incredible journey through the void of zero energy, when she and Ormus had first returned from the world of the Mers. Today's journey had not been dissimilar, other than that her body was older and the experience even more exhausting.

With Lia's thoughts of Ormus, he appeared in the kitchen before her while those about her were unaware of his presence. He greeted her with a wry smile and she knew for certain a new cycle was beginning, a new adventure in which her son, Deron, was to be involved. Lia looked at Ormus with a troubled expression. Ormus waggled a finger at her and then disappeared, his voice floating through her mind. *Lia, don't go jumping to conclusions, you should know better!* She heard his laughter and then his voice faded along with his silhouette.

'Here you are, my dear, this will set you up, tea, strong and sweet. Once you have downed that you will be ready for a good meal.'

'Thank you, Dorri.' *Tea: now even more prized than before the holocaust*. She did not particularly like Dorri's strong brew but drank it gratefully, the heat warming a chill inside that she seemed unable to lose.

The boys, having stopped to listen to the two women's conversation, were aware that their grandmother looked pale and tired. Lia was now 71 years old. When Ormus had first become acquainted with her, she and her twin, Ette, had just celebrated their twenty-first birthdays, such a long time ago: so much tragedy, and so many happy memories that had never faded. Lia concealed the cut upon her head, pulling her red head scarf over it as the boys stood quietly watching her drift within her thoughts, both having decided that today they would not bother her but let her rest. Tomorrow would come soon enough and they knew that rest and sleep would bring them back their grandmother of adventure.

The next morning Lia awoke having dreamed of a time long before the migration, a time when she and her twin sister, Ette, were staying in Torquay. Lia was not even married then and now she was a grandmother, her own two children grown adults, which in itself was an achievement considering the time of their birth. Lia trembled as she remembered how near her race had come to extinction but for the intervention of the Mers, without whose guidance the Otom would not have survived. Lia opened her eyes to see Ormus beckoning her to the window. She left her bed and walked towards his outstretched hand; once there she followed his gaze towards the golden haze of the rising sun. The sky was becoming clear again after so many years of devastation. Ormus gently wrapped his cloak around her shoulders and they lifted away towards the rising sun. It was many years since Lia had flown with Ormus to see the beauty of the Universe above them.

Ormus and Lia flew far beyond the Earth's ravaged beauty, all the while the scenery changing, much more water now, far less land, and what land could be seen was still mostly scorched and blistered, no longer green and beautiful as before the holocaust. Lia felt anger well up inside her. Why had the Cunmen been saved to cause more damage in the future? Suddenly she felt weary knowing that another challenge was about to commence, that life in a physical body meant just that, a continuous cycle of challenges until the final experience, passing beyond life through the veil of death, otherwise what would be the purpose to it? A monumental image of Aspheseuos' angelic reflection, revealed once to her by Hafnium, materialised before her with a throng of dying Cunmen cradled in his outstretched arms. The words *reveal to me those that judge the deeds of others, and I will show you their myriad of flaws,* cast a shadow over Lia's mind.

Ormus, who was listening to her thoughts, cut in to enquire, 'Lia, you have not asked where we are going, my dear.'

Lia heard Ormus' words but remained silent, shamed by the words in her head.

'You must not become disheartened,' he continued; 'remember, Lia, Rome was not built in a day. The Otom have gone through a quiet, a restful period and must now move on, and progression always involves much effort.'

Lia thought of Rome and Ormus laughed. 'It was mighty while it lasted, Lia, and produced an incredible step forward for man and civilised law, however brutal an empire.'

Lia smiled. She could feel the warmth of the sun on her face, even though it was physically impossible while so far away from the Earth's surface, but then she could breathe; was that also *impossible*? The word seemed without substance or true meaning, as anything was possible in one's mind, which, the Universe had proven to her, becomes factual in time.

'Where are we going?' Lia asked.

'Ah,' Ormus answered, 'communication at last!'

Ormus withdrew into the past, taking Lia with him. Fleetingly, she saw the Halls of Chequers before her. Her last visit to Chequers had been to attend the Neophytes' Ball, where her first real challenge had begun. Now she was to take up another, only this time her son would work alongside her, with the help of Ormus by their side. The Halls of Chequers disappeared, leaving Lia and Ormus spinning in the deep blue of space.

Below them the Earth's magnetic field blazed lights of fluorescent blue and green around the celestial sphere; the Earth lady,

Gaia, was healing. Lia realised that the resplendent colours the Earth was displaying were a sign of the unseen new growth which flourished beneath her surface. Tears began to flow as her heart filled with hope; this was how she remembered the vastness of the Universe when first the challenges had begun, one moment clinging to hope on the board of chance and the next at the door of Chequers saying goodnight, her challenge over. The evening spent at the Chequers Ball, accompanied by Ormus and her friends Odelia Cavil and Glashadou, her sister, Ette, and Edward, drifted through her mind and finally disappeared.

Chiron, master of the challenges, appeared upon the blue and silver chequerboard. Lia glanced at Ormus to see him as his true self, a Holocene, the shimmering light of silver radiance that danced back and forth over his form no less reassuring than the figure with the encumbrance of matter.

Chiron greeted Lia before summoning forth the hologram from which events of the past would be portrayed. Lia's body weakened as the memories of the holocaust rose up before her. Then Ormus' thoughts reached out to her. *This is the past, which is so necessary to the future. You must take heart, Lia; the coming challenge that the Otom face will be your last real challenge in this Earthly life, and with it a future will be made possible for your grandchildren, and all that come after them. You and the 'chosen ones' have survived. Your daughter has just given birth to her first child. There is much to be thankful for.*

Lia's daughter, Carlen, was forty-five years old, and one of many women who had remained childless throughout mankind's period in the underworld. These women were now giving birth to a new generation of Otom, children who would grow to adulthood on the Earth's surface. Ormus spoke the truth about the newborn child, Rosalie. Lia had felt so much joy at the birth of Carlen's infant, whom she had seen in her dreams long before her own daughter was born. The newborn infant, Lia's grandsons and their generation were the future, a new beginning for the Otom.

Lia's thoughts drifted to the coming battle with the Cunmen and she wondered if it would be as frightening as the final stages of the holocaust ... Suddenly she realised that her life had had its trials and terror, but it was never dull. She had walked a pathway of never ending experience, which, if she was honest, she would not have changed. And it looked as if the future would be just as exciting.

The experience of the holocaust had become a distant memory, one that was easier to accept each time she returned to her home, the Causeway.

Lia's attention was drawn back to Chiron, and the history within the hologram. The vision within was no less horrifying but something had changed within her. The past was done with; there was a future to be earned for the children born, and being born, and this was the time to be earning it.

Chapter 6

The Holocaust

The final stages: Hafnium, the grand master, stood before the assembly of planets. Down below, the blackened Earth lay beneath a cloud of radioactive dust that blotted out the sun's rays. Hafnium's silence was commanding; held within his presence the twelve archangels waited silently; the moment for mankind's atonement had come. All assembled held a joyous light about them as once again a time of liberation was upon the Earth, a change of magnitude that Hafnium had foretold. It was time for mankind to surrender his hold upon the Earth.

It was the month of December: a time when long ago a 'gifted one' had come to pave the way for mankind's further enlightenment. Now, two thousand and more years later, only destruction remained. The soil was toxic, the sky blackened and the heat of the sun shut out. The holy land into which he had been born had ceased to exist. Silenced and blackened, not a breath of life remained; only the cry of the scorched earth lingered. Religious conflict had reached its conclusion, initiating the deadliest war ever known to mankind.

Gaia, the Earth woman, listened to the laboured breathing of her death-infested body, while upon the Earth all life, which she had created in her watery womb, struggled to breathe to her resonance. Of mankind, many were dead and more were dying. In the east, Iran had unleashed a fury of madness upon mankind which few would survive, leaving the land on all continents contaminated for decades to come.

The chosen ones: the 'lightworkers' made their journey through the void of zero energy to the valleys below the great oceans, deep within the bowels of the Earth where the holocaust would not harm them. They joined those who had been the first to leave many years before: teachers, philosophers, those who would guide the new mankind without control or autocracy. In the City of Memories, they would learn the customs of the Mer race and rear the new generations in a peaceful and loving environment while they waited for the day when the 'chosen ones' would return to the Earth's surface.

Gaia trembled, her life form racked with pain from the torture inflicted upon her body, mankind's greed for development and war having slowly destroyed her. The Earth woman's cries of pain could be heard throughout the universe. Below the oceans, the whales and dolphins cried out her anguish as the land lay scorched and dying. Above her cries of pain, she heard the voice of Hafnium, the grand master of Universe Four.

'I have asked you to suffer enough, on behalf of mankind. I ask no more of you. Listen to your breathing, Gaia, feel how laboured it is. Begin your healing. Lengthen your breaths. I command you to do so.'

Gaia cried out, 'My beloved master, I cannot, for lengthening my breathing will swamp my body.'

'Do so, Gaia. It will bathe your tortured body with the healing fluid from your oceans. Be done with it; man will have to face his punishment.'

Gaia sighed, longing to surrender to her needs. For so long she had been held back by her conscience. Held back by the throbbing mass of life that depended upon her; she wanted to lengthen her breath.

The full moon gazed down upon her, waiting for the moment to help lighten her pain. Together they would turn the tides upon her tortured body, spilling the oceans as far across the land as they could manage. Gaia held back for but a moment, and then in one long sighing out breath she let go the forces that would save her and destroy the worst of man.

The tsunami swept around the world gathering speed and height as it went. A gargantuan wall of water gathering such strength that nothing remained in its wake, burning cities, ravaged continents, all devoured by the oceans' spinning wall of water . . .

The Cunmen: amidst the chaos and lawlessness, many that had secured a place in the secret underground sites perished before reaching safety.

It had been prophesied that decades later the challenges would continue between the chosen ones, the Otom, and the surviving Cunmen, those who would again pose a threat to the forces of good and hinder the Otom's return to the surface of the planet.

During the decades that followed the holocaust, the spiritual forces watched the Cunmen with interest as they emerged from the underground sites. They planned to regroup across the Earth, helped by a force of darkness that was not to be ignored, if the Otom were to live upon the surface again.

Below the oceans' valleys, in the City of Memories, those who had believed in the coming of a new world were safe. They had left the Earth's surface as the holocaust began, many questioning how they would make the journey and survive. The guidance they received from the other-worlds; the masters from the other-worlds reminded them to listen to their thoughts on the changes they had made in their lives, the constant thought on every detail of their daily actions. These changes had been part of the preparation for the journey that was now complete. The new race of man, the Otom would remain beneath the oceans for forty-five years, while the surface of the Earth was unable to support him; the wildlife would remain but in spirit form only, their physical life suspended in time.

Chapter 7

Unlocking the Code

Raphiel welcomed Lia and Ormus on to the universal chequer-board, his presence an indication that Lia was to access the universe's secret language: a language locked deep within Lia's consciousness that would enable the Otom to provide their own safe passage to and from the world of the Mers.

Ormus and Raphiel focused their attention on the Earth below to observe the progress of the lost souls, those who would not be separated from their Earthly existence and had remained in the moment of the holocaust that had torn the world apart and destroyed almost everything. The souls without their physical bodies continued to look on in awe at what was once town and country, their homes that were now part of a world of dust clouds mushrooming up towards a darkened sky. Ormus and Raphiel entered the past to stand among them, leaving Lia to stand alone.

'Shall I tell them or will you?' Raphiel remarked.

Ormus looked at the lost souls, who thought they had survived unharmed, as they continued to witness the non-stop cycle of destruction. Time and again the moment replayed, like a camera capturing a moment in time.

'Time enough, my friend. Time enough to tell them they are physically dead.'

Ormus looked across the arc of the Earth at the devastation mankind had perpetrated, forty-five years before. His twinkling blue eyes showed no compassion for the lost souls; the confinement that had been part of their destiny was coming to an end now the challenge between the Otom and the Cunmen was imminent.

Below the oceans, the Otom were preparing to leave the world of the Mers and live on the Earth's surface again. They could feel the power of the Earth as she healed from mankind's last conflict, and Ormus could sense their fear of what was to come.

Lia, having been alone with her thoughts, was unaware of the scenes that Raphiel and Ormus were witnessing or the communication between them. Below her the Earth's magnetic field transmitted a luminous green and blue radiance into the cosmos; then she saw it, a giant widening mushroom slowly expanding, blotting out the colours that encircled the Earth. This was how she remembered her world after the holocaust. No more a beautiful Earth firing her life-giving colours into outer space, only a sickening greyness remained. Lia realised she was reliving the memories of forty-five years past. When the challenges had begun, she never imagined that in order for mankind to survive, he would first almost destroy himself. She felt no empathy for the devastation she was witnessing; it was now in the past. Suddenly she remembered the initial fear of the confinement that she and her family had experienced below the oceans. The memory overwhelmed her and she let out a cry of terror.

A hand came to touch her face, another to cradle her shoulders. 'Lia.'

Lia felt the fear melt away as her father's arms enfolded her. René looked down upon the upturned face of his child, now a woman.

'Calm yourself, Lia, you are safe. How could you be anything but safe? You are of the chosen ones.'

Lia's thoughts went to those who must have suffered upon the surface; a child is a child, however its mind is twisted and maligned.

René's answer to her thoughts was austere. 'We are all part of destiny, and that was theirs. Their choice was to return to spirit having touched evil, to have witnessed and be familiar with its force. When those who are suffering have made their way beyond the psychic plane, they will use their knowledge for the good of all to inspire the collective universe. During your life you have gained immense wisdom, Lia, but when you truly witness the bigger picture, then you will understand. It is part of mankind's evolutionary development to love and suffer on all levels without the encumbering passions of Earthly emotions. Hate, anger, jealousy, fear, all these emotions result in grief and desecrate the universe, which is manifest of love, no matter what. When reasoning becomes balanced, unconditional, then the emotional devastation that you are feeling becomes transient and ceases to exist, because you understand why it exists.'

'Why have you come now, Father?' Lia asked, feeling trapped between the extremes of fear and acceptance.

'It is time for you to unlock the code to this universe, to begin your final journey, to see the bigger picture. Time for you to remember who you are in order to help mankind advance his code, for he has a code contained within Universe Four, as we all do, here and in the universes beyond.'

Lia remained silent; she was waiting for her father to explain the meaning of his statement, but like Lia, he appeared to be waiting.

Chiron, master of the challenges, appeared before them. The purple turban that covered his head contrasted sharply with the flowing silver and blue of his gracious figure, his flowing robes fusing with the dazzling blue and silver chequerboard of the universe. Almost simultaneously a luminosity that overshadowed all other light appeared above them. Hafnium, the grand master of Universe Four was in their presence. If Lia had been able to see beyond Hafnium's radiance, the planetary forces surrounding them would have been revealed to her.

Lia drew closer to her father; she still felt as in awe of Hafnium as when first in his presence at the start of her challenges. Fleetingly she recalled flying with Ormus high above the craggy landscape of Cornwall; the breathtaking scenery that moved slowly past them, as they kept company with the seagulls below. The amphitheatre where they had landed, hewn from the cliff-edge stone, it was there she had first listened to Hafnium and the twelve Initiators; the arrival of Aspheseuos, Satan himself, whom Hafnium had created to challenge his will within Universe Four. She had learned that for all the evil Aspheseuos manifested in mankind, he was an angel, the thirteenth Initiator, which Hafnium had revealed to her. In that moment of truth, she had realised the love that Hafnium had for Aspheseuos, his brother, sister. Aspheseuos was the dark fragment of the creator that examined and challenged all in existence for perfection, and for that purpose free will had been bestowed upon mankind to experience all facets of the Godhead within. Lia heard her father calling her back; the Master was about to speak.

Hafnium, subduing the radiance of his omnipotence, commanded the planetary forces to reveal their magnetism. Spheres of coloured splendour became visible, enveloping Lia and her father in their light. The planets, suspended in the universe, were immeasurable in size as they fused into one divine circle, each one flawless in their magnificence. In their midst shone twelve stars, their colours gently caressing those of their ruling planet, each star imbuing the energy of the planet they were inherent of. Each planet and star with their own unique qualities and characteristics, a dazzling magnificence that appeared without end. Below them the Earth turned on her axis, revealing the healing of her wounds.

The resonance of Hafnium's voice echoed like thunder rolling across the universe. The planetary forces knew his voice and were eager to hear his plans for mankind, his beloved and naive mankind.

'You have been called to help the new race of mankind that is emerging from Earth's oceans, the one tribe of man, the Otom. The inhabitants of your planets have watched closely the destruction of the Earth, and wondered: will the last of mankind next turn his attention to your worlds, and in doing so, will he bring about the same destruction? Let me assure you that the Otom are a peaceful race. The Cunmen are the last warring human species in Universe Four, and should they attempt to wage war upon your own evolved races, it would mean total destruction for them. However, this will not happen. The Cunmen have ceased all intelligent advancement in the last forty-five years, and do not understand that life exists upon and within you. They understand life in their likeness, while life without a physical body is not a reality to them.' Hafnium paused reflectively. 'Such are the defects of my Earthly children, the Cunmen, who will remain upon the Earth, unto death. However, the Otom, the "lightworkers" of mankind, are an evolved species, and they acknowledge your existence. They are now ready to return to the Earth's surface and learn how to survive upon the land. Therefore, I ask you, the planets and the star tribes, to watch over the Otom. Guide them, and with your influence, help them bring to justice those of the Otom who show signs of manifesting the old ways of the ego. This time they must evolve and live as one with their spiritual nature, for I am tired of this challenge and I wish to go another way, to create new challenges upon the Earth that are no longer of a material nature. It is time for advancement, time for the planetary species to interact with the Otom, to help their transition from the underworld to the surface of the Earth. The one named Lia will receive the code to the universe, on behalf of the Otom elders; from this time forth all travel through the void will be accessed through their knowledge of the code.'

Lia felt her physical body fall away, the particles dispersing into trillions of atoms, each atom seeming to have a coded symbol within one to nine before becoming a whisper of itself, herself, a memory of Lia. She was seeing the completion of her physical life: her thoughts, her choices having become progressively more balanced before the moment of physical death. Within the surreal experience of the fragmenting atoms, she realised that each thought or emotion activated within her had been a balancing of opposites and the means of bringing balance to her soul; the closer the two opposing emotions happened, the quicker balance was restored. Above her appeared the clocks of the past, present and future, revealing her genetic code, a code written into the seasons of Earthly life with the term of her life expectancy. Lia's genetic code was divided between the three clocks; three sets of numbers from one to nine danced within, each number a magnitude of moments, of experiences within her lifetime. The zero within each clock remained static – the void, from where she had entered Earthly life and would leave it, and the third, a premature ending of her choice, should she will it.

Her body continued to disintegrate and form into several right angles, the bends of arms and legs, the eyes to the end of the nose, the nose to the mouth. Throughout her form, triangles appeared and dissolved into the nothingness of the void, allowing Lia's mental energy to merge peacefully within the flow of movement. Lia watched in wonder the sum of the seasons her genetic code had been allotted, the time of her death, and then the symbols vanished.

Ormus appeared and took her hand; another female stood beside him. They were as one, and she could feel their wholeness as a force of absolute purity. Lia thought how perfect they appeared together, man and woman, male and female, balanced to the point where they merged as one. The vision disappeared and Lia sensed her body returning to normal. Another figure appeared before her, his silhouette a dazzling mantle of silver suffused with the Saturn colour of orange flame, the nature of this life form a stranger to her. It was René, her father.

'The Holocene woman is Ormus' female equal,' he said, answering the question she was about to ask. 'They are elders of the Holocene race, and are known as the "Choice Absolute" to their race.'

Lia did not question their title, it seemed perfect to her.

Raphiel appeared beside Lia, his body manifesting as recognisable matter to her in the nothingness of the universe. 'Let me explain to you why balance is the purpose and the goal of the challenges. Within the emergence of a human life the spirit of the soul is split into many characters, and each of those character traits will be found in strength within one or more members of the family to which you are born: the family with whom you will learn to be at peace, or do battle. Each family unit provides life's situations from which outside experiences are gathered whilst growing to adulthood, and each place or event provides the conditions where life's challenges take place. The challenges are put into action upon the board of chance, to allow the multiple characters to compete and accomplish a balanced view of mortal life, in order for the spirit of the soul to evolve. Pythagoras, the Greek philosopher and mathematician, found the code of the universe when chancing upon numerology, but failed to see the truth that lay written there. For example, one species, human, with its unique genetic code, containing a series of numbers reduced to a single unit. However, the entirety of the sum total is important; it contains a mortal's life lessons, and if any numbers are not present, particularly the nine – the number of unconditional love – then the body experiencing that life cycle must find the means to embrace the missing lesson. Otherwise, the life experience will remain incomplete and present a difficult passage through life; consequently, that life will not achieve its full potential. Mortal life has a limited amount of free will, and those who continually live on the outer edges of balance by choice, freely embracing a multitude of negative experiences, will find when they reach the furthest point from the centre of equilibrium that a sudden exit from life will show itself. However, there are exit clauses whereby the genetic code allows death in order to promote a turn in mankind's way of thinking, the Christ-like sacrifice for instance, which applies to animal, plant or human life. The circumstances of these exits, such as illness, suicide or violent death etc., are a gift to the evolvement of all life because they bring about great change within conditions.'

Painful as that may be for the mortals' loved ones, thought Lia. She tried to remember what her life span was; the memory of the code that had been revealed to her was now forgotten, and the code for her people to move through the void, *what of that?*

Her father stood before her. 'You have the code; every human, every species within Universe Four has their unique code buried deep within their memory. Hafnium has given you the key to the universe, but in truth, Lia, you have always known it. When the Otom travel to and from the surface, wherever they are, you, the elders will know their minds and the void will unlock from within your consciousness. Be assured of this.'

Lia felt her father's love embrace her.

'It is time for me to return, Lia.'

The strength of her father's love remained with her as his form disappeared; without regret or fear she was ready for the challenge looming before her. The silhouette of a white dove appeared in the cosmos, a sign of peace for the Holocene race, and symbolic of absolute wholeness.

Ormus took her hand. 'The planetary forces are waiting for us, Lia.'

Chapter 8

The Planetary Forces

Serenity emanated from the omnipresent love reaching out to mankind; a generosity of spirit had settled over Universe Four. The energy of hope pulsed outward from the planet Jupiter, the low humming resonance adding a slow magnetic rhythm to the silent orchestra of outer space.

The planetary forces of the Milky Way galaxy were highly evolved spiritual entities that existed in the realms of pure consciousness, expressing the beauty and perfection of the star formations. They had waited for Hafnium to command them, having predicted this moment, longing for the freedom to use their inspirational forces to guide mankind through his final chapter upon Earth.

Hafnium began. 'I call upon Aries, the activator, who emanates the vision of Mars. To you I give the responsibility of seeding the minds of the Otom with my ideals, but thereafter it is not your job to nourish them; you will endow them with the gift of self esteem, not ego, in order that mankind may use wisdom with courage to attempt new concepts.

'To you, Taurus, endower of love in all guises, who emanates the spirit of Venus in all things, to you I give the power and responsibility of building the seed of Aries into substance. You must remain strong, and not waver in your duty until the task is complete.'

Hafnium then called to the twins, Gemini, whose work it was to conceptualise the intellect of Mercury, the messenger. 'Go forth and spread your gift of awareness upon the Otom. It is your destiny to call men's thoughts to order, making them work for the answers they seek.'

The moon turned her smiling face towards her luminary, Cancer, as the Master spoke to her. 'From you, Cancer, I ask that you make it your duty and purpose to bring to the Otom a clear concept of the higher mind. May you also reveal to them laughter as well as tears in order that they may develop a fullness of heart within.'

The sun, whose energy powered the will of all matter, turned his powerful rays towards the east to gaze upon Leo. Hafnium's voice cut clearly across the universe for all to hear. 'Leo, it will be your task to express my magnificence in all its power and goodness for the Otom to see, for honour is yours, and I know you can carry this responsibility.'

Ormus, born under the star sign Leo in his time upon Earth, smiled as he remembered the tasks he had performed, and the adventures he had experienced under the watchful gaze of the star tribes. He looked to where Lia watched enthralled by the beauty surrounding her, still bound by Earth-time and fifty years older since his passing. Lia felt his nearness and her thoughts flowed out to him as she remembered her youth and the adventures they had shared at the beginning of the end of days.

Mercury's brilliance flowed out to embrace another that emanated his virtues, Virgo, one who was always absorbed in the labours of the universe.

Hafnium spoke. 'Virgo, the work set aside for you is perfect for your temperament. You will have the task of making man examine everything he undertakes, especially when seeking guidance for the Otom. You are to encourage them to scrutinise every decision that they make.'

Hafnium became silent for a moment, as the radiance of Venus grew strong again for her second star, Libra.

'Libra, star of gentle manner, you will do mankind a great service. You are to see that man is mindful of his duties to others, that he balances the scales of life and learns to reflect on the other side of his actions in order that he may become skilled at cooperating with all.'

Pluto raised himself, his eminence that of one who knows of all deceptions, his task to imbue mankind's senses with intuition. 'Scorpio,' he called, 'listen to what the Master is about to say to you.'

Hafnium spoke. 'Scorpio, you know the minds of men, and what you know you keep secret. You share their pain, their secrets and their perversions, and for this gift of silence, which is a heavy burden, you are given no thanks. Your task will be to stay with man until all that remains of his darker side is conquered, and he is ready to return to the other-worlds. You must help man carry his burdens until he can discharge the darker side of his soul.'

Dynamic Jupiter looked at her charge shooting through the sky like a giant flame. 'Sagittarius, stop your play; come, listen to what the Master has to say to you.'

Hafnium's resonance was forbearing of the playful Sagittarius. 'For you, Sagittarius, the task will be to bring laughter to mankind when he is deep in bitterness; there will be many that will need you, and you are suited to the task with your abundance of energy. Do well, Sagittarius, fire your arrows of hope right into the heart of the matter.'

A warning voice rang out, calling the star Capricorn. Honourable Saturn's words were short and to the point, advising the star to pay attention, but there was no need; Capricorn was well versed in the responsibility and serious nature of life.

Hafnium spoke gently. Capricorn responded well to this approach. 'Capricorn, for you the labour will be hard but the rewards great. I give unto you the responsibility of man's actions and into your hands the safe keeping of his soul.'

Uranus held her breath; she knew that her progeny Aquarius was headstrong, and worried that he might wander from his duty to mankind's continuing evolvement. Saturn also had words for Aquarius, entreating him to remember his duty to collective thought and loyalty to others. Hafnium waited, knowing the headstrong Aquarius would not listen for long; his mind was always flitting here and there visioning new possibilities, rarely aware of the needs of those around him because of his gift for seeing the bigger picture.

'Aquarius, I hand to you the responsibility of future potential. Help mankind further his development in all ways possible.'

Neptune called to the star Pisces and she came laughing before the Master, her brightness a mask to the confusion that personified her being.

'Pisces, last of my twelve star warriors, I ask that you commit to memory all of mankind's sorrows. This will reflect upon you gravely, but I know you can carry these burdens for me.' Hafnium breathed a deep sigh that resonated out into the eternal space of Universe Four, touching all that had come forth from him. Hafnium's light strengthened again and those gathered were bathed in his radiance.

'Let the light and love of Hafnium, the grand master of Universe Four, restore the plan on Earth.' Chiron and the universal chequerboard disappeared, leaving the stars and planets to settle back into position within the universe.

Chapter 9

The Snowstorm

Lia stood by the bedroom window; Ormus was no longer with her and she wondered if she had been daydreaming, then she noticed the white heather on the window sill, a gift from Ormus, picked from the Heavenly Mountain that arcs the world. Lia lifted her hand to the open window; outside the snow was falling heavily and the sky looked grey and laden; it was a January morning, and bitterly cold. Lia smiled as the cold snow touched her hand and began to melt; it was the first she had seen since Ormus' passing, some five years before the migration. The snow, encouraged by a strong north wind, was showering the sparse winter greenery with flurries and swirls of white angel's breath, while beneath its mantle, the earth's vegetation struggled to renew itself. A beautiful transformation was turning the darkened earth to pure white. Was this purification a sign of new life that would spring forth when the days became longer, and hopefully warmer? The faint rays of dawn were beginning to penetrate the still-toxic clouds that shadowed the healing Earth, and with the emerging light came hope of the Otom's return to the Earth's surface.

Lia heard the kitchen door open below her, and her two grandsons ran into the garden, the boys still pulling on their coats as they ran out into the snow with Dorri close behind them.

'Now don't you go waking your grandmother yet, she needs to rest this morning!'

The boys looked up to see Lia standing at the open window.

Kiron called up to her, his face now wet with the snow that

settled upon his upturned cheeks. 'Gran, look at the sky, it's snowing, it's frozen water! It's so beautiful.' He held his arms out and spun around. 'Gran,' he shouted up to her excitedly, 'this is the happiest day of my life!'

Haydes echoed his brother's sentiments by gathering the snow and throwing it at him, both laughing as he did so. Excitedly they danced together in the snow, while experiencing a childhood memory that they would never forget.

Lia remembered her own childhood when the landscape had been covered with trees and high-growing shrubbery, a winter's snowfall making them appear magical and mysterious in the twilight. As she watched her grandsons, she prayed that the world would return to its former glory.

Lia's thoughts were interrupted by a knock on the door. Dorri waited for a moment and then entered. 'My dear, why are you still by that open window? Shut it and come back to your bed,' she said without waiting for an answer. 'I have spoilt you this morning and brought you a breakfast tray. The boys won't be bothering you for a while, not while they can play in the snow.' Dorri suddenly slowed, her eyes taking in the flurry of snow outside. 'It makes you want to cry to see them,' she said, 'never having seen a snowfall before. It was so normal in our younger days.'

Lia nodded in agreement, and smiling at Dorri's fussing she did as she was told and climbed into bed, pulling the bedclothes over her to receive the proffered tray.

Some time later, Lia appeared in the kitchen dressed and ready for whatever the day had to offer. The boys were still in the garden, and having completed a snowman with instructions from Dorri, they were busy throwing snowballs at one another while the snow continued to fall relentlessly.

The phone rang and Lia moved into the hallway to answer it.

'Hello, Mother, how are you, how are the boys?'

Lia's heart jumped happily at hearing her son's voice. She often worried about him, especially when there was trouble at the coastal farming projects; she knew only too well the danger that presented. For the preceding four decades, the Otom and the Mers had sustained a plan to put down acres of oxygenating plants near to the world's shorelines. On some continents, the Cunmen had gained access to this vital source of plant food, and while sabotaging these they were damaging the acres of coral reefs that lay beneath them.

Only after the usual family matters had been spoken of, and the boys' encounter with the snowfall had been told, did she ask about his work and the trouble that was brewing in the Philippines. Deron played down his concern for the damaged coral reefs, and made light of the time needed to replant the acres of plant life that had been destroyed. He knew his mother's life purpose was to see the Otom live upon the Earth's surface again, and each time the beds were damaged, it meant a further wait was possible: the shoreline oxygenating farms that encompassed every continent were essential to the move.

Lia asked for news of the other new sites; she longed to hear that one of the new communities had caught sight of some form of wildlife. Deron answered his mother with words that were of Ormus' rationale.

'You know they will be sighted soon, Mother, have patience,' he chided gently.

Lia smiled. 'Yes, you are quite right. It's just that I long to sight a flock of birds, or see an animal roaming the land again. I miss the world as it was, and my heart cries out at all this barren countryside. When will we see the new future begin, for myself I am like a child, I cannot wait?'

They said their goodbyes and Lia put the phone down, picking up her shawl as she did so and moving towards the kitchen door. 'Boys,' she called out, 'come inside and let's plan our day.'

The land sites for the new communities had been carefully chosen, and were now up and running, each community capable of housing one thousand Otom. Lia's old home in Cornwall, the Causeway, had been home to Ormus during his lifetime upon Earth. Just before his death, the property had passed into Lia's father's estate, and later it had passed to her. At the Causeway, Ormus had taught Lia the wisdom of self-healing, and of her

Holocene lineage with the universal light forces, whom she would engage with to continue his work when he was gone. Some fifty years had passed since that time, and Lia's long-held wish that she would return to the Causeway had finally come to pass.

The Causeway perimeter appeared barren as if cradled in winter's busy cloak, while beneath the surface new growth prepared for the spring. Lia only hoped that was true. The landscape was truly dead, and the snow's pleasant mantle of white that covered its bareness was a joy to behold. For all the barrenness, Lia still loved her home and dreamed of the future when her children and their families would live at the Causeway. The land, and her precious gardens, would be filled with the sounds of birds, insects and animals again. Children's laughter would ring out amid the vibrant growth of an English countryside once more. Lia was happy; she had her memories of what was and thoughts of the Earth's future, and one day she hoped that her children and grandchildren would witness what she had seen, that which she could still see when daydreaming.

The other sites chosen were spread across the world, areas that had been the least affected by the holocaust. Regions that had been richly populated with numerous species of wildlife, forest, and plant life, and land that was rich in crystal minerals. The latter was to play a large part in the Otom's future, powering spatial energy science coupled with the new age energy that had emerged prior to the holocaust: man's ability to harness his own magnetic energy, the god fragment that had given life to his flesh, this was the energy he would use to communicate with those about him, with the aid of crystal power waves.

Lia felt confident that there was a future for the Otom upon the Earth's surface; her only misgivings were her son's part in it. She was having many dreams now, dreams that often became nightmares. Some were of her son and his work in the marine trenches, but predominantly Lia dreamed of another danger, the extraction of the fire enzymes from below the Mer world that lay deep in the bowels of the Earth. Lia felt sure she was being prepared for something, and did it involve her son? Deron was a grown man, but still her child; she could see him no other way. Lia suddenly felt afraid.

Ormus stood before her. 'Cease your worrying, Lia; have I not told you over and over, destiny must lead us…'

Ormus disappeared and Lia stilled her thoughts.

Chapter 10

The Gift of 'Enzyme Fire'

Lia had been troubled by a recurring dream in which Deron was one of a crew lost deep within the bowels of the Earth. Now she was living the dream as she waited on the beach below the Causeway for news of him.

For the past few months, she had worried for her son's safety while he worked in the Philippine Trenches. The persistent dreams, warning of danger, had now become a waking reality. The morning was grey and dull, the rain drizzling down steadily. Lia pulled the long dark weatherproof mackintosh close up around herself; on her head she wore a wide-brimmed matching hat. Her profile looked fragile, her long slender body bent forward, taut beneath the dark coat pulled tightly around her.

Ormus appeared before her. He felt no concern for the present situation while seeing a little into her future; this condition was part of the Otom's ongoing challenge and her son's destiny.

Lia waited all night for news of Deron who was trapped beneath the ocean trench, the Marianas. Deron's wife, Mariana, named after the deep water valleys, waited with Lia for news of him and the five members of crew still trapped deep in the bowels of the Earth.

The crew had gone to harvest fire enzymes, a food extract that was essential to the Otom's good health: life-giving proteins that they could not produce themselves and that in the past had been supplied by whole proteins generated from the land. Lack of the health-sustaining proteins was one of the many misfortunes that had befallen the new ocean people. In the early years of the migration, another condition began to cause serious problems among the Otom; the lack of sunlight began to cause attacks of depression and weakness among the older generations, and it was realised they would not achieve the longevity of their forefathers. And the women of childbearing age were failing to bear children. Something had to be done!

The Otom elders had presented their problem to Zrsiofour who, knowing little of human physiology, decided that the only way to help the Otom regain full health was to create an extract from the fire enzyme that would give them longevity, but that would take time.

Chapter 11

Zrsiofour – King of the Mer People

Zrsiofour had been deeply troubled when asked by Hafnium to take the Otom to live among his people. To allow mankind, creatures that were capable of such violence, to live alongside his own people: how could he agree to such a thing? Within the ocean world, he had seen much evidence of their murderous ways; the sea dwellers had been tortured and killed unnecessarily in mankind's plundering and exploitation of the sea. His fear of their destructive nature had made him want to refuse, but how could he? Wasn't this the destiny of both races, to live and evolve as one kind? Zrsiofour recalled uneasily the sacrifice that the animal kingdom had made for man, and with a heavy heart he reluctantly agreed to Hafnium's request.

The Mers were beings half man and half fish, and natural inhabitants of the world's oceans and the subterranean world below. They lived in harmony with the sea dwellers, their nourishment coming from the vegetation that grew in abundance in the deep ocean valleys and forests. They were able to survive conditions of extreme compression when entering the deeper regions below their cavernous world and beyond where the fire enzyme grew in abundance. Extracting the fire enzymes for research had been easy for the Mers, but when a formula had been found to help the Otom, the harvesting of enzymes had begun on a vast scale, and to achieve this they had need of mankind's past industrial skill.

Harvesting the fire enzyme was a dangerous venture for the Otom crew. Their bodies could not withstand the same pressure as the Mers, and the outdated pressurised vehicles they used in the deeper oceanic regions would not support life in depths such as Subterrania. A deep sea vehicle that was lightweight and efficient at boring through the fragile cavernous terrain was needed to build tunnels wide enough for smaller transporters. Hundreds of vehicles built for deep sea excavation had been found when opening the landsite in Wiltshire. These, they decided, would do the job and protect the Otom; a prayer had been answered.

Below the world of the Mers, the lichenin algae plant, which produced the fire enzyme, was at its most pure and came from an uninhabited source deep within the Earth's crust. The fire enzyme grew in one place only, the subterranean valleys below the entrance to the Mer world. The Marianas Trench concealed a cavernous world of fragile volcanic rock that reached up towards the surface from the Earth's seabed, thirty-six thousand feet beneath the South Pacific Ocean.

The Otom's home, the City of Memories, was all that remained of the Holocenes' time upon Earth and a past civilisation of mankind's iniquity that had been cast into the sea; the city now lay protected by Zrsiofour beneath the ocean bed of the Marianas, and for nearly fifty years it had been re-inhabited by the Otom, the chosen ones. Zrsiofour remembered it as a time fraught with minor and major disasters. The Otom had gradually adjusted to their new diet; however it had failed to provide a complete food source, and the lifestyle changes that the 'lightworkers' had made, in preparation for the migration, could not prepare them for the extreme adjustments needed within their new environment. In the proceeding years this proved extremely painful for them. In the decades that followed they longed for the old ways, the light of the sun and oxygen in their lungs, which moved some of the older ones to give up the fight and return to spirit.

The incoming Otom infants, like the elders, were returning to the other-worlds before time, some taking their mortal mothers with them, both mother and infant unable to sustain the challenges of the flesh. Child spirits that had eagerly awaited the challenge of mortal existence had, when the time came, decided to terminate the experience. Hafnium, the grand master, knowing this would come to pass, allowed the souls that wished to relinquish the Earth challenge to do so. Everything needed to balance in Universe Four, even chaos and disaster. The challenge had continued, and the spirits returning before their time had come again to play their part in the future. Zisiufour felt blessed, those times of hardship were now behind the Otom thanks to his people, the Mers.

The Cunmen, living on the Earth's surface, were receiving information on the Otom's resources from a conspirator within the Otom race. They frequently sabotaged the coral and vegetation beds in shallow waters, harvesting the fresh food for their own needs; their bodies were ravaged from living in a climate poisoned by radiation, and the rich source of food was invaluable to them. The Cunmen being unacclimatised to harvesting in the deep ocean, their attempts to sabotage the marine beds on a large scale were unsuccessful, but each attempt on the shallow beds near to land was enough to slow down the return of the Otom to the Earth's surface.

There was one other source of nutrients that the Cunmen needed to help them recover sufficiently and possibly to repopulate their dwindling race. The fire enzyme that grew deep within the bowels of the Earth. Its properties were known to include miraculous healing powers, and there was one person who could supply their need.

Chapter 12

Mikell Lang

The Cunmen's conspirator, Mikell Lang, was trusted by all who had elected him as a delegate to the council of elders in the City of Memories.

Mikell was the same age as Deron Debarc-Major, forty-eight years old, and an associate by common benefit, but not a close friend. Deron, although brought up in a non-judgemental society, found something lacking in Mikell that was to prove ill-fated for the Otom.

Zrsiofour had known for many years the treachery instigated by the one, Mikell Lang. He had watched the Otom's struggle with great sorrow as they overcame each problem, never suspecting Mikell Lang, a trusted advisor, of treachery. Zrsiofour had remained silent on all problematic issues, intervening only when the council of elders asked him, reminding himself many times over the passing years that his task was to watch mankind's progress in the new world without intervention.

Deron and his crew's current assignment was to harvest the fire enzyme algae from the underworld, a world the Mers called Subterrania. For some time the fields of fire enzymes had been in preparation, Zrsiofour's people, the Mers, having worked hard to bring about a subtle change in the enzyme's properties. The lichenin-algae containing the fire enzyme was so pure that the Otom's digestive processes could not tolerate it in its natural state. With the process completed, the fire enzyme extract was easy to digest for the Otom and their sickly infants. New algae beds had been planted by the Mers, adding man's genetic code to the fire enzyme in order to promote a protein synthesis that was digestible for the Otom. When a suitable extract was found, the Mers gathered the first harvest and the new enzyme was tested on the adult Otom, and then on the children who had grown beyond infancy. Eventually they were able to infuse the nursing mothers' milk with the tested extract, which the infants consumed with good results; they began to show signs of healthy growth.

The deaths among the adults and the low birth rate had put the new race of man at serious risk. With the harvesting of the fire enzymes, they were beginning to flourish again.

Deron Debarc-Major and his team of Otom and Mers were working to achieve two things: the survival and healthy growth of the Otom race, and to stop the Cunmen's attempt to keep their race below the oceans. The latter could only be successful if they could deliver a message of strength to the saboteurs and stop them destroying the coastal vegetation and coral beds.

Mikell Lang had other plans, having been offered a far greater reward than equality as an Otom: power and leadership, a reward that Mikell Lang was unable to resist. The leaders of the Cunmen, his co-conspirators, were offering him a powerful position in their goal towards global rule, their objective being to have one world race, bringing the Cunmen, Otom and Mers under one rule, with which to plunder the Earth's remaining resources.

Chapter 13

Subterrania – The Mastermind Explorer

The Mastermind Explorer had been missing for eight hours in the subterranean trenches of the Marianas. Deron and his crew had entered the Earth's innermost world, Subterrania, carrying on board the machines that would harvest the fire enzyme needed for the Otom; now all waited for news of the Mastermind and crew.

The Mastermind Explorer was a powerful load-bearing machine that was used for excavating and transporting heavy loads of rock deposits; it was able to bore through the Earth's subterranean core at enormous speed, creating tunnels to link up the dangerously water-saturated caverns where the fire enzyme algae grew.

A catastrophic miscalculation involving the weight of the new harvesters taken onboard had sent the Mastermind Explorer plunging deep into the fragile interior of Subterrania. The harvesting machines were to replace the Mers that had been harvesting the fire enzyme manually.

The harvesters had an unlimited power supply that was provided by the same sourced crystal energy harnessed from the oceans for the City of Memories. Unlike the Mer people, they were virtually indestructible in the fragile terrain – computerised vehicles that could obey commands and harvest the algae beds in half the time taken by a Mer crew.

The Mastermind Explorer had been brought from the Wiltshire landsite, and the harvesters had been salvaged, along with other machinery, from the world's oceans which after the holocaust had been littered with freight cargo, the final tidal wave having sent all shipping to the bottom of the oceans, later to be salvaged by the Otom and the Mer and stored beneath the ocean in dry volcanic zones.

Subterrania was a sacred place where the Mer people never ventured unless their king commanded it. The fire enzyme, which the Mers had been harvesting, sprang from a fragile world where the atmosphere was extremely humid and volcanic. Molten rock spewed out mineral-rich magma deposits to which another element was added, the sediment that came from the sacred burial grounds of the Mers. The combined rock mineral and decomposing sediment were the elements that gave the fire enzyme algae its unique healing quality.

The Lacofpartin valley where the fire enzyme grew was a vast landscape, its lower valley basin an immense lake filled with thick brackish water where the mineral-rich fire enzyme grew abundantly in channels which ebbed away and upwards from the lake, allowing the algae to grow in the cavernous channels' moist hot atmosphere.

It was into this watery womb at Lacofpartin that the Mers placed the bodies of their loved ones after they had passed from physical life. The ceremony of farewell was initiated ten days after the death of a Mer, with only the higher elders of the race and King Zrsiofour travelling down into the world of Subterrania to accompany the dead for burial.

The Mers, at Zrsiofour's command, had worked diligently to section off a part of the lake at Lacofpartin, in which they began to bury the Otom's deceased. The bodies decomposed quickly to become part of the mineral-rich water, which later produced a dark purple culture of the fire enzyme as opposed to the natural black culture. As soon as it was possible the Mers began to harvest the purple algae from the caverns, and the trials began …

The Mers had no need of the fire enzymes, nor would they ever contemplate eating the algae that grew there. Their food chain was supplied by the world above, the oceans that merged and receded throughout their world with the rise and fall of the deep ocean tides. They gathered their food by means of the oceans washing the beaches of the Earth's crust, the tides emptying and filling their world to bring an abundance of health-giving vegetation to their door.

The subterranean world of Mer was a place of outstanding beauty; near to the centre of the Earth, the mountainous seascape was a deep coral red and rich in luxuriant plant life. The Mers lived among the sea forests where they constructed their family dwellings from the abundant flora and overhanging ferns. Vegetation of multifaceted greens and emeralds inhabited the red rock valleys, lucid intermingling colours of all shades both vivid and pastel, colours that reflected panoramic rainbows onto the ceiling of their world. The trees, black as jet and burgundy, grew tall and proud with long dark green roots that were gnarled with age and protruded from the water-logged ground; evergreen foliage that stirred continuously in an ever-flowing movement with the tidal water. The tidal waters enabled the Mers to move freely within their precipitous world, a race of mermaids as real as all things living, a myth to man until the time of the holocaust.

King Zrsiofour's citadel lay in the valley of the sea orchids, near to the City of Memories. It was here that the Mer peacekeepers, chosen from each subcontinent, would go to mediate on behalf of the oceanic race. This ancient race would gather among the multi-coloured sea orchid beds to speak with their king on all matters concerning his people, and while they mediated with their king, they would dress each other's long flowing hair with white flowers from the orchid beds as a sign of peaceful arbitration.

When the Otom had come to live in Zrsiofour's kingdom, they had survived as did the Mers on vegetation from the oceans, but as the years went by the need for the fire enzyme supplement had become critical; they also lacked the light of the sun, which had changed their outwardly appearance considerably. But the sun was now penetrating the dispersing toxic layer surrounding the Earth. It was time for the Otom to return to the surface.

Chapter 14

The Challenges Begin

Lia had risen early that morning; unable to sleep she had left the Causeway and made her way down to the beach. Knowing it was forbidden and without thinking of her safety, she had slipped beyond the perimeter gates unnoticed by the duty guards.

The Cunmen were always watching, always looking for a weak link and this morning Lia had broken the golden rule, although today it didn't seem to matter; she trusted her spirit guides and knew she would be safe. Lia felt she had good reason for breaking the rules, reasons that were unexplainable other than that she knew her son was possibly facing death and would be tested severely.

Lia looked out from the shelter of her cloak to find Ormus standing beside her. 'This is the moment Mariana and I have been dreading,' she said. 'For us, for the Otom, this is the beginning, the first of the challenges, isn't it?'

Ormus nodded in agreement. Behind him the sun was trying to break through the heavy cloud, the weakened light bathing Lia's face in warmth, then it was gone again.

Raphiel appeared beside them, and turning to Lia, he said, 'My dear, for what comfort it is, I will be with you for the duration of this challenge; I will be here to support you.'

Raphiel's beautiful voice drifted through her mind like that of a poet versed in Shakespeare, his kindly words reminding her of the comfort he had been after Ormus' passing.

Before Lia could thank Raphiel for his support, Ormus said, 'And I will be here with you when I can, Lia.'

Lia turned to look at him.

'For the rest of the time,' he continued, 'I will be with your son as an invisible support, hopefully encouraging him to make the right decisions. Time is short now, and if he is to succeed in his bid for freedom with one other, then there is no time to lose.' Ormus looked down at Lia's face, the fine lines of age taking nothing from the beauty that manifested from within.

Lia looked at Ormus, her eyes searching for an answer, but before she could question him, he spoke again.

'Lia, I have not the foresight to tell the outcome of this challenge; I do not have the answer that you seek. This is your son's destiny, and whether he will pass through the test of fire is entirely in his hands. If his trust is strong enough, then the outcome will be good.'

Lia's thoughts went back to Ormus' turn of phrase, 'one other'. Ormus did not make statements that were without meaning; she already knew that four of the crew had perished: lost friends whom she had shared her life with. The times spent together as one family, and the children who would now experience the grief of losing their parents. The four crewmembers who were known to have died were husbands and wives, each with children who were now orphans. Lia closed her eyes, trying to rationalise this new cruelty, this loss. She suddenly felt angry, the heat rushing through her body. 'Why do the assumed innocent suffer? It may be only another experience to Hafnium, the grand master, but it is pain and grief to the afflicted.' As soon as the words were spoken her anger subsided, leaving her feeling cold and drained. 'I'm sorry,' she whispered, 'I know we cannot hope to evolve without these experiences.'

The empty beach suddenly came alive with the sound of footsteps as Mariana came hurrying towards her with the guards following close behind.

Eight hours earlier Deron had taken charge of the Mastermind with the harvesters on board, his mission to transport the cargo down to Lacofpartin. The success of the mission was important to maintaining the Otom's good health, the project having been in progress most of his adult life and, after years of faltering progress, having finally been successful. Since that time, the Otom had emerged from the underworld; the land sites were up and running and waiting to be fully colonised, and the newborn infants were growing up strong, their immune systems continuing to show positive signs of vital health.

Eight hours earlier, Deron had felt absolute joy as the Mastermind Explorer began its journey below the world of the Mers to Subterrania; he felt his crew had done everything to ensure success.

Deron's family had become accustomed to his long periods of absence while he worked in Subterrania or on land at one of the community sites. Like many scientists, his work directed his life, and his ultimate purpose was always the Otom's return to the surface. Deron's wife, Mariana, was used to the single-mindedness of her husband; she accepted the nature of her marriage and made it work, especially as their survival beyond the great disaster was attributed to his work. That alone helped her to accept the little time he spent with her and the boys. The success of the project was vital, not only because the source of food was invaluable to them, but it was out of reach, being so far down in the depths of the earth. She had accepted that the project would mean another long absence from the family, but she was used to that now. With a plentiful supply of the fire enzymes, they would continue to increase their population. Mariana wanted a peaceful life upon the surface for her sons and her family; she constantly thought of the unopened underground sites, knowing the Cunmen would rise up again if they gained access to the machinery and weapons held there. Her thoughts would often become shadowed as she thought of the possibilities that the future held. The beginning of a new and peaceful life for all of them; if the Cunmen ceased to exist. But someone within her race was helping them, and did they have the knowledge to open the sites?

Mariana remembered nothing of the time before the holocaust when her race had been countless races. Many viewings were shown of the surface of the Earth before and after the devastation.

These viewings were shown for teaching purposes, and were a lesson in cause and effect. She recalled the first time that she had travelled to the surface of the Earth; awaking to find herself lying upon her side, her hands touching the ground beneath her, and the gradual awareness of a light that dazzled her eyes, and the distant memory that made her realise she was seeing and feeling the sun. As her eyes had focused from the sleep of zero travel, she could see that the land was still blackened and scarred but that here and there, new growth was showing. Then she had noticed, in the sandy earth among a clump of dry tough grass weed, a single purple flower billowing gently back and forth in the wind current of the incoming tide. Mariana had felt her heart surge with hope and excitement. Since that time, she had seen great change at the Causeway as her work took her back and forth. The weather conditions were still freezing for most of the year because of the lack of sunlight upon the Earth. And only when the summer months came around, and if the weather conditions were right, would the children be able to live comfortably above the oceans; then the children would accompany their parents to the new community sites.

Mariana was a delegate to the council of elders, and it was for this reason she had been chosen to work on the surface when the Otom set up the first community at the Causeway, the site of Lia's old home. As a result, a large community now flourished inside the five-mile perimeter that was protected by a military guard, who monitored the movement of the Cunmen upon the surrounding land and shoreline. Since that time, twelve more sites had been established, the Causeway being site one where all decisions were taken to make the sites work efficiently. Site one included a court that convened to make vital decisions regarding the inhabitants, and any new procedures regarding safety. The court was simple in structure and procedure, the Otom having raised themselves from below the oceans still aware that unity of spirit was their only chance of survival.

Mariana had not neglected her duty; she was as dedicated to her work as her husband was to his, both seeing the purpose of their life at an integrated level beyond the individual. As part of the new race, they were to see the dawning of a new world from which their children would enjoy the worlds beyond their universe. Now Mariana waited for news; Deron was missing, the Explorer having plunged deep into a ravine below the surface of Subterrania.

The Otom council of elders were aware they had a conspirator in their midst; how else had the Cunmen been able to locate and plunder the food beds, and damage coral reefs? In the arctic conditions that followed the holocaust's initial fires, the surviving Cunmen had been drawn to any source of heat that would keep them alive. Over decades, the world's great cities had burned; lakes and deserts saturated with oil, and other toxic materials, fuelled the blazing fires which provided heat to keep the Cunmen that had left the opened sites, alive. When the fires had eventually expired, they had been saved from extinction by the betrayer, Mikell Lang. He had given them access to the shallow water food beds, which they pillaged and partially destroyed, and with the sun's growing strength to penetrate the radiation cloud around the Earth, and the fresh source of food in the waterbeds, they were growing stronger, although the few infants that were being born were still dying.

Chapter 15

Senithe – Custodian of Subterrania

The crew of the Mastermind were enjoying some light-hearted banter as they bored through the rock; just a few more feet to drill before entering the fire enzyme caves. So confident were they that they had decided to carry four of the harvesters inside the belly of the Explorer and begin harvesting the fire enzymes immediately. The crew showed none of their usual tension; they had come to know the density and properties of the rock mass that they were drilling through, rock mass that was fragile and lighter than the rock formation found in the Mer world, and twice as fragile as the rock formation found upon the surface of the Earth. The crew had just an hour's work left and felt boosted by the confidence their captain was showing, each of them feeling his excitement as one of their greatest achievements neared its close. They stood laughing and making jokes with one another, talking of their next assignment with the Mastermind Explorer. Paul, Deron's second in command and his closest friend, was especially cheerful, having been told he was to accompany Deron on his next visit to the surface. The fire enzyme project was coming to an end for the crew, and a new team to man the harvesters had been chosen.

Paul was a dedicated worker, which had gained him a credible insight into the ecosystems below the Earth's surface. He had marvelled at the world beneath Mer. Another hidden world, so hot that it was a place where few living creatures would be able to survive for long, only the fire enzymes seemed to thrive on the potent energy. He remembered the books brought from the surface to the valleys, the books depicting a soul known as the devil who lived within the very centre of the Earth, so hot a place of dwelling that only the very wicked survived to burn there in hell alongside the one called Satan. Recalling this myth brought a smile to his face.

Deron turned towards his friend. 'Paul, what the devil are you smiling at?'

'You don't want to know, lest it catch up with you.'

No sooner were the words out of his mouth than the sound of tearing and grinding came like a pitched scream to their ears and the Explorer lurched into a ninety-degree turn and plunged downward. The machine pitched downward through the widening gap, the crew flying across the cabin like rag dolls being tossed into the air, each one trying to hold on to something, but in vain, their bodies being smashed against the dislodged equipment. Down they plunged into the unfamiliar world of underground caves.

The Mers' world heard a distant shudder and then stillness; instinctively they knew that something had gone seriously wrong.

Senithe, the custodian of Subterrania, had watched over the work being carried out. She had seen the Explorer plunge, and the crew working on the outside of the cabin plummet down alongside the machine. They now lay dead, their smashed bodies caught upon the ledges where the Explorer had dropped out of sight into the fathomless cavern below them. Immediately she sent out a call that informed her race of death and injury, a sound like that of the whale, low and hollow. The sound was picked up and repeated, rapidly travelling along the ocean floor like lighted beacons that give a signal of importance on land.

Zrsiofour was the first to receive the news and came immediately to the site of the disaster.

Senithe came forward to welcome her king, and bringing her arms across her chest she greeted Zrsiofour, who returned her greeting with the sign of peace that was used with reverence in the Mer kingdom.

Senithe said, 'Zrsiofour, I have sad news. Four of the Otom crew have passed to the other-worlds, and the remaining crew inside the Explorer may have suffered injury or death. The Explorer is out of sight and out of reach for us. We have not the means to enter the deeper valleys of Subterrania, beneath the fire enzyme beds; to do so would mean certain death for a Mer. The crew's only hope is that they have survived without serious injury and may be able to find a way back. They have the advantage that their bodies are heat-absorbing, and they have the equipment to protect them against fire; although they have lived many decades here with us, they were born to live on land and absorb sunlight, whereas our people could not withstand the intense heat below Lacofpartin.'

Zrsiofour listened to Senithe knowing her words were wise; she had a great standing in the community because of her wealth of wisdom. His thoughts went to Deron and the crew, and his heart grew heavy for Lia and her family. The disaster would bring much despair and a loss of faith for the Otom and a further delay to their return to the surface.

'Why, oh why, has this happened now?' he questioned.

An image of Ormus appeared before Zrsiofour and then disappeared as quickly, the fleeting vision bringing him peace; this was a sign that the accident was the beginning of an important challenge. He turned to Senithe and asked her to summon the Mers who were working in the fire enzyme beds.

'Tell them they are needed to free the ones dashed upon the ledges below; they must be taken to the City of Memories for burial.'

Senithe made the sign of peace and left him.

Zrsiofour looked down into the gaping hole where the Explorer had fallen, and wondered: how was Ormus going to help the men and women trapped below? A woman he had not seen before began to materialise in front of him. Zrsiofour had a good memory for faces, even those of man, but this woman was different, having the silhouette of a cat around her human form like Ormus and Lia; the creature standing before him was a Holocene.

Chapter 16

Odelia and Glashadou's Vigil

The woman standing before him introduced herself as Odelia and gave the Mer sign of peace. For a moment Zrsiofour remained silent, absorbed in her appearance and the tail that flickered above her head. The tail disappeared and she smiled at him, her Earthly apparition portraying quick twinkling grey eyes above rounded red cheeks in a face that radiated charm. The image of rosy warmth was held beneath a thick mop of green hair that reminded him of a land plant, the strawberry.

'Hello,' she said, aware that Zrsiofour was preoccupied by her appearance. 'My Earthly name was Margarita Odelia Cavil, or Strawberry to my family and close friends. And this is . . .'

Within the blink of an eye another Holocene appeared before him, whom she introduced as Glashadou, known as Glas in his lifetime as a human.

'Nice to make your acquaintance,' he said brightly, looking at Zrsiofour with great interest. Glashadou had vanished from the Earth at the time of Ormus' passing, to return with him to Holocene, and Odelia had followed them not long after. Since that time he had travelled to several universes, to dimensions where complex civilisations existed, which for his and his travelling companion Odelia's inquisitive nature had been just perfect. The silhouette of Glas the human grew stronger, his manner presenting a friendly and good-humoured individual, whereas Glashadou the Holocene was serious by nature. Glashadou continued, 'Hope you don't mind us turning up; we're just going to pop down to the bottom of that hole and see what's what.'

Zrsiofour looked at them oddly; what were these two thinking of? They appeared by the jovial nature of their banter to think that this was some sort of away day distraction, and not at all serious. The trapped men and women below them needed help and might already be dead.

Intruding on his thoughts, Odelia became serious for a moment. 'Please don't think we are being disrespectful to the dead or dying, indeed we are not. We have been awaiting our attendance here for forty-five Earth years, and know exactly our part to play in the coming challenge. While Glashadou and I have been preparing for this day we have been travelling among the universes, and have yet to remind ourselves how it felt to have physical emotions. As Holocenes we are of one emotion, which is unconditional love, as well you know.'

'So much easier, much easier,' Glashadou repeated the statement, as was the way of Glas the human.

Zrsiofour smiled, having forgotten himself; as a Holocene he should recognise the truth told to him by the one called Odelia. 'Thank you for reminding me. Living with mankind's emotions for forty-five years can colour one's logic. I look forward to your return and news of the Otom crew ... and of Deron.' Zrsiofour felt his watery old heart ripple; he was very fond of Lia's son who had adapted easily to life below the oceans, adjusting with a natural familiarity to the water world, which he had personally encouraged.

Zrsiofour looked up from his thoughts to find the two newcomers gone. Motioning to his oarsmen, he bade them to take him back to his citadel to wait for news. As they rode out upon the ocean's flowing current, he could hear the sea dwellers singing their songs of lament, calling the angels from the other-worlds to come and take care of those who had terminated their life in the physical world.

Senithe looked up from her work with the Otom crew; she was aware of their grief at losing their friends and their fear of descending into the chasm where the Explorer had disappeared.

How would she instil in them the courage to climb down and retrieve the bodies of their friends? The Mermen working on the fire enzyme beds were strong enough to hold the ropes, but could not climb down. Senithe had an idea; she stilled the boat and turned it towards a cave nearby. Steadily she pushed the boat along the shallow canal towards the cave, the men rowing in the direction in which she pointed. Once outside the cave she sought, Senithe let go the boat and motioned the crew to enter the water and follow her. Passing through the narrow entrance, she warned the men to hold onto the sides of the cavern and pull themselves along; the water was deep with strong currents and to be cast adrift was dangerous. They entered a high domed cave, the water's reflection revealing walls veined with silver. Senithe reached for a ledge and pulled herself up, beckoning the Otom crew to follow. The argentite ceiling was rich in silver sulphide and hung heavy with fruits of deep purple and white, which grew among the stalactite crystalline formations endemic to the silver caves of Subterrania. The fruits' inexplicable dual qualities lay in the high concentration of iodine-rich kelp, providing a natural hormone, and colloidal silver, both essential to the ecosystem of the Mer world.

The crew were reluctant to leave the water, knowing that in the world of Subterrania many of the reefs and platforms were unable to support the weight of man, but did as they were asked. The cave felt cool and pleasant as they sat facing the water's edge, the water's current rippling to and fro, throwing shadows upon the cave walls.

'Look up at the cave ceiling and make a wish,' she said, 'and when you have done this we will make a space in our hearts for those who have left us to journey to the other-worlds.'

The Otom crew looked up to see a throng of faces in the crystalline forms above them, faces that were both pleasing and compassionate. Senithe began to chant, her voice becoming stronger as the language of the Mers echoed throughout the cave and travelled beyond, filling Subterrania with the divine lament.

Odelia and Glashadou appeared above the opening where the Explorer had disappeared, their healing energy gathering the departed to them, lifting the bodies of the four crewmen up and onto the ledge of the chasm where they lay side by side: motionless bodies wrapped in gossamer muslin, their still expressions emanating serenity.

Senithe gathered the fruit that was near to hand, fruit intertwined with the purple and white flowers that initiated their complex duality, a female flower and a male flower, perfection in the one. Senithe offered it to the crew to eat. For the Mers, the fruit was a source of food that grew from Subterrania to the Mer world above, an invaluable food that supported the immune system of the Mers, which they had named the fruit of divine magic. As the crew began to revive, their courage returned. Senithe guided them back to where their friends lay waiting to be taken to the City of Memories. The crew, thankful for being released from the recovery, gathered up the bodies of their friends and began their journey.

Glashadou and Odelia, having recovered the four members of crew, were nowhere to be seen; they had disappeared into the gaping hole to find the Explorer.

Chapter 17

The Longest Day

The Mastermind Explorer lay in the ninety-degree turn in which it had started its descent. The right-side front of the machine was flattened and the cabin, which sat high up on the front, lay partially buried in soft ground beneath a cloud of bedrock particles. Odelia and Glashadou appeared inside the cabin, Glashadou grimacing at what he saw and Odelia recognising that it was not a sight for the faint hearted. Some of the crew were badly injured and some were dead, their severed limbs lying grotesquely upon what was now the cabin floor and among the machinery. Glashadou and Odelia could see the spirits of the departed standing by their dismembered bodies, their faces showing disbelief. The five spirits stood waiting for instruction from Deron, as if his voice would awaken them from their nightmare. Glashadou realised with relief that Deron and one other crew member were alive, both still strapped into the command seats from which they had been piloting the Explorer at the point of descent.

Odelia moved to where Deron lay, her shimmering light bathing his body in rays of healing energy, while Glashadou explained to the two women and three men that had passed to spirit that they were soon to be accompanied to the other-worlds. They accepted their fate as soon as they were told, and only the women asked of their children's future, to which Glashadou replied that it was part of their children's destiny to experience loss at an early age. That their untimely experience of death was necessary to the future when they would help others in similar circumstances, and that they had chosen their parents for this reason as the five deceased standing before him had chosen this particular death. As light began to fill the cabin, the crew members linked hands for reassurance as a new dawn emerged for them, its intensity shutting out all else about them, and then it began to fade taking the newborn souls with it.

Odelia looked down at Deron; the light of the spirit guides had boosted her own healing power and he was waking. It seemed a miracle that he was unharmed by the experience other than a slight gash on the side of his forehead.

Deron looked across at Paul, while trying to avert his eyes from the carnage that lay scattered about him. His heart was beating furiously, his head was throbbing and he felt sick from the stench of drying blood. The life support system was still working and the lights were on, but the warm air in the cabin was beginning to turn the lifeless bodies into foul-smelling corpses. Deron wondered how long he had been unconscious, and how far down they were. More questions flooded his mind; he desperately wanted Paul to wake up – he would go mad if he were the only one alive. This was the first time he had been close enough to human death to smell its pungent odour; he let out a scream, unable to stop the panic inside his chest.

Paul's eyes opened and then shut tightly again. 'Oh no, please let it be a dream.' He could smell the stench of blood from the broken bodies. He began to sob.

Paul's sobbing suddenly brought Deron to his senses, and, releasing himself, he slid onto the tilted floor. As he did so his hands touched on the fleshy tissue that had been one of his crew members only hours before. Trembling with shock, he kept his eyes on his friend just a few feet away, and then he was holding Paul.

'It's going to be okay, we're going to get out of here. Do you understand what I'm saying, Paul?'

Paul stammered back a reply and began to cry uncontrollably. 'They're all dead.'

'I know it looks bad, but there's nothing we can do for them. They are at peace,' Deron answered shakily. 'And we must look for a way of getting out of here. I expect they are doing all they can above, but I feel we are on our own in this.'

Deron spoke the last words gently, knowing that Paul would come through better with reasoning, rather than commands. Deron was no longer the commander of the Explorer but one of two people who would have to support each other if they were to survive. Odelia and Glashadou listened compassionately, while Deron and Paul were unaware of their presence.

Ormus and Raphiel had appeared many times to Lia in the presence of Deron as he grew up, but he had never shown an awareness of their presence. It was now up to Glashadou and Odelia to make themselves visible to Deron and Paul, trusting that the gift of vision would aid their safe return to the surface.

Deron was beginning to think clearly, the pain in his head forgotten. He began checking the support systems connected to outside. Deron checked the oxygen levels to see if they would need breathing apparatus outside the cabin. The answer that came back was disappointing; the atmosphere contained high levels of sulphur dioxide, and they would have to use the gear.

Deron gave Paul an order. 'Check the breathing apparatus and get the climbing equipment ready. I will check the cutting gear and the power torches; we will need them, and the fireproof suits. We'll be a bit weighted, but at least we will be prepared for the worst.'

Paul stood up unharmed and without a scratch on him, only his thoughts were in pieces at the horror all around. Deron's taking charge had calmed him down and he began to breathe more easily, while thanking the forces of destiny that Deron had survived and he was not facing this nightmare alone.

For the first time in his life Deron heard another's thoughts; they came to him as clear as a bell, and turning to Paul he said, 'I thank the forces of destiny that you survived as well, I would have gone mad if I had been left here alone.'

They hugged each other, each wanting to support the other.

'We'll be all right,' they said assuredly, and they turned to the work in hand.

Within twenty minutes the equipment had been checked and they were kitted up, ready to move outside the safety of the cabin. Deron looked around the cabin for what he thought was the last time. The Explorer was finished; they would never be able to bring it up. He thought of the great times he had had captaining the powerful machine; he would miss it, and although he would captain another, it would never be the same. The memories came flooding back of a crew who were now on their way to the other-worlds, he believed without question.

Paul interrupted his thoughts to ask, 'Have you got the climbing hooks?'

Deron began to concentrate on the present and answered, 'Yes, we are all set for the ascent.'

'Good.' Paul released the air lock on the outer door in the belly of the machine and climbed through, the weight of the gear he was carrying hampering the uphill struggle through the door hatch.

Outside, they immediately sensed the temperature increase; they would need to ascend as quickly as possible if they were to stay alive. They could see the damage that the descent had caused and wondered how they, unlike the others, had survived. Paul peered into the shaft above him and thought he could see a light, but it was a long way off, and after some debate they could only guess at how far down they had travelled. The heat was beginning to engulf them and they could see the sulphur vapour rising like smoke in a funnel, the cool air at the top drawing it into the opening above. Deron signalled Paul to return to the cabin to give them some resting space. They re-entered the cabin and pushed the door back into place, the red light on the life support system turned green, the air was safe to breathe again.

Deron opened the visor on his helmet. 'We will have to climb pretty rapidly if we are going to survive the heat,' he said; 'the problem is,' Deron pointed upwards, 'the wide ledges that are over-hanging the open shaft. As we climb we will have to go around them; if we try to climb onto them they will probably disintegrate.'

Paul nodded, his visor still down.

Deron told him to turn off his air supply and open his visor. 'You will need to conserve your air,' he said.

Paul did as he was told.

Deron decided that this was as good a time as any to tell Paul what he was thinking and said calmly, 'You will have to think for yourself when we get out there, Paul; both our lives are going to depend on each of us using our wits.'

Paul apologised for wasting his air supply; he understood that Deron was counting on him for their survival. Deron brushed his anxiety aside and decided he would take another look at the ascent before they started out; he needed to work out an exact route to the top. Picking up the power torch he made his way outside. Paul decided to try the communicator to see if he could get a response; he did not like the idea of being in the cabin alone with the remains of his friends. Gently he half slid, half walked towards the command panel, his sense of smell rebelling at the odour that was penetrating his nostrils.

'I must keep my mind on the job,' he muttered repeatedly.

Suddenly he heard a man's voice. Paul's hair stood up on the back of his neck, and although he did not recognise it as one of the crew, his mind played a most horrendous trick on him; he froze to the spot, terrified he might turn to see one of the dismembered bodies alive. Glashadou waited for Paul to find the courage to confront his fear and acknowledge his spirit form. Eventually, when Paul opened his eyes he found a man of his age standing beside him with an elegant lady, sporting an amazing crop of green hair, by his side.

Paul's body trembled but his spirits lifted. 'Where did you come from?' he asked incredulously.

Glashadou introduced Odelia and himself, and then said, 'Well, we're jolly glad you can see us, aren't we, Odelia?'

Odelia nodded, and Paul wondered if he and Deron were dead.

'What do you mean?' asked Paul. 'See you, of course I can see you, but where did you come from?'

'We have come from the other-worlds,' said Odelia.

Again, Paul believed that he and Deron had died with the others.

'No, no, no,' said Odelia lightly, reading his thoughts. 'You are still in the land of the living but have entered another dimension in order to communicate with us; that is all.'

Paul remained silent, absorbing this new information. His emotions were jumbled, there was too much happening too fast, and he wasn't sure if he and Deron were going to join their dead friends, or make it back to the surface. *Why is Deron taking so long?* he thought. Paul wanted him to return so that they could make sense of what was happening. *Was he dreaming, never having left his bed that morning?*

Glashadou began to explain why they had appeared; they were there to awaken Paul and Deron's senses to life beyond the physical, and to show them how to use their supernatural senses in their hour of need.

Deron had made his way around the perimeter of the shaft that had opened up and swallowed the Explorer. With the aid of a power torch, he decided which would be the quickest and safest route to the surface, knowing that they must climb quickly otherwise the intense heat would be the end of them, if not the climb itself. Suddenly feeling exhausted, his hope of survival took a terrible plunge. Mariana and the boys came to mind and he cursed, his mind flooding with anger.

'To hell will I die!' He spat the words into the air and turned towards the cabin to get Paul.

Lia barred his pathway; Deron could not believe his eyes, and like Paul he thought he was dreaming.

'Mother, what are you doing here?' He looked at her with unbelieving eyes. She was dressed in her weather proof and he could see rain falling around her; she looked cold and frail, and for a moment, in his confusion, he wondered how she was breathing without apparatus in this atmosphere.

'I am not here in the flesh, Deron. It is only my spirit that you see. Surely you are at ease with such knowledge now.'

He felt relief, even though her logic appeared strange. 'Mother, what is happening? Am I dead?'

'No, but how you and Paul accept and master the challenge before you will decide your fate. However, you will come through, I am sure of it.' Lia looked deeply into her son's eyes and he felt reassured by the strength he saw reflected there. 'Look, Deron, see your challenge reflected there. You have looked at the ascent and know that your chances of survival in this atmosphere of heat and sulphur are slim. There is another way, but it will take all of your courage to surmount the fear that this pathway will provoke; however, it is the better of the two.'

Deron gazed into his mother eyes, the fluorescent pools of golden liquid shimmering like a haze of expanding light. His eyes focused into the light to see an opening where the Explorer had become embedded in porous bedrock. The opening appeared so narrow that he would have to crawl along the ground to enter the tiny gap. Beyond the opening he could see nothing, but he remembered his mother's words, that of the two avenues of escape the shaft was the better choice. When he looked away from the pool of light, Lia was gone and Paul was signalling him to return, having managed to get the communicator working. Signalling that he was on his way, Deron started back towards the cabin doorway. Paul was opening the door hatch as he pulled himself up the last few feet; he dropped into the open space and lifted his visor, choking at the putrid smell of dead flesh that hit him.

Deron leaned against the wall, wondering what he was going to say to Paul: *By the way, I've just seen my mother and she advises ...* Deron looked at Paul, his face ashen, while Paul was wondering how to explain his encounter with Glashadou and Odelia. He felt tense; what if Deron thought the recent events had sent him over the edge?

They both looked at each other. 'Let's rationalise...' they said together. 'What's happening?' Again they spoke simultaneously.

Deron said quickly, 'Okay, I've just seen my mother.'

'Okay, I've just seen two people from the "other-worlds".'

'Fine,' they said in unison.

Deron and Paul found themselves a drink among the smashed remains of the storage unit, and then sat down to go over the events of the past thirty minutes. Slowly they reconciled this new experience with the past. Lia, Deron recalled, was often seen talking to herself; he could remember this happening from his infant phase and upwards. Their migration to the ocean worlds was an event that they remembered little of, and they accepted their life in the underworld as normal, and now, well, now they must accept another reality. They had accessed the other-worlds beyond physical life, before their physical death. Deron and Paul finished their drinks and looked at one another, both having made the same decision.

'It's the shaft, not the climb, then. So let's sort the gear and get going.'

Lia heard their decision and cried with relief. The rain continued to pour down upon the beach and the cold to consume her frail figure, but their decision had given her renewed strength. Today would be remembered as one of the longest that Lia had known.

Chapter 18

Initiation by Fire

Raphiel alighted on the beach, his energy moving rapidly towards Lia and gently engulfing her; immediately her vitality began to return as the healing rays encircled her, energising a recovery within.

Lia opened her eyes to see Glashadou standing in front of her, her dear friend who had returned to the other-worlds while still a young man. She smiled at Glas, who had escorted her on her challenges with Ormus and Odelia, such a long time ago when she was just a girl. Glashadou looked into Lia's face and realised that she was tiring of her Earthly life; he moved within the healing light to hold her.

'How are you, my dear? I'm told it won't be too many Earth years before you'll be joining us in the other-worlds again. I can't wait, can't wait,' he said in his usual jovial manner.

'It's lovely to see you, Glas,' she said quietly. 'I'm sure you are right, it won't be too long, but first I have unfinished work here with mankind, and then I will be ready for my rebirth into the worlds beyond this universe.'

Glashadou gave Lia a long embrace, and then, releasing her, he said, 'I will return to see you soon, but for now I need to keep an eye on that boy of yours.'

Glashadou disappeared, leaving Lia to her vigil.

Deron and Paul were now at the entrance of the shaft, the Explorer's descent having made an opening big enough for them to squeeze through. Deron signalled that he would go first and began to crawl on his belly into the opening. Once through he pulled upon the rope and shortly afterwards Paul's head appeared. If they had been optimistic, they could not have wished for a better environment, for once through the hole and into the shaft beyond they could stand up, and the instruments were registering a life-supportable atmosphere. They could not believe their luck.

Having removed their breathing apparatus, they moved along the shaft, which inclined steadily towards the surface and optimistically the fire enzyme beds of Lacofpartin. They were now feeling buoyant; it could not have been easier, they could breathe normally and although their fireproof suits were bulky and extremely uncomfortable in the dry hot atmosphere, it was nothing compared with the climb they would have encountered before being given a choice. The shaft sloped steadily upwards, turning on its axis every one hundred yards or so, giving the slope an easy forward and upward pace.

Deron knew they had been lucky, but there was just something that niggled in the pit of his stomach. The atmosphere was getting hotter and the air began to smell of sulphur again; he slowed his pace and waited for Paul to catch him up.

'Paul, I think we should have held on to the helmets. I am going back down to get them.'

Paul was now exhausted from the climb and the increasing heat, and sat down, waving a hand to say he would stay. Deron began the descent immediately; suddenly he felt he needed to make haste. Once at the bottom, he grabbed the helmets and a rope and began his ascent. As he neared the spot where he had left Paul, the sweat was pouring from him, soaking his clothes, which rubbed against his body, the soreness slowing him down. It was over an hour before Deron returned to the spot where he had left Paul, only to find him gone. He felt his soaked body chill in the heat, then optimistically he thought *maybe he has found a way out?* Deron continued to climb to the next turn; his stomach felt tight, a sensing, fear, something was wrong. As he mounted the turn, there barring his path stood Paul. Paul turned to stare at Deron, his face wet and ashen.

Deron's voice came up from his throat in a loud forceful boom. 'What is it?'

Paul moved sideways for Deron to pass. Beyond the next turn lay another shaft, the one hundred foot passage far wider than any already passed, and at the end an inferno of white heat that blocked their path, the intensity of which they could feel burning into their fire-protective suits from where they stood. Deron took hold of Paul's arm and led him back down the shaft from where they had just come; they both sank to the floor, neither able to say a word. Minutes passed and Deron began to think about the alternative. Maybe the first option hadn't been so bad after all, falling to your death was one thing, but burning alive ... He sat there unable to think, unable to move. Had seeing his mother been a falsehood? *Why, when you think you're near the finishing line, do the rules of the game change, why?*

To Deron's relief his mother appeared before him. 'Now you understand my words; your life experiences must become more challenging, otherwise your soul will not experience soul growth. Have faith, Deron, and listen to what I have to say. The challenge that you face exceeds physical logic. To you at this moment there seems no alternative but to go back and attempt the near-impossible climb to the shaft's surface. The way here appears totally barred to you; however, you are talking to me and I am on the beach at the Causeway, is that not so? Follow me.'

Deron pulled himself to his feet, his mind not willing or able to comprehend his mother's words. In fact, she was beginning to make him angry and he could feel the anger mounting at his entrapment. Harsh words were beginning to work their way to the surface of his mind, which at any minute would erupt into a violent outburst at this cheating, miserable disappointment to all the hard work he and his crew had endured, which was now in ruins. Deron walked behind his mother, closely watching her silhouette, which seemed to be as solid as when he was walking with her normally. He reached out and touched her shoulder to reassure himself that he wasn't dreaming; his hand vanished beneath the cloth. He closed his mind to the moment, not understanding, not even caring, only following her footsteps.

Lia stopped near the entrance to the shaft. 'Stay here,' she said, and she continued along the shaft towards the wall of white fire, then, turning to look at him, she walked into the flames.

Deron screamed out, 'Mother,' his heart hammering fit to burst. He wanted to run after her, but the intense heat terrified him; he stood sobbing, angry at his fear of the fire, angry at his cowardice for not going after her.

Lia stood once more by her son, she put her arms around him and cradled his sobbing body. 'It is all an illusion, Deron, and today you will know whether you have the gift to see through illusion or not. That wall of fire is as intensely hot or cold as your mind will have it. How you prepare for this challenge will determine whether you succeed or fail; make this challenge the one that will guide your decision-making for the rest of your life.'

Lia returned to where Paul was sitting motionless; having heard Deron scream out, he now wore an expression of overwhelming defeat.

As she made herself known to him, Paul acknowledged her by asking, 'Lia, is it you?'

'Yes,' she answered gently, 'and I have come to help you get out of here, but you are going to have to change your concept of what is real and what isn't.'

Paul looked at Deron, whose previous moments were etched deep within his face.

'My mother is here to help us walk through the wall of fire.'

Paul withdrew further, his mind barely acknowledging the words that Deron had spoken. 'But how?'

'We just walk, walk through the fire.' Deron stood over his friend, the combination of tiredness and fear having given way to calm.

Paul began to laugh. 'That easy, huh?'

Lia watched them but said nothing; her cold tired body, standing on the beach, was having difficulty holding its position; if only she were here with them in the warm volcanic heat. Lia gathered her thoughts; it was important that she support them.

'Come and rest your backs against the wall. Open your suits a little and get as comfortable as you can. I wish to explain to you the order of meditative walking. It is a process that you have used many times but would not have recognised as such. You will need to hold a deep meditative state whilst continuing with the form of exercise that you have chosen. In this case, it will be walking.'

The Otom were used to diving in the deep ocean; they would collapse their lungs to the size of a fist, having first flooded their body tissue with oxygen. With this meditative process they were able to delay breathing for long periods of time.

Lia took them back to their classroom days, when they would prepare their bodies to work in the oceans without apparatus. 'Using the same meditative state, you must slow your breathing down to the minimum life supporting level. Once you have achieved this, your state of mind will enable you to walk into the wall of fire and emerge on the other side.'

Deron and Paul began to clear their minds by concentrating on the inflowing force of light that was suffusing their bodies; their breathing began to slow and their heart rate lowered as they breathed slowly in and out to each count of one. Their minds began to fuse with the purity of the energy field that surrounded them and their physical bodies elevated as they reached the required state of meditation.

Lia watched their energy fields expand and their bodies take on a profile of transparency. Within the force of energy, their slumped bodies straightened and their heads lifted slightly as the beam of light entered the crown of their head and flowed downwards, overwhelming their bodies with light. The process continued, the men becoming enveloped in their own protective energy field, until the moment when they were ready to receive the powerful healing rays that were the blessing of meditation. Only then did Lia continue, her words penetrating their energy fields with clarity.

Deron's energy field remained strong, while Paul's, having been distracted by Lia's voice, began to fade. As his energy field weakened, Lia urged him to re-enforce his meditative focus. Paul was tired and frightened, but if he could not maintain a meditative state the wall of fire would engulf his physical body. Lia waited for Paul's energy field to become strong again before motioning to them to stand; they were ready to set off into the shaft.

Lia walked in front of them, her silhouette moving silently towards the wall of fire, her thoughts urging them forward. Deron followed behind, so close that he could almost touch her. Lia's body disappeared into the white flame with her son still following. Without hesitation Deron had followed her, and Lia was aware of Paul's presence close behind him. Once they had stepped into the flame, the colour turned to a violet ray and the lack of heat or cold was uncanny, only the purest feeling of love could be felt, and both Lia and her son immersed themselves in the joyous feeling, having forgotten Paul. Lia suddenly became aware that Paul was in pain, and drawing her son through to the other side of the shaft, she travelled back to where Paul lay. His fire suit had been damaged as his energy field had weakened, his feelings of terror having overcome his meditative state. Lia roused him and he managed to get back down the shaft, away from the heat.

Paul opened his eyes and looked up, but it was not Lia kneeling over him, it was Deron. Realising that Paul had not come through the fire and that his mother had returned to find him, Deron had made his way back through the flames. Now unafraid, he had welcomed being engulfed in the pure energy of love that the fire offered. Deron had been strengthened by the experience, and Paul could see the transformation in his eyes.

Even so, Paul stammered, 'I cannot go through, Deron. You must go on without me.'

Deron did not answer; he was aware that his mother's image was beginning to fade and that in her place an elderly man with twinkling blue eyes had begun to materialise. Deron recognised him as the one called Ormus, his mother's teacher of many years past.

Ormus spoke to Paul, who could see him clearly. 'I have been with you both through this challenge, Paul, and now make myself known to you, in order to bring you through this challenge by illusion. Look into your friend's eyes and trust what you see there, then follow him.'

Deron and Paul sat facing each other, Deron looking anxiously at his friend, who was easing the collar of his suit from his neck to reveal the burn sores that were beginning to form.

'Paul, I'm going to get the rope and tie it around us, and then we will go through the fire together. I want you to look into my eyes and stay fixed on what you see there, while we pass through the flames.'

The two men began to clear their minds until their energy fields were again strong and pure. Paul's gaze remained fixed on Deron's eyes, which slowly merged into the centre of his forehead to reveal the third eye of his psyche. Slowly they began their walk towards the flames, Deron's trust motivating Paul to keep his energy field strong. They began to merge with the firestorm that raged about them, becoming one with the void of pure energy. Every fear, every horror that Paul had experienced during the past few hours disappeared, as suddenly he felt lightened by the force of the violet rays that flowed through his body. A feeling of perfect joy flooded his mind, healing the burns to his physical body. The awesome expansion of energy left him transfixed, bathed in love of the most perfect form.

All too soon they could hear Ormus calling them, and they made their way to the other side, knowing that in meditation, discipline was of the greatest importance, and that when your teacher called you, you must return.

Senithe was waiting at the top of the shaft as Ormus appeared. As she looked at him, she knew that Deron and Paul had survived.

Lia was waiting on the beach with Glashadou and Odelia for Ormus' return. Ormus appeared and said brightly, 'The long day is over, Lia; Deron and Paul are safe. It is time to get you back to the Causeway.'

Lia nodded gratefully.

The four companions lifted into the air stream, their silhouettes disappearing into the background of the incoming tide.

Lia was scarcely back in her room before Dorri was knocking on the door. Lia opened it, her cloak having been thrown into the closet quickly as she walked across the room.

'How are you feeling now, my dear? You have been asleep all day, even the boys playing in the garden did not wake you?'

Lia had spoken to Mariana before her departure to the court that morning; she had disclosed to her the situation just passed, asking her to join her on the beach. Mariana had asked Dorri to let Lia sleep, and Dorri had been unaware that Lia had in fact left the house to wait on the beach, another aspect of herself having played the part of an ailing Lia in bed.

'I'm much better now; thank you, Dorri, and I dreamed that Deron and Paul will be here tomorrow.'

'Well, let's hope you're right … Here's some tea,' Dorri said, putting a tray by the bedside; 'can't have you wasting away, can we? And then it's a good night's rest for you.' Dorri continued to fuss for a while and then left Lia in peace.

Lia picked up the phone and rang her daughter-in-law. She knew that Mariana had been informed of their safe return, but wanted to reassure her that all was well and that tomorrow, when she returned to the Causeway, Deron would be home, of that she was sure.

'Thank you.' Lia spoke the words softly, her eyes closed. 'Thank you for my lovely warm bed and thank you for everything I have received today and that which I have given. And with all my heart, I give thanks for my son having completed this very important challenge.' Feeling extremely happy, Lia lifted the cup of tea to her lips and sipped the hot sweet liquid slowly, and then she said solicitously, 'Thank you for my children, and for my family and wonderful friends, those who are here with me and those who have gone on to other-worlds, thank you.'

Lia switched the light out and looked at the open window. Was that a star she could see? Each day the cloud vapour that encircled the Earth appeared to get thinner and another miracle of nature appeared.

Chapter 19

Getting Started

Lia sat in the garden looking out at the ocean. The sun was setting and the garden was bathed in the golden glow of the late afternoon sun. In a while it would be too cold to sit outside, even though she was dressed warmly against the winter's harshness. Even so, it felt good to see the sun unhampered by thick blackened clouds, and she wanted to linger as long as possible. It seemed so long ago that the holocaust had taken but a moment to overwhelm the Earth. Now, in its re-awakening, it was taking decades for the damage to disperse. The Earth was slow in its recovery, or so it seemed to her in her human cloak of seventy-one years. Lia considered the more evolved life dwelling in other universes, and surmised that this era upon Earth would for them be no more than a brief occurrence. 'But who knows?' she murmured, her eyes surveying the snow-covered garden that was a picture of tranquillity. Her thoughts continued to ponder upon the nature of Earthly life, the unseen vegetation that was now peacefully dormant, that would again surface and struggle to survive.

When the garden had been productive, forty-five years ago, she had cut back the vigorous plants in order to help the smaller ones, which were crying out for space to survive. *Wasn't that culling life?* In the undergrowth the weeds had quietly smothered the weaker plants until she had come to rescue them, and below the surface the insects had fought for supremacy, especially the ants. There was not one source of life she did not think about deeply; the earth had looked peaceful enough, but on closer inspection she had witnessed the aggression that prevailed, each level of life struggling for their share of freedom, and at any cost to their neighbours. The Cunmen came to mind. If the human race could live without affecting or disturbing other species, there would be nothing to war about, but how to achieve this? The words, *live and be guided by the soul, not by the ego*, came to mind. Lia then realised that the Otom had achieved this state of being, which at first had been forced upon them by circumstance, but was now a way of life.

Lia lifted her chilled body from the bench and walked slowly towards the beckoning warmth of the house. She realised that over the past forty-five years in the underworld, the Otom had given much time to meditative awareness as a way to survive the doubts and fear in their minds. Meditation had become a discipline for them during work as well as when relaxing in order to eliminate negative thought, but since returning to the land, she realised, her mind had begun to fill with unnecessary worries.

That night as Lia slept, she had two dreams that were to help her. Lia's first dream was allowing her to change a past event. She was taken back to the day before Ormus' death. Lia was pleased for the opportunity to change his last day with her from an unhappy to a happy one, when he had passed to the other-worlds in a state of pain and disillusionment. Lia now understood the lesson he was trying to convey, that destiny held the cards to all final solutions concerning the universe, and that the free will of the people was in the choice of how it came about, and the possibilities were endless. That whatever one's choice, the outcome would include the choices of all universal life fragments, in order to remain perfectly balanced.

Ormus had spoken to her. 'My last day with you was filled with doubt and sorrow, only because during my physical death I lost sight of the other-worlds. Once having passed through the veil I was able to see clearly again. Destiny is the bigger vision which keeps the universe as one.'

Lia was not disappointed by this brief explanation that told her it was not in her power to change Ormus' last day, and that he had chosen the circumstance of his death from the endless possibilities of his choice.

In the second dream, Lia was entering a relay race. Five lines of four people waited at the starting point, and Lia was the last person in the last line. The race began; the first person in the first line began and disappeared, then the next, until the second line began, first runner, second runner. Lia began to get anxious; she was the last runner. How could she possibly win? At last she was running, but in front of her people were blocking her path, and from nowhere obstacles appeared strewn upon the ground, giving her no clear line to run ... Lia woke up; the room was light and she could hear the boys in the garden below. She lay still for a moment, and then sat up in bed. Reaching for her dressing gown, she got out of bed and went to sit at the dressing table, taking her book of dreams from the drawer as she did so. Lia wrote the first dream down and then she started the second. The first she understood, but not the second. As she wrote, she read the words aloud: 'Five lines merged into one, and no finishing line?' Suddenly she understood. There was no race, only a journey that each contestant started and finished in their own time, a journey of experiences and obstacles in physical time. The ranks did not race against each other but were there for support, and her concern at letting them down was unfounded. As with the first dream, Lia was not the cause of destiny, she had not the power to change it, for Ormus or for any given situation. The power of destiny presided elsewhere, its force guiding all living energy on a predestined course. Now she understood that her destiny and the destiny of all life was to follow one's instinctive direction back to the source of the 'one' by using the paths of goodwill and love, however difficult the circumstances.

'We run at our own pace, we do not compete against each other, and the troubled thoughts that invade our minds are meaningless if we understand that we are powerless to change the bigger picture of the universe.' Lia's thoughts lifted, giving way to the sound of laughter outside.

Haydes and Kiron were playing in the snow again, their

laughter rising up to the open window of their grandmother's bedroom. Lia pulled her dressing gown close about her and went to the door. 'Meditation, not anxiety; destiny will decide for itself.' She left the room ready to embrace the happiness downstairs.

As Lia started down the stairway, she could hear the boys shouting excitedly; their father was home and with him their mother. Dorri's attempts to quieten the boys went unheard, and Lia was so relieved to see them standing in the doorway that she rushed forward to give them a big hug. Everyone began to laugh as the boys jostled to take middle place; it was good to be together again. Lia stood back to look at her son; there was none of the tiredness that had shadowed him during his ordeal. It was time to enjoy a family reunion.

Dorri called them to the kitchen; she had prepared a special breakfast and was busy fussing over her presentation. Lia pulled the boys towards the kitchen to give Deron and Mariana a little time to talk. They had arrived at the Causeway at the same time and had barely had a moment together. Lia understood that they needed to talk, to reassure one another, and then the ordeal they had been through would be put to rest. The door to the kitchen closed, and the boys were told to give their parents some time alone. The boys' long faces lasted all of two seconds before they were busy chatting with their grandmother about the day ahead. Lia did her best to answer amid their eagerness, telling them that Paul was arriving later and that their father would be busy for a while. During that time, the boys would accompany their mother to explore within the Causeway's perimeter the changes that had taken place since their last visit. The boys seemed happy with Lia's answer once they had pinned her down as near as possible to the time when their father would be back with them.

Dorri's special breakfast was now laid out and waiting for the family to sit down to eat. Breakfast was always special when they were gathered at the table together. The food was not a feast but it was light and tasty and the recipes ingenious. The Otom had come to terms with mankind's overindulgence in food, and nourished their bodies with a lighter and more nutritious diet. Before they ate, Deron gave thanks to the plant life that was to become part of their life forms, after which they began, each one eating in unhurried reverence to their body's sustained health.

At the boys' prompting, Lia began to tell them another story of the fast food chains that had been a major part of the human eating problem before the holocaust. 'It was quite normal to eat your meal in a bag, while walking on the street,' she said.

The boys began to laugh, always fascinated or amused by the strange stories of their ancestors' civilisation, so unlike their own.

Lia continued, 'Many children ate their breakfast on the way to school, which often consisted of processed food in the form of potato crisps or chocolate, and fruit and nut breakfast bars, which, it has to be said, mankind found irresistibly delicious.'

The boys looked at Lia in a questioning manner. 'Tell us all the processes that produced those foods, Gran.'

The family had heard the story many times from both Dorri and Lia, and each time it held something extra, something new would come to light that would enthral the children, and occasionally their parents – stories about the people from a world that had disappeared, a world that the older generations of Otom still remembered clearly.

For over an hour Lia and her family sat at the breakfast table, talking about the accident and putting the Explorer's fate to rest. Eventually the boys were eager to get on with the day. They stacked the plates in the sink and then cleared the table. Mariana thanked Dorri for the wonderful breakfast and at the same time for the grand job she did of looking after the boys.

Mariana was to have a few days with her family while preparing the Causeway's courthouse for occupancy. When next she returned she would instate the laws of the Mers, which had become the Otom's law for the past forty-five years; these would replace mankind's Ancient Roman laws that had been established in the early years of the first millennium of an era now past.

The rest of the morning was spent on the beach below the family home, waiting for Paul; the cottage was positioned on the rugged cliff edge above a sheltered cove and weathered rock platform, below which the tides of the Atlantic Ocean rose and fell upon a small stretch of beach that was only accessible from the sea.

Later that morning, Paul arrived accompanied by Glashadou, Odelia and Raphiel, Lia's friend and late mentor, who had passed to the other-worlds a few months before the holocaust. Paul sauntered down the sloping garden, making his way past the rectangular conservatory – a building made up of three walls of glass and one of local stone, which housed a large fireplace with a welcoming fire burning in the large grate. Paul had heard much of the Causeway and looked forward to the time he would spend there with Deron and his family, especially looking out from the conservatory at the swirling Atlantic Ocean, which Deron had said was his most favoured time with the family.

Mariana was the first to see Paul climbing down the cliff path towards them and called the boys; it was time to take them on their tour of the Causeway. She ran through her plan; their first stop was to be the domed courthouse where there had been many changes since the boys' last visit, and then on to the new homes being built within the community area, of which one was to be their new home.

The boys, when seeing Paul, ran along the beach waving and shouting, their eagerness never seeming to wane. Paul waved back and jumped down into the sand, the grains slipping into his shoes and making his feet uncomfortable. He stopped to slip his shoes off, a new hindrance to his acclimatising body, and the sand felt rough beneath his feet but his mind sensed a freedom that felt natural and right. Deron came alongside him and they gave each other a hug. Deron and Paul had spoken for hours of their experience after the accident, each one not wanting to stop lest the reality be diminished now that their lives were back to normal, both knowing the experience had been unique.

Lia was the next to greet Paul, and then Dorri, who gathered him into her arms and gave him a long hug. Paul was her sister's son, and when she had been told of the past day's events she had been distraught with worry, even though she had been spared the whole truth. That, however, had not kept Dorri from her duties; she was a Scotswoman who hid her feelings well.

Lia greeted Raphiel with a discreet smile, and Deron, sensing another's presence, turned to see a rather portly gentleman with a large white whiskery moustache standing next to his mother. Raphiel offered Deron a slight bow. Odelia and Glashadou appeared and greeted him likewise. Deron discreetly nodded back.

The boys, unaware of the unseen visitors, were eager to be off and ran to the steps with the others following. They began their climb up to the cottage where they would go their separate ways.

Chapter 20

Master Raphiel

Mariana and the boys left to visit the courthouse accompanied, unbeknown to them, by Odelia and Glashadou, while Dorri disappeared into the kitchen to busy herself with unpacking the deliveries.

Raphiel felt more at ease after their departure; he found it difficult working around those who were not aware of his presence, the situation always making things complicated. Now those that remained could get on without being interrupted.

Raphiel, whilst Earthbound, had been Edward's father and Deron's paternal grandfather, Ralph Major. Ralph was an hotelier and writer who, like many of his kind, had returned to the otherworlds shortly before the holocaust.

Raphiel, Lia, Deron and Paul entered the library where many of Raphiel's books sat upon the well-stocked shelves that filled the comfortable room, all having been safely stowed away in the caves beneath the Causeway, before the death of Ralph Major. He had been an accomplished author before the holocaust; his works conveyed his belief in the restoration of the mind and body through the natural process of self-healing as a positive method of alleviating one's ills.

Raphiel sat down on the chair placed in the centre of the room ready for him, while the remaining three reclined on reading couches placed around the room. Raphiel waited until they were settled and then he began.

'Today we are to visit the University of the Third Eye.' Raphiel continued to explain that they would be travelling to the third dimension of Universe Four where all learning took place. 'Before your trial by fire, your visits there were made in the dreamtime. Since then you have gained the right to visit the third dimension in your waking state but only when accompanied by a mentor, such as me.'

There was a pause, a chance for questions, and as none were forthcoming Raphiel continued, his large deep brown eyes moving from one to the other with an unequivocal gaze that all three found hard to hold. 'There are two things that I wish to speak of before we make our journey. They are the nature of zero energy and how it came into being, which will give you an understanding of universal energy, and why grasping an opportunity is important only as long as the end creation is good for mankind as well as yourself.' Raphiel got up and moved around in order to collect his thoughts, listing points so as not to miss any detail of importance. He continued, 'The Healing Globe gave birth to all universes, and when Hafnium, who is Universe Four, was born, he immediately began to create. He played with the energy at his disposal, combining the various forces at hand to become a multitude of formations and energies. When he had exhausted his thought on the macro-scaled universe he turned to creating the micro-worlds within. This decided, he began to create life upon and within the newly formed planets and stars, and each micro-life created was to absorb and be absorbed in order to continue the creation. Like a child with a creative toy, he varied the substance antimatter in order to create matter, and in doing so he created the cycle of birth unto death within his universe.' Raphiel waited for questions to arise but his three companions remained silent, each one listening from within a state of deep meditation. He continued, 'I would like you to think back to your school days when you learned of the motorways that your ancestors built for travel, particularly the one identified as the M25 that encircled the lost city of London, which is still visible beneath the shallow ocean that covers much of central Britain's landscape today. Imagine this vast circle as a river with a bridge crossing the axis, upon which you are standing centrally and from where you can see the entire city. Now, here you have the key, the key to opportunity. Let me explain.' Raphiel asked Paul to visualise the city with the vast bridge across the middle, then asked him, 'What is the colour of the water that flows around the city?'

Paul replied, 'Well, it appears to be two colours. On one side of the bridge the water is gold and vibrant, but as the water flows beneath the bridge to the other side of the circle, it becomes grey and lifeless.'

'And you, Deron, what do you see?'

'The same,' he replied simply, now deeply relaxed but attentive to Raphiel's voice.

'What you see there are the opposing sides of opportunity and opportunity lost, which the circle offers but never in the same format. The cycle of life in London and worldwide was exactly like that, creating opportunity wherever life revolved between the regions of gold and grey energy, two forces that would compel those involved to act post haste or lose an opportunity for always. Once time had taken an opportunity beyond the bridge to the region of grey, the chance of having what was offered was lost. So remember, as you begin your challenge to return the Otom to the Earth's surface, you must take the opportunities as they are presented, of course rejecting an opportunity when it appears morally wrong, because countless lives will be changed for better or worse with each decision. Some are born with the key of opportunity grasped firmly in their hand, which mankind calls natural good luck. Whereas the souls who have chosen a difficult pathway in life will find that their key is hidden, and it is left to them to seek out the veiled opportunity. This is the secret of mankind's life: he is born into this world with or without the key to make his journey. During that lifetime he will endure seven yearly changes to his physical and mental health, experiencing cycles of opportunity until death comes to call.' Raphiel paused. 'It is time for us to take our places in the Halls of Learning.' Without another word, Raphiel disappeared from the library, taking his three companions with him.

Deron and Paul felt the same surge of energy they had experienced when rising from the fire to the top of the shaft where they had found Senithe waiting for them. This time the surge was followed by a feeling of suspension in which they could neither hear nor see anything other than the white light that surrounded them. As they travelled within the light – the zero energy of Universe Four they realised that the trial by fire, which had been unique, was only the beginning of their adventures.

Chapter 21

The University of the Third Eye

The white energy surrounding Deron and Paul began to fade as they appeared on the outside of a walled citadel. From where they stood they could see a vast structure that rose as a labyrinth of buildings, passageways and towering auditoriums that could be seen for miles. The ethereal citadel appeared unworldly in form, but when Deron and Paul reached out and touched the towering wall in front of them, it was as solid as they were. This strange place without substance, where all souls gathered to expand the knowledge of their world and other-worlds, was the University of the Third Eye, the nucleus of learning for Universe Four.

Lia and Raphiel were nowhere to be seen, and as Deron and Paul waited in the eerie silence they began to feel afraid. At last came the sound of others present; the knights of Aspheseuos and Hafnium appeared inside the open gates of the citadel, both mounted on winged stallions of pure white, the noble beasts rearing and bucking. Behind them walked Lia and Raphiel. Deron and Paul were in awe of their presence, the stallions' trappings of silver and blue echoing the colour of the knight that rode them. The knights held their lances aloft with their colours held high, their radiance emanating as one. Both extended an arm and their gauntlets met in a clasp of friendship. Next to appear were the twelve Initiators robed in shimmering white, their presence forming a semicircle behind the knights. Hafnium's knight moved forward, summoning Deron and Paul to enter the citadel and stand beside him. As they entered the gates, the fragrant coolness of a spring morning began to filter out around them, stirring the senses of Deron and Paul with an unfamiliar smell.

Paul felt a foreboding within and longed to be back in the library at the Causeway. The citadel and the strange fragrant coolness were not something that he recognised, or wanted to remain a part of. He liked his physical life and everything in the citadel seemed strange – if this was the afterlife he was not ready to embrace it.

'Why are they here, Mother?' Deron called out, taken aback by the strange splendour.

'They are the Knights of Good and Evil, and the twelve Initiators represent mankind on behalf of Hafnium, creator of Universe Four. Each one is a protector of the twelve original spirals that gave life to mankind.'

'But mankind's beginning manifests from a double helix, only two.'

The Initiators responded, 'Not in the beginning when man's future hopes were high, when the soul nature was first manifest in the physical body. The physical body was to have lasted for hundreds of years, but the soul-kind that inhabited it became immersed in experiencing the ways of Aspheseuos. In doing so, they damaged the physical body, which needs Hafnium's radiance to survive. Ten spirals of knowledge have been destroyed, lost, because of this folly. Now, when a soul enters a new physical body, the life span is short and is quickly supplanted by another. The physical body of mankind is expected to live on average for three score and ten years, but it is unnatural and against Hafnium's original plan, which was to create a more permanent physical vehicle for the spirit and soul to experience cause and effect in the micro-world.'

The twelve Initiators' words were heard clearly by those entering the dreamtime to gather in the Halls of Learning, but not all would remember their words when waking. However, for all those who continued to believe life was possible without Hafnium's existence, there were many more who understood this to be untrue having gathered in the Halls of Learning.

'Deron and Paul, you and the Otom, along with the Mers, will soon join forces with the star tribes to take up mankind's challenge for his continuing existence, and in doing so, you will work to restore the Earth to her past beauty, before you leave her for always.'

Deron and Paul shuffled uncomfortably at this reference to them, while Raphiel beamed, and Lia, reminded of her first meeting with the Initiators and the journey that had transpired, felt a glow of parental pride. She now felt confident that Deron and Paul were ready for their next challenge. The future that she had dreamed of for the Otom had at last begun to manifest.

The Initiators continued, 'Each one of you is ever present in a seven year change; it may be your sixth, or seventh cycle of change, but whichever, you are finding that habits or situations that suited you in the past are habits that you have broken, or you wish to break with people, or places that you no longer frequent.'

Deron thought of Mikell Lang, his childhood friend and adult acquaintance with whom, these days, he never felt at ease.

Paul's thoughts drifted to his love of dangerous water sports; he had loved the thrill of the dare, but now his need for these pastimes was waning and he felt there must be something more fulfilling to do with his life. *Love, marriage and children of my own, if only?* Paul closed his mind to the despair he felt at falling in love with Senithe, the marriage between a Mer and Otom being impossible as far as he could see; he returned his thoughts to the voice of the Initiators.

'These seven year changes are always accompanied by feelings of guilt or concern because of that which must be left behind, although this process of change is completely natural. However, man usually extracts himself from the old by judging those or the situation that he is leaving ... man always needs a reason, but why we do not know. The physical emotions of man are very interesting but also very complex and are only truly understood by mankind's creator, Hafnium. Try to remember this wisdom as each new challenge appears, and do not judge yourself too harshly at the result of your choices. Deron and Paul, you are here today to take up another challenge that when completed will allow you to join Lia in bringing the Otom upon the land.'

The voice of the twelve Initiators stilled and the vast citadel transformed into another landscape; Raphiel and his three companions were standing on scorched barren earth high above a vast red mountain range. Above them they could hear the screeching sound of three giant eagles that soared overhead while casting large shadows upon the red valley below.

Chapter 22

The Other-worlds – The Three Great Eagles and Great Bear

Below the ridge where Raphiel and his companions stood, a dark-skinned man with long black hair held back from his brow by a red bandana sat motionless, gazing up at them. Lia, having recognised the figure as Inti, made her way quickly down the rim towards him.

Inti, an Indian shaman, had crossed to the other-worlds when his life had ended with the earth erupting in the wake of the holocaust, some forty-five years past. Now his soul's purpose was to help disembodied spirits find their way through the psychic plane to the other-worlds that were waiting to receive them.

Inti and Lia were old friends, Inti having taught Lia the healing ways of the shaman in his birthplace, Peru. His students had called him Coyote, as it was his wily nature to observe his pupils while they struggled unaided to let go of their limited beliefs and seek the truth. With her arms outstretched, Lia greeted him while her companions followed cautiously behind.

Inti smiled as he listened to her thoughts of their time together, and answered, 'Yes, you were a challenge, Lia. But for you, learning the hard way most always gave the best results.'

Deron and Paul came forward to greet Inti and he embraced them warmly. 'Son of Lia, it is a pleasure to meet you and your friend, Paul. And Raphiel, my friend, it is good to see you again.'

Inti and Raphiel made the Holocene sign of peace, bowing their heads and crossing their hands over their chests while entwining their thumbs to form the shape of a dove.

'It is good to see you, Inti,' Raphiel said as they embraced.

'May your journey here bring peace of mind to our friends from Earth. Peace in the present and peace in the future,' Inti replied.

'Truly a "wise one's" blessing,' Raphiel replied.

Inti sat down to absorb the warmth of the late afternoon sun and invited them to join him. Beneath the ridge shelf was the entrance to a cave. Nearby a small fire of brushwood smouldered, sending wisps of grey smoke into the air. This place, they were told, was where they would spend the night.

Inti continued, 'Tomorrow you will experience a challenge of faith, of trusting in others to support you. This is to be the foundation upon which the Otom must build their future. A future built on trust without rivalry, a race of one in mind, body and soul.' Inti ended his statement with words that surprised both Deron and Paul. 'Lia has asked to undertake the challenge with you when again you confront your fear of death.' Rising from a crossed-leg position, Inti moved towards the fire where the smoke had been replaced by a welcoming heat over which supper was cooking. 'Soon we will eat and then we will sleep,' Inti said, holding up a water flask for them to drink from. As the golden liquid poured from within, Lia recognised it as the chalice water given to the seeker ... of which there were now three to receive its strength.

In the morning Lia awoke to the light of the sun rising in the east, a blazing orange hue set against a blue sky, a time of the Earth's earlier beauty that had passed long ago through the veil of death to manifest its splendour within the other-worlds. The memory caused Lia to draw her breath in sharply as she wondered if the Earth would ever look this way again.

Within the other-worlds there was nothing of substance, other than a temporary manifestation of visual experience for the journeying soul. Lia gazed at the surrounding landscape, which was still and naturally barren, untouched by the disaster of the holocaust. The land remained unchanged from her time there long ago when the wildlife was not sleeping, at Hafnium's command.

Lia shielded her eyes from the sunlight; she realised that she could see moving shadows in the valley beneath her. Looking up she saw the first of the three eagles flying gracefully above her. Lia's heart gave a jump. The three eagles soared high above her. *Have the boys seen them?* she wondered excitedly.

Lia moved cautiously towards the edge of the great canyon ledge as Inti appeared beside her. Behind them, the boys stood motionless, their upturned faces bathed by the blazing sun. Deron and Paul had never seen a land creature before yesterday, when these great creatures had appeared in the sky.

Inti spoke first. 'You have been many moons in the underworld and have mastered your fear of confinement. Today you will discard your fear of altitude without the help of levitation from those other-worldly beings that seek to help you. You will fly with the eagles, and not with the powers of a "wise one". By entrusting your life to the eagle you will be preparing for the challenges ahead.'

Lia, as a small child, had feared both heights and confined spaces. Living below the oceans had tested her almost beyond endurance as each day she had battled with the panic that rose inside her. Eventually she had become at ease with her new surroundings, although her fear was never far away. When the time had come for her to return to the Earth's surface her feelings were those of exalted relief.

Lia fixed her gaze upon the one she knew as Coyote and, smiling, said, 'No trickery today, my friend, I want to embrace this challenge with all my heart. And I know that I can only find my strength in letting go completely, allowing the great eagle to carry my human cloak into the valley below where my spirit will find the courage to soar beyond fear.' Lia looked deeply into Inti's fathomless black eyes as if searching for an answer there. She continued, 'I dreamed last night of the void, a deep dark nothingness in which I roamed guided solely by my instinct and the knowledge that my body would be safe upon the Earth.' She paused and then said with conviction, 'Because I believed it would be. Then I was thrust back to Earth and all was chaos as I tried to find my human cloak.

It then became clear to me that if I could not return to my body I would re-enter the divinity of the void. The chaos stopped! Perhaps the dream was telling me to go in peace to the challenge because I have already surmounted it?'

'I think that you are right, Lia. I cannot cause entrapment for you; only your thoughts can do that.' He smiled at her, allowing her to observe the radiant spirit behind the eyes of the dark-skinned Indian.

A moment of serenity passed between them and then was broken as the boys and Raphiel came to join them by the fire. Breakfast was cooking and the aroma of fresh coffee had stirred their appetites. Lia held out her arms to the boys and gave them a hug, while Inti invited them to sit before the fire. He began to chant the morning prayer of the ancient Indians, a tradition of early morning thanks-giving for the new dawn and for the food they were about to receive. Inti's forefathers appeared and came close to the fire to observe the divine beginnings of the new tribe of man, the Otom. The chosen ones were about to leave the Mer underworld and re-emerge upon the Earth's surface; this was an important time in the history of mankind.

After breakfast Raphiel disappeared, and he did not return until the sun was passing to the west horizon. Deron was first to see Raphiel moving swiftly across the sky with the three great eagles. The well-dressed, rather portly man was flying beneath the birds of prey, a sight which looked rather bizarre to the onlookers.

Inti immediately gave Lia a command. 'Come, Lia.' Lia stood up, her body suddenly stiff with fright. She followed Inti to where the first eagle had landed upon the ridge. Lia had never seen an eagle of such large proportion, with a body and legs the size of a man and a wingspan the length of three men. Inti took Lia by the shoulders and positioned her beneath the creature's body, its hooked talons resting upon two boulders three feet from the ground and two feet apart. Above the first eagle hovered two more, one to the right and one to the left and some twenty feet away from each other. Inti helped Lia to place the support harness about her body. Behind them, Raphiel waited to help

Deron and Paul into their harnesses once Lia was airborne.

Inti looked into Lia's eyes; her fear had turned to acceptance. He faced her and made the sign of peace, then stood aside. The eagle's wings lifted and the oyster shells of goodwill hanging from Lia's harness jangled at the motion; the creature was ready to carry his precious cargo down into the valley below. Inti began chanting his ancestors' words of ancient wisdom as the great bird lifted away from the ledge, his mighty wingspan soaring towards the azure sky. Inti stepped back and forth, his body moving slowly in the rhythmic dance of the ancient ones, his chanting drowned out by the sound of the creature's great wings as it began its journey downward.

The three eagles had lifted away from the ledge and turned until they were airborne over the valley wall. Lia dared not open her eyes until her heart had quietened and her anxiety had disappeared; only then did she dare to look down into the valley to marvel at the miracle of breathtaking beauty surrounding her. The breeze flowed gently about her and was not as she had imagined it to be, harsh and cold. The eagle's flight seemed effortless and at times motionless. Lia, having mastered her fear, looked around at the two eagles that followed behind with Deron and Paul. The eagles were following in the order in which they had begun, one to the left and one to the right of the leading eagle. She could see the boys' faces were turned towards her as they watched the leading eagle flying effortlessly with its cargo. Over the valley they soared, the scenery of red rock and dusty floor merging as one only to be broken by the perpetual change of valley brushwood and a winding river interspersed with roaring foaming waterfalls, the unending beauty warmed beneath a late afternoon sun in a pale blue sky.

The eagles, having followed the river towards the western horizon, began their descent into the basin of a waterfall upon the valley floor. Immediately, the eagles' cargo felt the raging iciness of the river's relentless spray as it forced its way upwards, making it difficult for them to breathe. They clung to the eagles' giant talons as they glided downwards buffeted by the forceful downpour that thrashed the sides of the gorge. Moments later, they felt the full force of the river's power as the creatures turned into the spray and began to descend beneath the canopy of water to the basin below. Lia's eagle glided down behind the raging curtain of water, the two eagles behind them following close by. Beneath the rushing torrent of water, Lia shuddered against a fierce rushing wind that forced itself against her soaked body, making her strain against its power, but then it was gone and they were flying over the basin of the waterfall upon the valley floor.

The three great eagles alighted upon the far side of the river, far enough away from the waterfall that they could no longer feel the water's forceful spray. Thankfully, the three companions lay down to rest in the warmth of the late afternoon sun. Slowly their clothes began to dry, restoring warmth to their bodies. The creatures stood in silence; just an occasional ruffle of feathers and the jangle of the oyster shells could be heard. Raphiel appeared but remained silent as he went among the eagles to remove their harnesses. Now was a time of quiet reflection for the seekers, Lia, Deron and Paul, they having been left to their thoughts.

Once free of their harnesses, the three eagles took flight, gradually rising towards the roof of the valley, their giant bodies throwing shadows across the river basin as the three seekers watched them from below. When the creatures were no more than dots on the horizon, Deron and Paul lay down to sleep. Lia moved to where a large flat rock rose out from the riverbed, the rhythmic splashing of the water upon the side of the rock inviting her to rest there. Lia had noticed a partially shaded overhang sheltering the rock's flat top and thought it a perfect place to rest. She climbed upon the flattened rock and lay down upon her back to view the darkening sky high up beyond the valley walls, the tranquillity of her surroundings easing her breathing to a slow and peaceful rhythm.

Lia drifted to sleep, while above the ledge where Lia lay a large brown bear came to rest. He sat quietly, watching her sleep, his paw occasionally stretching down to paddle the water, and as was his luck, from time to time he would retrieve a large fish that had become attached to his claws. The bear sat and ate and watched and listened.

Inti entered the valley basin, having made his way down the well-worn pathway used by his ancestors long ago. He too was watching the scene below. The large brown bear continued eating and watching Lia, Deron and Paul as they lay sleeping, while the universe took care of them as they drifted in the dreamtime. Inti pondered on his inaction, which in his Earth time would have been foolish, but the outcome of the challenge was in each one of their keeping, not his. Their bodies of matter and spirit were now closely entwined in the one experience. Inti pondered on the Earth's merciless nature of many moons past when most animals that had roamed thereabouts were dangerous, including man. The spirits of the animals that had roamed the Earth had never gone away; only their physical cloaks had disappeared when Hafnium, the grand master, had commanded it. For Inti, the Earth of yesteryear that existed in the other-worlds was still as busy with insects, birds, fish and animals as it had ever been; nothing had changed for those with his sight. He wondered what gift the bear had brought the three companions today. What wisdom would it be? What would he teach them, and would he change their way of thinking? Inti smiled, for the bear was as crafty as he could be. He dropped a stick into the water below where the bear sat; the splash woke Lia as it burst upon the running water beside her. Inti watched motionless as she sat up with a start. Lia could not see anyone and yet she knew that someone was near, she had felt the presence on awakening.

Above her on the ledge, the bear finished his dinner and threw the remains down into the swirling pool, the resounding plop urging Lia to look up. Lia gasped with horror, not knowing whether to run or stay. Immediately Raphiel was sitting beside her and she began to relax.

Lia turned to face the bear and his black-brown eyes stared back.

'I have never been this close to a brown bear before, Raphiel, he is enormous!' Lia said, feeling a little anxious.

'Yes, isn't he?' said Raphiel, observing the bear respectfully. 'But quite harmless.'

'Thank goodness for that,' said Lia, and she swivelled round to get a better view.

Inti made a hooting noise and both Raphiel and Lia looked up to see him climbing down to where they sat on the large flat stone. When Inti reached the ground he beckoned to Deron and Paul to join him. They were now watching the bear's movement nervously, having been roused by Inti's call, the soft hooting noises sounding like an uncanny warning. The bear started to move to where Lia and Raphiel sat, his ample body scrambling effortlessly down towards them until finally he stood upon his hind legs in front of them on the large flat stone, his shoulders towering way above them. The bear's image began to disappear as the silhouette of a young Indian brave began to emerge until only the young brave remained standing on the ledge with them.

Flying Hawk inside Great Bear greeted them and sat down to speak; his dusty nut-brown body was clad only in a cloth about his waist and his hair was roughly braided with hawk feathers. 'Soon the challenge to resettle the Otom race upon the Earth's surface will commence. It will be a time when they will experience their worst fears but will face them with great courage because they will have the support of the star tribes, the heavenly forces that are our ancestors. The Otom have the ability to emerge victorious from the challenges to come. Mankind has, so far, been on course with his evolutionary destiny, even when in danger of becoming extinct, and the next challenge will decide who will continue Hafnium's Earthly experiment, the Otom or the Cunmen. To win, the Otom will do well to remember that when making incautious progress, there will be sacrifice,' Flying Hawk inside Great Bear looked up towards the summit of the canyon. 'My people say,' he continued earnestly, 'that if you cause an avalanche you must expect to get buried beneath it. The great bear is always wise in the face of an unsafe overhanging rock ledge, and how did he come to know this? Because in the beginning his ancestors were unaware of the dangers upon the mountain, and in the process were buried alive.

This knowledge, wisdom, is passed down among the bear tribe, which is crucial to the continuing evolution of his kind. The Otom must be wise in their choice of advancement and hold judgement whilst they seek to see through the illusion of fear.' The young brave stood up and moved towards the edge of the flat stone; suddenly his body flipped and he disappeared into the cold rushing foam below, his last words echoing around them. 'The Otom will see much chaos and disaster when returning to the surface of the Earth, and this will continue until peace and healing have renewed Gaia, our Earth mother.'

The silhouette of Flying Hawk emerged on the other side of the pool and leapt from the water. Slowly the image changed to be replaced by the large brown bear, which ambled over to a nearby rock and shook his body vigorously.

Lia watched the bear shake the water from his thick fur. *I wish I could have touched him.* Instantly she was on the other side of the pool sitting next to the great bear. He put his paw out and gently touched her face and she laid her hand upon his body.

'You know,' he said, 'we two are no different, Lia. We are born of the animal kingdom and live within the power of the creator, Hafnium.' The bear fixed his eyes upon the now darkened sky above the canyon roof. Lia followed his gaze to the star constellation of the Great Bear. 'Remember, Lia, we are all the same,' he said before ambling off towards the waterfall.

Lia felt the drawing back as her silhouette rippled and then re-emerged where her companions sat around Inti's welcoming brushwood fire.

Paul asked Raphiel, 'Do we all live on in the other-worlds after physical death?'

'No, some are forgotten by Hafnium and cease to exist,' he replied. 'Each one of us is part of Hafnium's creation, from the beginning of Universe Four's existence. We are a part of his being. A fragment of the mathematical sum of the "One" that is Hafnium, and each fragment is on a separate evolutionary path. As I have explained to you before, in the beginning, all life was created to exist for eternity; however, that was not enough for Hafnium, who marvelled at his new creation but wanted more. Therefore, he changed the fragments to experience death and transformation many trillions of times until the planets, stars and galaxies were formed within Universe Four. Hafnium then began to create microcosmic life within and upon those worlds, one being Earth to whom you are bound. The planets became the mother, the womb, from which all physical life took form and continued to multiply and evolve, while Hafnium experienced all that was and is being created. At the time of mankind's death his physical body returns to the earth but the fragment that is Hafnium, the God fragment, lives on in another generation of life. Like the leaves upon a tree: when they die the tree sleeps to prepare for the next cycle of life, which will bring new experiences with the new growth. When a physical being dies, the memory of each lifetime remains within the host fragment of Hafnium, unless he chooses to forget them and eliminates them from his memory. Inti is one such lifetime memory. He appears to you in the form he does because Lia recognises him as such and is at ease with him, and because of her acceptance of him, you trust him also.'

Paul poked the fire thoughtfully; he had learned many things since emerging from the world of the Mers but none more absorbing than the knowledge of the universe beyond the Earth's surface. 'Why does Hafnium choose to forget them?' he asked.

Raphiel replied, 'There are those like the Holocene race who have almost completed their cycle as an experience for Hafnium. They have emerged from trillions of physical and non-physical life forms, and their next journey will be to return to the "One", the globe of living energy from which Universe Four was created. Then there are the life forms that refuse to evolve, their mental energy stagnating upon the psychic plane of the world they will not leave, resisting Hafnium's plan for their return to the One. They are returned to the One by Hafnium if the cycle of experience cannot be completed. The life forms that follow Aspheseuos, Hafnium's beloved brother, will most often journey back into the light after many lifetimes of evil, but if not, they eventually cease to exist in Hafnium's memory. Man lives on in those that come after him, his continuing family, whose souls' destiny it is to par-ticipate in and experience the life cycle of Universe Four.'

Deron sat quietly listening to all that was said, while his mind was curiously fixed upon another thought. He could not help but compare his pallid, muscle-fatigued body with Inti's muscular half-naked one. His own appearance was more in keeping with the Mer people than with the human sitting beside him.

Life below the ocean bed for almost half a century had changed the Otom's outward appearance dramatically. Their lungs were now able to sustain them in or out of water and their toes had become webbed. Their human muscular appearance had wasted away and the lack of sun had caused their bodies to become pallid, with skin that was almost translucent.

Raphiel, having become aware of Deron's thoughts, turned his attention to answering him. 'It is true that the Otom do not look as they did when first they entered the world of the Mers, which causes you to ponder on whether you will return to a state of physical strength. Your physique at present is perfect for life beneath and in the oceans but is questionable for living upon the surface. I will tell you how it will be, in order that you can proceed with assurance.'

Raphiel took them back to the time when mankind had begun to eat animal flesh in order to survive and explained how he continued in this way because of his liking for the taste of meat, which gave him the appearance of physical strength.

'Hafnium does not intend to reinstate the old ways of life upon Earth. The Otom will discover a similar food substance that was created from stem cells years before the holocaust. The secret lies buried beneath the Wiltshire land site. Deep below the maze of underground tunnels there is a city of laboratories and living quarters. The city was built for the scientists in charge of all data needed for the continuing existence of mankind, a city that could support life for a hundred years. Since the holocaust the scientists, both male and female, have delivered forth further generations of scientists. When found, they will be an important key to the Otom's continuing existence. This find will not take place before the Otom race is settled upon the surface. Then the Otom will again take on a human appearance as their diet changes. The future will not be easy, Deron, but the answers are to hand if you look for them.'

Deron and Paul thanked him and slipped beneath their blankets, their uncovered faces warmed by the brushwood fire nearby. Now was a time for solitude to consider Raphiel's words.

Mankind once thought the world to be flat, and that the sun revolved around the Earth. Raphiel smiled as a surge of optimism spread through him. *When the family of scientists are found*, he pondered, *it will be also be time for mankind to be acquainted with the fact that Universe Four is teeming with life, albeit life different to their own. Then the universe will open up to them, as I hope the Healing Globe of Energy, the 'One', will open up to my kind, the Holocene race of the ninth and final universe.*

Chapter 23

The New Masters

With the break of dawn the three companions stirred upon the canyon ledge. The challenge they had come to face was over and they could move to the next phase of their journey. The night before, Raphiel had informed his three companions that come morning they would be returning to the Causeway.

Ormus waited in the caves deep beneath the Causeway, a place that had been his secret abode during his life upon Earth. It was here that the next stage of Deron and Paul's journey was to take place.

The Mer angels that were to preside over Deron and Paul's initiation into the Holocene wisdom were gathering; from this time on the two men would take their place among the Otom elders as '*wise ones*', as mediators for the Otom race. They would share the responsibility for the Otom's return to the surface and any decisions made in the future that would manifest as a gain or sacrifice for their race.

Inti was preparing to leave them. With the challenge over he would continue on his journey through the other-worlds, helping mankind as they entered the dreamtime to seek answers and gain knowledge. He bade them farewell as his dark brown body began to merge with the scenery around them, the shadow of his body and long flowing hair standing out against the valley's summit, the bright red bandana tied about his head still visible. Inti's silhouette rippled and disappeared as he passed beyond their point in time to journey within the hologram of past and future events. As Inti's silhouette passed to the dimensions of the other-worlds, Paul glimpsed the future that was revealed to his unfocused eye, a view of the world without man through the window of destiny.

Raphiel raised himself from the ground and eyed his three companions. It seemed that he was about to speak but instead he closed his eyes and the four companions disappeared from the ledge top, leaving the valley to hold the secrets it had held for all time . . .

Below the Causeway Ormus waited to greet Raphiel, whom he expected to appear at any moment with his charges. Ormus looked up to see a rapidly expanding hole appearing in the cave roof. 'Greetings, Odelia,' he said as she made her grand entrance.

'Greetings, Ormus,' she answered brightly, her larger than life personality filling the cave with exuberant warmth.

Glashadou followed with an equally boisterous greeting. 'Hello, Ormus. It's good to see you, my friend.'

'And you, Glashadou,' Ormus replied.

Raphiel appeared in the cave with his three companions. Lia on seeing Odelia and Glashadou greeted them with a big hug, surprised and pleased that they were to be present at her son's initiation.

'Was your stay in the valley successful, Lia?' Ormus asked when she turned to greet him.

'It was, and just as I dreamed it would be,' she replied happily. 'I'm truly glad I found the courage to fly with the eagles.'

Ormus nodded. 'All illusionary fear is surmountable, given the right time and circumstance to challenge it,' he replied.

Ormus greeted the boys and then focused on a small sphere of blue flame that burned in the centre of the cave. The sphere began to radiate outwards to the cave's perimeter, illuminating the darkness to a brilliance that equalled the daylight over the cliffs above. At Ormus' request the seven sat down around the sphere, but it was Raphiel, not Ormus, who spoke.

Directing his words at Deron and Paul, he began. 'Today, you will revisit your past. You will then move forward for all time. As you journey, the shadows of the past will be left behind you. You will become elders of the Otom, mature and wise in your thoughts, words and deeds as you receive the Holocene knowledge. From here on you will be in no doubt as to the infinite power of Hafnium, creator of Universe Four, and will use his gift of wisdom wisely in the decisions made for the Otom race.'

The flame's ethereal mist spread outwards to embrace the other-worldly entities entering the cave. Within the vaporous cloak, the Mer spirits began to form. As they entered, the sound of the ocean echoed about the seven motionless figures encircling the blue flame.

The voices of the Mer spirits echoed softly about them as the initiation began. 'When inspired with the Holocene knowledge of a "wise one", you will bring your people to the Earth's surface. This wisdom guided your people to the City of Memories at the time of the holocaust, and with the knowledge of zero energy imparted to Lia, they are able to move at will between the two worlds. You are the new generation of "wise ones", elders of the Otom. Teach the new generations of Otom the symbols and meanings of enlightenment until their disciplines are complete, as they will guide the Otom when you are gone.'

Memories of what the two men were to experience came flooding back to Lia, as though it were yesterday.

The Mer spirits began to chant the invocation. 'From within the healing globe of all knowledge, let the Holocene wisdom draw close to the mind of man…'

The seven companions were now as one while they drifted deep within a spiritual world without substance, Deron and Paul's energy field intensifying to equal that of the other five. The Mer spirits chanted the invocation while the transformation of Deron and Paul's consciousness to that of a Holocene "wise one" continued.

Deron's hands were brought together by an unseen force as the Holocene symbols appeared in the air above him. The symbols began to spin about him and then penetrate his physical body; Deron's journey of enlightenment had begun. He watched his soul body fragment and reform into a small child of three years old. The child lay in his mother's arms wrapped in a dark-coloured blanket. He recognised the mother as his own; the child was him. Beyond her shoulder he could see their home; there was shouting, lots of noise, frightening noise, and the stealth of those around his mother silently hurrying into the blackness of the night. The scene fragmented and he realised that his soul was showing him the past. Deron had seen glimpses of those memories when growing up, memories of another world, a world that had been taken from him, something he now realised he had resented very much. He had missed his former life, where he had felt safe and secure before it had been torn away from him. The soul fragments, his soul fragments, drifted about him. *How can I piece them together again?* he wondered. A feeling of numbness, of deadness seemed to encompass him, nothing more, no reality about him. He tried to gather the pieces with his thoughts but as they came together the difficulty of the task made it impossible for him to stay as one bodily; he gave up and let the pieces drift haphazardly. He had a longing for something to fill up the sense of emptiness within.

Deron had always been an achiever but also an adventurer; he would be the first to attempt anything with risk. His move to the underworld, coupled with his mother's hidden fear of her surroundings, had continued to manifest a sense of loss throughout his growing years, a loss which he had fought hard to block out. This feeling had been kept well hidden behind a personality with a great longing to succeed. Now he was facing his demons. A scene came into view of the years that followed when the world he had known fell apart, leaving nothing of the old to hold onto. He began to realise that what had taken place had given him a chance to survive and flourish in a world where he could achieve a sense of self, which could not have been possible if they had remained. He also realised in that moment that he longed to let go of the resentment that he felt. The fragments of his soul began to mend together as the collective law of cause and effect healed a place within his mind. The path that had been chosen for him was offering him an accolade that others respected and loved him for, and from where his character had been formed founded on his childhood loss.

Paul drifted peacefully in the emptiness of the void, unaware that his mother stood beside him. Soon he would be a 'wise one', an elder of the Otom and a teacher of the ancient wisdom ... Dorri, her sister, had taken good care of him during his childhood, a joy which she had been denied. Bending forward she kissed his upturned face. Since her death, she had played her part as his guardian angel. Now everything that was lost to her would be returned. He would see her again.

The initiation chant began. Paul was ready for whatever lay ahead. He opened his eyes to the touch of his mother's kiss upon his cheek, his childhood memory of her face still fresh in his mind. Then he was torn away, flying fast, flying high, as the spinning symbols penetrated his energy field, the joy of love and illumination, euphoria, strong as never before ... The pain of his childhood loss seemed to dissolve like melting ice. The meaningless void that it had left filled with warmth, love and trust ... Paul's transformation was complete.

The initiations over, all seven drifted in the peacefulness of the cosmos.

Chiron, master of the challenges, could now assign the next game to be played out upon Earth.

Chapter 24

The City of Parables

Lia sat alone in the conservatory, looking out towards the darkening Atlantic Ocean. The winter sky was shrouded in an eerie blanket of white cloud that had blocked out the sun by day and lightened the sky well into the night. The light was almost gone but in the greyness she could see the waves rolling in upon the swell of water before crashing against the cliff edge, the sound forcing its way up to her from below. She turned towards the large fire that burned brightly in the open hearth, mesmerised by the sparks that swirled into the chimney above.

Lia had been thinking of her youth, when she had been imbued with the Holocene powers to become a 'wise one'. She recalled the symbols flying and twirling around her before they merged with her being. She had gained much during those early years but had lost her mentor, Ormus, and then her family, which was still painful to recollect. Ormus had returned from the other-worlds but her family, whom she longed to see again, never materialised before her. Closing her eyes, she thought of the time that had altered her life completely.

Lia drifted, journeying through her past, to a place where the smell of apple blossom filled the space around her. The time was spring, her favourite time of year. Ormus and the mermaid Senithe were seated outside the old cottage that had stood on the Causeway before the holocaust. Both carried baskets of golden daffodils, the memory of which was joyful and precious to her, the holocaust having wiped all seasons from the Earth. Lia reached in to pick flowers from the baskets but the contents changed into a blazing fire in which the records of her past lives were burning and diminishing before her.

Ormus took Lia's hand and together they entered the blazing flames of her past. A searing pain drew up through her body and then melted away as all past transgressions in her present and past lifetimes ceased to exist. Lia's journey into the season of beginnings, spring, was to be a journey of celebration …

Lia drew the cloth further about her head and veiled her face as a throng of people gathered round her. Some she did not recognise, but most she had known and shared experiences with during her many lives in many cultures. Beneath a searing sun they walked before her, clearing the path of any obstacles that stood in her way. Ahead of them she could see a walled city with a large gateway, which they would soon enter. She had been here, in the east, at the time of her initiation into the Holocene wisdom but as yet did not understand why she was here again. A child came to place a crown of healing herbs and flowers about her head, which lifted her spirits as she was guided through a gate cut in the towering sandstone wall before her. On entering the ancient Egyptian city, she heard the words 'divine sanctity'. The City of Parables held the chronicles of all allegories that had existed in Earthly time; this was the dwelling place of the soul of the Earth mother, Gaia, a place of infinite knowledge for the dreamer to make use of.

Lia left the throng of people inside the city gates and continued on through the town, acknowledging the strangers who greeted her, and listening to the many who were busy trading their dreams for further wisdom. The dusty roads were cluttered with stalls; the colourful sights and sounds made Lia feel that she belonged there as she walked on, passing through the narrow streets leading down to the harbour.

A large flat boat, weighted down with a heavy cargo, was sinking near to the harbour wall. Lia noticed that no one passed by without helping until the boat stood upright again. Amidst the cargo stood a magnificently robust man with a dark brown face, dressed in white with a gold turban about his head. Beckoning to Lia, he invited her to come on board.

Lia stepped on board, and thanking him she fingered the bales of brightly coloured silk that held the boat deep within the water, while the jars of spices piled on top filled the air with pungent smells.

He smiled and said, 'As yet you cannot see your future, Lia. You fear the pain that separation from your loved ones will bring, but this is a human emotion and will pass as you leave behind your Earthly life.'

Lia looked startled. Had she returned here to be told that her Earthly life was ending?

'Your time is not yet, Lia. You are here to accept that you will relinquish the responsibility of leadership within your tribe. Deron and Paul will take your place, as will others replace the council of elders. The journey to the Earth's surface will be strenuous and a new council of Otom will be needed when it is done. It is time to instil in the younger generation the wisdom they will need for survival as they face the hostile Cunmen upon the Earth's surface. After which you will need the courage to stand aside for others to choose.'

Lia listened to the words he spoke, partly with relief and partly with concern. Would she be able to stand aside and trust the Otom's future to the young?

'Now you must travel further, to receive a gift,' he said, interrupting her thoughts, 'to where the book of beginnings is held, in which your future is also held. Come, Lia, let me help you.' Holding out his hand he helped Lia mount the harbour wall. 'Take the road that appears before you,' he said, waving her goodbye.

Lia thanked him and made her way out of the city to begin her journey along the mountain track in front of her. The path seemed effortless as she climbed towards a village of houses set beneath clouds of pure white. Lia, although curious, passed by in search of the valley further up on the side of the mountain. A column of white energy had descended from the clouds high above her. The words 'the spirit of the creator is all good' were spoken as the column began to change shape, transforming into many forms of an immortal nature. Lia heard the name 'Elisha' as the clouds' form took on the shape of a robed prophet. She tried to remember who Elisha was. She could hear his name being called again as she ran through the stories of his time. Elisha had been the creator's servant throughout a lifetime of adversity. *What did it mean, and what did the future hold?* At the back of her mind a worrying uncertainty niggled at her.

Lia walked on towards the valley peak not knowing what was expected of her. The column of white light continued to change until twelve symbols had formed above her. Each symbol, she realised, represented one of the twelve primary nucleui that had begun life in the watery womb of the new Earth, and each one a fragment of twelve suns in Universe Four that now existed as stars. Lia continued to climb as she pieced the mystery together. The twelve symbols that she recognised as the symbols of transformation also represented the stars that mankind had used for guidance in ancient civilisations. Lia stopped to look up from her frantic deliberations. She was now at the peak of the valley and the clouds had disappeared to reveal a darkened horizon wherein the twelve star tribes shone brightly. Lia realised that this was the book of beginnings as promised, the map of the heavens that held the Earth's destiny, and also her own.

Two star formations appeared more radiant than those about them, one reflecting a pathway to the other. The archer's bow of the constellation Sagittarius appeared ready to release a gift of knowledge for Gemini to pass on: the hidden symbols of the void were to be set free upon the Earth ...

The transformation Lia had experienced as a young woman of twenty-one years, and the symbols, which she had forgotten, had revealed to her the pathway she would tread during her final years upon Earth. Lia was drawn back to her first journey with Ormus and Raphiel to the Heavenly Mountain that arcs the world, and her first sight of the multiple rainbows surrounding the Earth. At that time her challenges were just beginning. Now as she stood in this familiar place, fifty years on, she accepted that her leadership challenges were almost over, and that the Otom's two new elders, Deron and Paul, would take her place. Lia knelt down in honest gratitude for her release from such a burden. The karmic records of her past lives no longer existed. She was absolved from all past error and on her journey back to the 'one' divinity, which made her aware of the fact that she was entering the final phase of her Earthly life. The time was coming when she would watch over those in her charge but not lead them …

When Lia returned to the room the fire burned low in the grate but the conservatory still remained warm. Her mind and body felt at peace as she pulled the blankets up around her and snuggled down to stay for the night. 'Thank you,' she whispered.

Deron and the boys appeared at the door, and opening the sliding panel they came in to warm themselves by the fire. They, like Lia, loved to sit outside in the conservatory at night and be at one with the sound of the ocean and the stillness over the land.

Earlier that evening Mariana had been recalled to work. The family had had their supper together and afterwards Lia had left them alone until it was time for Mariana to leave. Now it was late and the boys were sleepy and they had come to say goodnight.

Deron came over to his mother and kissed her lightly on the cheek. 'Today's experience is beyond words, Mother. I'm so glad that you were with me.'

Lia smiled at her son, whose face was still glowing from his experience that day. What had been but a few hours' absence to her grandchildren had been an eternity of discovery for Deron and Paul, and she knew from experience that he needed time to himself to embrace his newfound level of enlightenment.

Lia said to the boys, 'Come on you two, time for bed.'

The boys stood up, too tired to argue.

'I think I will turn in as well, Mother. I feel really tired tonight.' Deron winked at her, not wanting anything said that might arouse the boys' interest.

'Good night then. See you in the morning.' Lia stood to kiss them. Then she was alone again.

Ormus appeared and sat down upon one of the large cushions that were scattered upon the large empty wooden floor, a space left uncluttered by furniture.

Lia went and sat beside him. 'And to what reason do I owe this welcome visit?' she asked, knowing that the pace of things would quicken now that Deron and Paul's transformation was complete.

Ormus answered, 'Lia, tonight we will travel to meet the star tribes. It is winter and Capricorn, the progeny of Saturn, comes before him to be told her duties in the month to come. You hold the key to the star tribe's role in mankind's challenges, and will be expected to reside at this and each of the eleven subsequent gatherings as the year's challenges are being met. Each star formation has a part to play in the coming rotation of the Earth's seasons. The cycle of winter has begun. December is making way for January and it is Capricorn's time to act.'

Ormus stood up and walked towards the door, which slid open as he approached it. Lia felt the cold air rush in to greet her.

Ormus turned to her and said, 'Tonight we will fly again! We will travel back in time to see the Earth in all her splendour, as she was many years ago.'

Lia smiled broadly as she walked towards her dear old friend, Ormus, whose worldliness often bordered on showing off, which had always made her smile. Ormus' cloak came around her shoulders and she felt the rush of cold air upon her body as they lifted high above the garden and out beyond the cove. Below, the ocean's mass rose up dark and powerful as if to claim them. Lia lifted her face towards the stars that were to guide the Otom through the next phase of their journey. *How have I been so lucky to have been born into the world at this time of such change, such wonderment, such excitement? Perhaps affectation becomes part of us all when life becomes so full of wonder that we cannot believe how fortunate we are.*

Below Lia and Ormus, the sliding door of the conservatory closed unaided, and the garden became as silent as a whisper again.

Deron Debarc-Major stood watching from his window as his mother and Ormus left the conservatory. 'I hope I will be joining you in future,' he said softly. 'Good night, Mother. Have a safe journey.'

'Good night, Deron, sweet dreams,' came the reply.

Chapter 25

Capricorn – Queen of Winter

The planet Saturn surveyed his progeny, Capricorn, his orange-red hue shrouding her icy intenseness and holding in check her ability to inflict a permanent death upon Earth's nature.

'Capricorn, come listen,' he called, 'you have much to do.' Saturn waited for her to ease herself awake. Capricorn's wintry nature was grossly misunderstood by those who judged her, those who were not aware of the strength they drew from her season of hardships. Saturn's influence, contained within Capricorn's nature, bestowed upon mankind a sense of honour and substance, professionalism and authority, especially in times of adversity. Saturn's guidance of those beneath his gaze was unyielding and harsh while they learned their role in the universe. Capricorn's nature was cold but not inaccessible, and she always sensed the universal love that surrounded her and was content in her winter cloak of obscurity. To Saturn, her mentor, she was a joy to behold, a jewel hidden beneath the onslaught of winter's barrenness. Capricorn, queen of winter, imposed a time of rest upon nature.

Lia and Ormus appeared on the blue and silver chequerboard of Universe Four. Above them, within the brilliance of the star Capricorn's icy glow, they could see the form of a young woman, her long slender body surrounded by flowing ebony hair that fell about her waist: Capricorn, a delicate spirit dressed in flowing white and blue robes, with a face as pale as a winter sky that contrasted starkly with the warmth of her intense golden eyes.

Lia thought her beauty awesome as she gazed into the deep pools of gold.

'Welcome, Ormus and Lia,' said Capricorn.

'Greetings, greetings,' said Saturn, his golden radiance flowing out to bestow upon them his abounding, although a little authoritarian, love. Saturn came straight to the point. 'Ormus, I have taught my progeny, Capricorn, to concentrate on her strengths, not her weaknesses, and to hold firm to her beliefs. She is the spirit of winter and beneath her mantle she nurtures all that is to be born in the future, while teaching strength within hardship as they wait. My progeny, Capricorn, will be a good intermediary for those of the Otom who fear the coming change. When winter turns to spring they will see a miracle unfold upon the land that will draw them gladly to the surface of the Earth.'

Ormus looked upon the star, Capricorn, her silhouette of beauty mirrored within the blueness of his eyes. 'Capricorn,' he called, 'you know what is to be done. Take Lia to her karmic past, a past that is now absolved but must be acknowledged. Take her to the lifetime that she shared with me, which resulted in the loss of her soul for many lifetimes. Help her to understand why this lifetime has been burdened with so much responsibility, pain and grief. Yet like you,' he said softly, 'she bears it with dignity and grace. Such is the wonder, Capricorn.'

Ormus' words of compassion warmed Capricorn's cold heart with a benevolence that she thought she had long forgotten. She answered him, 'After Lia has returned to her past and relived the pain that shadows her, she will be free to live in peace.'

Capricorn held her arms aloft and enveloped Lia in her cloak of icy energy. Immediately Lia felt an unbearable pain within as Capricorn's touch of death enveloped her. She began to drift across death's icy wasteland back to a time when she had been responsible for the death of many. Warmth began to touch her again as she stood looking over the high peaks of a mountainous region that she recognised, a place, a lifetime where, as a high priestess, she had willingly sacrificed her people to the worship of the gods.

Lia touched the white flowing robes clinging lightly to her body, her mind rejecting the fact that they were real; this lifetime had been an atrocity to mankind, and from which her soul had been exiled from the path of evolution, but not forgotten by Hafnium.

The walls of a temple citadel rose up behind the parapet where she stood. Below her a woman looked up at her with a fixed and hostile stare. Lia felt the sense of loss that had shadowed her all of her life, but now she felt a heightened sense of dread. The woman remained motionless as a man appeared from the shadow of the ramparts and walked towards her. Lia stepped back, but he had seen her and his clear blue eyes conveyed veiled anger. The man of obvious authority gazing up at her was dressed from head to toe in feathered gold. Lia recognised him instantly, and the memories flooded back as Ormus stood below her.

Ormus, high priest of the temple, was a man of deadly influence, and her husband. Lia's heart raced with fear as she realised he was part of the dread that she carried inside. The fear strengthened its grip as she sensed there was something more. The temple buildings rose up behind her, the mighty sandstone walls casting shadows before the blazing sun. Lia felt terror as never before, and turning to face the fortification behind her, she ran inside and made her way up to the highest point. The shadows seemed to chase her as she ran up the winding stone steps, her heart pounding wildly as she ran from her fear. The stairway ended, and a door barred her way. Standing still for only a moment, Lia reached out and pushed the door ajar. Upon the floor a man lay motionless, a man that she recognised as once having loved, and who had loved her in return. A centurion dressed in red and gold, one of her personal guards, lay still in death. Lia stood frozen to the spot as the memory of that lifetime, when her character had been so cruel, so merciless and evil, slowly unwound before her. The cloak of forgetfulness had been lifted upon a lifetime when Ormus' race, the Birdmen, beings of both man and bird, had ruled over her enslaved people for centuries, and she, as high priestess to the Temple of the Sun, had sacrificed them to the gods. Ormus had ruled supreme; he had manipulated and betrayed her throughout her passage from child to womanhood. He had been her protector and her incarcerator, grooming her for her place as high priestess to the Temple of the Sun, a place of human sacrifice.

Lia had been taken from her parents and given to the temple when still a small child. As Lia had grown to adulthood, Ormus, a man of many years, had been kind to her, and encouraged by this, Lia had consented to their marriage taking place. Lia had felt betrayed, angry, and jealous when she had found that this centurion was to marry her handmaiden. Her anger had turned to malevolence. Now he lay before her upon the floor, his body pierced and bloodied. Lia was responsible for his death and she realised her happiness had been lost forever. Suddenly the picture changed, and Lia waited for the attendance of Ormus in a marriage that she had decided would not continue. She watched the Lia of thousands of years past begin to fall, tumbling backwards into a darkening infinity, until finally coming to rest in a prism of ice where she had remained for what seemed eternity.

Lia looked into the face of Capricorn and asked, 'Why did I do it? Take his life?' Lia could not see the truth, that a child reared in cruelty understands the brutality of those about her as her truth.

Capricorn replied, 'You experienced a life in which you took the lives of many as high priestess of an ancient civilisation, and you were beguiled to accept marriage with Ormus. Ormus loved you but he knew only the ways of evil, which you came to know also. The love of the centurion was not yours to have, and in your jealousy you took his life and then your own. While you healed from this experience I held your soul entombed within my citadel of winter, as I do with all souls that experience the taking of life within the worlds of emotional transgressions, which mankind calls death.'

Lia's head was spinning; to take another's life, surely not; it wasn't possible that the dark shadow that had pursued her from her past was the murder of another being. She could never ... and Ormus her dear friend ... Lia began to feel violently ill, her heart pounded. She could not breathe. Her throat constricted as she tried to draw breath. Ormus appeared beside her and put his cloak around her form. She began to breathe easily again.

'Lia,' he said gently, 'all experiences are universal. Do not think that you are different. I told you long ago of my time upon Earth when I succumbed to the material excesses of a worldly life. For that life I served years of purgatory, and others with me. The life you have been shown was but one that you shared with me, which, for my transgressions, turned you into a murderer. Now the truth is known my wrongs have been absolved. Every soul will experience all there is to experience as it passes through each phase of life. Finally, when the soul's journey is complete, it returns to the divine spirit of the One and the journey of experiencing "all" is at an end.'

Lia began to sob. She wept with relief for the unburdening of her past, and for the souls who would follow her racked with pain and guilt in the processes of returning to the divinity of the One.

'Capricorn,' said Saturn, 'see the rewards that your gifts bestow upon you. You are responsible for souls such as Lia during their darkest moments, but look at the precious jewel that finally emerges from the uncut stone. Shine with pride as you gather the burdens of all souls to you, and when you tire of your duty, remember Lia as she is today. She is the result of your duty to her continued evolvement during the darker episodes of her soul.'

Saturn turned to Lia. 'The universe has not yet done with the challenge to your heart, Lia. The one whose death lies at your feet is to challenge you again, and he lives now as the one called Mikell Lang.'

Lia's thoughts went immediately to her son's companion, Mikell Lang, a young man whose character was dubious and whose position as a delegate to the elders of the Otom tribe questionable. Lia suddenly felt calm; his presence may be dangerous but not to her peace of mind; she would accept his challenge as and when it came.

Capricorn had blossomed at Saturn's' words, her exquisite radiance enveloping those about her.

Saturn felt a resonance of concern deep within his stern old heart, knowing that mankind's preparation to ascend to the sixth universe would make Capricorn's duties burdensome, but there she was, her beautiful star formation dazzling in the heavens as he had never seen before. Saturn blazed with pride at the tranquil beauty of his progeny, Capricorn. She would not let him down.

Ormus stood Lia gently upon the bedroom floor, holding her shoulders while she became used to her surroundings, and then he sat her gently upon the bed. 'You must get some sleep, my dear. Tomorrow will bring another busy day, as life for you is always at a pace. Think no more about the past, for the past is truly over and you are what you are today, at this moment, not what you were so long ago in your many lifetimes.' Ormus passed his hand over Lia's face, stopping to touch the centre of her forehead. A deep violet energy began to merge with Lia's energy field. The healing ray that Ormus bestowed upon her form slowly began to do its work. Lia lay upon the bed and was soon fast asleep. Ormus pulled the covers around her. 'All karmic debts have been repaid, my dear, and are now forgotten,' he whispered before slipping quietly from the room, glad that Lia's darkness would finally leave her.

In the heavens above, Capricorn waited for Ormus. It was time to do Saturn's bidding. Mankind's next challenge would not wait.

The Earth's wildlife had been called upon by Capricorn, queen of winter. They knew the time was upon them when once again they would have to live with man. Some forty-five years had passed since Hafnium had thrown his cloak of invisibility over all wildlife that lived upon the Earth's surface. Man had been driven down below the oceans to live among the Mers. Now only Cunman roamed the Earth's surface, and he could neither hunt nor kill the wildlife as they were invisible to him. The spirits of the wildlife and the other-worlds roamed the surface of the Earth unobserved to watch the Cunmen's struggle to survive.

At Hafnium's command, Capricorn was to lift her cloak of sleeping darkness. Life would begin to manifest again deep below the Earth's frozen surface. The seeds of life would begin to force their way towards the ever growing strength of the sun's rays and later, when vegetation covered the land, the wildlife that was stilled in deep hibernation would awaken and roam the Earth once more.

The wildlife spirits, being aware of the change to come, recalled with unease the time before the great destruction when man had destroyed most of their natural terrain, which had led to their virtual extinction. As the world had felt the first tremble of the holocaust, Hafnium had thrown his cloak of invisibility over the wildlife and moved them within the safety of the void, where their spirits were left to watch over the Earth as she healed.

A 'wise one' and leader of the herds stood before Capricorn, his great nostrils flaring, his breath frosty within the presence of the winter queen.

'Greetings,' said Capricorn. 'It is with great happiness that I come to speak with you. Soon all that has been beneath my mantle will manifest and the Earth world, Gaia, will again be teaming with life. Does this make you happy?'

For a moment the great beast stood silently thinking of how his herds had suffered, how every living beast had suffered at man's hand. He replied, 'I hesitate in my answer to you, Capricorn. We have encountered hope from your words in the past as we lay beneath your mantle of death, after much pain and suffering. Now we are to be reborn to experience more pain and suffering. We have seen no change in the Cunmen, after this great time of barrenness, and yet you ask us if we are happy to trust our lives to man again. I am not able to say it brings me any contentment. And what of the Otom, how have they spent those years below the oceans, have the one tribe that will emerge really changed? And if they have changed, then what of the Cunman, what of him? He still roams the Earth for all the wildlife spirits to see. How can you say that we will find any love in the new world, any compassion? Perhaps we would be better living in the spirit world forever.'

Capricorn felt the usual feeling of rejection that she stirred in those who were to be challenged by possible hardship. Capricorn's radiance began to diminish as she hesitated, not knowing how to answer him. The animal hung his head in anguish at her reaction, and what appeared to be another hopeless situation. Ormus appeared beside him to speak on Capricorn's behalf but his voice was carried away by the snowstorm that came rushing in towards them, spinning them in its wake. The snowstorm carried them overland to the Siberian taiga where a vast region of healthy unbroken forest and wetlands lay before them, land enough to allow populations of large predators to survive and roam at will. As they were held in the storm above the landscape, species of water fowl and shorebirds appeared alongside Siberian crane.

'This is my answer.' Hafnium's voice echoed about them. 'They will be safe this time, as will the Otom be compassionate.'

The spirits of the wildlife felt encouraged that all species would return to the Earth's surface and that the Otom were preparing for a new and peaceful time alongside them. Hafnium's word had been given. The wildfowl vanished to reappear later with the return of the forests and plant life.

Ormus turned to Capricorn and said, 'Why do you give up so easily? Why become downcast? Let your radiance remain constant, and your ideology sound within, then you will convince those who have a need to change.'

With the kindly guidance of Ormus, Capricorn's light returned to its former brilliance and the leader of the herds, having seen the vision of a better world, listened to her request.

'You have now seen the mantle of hibernation lifted from one region of the Earth. Now I will tell you how the work will be done. With the coming seasons, each star's time of manifestation will bring an awakening upon the Earth. Nature will reveal itself in abundance, and with its coming, every species of wildlife of the air and ground will follow. Be at peace, for the Otom have been cleansed of their need to eat flesh. The one tribe of man arises from the world of the Mers without the desire to hunt you down for food or sport. He will live in peace with you and be joyful of the beauty you provide to the Earth. The Cunmen's future is yet to be told as the new world arises, but for now that is for Hafnium to know.'

The lonely beast held his head proud above his body, his countenance one of joy. 'At last,' he said, 'at last our gift to man, our sacrifice to man when the world was covered in ice, is finally over. No more will man slaughter my kind in order that he may live. We can live in peace beside the Otom, as those of our kingdom that once fed upon each other have also changed while held within the land of spirit.'

Ormus looked on as the 'wise one' of the herds thanked Capricorn for nurturing all of nature beneath her mantle. All would now gradually emerge from beneath her icy gaze. Capricorn shone with a brilliance never seen before. This time they had listened.

Chapter 26

Mary

At the beginning of the new millennium people of the western world spoke of the coming Age of Aquarius as a time of great change and renewed hope, not realising the world as they knew it would change beyond recognition in order for a spiritual awakening to manifest within mankind.

Three years before the holocaust, Lucille Lang, a single parent, had borne a son, Mikell. Mikell Lang had been a quiet but disruptive child, and later an inventive teenager, but his opinions were cold and radical as he moved towards manhood.

Mikell had been orphaned when still an infant, leaving him in the care of his aunt Mary. Mary was a firm believer in the coming change that was to be a spiritual awakening for those who acknowledged it; she spent much of her time with the lightworkers, healers who were to witness the new world.

The lightworkers' lives were often difficult. They were considered dangerously unconventional by certain religious orders and medical institutions alike, the latter proclaiming the success of their work coincidental rather than factual and the former that the right to heal the masses sat with the ordained. For the new healers, life was a series of worrying contradictions in a world where material success was considered the value of one's worth. The spiritual philosophies of the lightworkers made life impossible in a society where corruption ruled without justice or righteous law, and those who championed principled fairness were dealt with harshly. The law of human rights had been manipulated in favour of the criminal with the introduction of a Human Rights Bill that allowed the unlawful to rain war upon the innocent. The silent din of mankind's inventiveness bombarded people's daily lives with energy waves that afflicted them constantly, making them stressed, ill and angry. Time was running out. The day when time would cease to exist was drawing near. Mary believed this to be true without any doubt.

The lightworkers continued with their daily lives as best they could, waiting patiently for the day when they would perform an exodus from the world they knew and journey below the Earth's surface to begin a new life. Most were concerned about the future that would take them beneath the oceans to the City of Memories, a place seen in their dreamtime as a shroud of white energy, which they imagined was a place of peace – or heaven to be. But this was different; they knew instinctively this was not heaven, death, whatever it might be.

The lightworkers' main worry was over the coming change that would mean life without soil, sun or sky, and if their dreams were to be acknowledged, a world that they feared.

Mary's thoughts were constantly troubled; would the lightworkers allow Mikell to go with her? She loved her sister's child deeply, but his behaviour for one so young was unnaturally worrying. Constantly she dreamed of a future time when Mikell would try to destroy the lightworkers. Mary's concerns continued to flourish as the growing infant showed all the traits of his father's aggression, and his mother's weakness. It was only her sister's memory that kept her sense of duty clear. She would not leave her sister's child to the mercy of a disintegrating world; she would not go without him.

Mikell's mother Lucille had been an alcoholic, his father a scheming bully, both partners drawn towards each other by an unseen bond, the weakness in their characters having drawn them together like a magnet. Lucille had been a lovely child, quiet and gentle, but deeply disturbed. As she grew to adulthood she was drawn into a life of excitement way beyond the sanctuary of her parents' support. With the security of her childhood over, Lucille became pregnant, dependent on drink, and trapped within a violent relationship.

Mary had hoped when her sister's child was born that he would grow in her favour, quiet and gentle but without his mother's weakness. She realised very quickly that what she wished for was not to be. Mary was reminded daily that Mikell had been created in his father's likeness both in temperament and appearance, his deep dark eyes observing her with a defiant look, while his body language remained constantly challenging. Life, she realised, would become an enormous challenge for him as he struggled to accept the new world where she must take him. But take him with her she must.

Ormus had appeared to Mary in her dreamtime, bringing her the news that Mikell would be going with her to the City of Memories. In the dream, Mary stood before the council of elders who gave her solace, telling her that Mikell would grow to manhood among the children chosen for the migration. Mary had been overwhelmed with relief as the council gave her the good news, until they made clear that he would become their betrayer. Mary had wanted to stay behind but the council had soothed her fears. They would watch over the growing children as they were challenged by the evil that Mikell emanated; it would be the greatest challenge the children faced before they returned to the Earth's surface as the new tribe of man, the Otom. Mary's role, they told her, in the coming challenge was a blessed one. She must rear the betrayer with love and compassion while mindful of his role in the destiny of their race.

Mikell was to grow to adulthood among them in order to help the Cunmen, those of mankind who remained on the Earth's surface after the holocaust; this, they told Mary, had been foretold.

Mary had awakened from her dream sobbing; she was to take Mikell among her kind to betray them.

Chapter 27

The Lightworkers

During the early decades of the twenty-first century AD, mankind's awareness of telepathic communication began to open up on a worldwide scale; people in search of an altruistic way of life began to gather together, and spiritual awareness groups burgeoned on a magnitude never known before. With this growing energy phenomenon, there arrived an upsurge in loss of life worldwide, as disease, warfare and natural disasters continued to escalate on a massive scale; for mankind, the new age cycle of change was well under way.

Maddie, a dedicated lightworker, found it hard to maintain her belief in a better future as the years moved into the so-called Age of Aquarius. She worked for her local council managing a support group for the carers of the elderly and disabled, and in her spare time worked with fellow lightworkers at the local healing centre, giving the same supportive help.

Maddie's local council was constantly under fire for its mismanagement of public funds, but all attempts to correct the problem had failed. It was widely rumoured that most of the senior officials working for the town's council had been selected through the good word of a 'friend', most being unqualified for the responsible position that they held. A handshake here, a handshake there ... a voice would continually engage her mind in warning of the obvious mismanagement of public funds that was about to disband the carers group. By the time Maddie had realised how seriously wrong things were, she had been drawn into the circle of corruptness by her silence. The funds for her carers group were about to be placed elsewhere.

Maddie turned to her friend Robert, who lived not far from her. Robert was a lightworker, and organised the running of the healing centre where Maddie worked. He was a tall man of indefinable age with a love for dressing in dark green garments; his dark hair was always combed sleekly back, and his large fluid eyes looked back at you with an unequivocal gaze.

Robert was waiting for her when she arrived, even though she had come uninvited. 'Come in, Maddie, I have been expecting you.' As they embraced, the word 'misappropriation' entered his mind.

Maddie entered Robert's ground-floor apartment and was immediately ushered out to the garden where he had set out lunch for them: fruit, a vegetable flan, some nuts and something to drink.

'Sit down, Maddie,' Robert said politely, pouring them a drink. Then taking some fruit he went to sit on the grass.

Maddie filled a plate and joined him. Putting her food down, she started to talk; she felt so full of worry and discontent, and wanted to release it all from her mind. She began to cry.

Robert, realising why she had come, spoke gently to her. 'When I was a young man, I worked as an IT manager at my local sports centre. The council had contracted a local small business to replace and monitor the IT equipment. The project was financially massive to the small company, and for the contract, the senior council officials asked for a vote on the board, their reason being that public funds would have to be provided for the project, for which they would be responsible. When all was up and running, the company's director called on me one day with the news that he had been voted off the board by a majority vote of the council members, and that the council had other plans for his company. He said there was nothing he could do, and then advised me to look elsewhere for employment, that if I was to stay they would coerce me into doing things that would go against my principles. This was all he would say as to the reason he had lost his position in the company. We had become good friends, yet in my unsure judgement of him, I ignored his advice and stayed; I had managed the IT office for many years, and I held on. Another came to replace him whose reputation for winding down companies went before him as a beacon of light. From that time on the company assets were gradually stripped, and I made an enemy of my new boss by questioning the integrity of his decisions. My health began to deteriorate as I realised that, like you, I was becoming part of the deceit by remaining silent.' Robert paused reflectively. 'But you see, Maddie, the experience was to awaken me to the growing evil that rules mankind's way of life. It mattered not what they did, they were protected by Aspheseuos; his army of centurions are a force of evil that rule in every public organisation across the country, across the world. Finally, I made the decision to leave when my principles were questioned; I was asked for the invoicing data of a company they no longer wanted to use, and for which they intended to contrive a dismissal without payment for their software. This I can tell you went against all that I felt was just, and so I left, but not before ringing the company in question and telling them what had come to light. So tell me, Maddie, because you are today where I was once. What will be your choice?'

Maddie sipped at her drink. The tears had stopped long ago as Robert recalled his story.

Maddie began to unburden her worried thoughts. 'You know that I am a therapist, Robert, and that I teach an alternative health programme for the local council. Well, I was approached by a charitable organisation to prepare a course for a new project helping carers of the elderly – to be funded by our local council. If it was successful the council would be able to apply to the government for a permanent grant for future years. The project has been a success. I have held two-hour sessions each week at three centres for the past two years, and the carers appreciate having that time as their own. They enjoy the various relaxation activities that we work with, especially meditative healing. Within the first year, I was told that the application for funding was going well and that I was to continue updating them with a weekly report. But once the funding was passed the classes were cut back, and it was rumoured that they were to be discontinued. The carers that had fought for the funding decided to complain, and they each received a letter reprimanding them for interfering. But it left the council shaken and the classes were reinstated. And so we struggle on, but the work no longer gives me the pleasure that it used to. This has left me feeling unsettled and compromised, and that I am not supporting the group as much as I should.' Maddie looked at Robert guiltily. 'The healing centre is so dissimilar to the employment that pays my rent, and I often wish that I could find the means to work as a volunteer full-time.'

Robert spoke quietly. 'Maddie, it's time to give this up. Someone else will step into your place. Sadly, you cannot win against this corruptness; the grant they have claimed will be channelled elsewhere as soon as they are able. You must trust your feelings in this and be patient, which is the way of the lightworker.'

Maddie and Robert sat in silence on the sunny embankment at the bottom of Robert's communal garden, watching the slow running stream that flowed past them.

'Patience, Maddie,' Robert said again.

Life had not been easy for Robert in the beginning, his values had not nourished him and he had felt anger in his heart for a very long time, but time had healed those things, and now he held faith in what was guiding him forwards. Robert smiled. 'Destiny is always in charge, and will take care of your problems while you listen to what is right for you.'

Maddie lay down on the grass and looked up at the clear blue sky; suddenly a cloud came into view and shadowed her body, and then it was gone just as quickly. *That,* she thought, *is like my problem – the quicker it is dealt with, the sooner it will go away.*

Maddie decided that she would not continue with her work; she would let it go. Her heart felt happy with the decision. Turning to Robert, she asked, 'Do you have any permanent work at the healing centre?'

Robert replied, 'Well, I was going to speak to you about that; as a matter of fact ...'

Chapter 28

Aquarius

Hafnium, the grand master, commanded Aquarius to look into the hologram of the past; the psychic world was gathering en masse the ethereal bodies still shackled to the illusion that their Earthly life continued. Those that had released their ethereal body at death were passing by the psychic plane to the other-worlds, leaving the physical plane of illusion and distorted reality behind to advance their soul's nature on a higher plane of existence.

Many souls had exited the Earth at this time, their lives cut short by the holocaust. The carnage was indescribable as steel, earth and flesh disintegrated into dust. There had been little time to mourn loved ones before the final assault upon mankind, which had been incurred by many things – different cultures, religions, and corrupt systems of law.

Hafnium asked, 'Is this what you want to bring forth again, Aquarius? Think on this: the one called Mikell is the progeny of Aspheseuos, and he is gathering his followers. I can see that you are tempted by the glory that helping him might bring, but have you thought of what it will mean? You will be turned away from the star tribes to exist alone, as was Aspheseuos, the angel most holy. Are you to join him in this challenge, or will you remain loyal to your kind?' Hafnium waited for a response but none was forthcoming. He continued, 'Can you not see that should Aspheseuos win, then the Otom will be destroyed and the opportunity for mankind to move on to Universe Six in the far distant future terminated? I will not let that happen to my plan. Change must come, Aquarius. Aspheseuos cannot stop it. We know the universe will appear strange when mankind and all things of a physical nature leave Universe Four, but the star tribes must return to the way they were, black holes that were allowed to reveal their brilliance as more dark mass was created to give equilibrium. All manner of life was brought into existence this way; mankind, the Earth, the planetary forces, the solar star of the Milky Way galaxy, all were created from the black depth of my being. When mankind leaves Universe Four, the twelve stars that brought him to existence must return to the void, for that is where they are destined to belong for a while. Universe Four will become dark again until my new plan begins. And then, new life will replace mankind in this universe, and the newly created planetary forces will shine forth again. Does this not please you?'

Aquarius remained silent.

Hafnium continued, 'Aquarius, do not let Aspheseuos tempt you into believing that you can move on to Universe Six with mankind, for you can never go from here; you are part of my creation, I am Universe Four.' Hafnium wondered how he might make Aquarius see the truth. 'There is a higher power far beyond us, a power that we are all part of, a power that creates continually at its own command, not ours. You will remain here, whatever you are told by Aspheseuos. I have told you the truth.' Hafnium's light faded and Aquarius was left alone.

'What have I done, what have I done?' Uranus listened to her progeny, whose tone was at first guilt-ridden, and then righteous. 'If Hafnium is not the lord of all then how can he be sure that Aspheseuos is wrong?'

Uranus listened with growing sadness; Aquarius was never going to listen. There was only one voice that he heard, and that was his own. Her visions had foretold that Aquarius would help Mikell, as Mary's dreams had warned her that one day Mikell would betray his kind.

Upon the Earth, the moon eclipsed the sun and the light was taken from the planet; it was the time for the devil to dance, and dance he would. The war between the Otom and the Cunmen was within Hafnium's control, but from the shadows of darkness came a wealth of learning for mankind, his bad thoughts becoming powerful, collecting together to manifest and experience another phase of evil. The Otom's guidance came in the form of meditation, whereupon they were continually reminded to care for their thoughts lest they become a challenge.

The world in the first years of the new millennium had been overflowing with the dark thoughts of mankind who sought out the like-minded and gathered like a swarm of insects, so dark that light could not penetrate, bringing forth violence of a manner so devastating that hundreds, and sometimes thousands, died in one dark moment.

The Age of Aquarius was to be the new beginning in which everything would get better, but what mankind had chosen to ignore was that change had to come from within himself. The Age of Aquarius meant a new era of self-inventiveness, of independence, freedom from oppression for all. This change would only manifest when mankind found the courage to speak out against the tide of corruption and violence that had swept through each continent upon the Earth; it was time for man to choose a new path to follow.

Uranus had observed Aquarius' years of control over the growing child, Mikell. She had spoken of her misgivings to Hafnium, the grand master, long before his gathering with the star tribe, knowing there was danger within their partnership. Uranus' progeny was headstrong, and she worried over his role in mankind's continuing evolvement; Mikell was showing the first signs of his influence to corrupt and his strong desire for control, and Aquarius, who would not listen to her, encouraged him in order to fulfil his own desire: to save himself, and the star tribe, from returning to the void. Aquarius was always flitting here and there, rarely aware of the needs of those around him. Uranus thought of Hafnium's words: '*I give to you, Aquarius, the responsibility of future potential. You will serve mankind to further his expansion…*' To see Aquarius' attributes manifesting in the one called Mikell, who would not be advised, but questioned and argued his point until he won, because to lose an argument was not within his concept. Uranus continued to worry; she knew of mankind's past dark history, and her progeny's love of freedom.

Mikell, Aquarius' mortal collaborator, made those around him feel ill at ease wherever he went. Mikell conversed with charm, but beneath the allure his bullying nature was never far from the surface and would often manifest, after which he would laugh and apologise insincerely.

Mikell had been a very sickly child; his soul was so imprisoned within the dark karma of his ethereal body that he could not tolerate his new existence among the two spiritual races, the Mers and the Otom. Mikell had experienced a solitary infancy, with Ormus watching over him, and mainly his Aunt Mary for company. By the time Mikell was interacting with other children in study groups his education had moved far beyond that of his peers; with Ormus' mentoring his presence of mind was strong, although his behaviour was disruptive and sly.

Deron had been fascinated by this rebel, the one who always seemed to place himself at the centre of attention during their growing years. Deron would stay close to him; he found his antics fun, although at times they made him feel uneasy. Deron's close friend Paul was quiet and serious, his nature kind but fretful. Mikell would play tricks on him and get him into trouble until the day that Mikell went too far. The three companions had gone swimming in the pools between the water caves; this was a favourite place that was quiet and away from the gaze of adults, where they would talk of manhood and their roles in the future regrouping on the surface. Mikell beckoned Paul into the water to race, teasing him to swim into deeper water. Paul, upset by his constant chiding, followed him; he raced out to where Mikell stood upon a submerged rock, and when he drew near, Mikell suddenly grabbed him and held him under the water. At first it appeared to be fun; they could all breathe below the surface for long periods of time, but then something told Deron to dive into the water below them. Mikell's hand was covering Paul's mouth and nose. Paul was slowly losing consciousness, his body slumping forward, floating like the cave weed that drifted around him. With one sharp wrench Deron grabbed Mikell's head and twisted it violently, immediately Mikell let go his grip and Deron pulled his friend from the water.

Paul came up gasping for air, and then began to cry. 'I have told you, Deron, I have told you,' was all he could say.

Deron turned to the laughing Mikell, his face like thunder.

'What's the matter? It was only a bit of fun.' Mikell said, laughing uncontrollably. 'You and Paul are just too sensitive.'

Deron said nothing; he could see the coldness and cruelty in Mikell's eyes, and it was the first time he had felt such anger, it was the first time he had ever felt the desire to hit out, the desire to hurt. Now he felt confused and ashamed, but he also felt fear, fear of Mikell whom he no longer trusted or thought of as a friend.

From that time, in his fourteenth year, Deron had remained at a distance from Mikell, his cruel antics no longer funny, his evil now seeded and in full growth.

Aquarius, whose duty it was to help the Otom achieve their goal, was interested in helping only one of their kind, Mikell. And with Aspheseuos, his master, having promised him a place in Universe Six, he would agree to Mikell's every demand. Aquarius could see no other way; Mikell would one day be leader of the Cunmen, who would destroy the Otom. Aquarius wanted to be triumphant alongside the victors.

Capricorn's time of influence was diminishing; it was Aquarius' time to shine forth.

'Not so wise after all, Hafnium, my brother,' Aspheseuos said.

Hafnium, the grand master, replied, 'We shall see.'

Ormus had mentored Mikell knowing that in the future he would become a Judas in the midst of his people. He passed on to Mikell every gift that his wisdom could impart, while in his heart he knew that what he gave would one day be used against him, but give he did, unconditionally and of the highest degree that his knowledge afforded.

Lia also opened her heart to Mikell, allowing him to spend as much time with her family as with Mary. Mary found it hard not to feel betrayed, having been prepared in her dreamtime for the events that were to unfold with Mikell. Her dreams she now shared with Lia and no other. When the time came for Deron to relinquish their friendship, Lia allowed Mikell to continue his visits, explaining to her son that his severed friendship could not include the family, for that was the way of fairness for all. Deron accepted his mother's decision, and at a very young age had shouldered the challenge well, always being polite to Mikell and never allowing his behaviour to sway his better judgement when anger filled his heart. Deron watched the boy become a man, knowing he did not trust him and that one day Mikell would become his enemy.

The children who had been fascinated by Mikell's behaviour still had much to learn of the legacy from their forefathers; the dormant seeds of temptation, cruelty, slyness and violence that were planted long ago would now manifest among them to cause disruption in the peaceful City of Memories.

It was forty-five years since the migration to the Mer world below the oceans. Deron was now a married man with two sons, and the Otom's return to the surface was under way. Over the years, Mikell Lang had made his presence known to the council of delegates, a circle of advisors to the council of elders, and eventually had gained a leading position within. Mikell's knowledge of all things within the City of Memories was now immense, and his covert journeys to the surface invaluable to the Cunmen.

Chapter 29

Uluru Mountain

Across the ocean continents the Mers existed as several races, each one different in appearance and culture but with a unified language. Their world was similar to the Earth's landscape, merely mirrored in water, yet also inexplicably different. Mountains, lakes, deep valleys and vast desert plains lay beneath the Earth's mysterious oceans, all teeming with marine life that the Mers called the ocean dwellers.

Beneath Australasia lay the continent of the Mer angels. At the mid-point of this mystical place stood the base of Uluru, a large flat-topped sandstone rock that rose up from the surrounding landscape to some three hundred and eighteen metres in height, while spreading out to a circumference of eight kilometres. The monumental sandstone rock was all that remained from the erosion of an original mountain chain, and was known to white Australians as Ayers Rock. The base of Uluru drove into the earth, continuing downwards to form an inverted pinnacle that lay embedded in the subterranean caverns beneath the ocean bed, the volcanic flow having continued until the mountain's all-seen form resembled two pyramids joined to form the shape of a diamond, before the erosion on the surface had flattened the rock. Before the holocaust, many had believed in a future time when Uluru would be completely eroded, and mankind would be free of his Earthly masters to stand on the inverted pyramid as master of his own life.

Uluru Mountain was a spiritual place for the tribes of the Australian Aborigine. Their ancient culture, cloaked in spiritual mysticism, was bound to the mountain's history, the Aboriginal people having used the place for ritual gatherings. They identified with its supernatural power to communicate with the spirits of all kinds: man, bird, animal, plant, and the spirits from other-worlds. They believed in the core of unseen power that lay beneath and above Uluru's surface, a power that would transform the rock's energy to rays of blue, violet and multiple reds; Uluru was central to their existence.

To the Mer race, this mystical continent was the most cherished place in their world: it was the last place on Earth where angels still existed and their magical powers were still understood.

The Cradling: Senithe sat among the amethyst rocks, her beautiful long tail trailing in the water. Upon her lap she cradled an infant, though not her own. Senithe often came to the place of Cradling where all newborn Mers spent the first two years without their parents, although parents could visit as often as they wished. The Cradling was a special place, where the infant Mers were welcomed into the sacred and spiritual knowledge of their kind, a magical place where the young were weaned in the bosom of the Uluru mountain underworld, and where the primary Mer knowledge was instilled in each child to remain with them for always.

The sacred mountain's base thrust downward into the earth to form an inverted pyramid of pulsating crystal power that descended into the ocean basin far beneath the world of the Mers. The pinnacle of the inverted mountain spliced deep into the layers of amethyst caves that gave the mountain its healing power, and the Mer people their healing energy. A flooded cavernous area stretched out and around the embedded tip, over which the tidal water ebbed and flowed among the amethyst rock. It was here that the Mer infants dwelled.

The Mer angels populated the honeycomb of caves that surrounded the Cradling. When the infants needed caring for, the Cradling would fill with the sound of a thousand wings as the Mer angels attended to their charges, after which the Cradling would fall silent again.

The Mer angels were translucent in appearance while emanating a violet light that healed all that they touched or touched them.

The Mer people would travel from all continents to meditate while cradling a newly born infant; this was the Mers' way of clearing their thoughts of doubt. They knew that all would be washed away by the powerful magic that nurtured the infants and their troubled minds would heal.

Senithe had come as soon as she could after the tragedy involving the Mastermind harvester. When the men who had died had been returned to the City of Memories for burial, she had immediately set out upon the journey that would bring some solace of her own. Holding the male infant to her breast, Senithe closed her eyes and began to drift in the peaceful silence; as her long dark hair fell across the infant's fragile rounded body, his tiny tail curved around her thigh. They sat in the stillness, Senithe clinging to the bundle of love that felt so cool and smooth, while the infant absorbed her need to release her troubled thoughts, his mind already able to understand the needs of those around him. Senithe and the infant's breathing became one as they drifted in the stillness to heal and rest. The infant was unable to communicate with words, his mind still too innocent to comprehend the cause for her sadness, but give his love he could. Senithe's thoughts drifted to the recent events that had caused her so much anguish, because of the human, Paul.

A Mer angel entered the Cradling and came to sit with her. Senithe had spoken to her before and recognised her as Madina. Senithe greeted the angel, whose pale luminous body was surrounded by a mane of flowing golden hair, while her wings remained open as if in full flight.

As Madina drew nearer, she asked Senithe, softly, 'How can you ever follow your heart in this direction, Senithe? The one called Paul is not of your kind, and to follow this pathway will end in heartache for both of you. You must let go of this love. Let go with an open heart, for your feelings are drawing him towards you, and he must be free for his part in the challenges that lie ahead for the Otom. Soon he will be released to the surface, and then his time here will become less and less. If you draw him to you, he will not want to go. You are to play a part, an important part in mankind's challenge, Senithe.' Madina thought of the sacrifice that Senithe would have to make. 'And be assured that you will not carry the pain of desire for much longer.'

The angel touched Senithe's beautiful silver face, gently stroking the brow above her large green eyes. Senithe became lost in the words of the angel's message; a light enveloped her, and the pain disappeared as she drifted within the consciousness of absolute love.

Lia had climbed down in the cove to sit at the water's edge to wait for her old friends the dolphins, Millie and Max, to appear. While she waited, Ormus appeared beside her. He had come to tell her that the night before, the council of elders had convened in the City of Memories, and that he was there as their messenger. The elders had decided it was time for Deron and Paul to visit the Cradling to study the divine healing powers of the Mer angels.

Ormus continued, 'Deron and Paul will be joining us this morning, Lia. Together we will make the journey to the continent of Australasia. The Mer angels are expecting us, and will welcome you into the City of Five Pathways.'

Lia looked up at Ormus with surprise; entrance to the city had never before been allowed to an Otom.

Lia's link with the Mer angels went back to the time she had been bestowed with the Holocene wisdom in the caves beneath the Causeway. In the years that had followed, and while living among the Mers, neither she nor any Otom had ever been taken to visit the Mer angels in the City of Five Pathways, a place that was linked to the Heavenly Mountain that arcs the world. As she stood smiling at Ormus, her thoughts returned to her visit upon the Heavenly Mountain at the beginning of the challenges. It seemed so many years ago that she had been a young woman of twenty-one years, when she had first met Ormus in her dreams; the second time on the mountain had been less joyful, when Ormus was passing from the Earth. Ormus' invitation made her feel extremely privileged that at last she was to see the city where the infant Mers were raised from birth to two years of age, and the Mer angels' sanctuary where they were kept in safety.

Deron and Paul entered the garden of the Causeway and made their way down to the cove.

Ormus sat quietly looking out towards the horizon. Having told Lia where they were going, he was now listening for the approach of the dolphins, Millie and Max. They would be bringing with them the Mer angel Tanithe, who was to accompany them.

Ormus could hear the two men approaching from the cliff steps, whereas Lia seemed unaware of their chatter as she sat quietly taking in the stillness of the cove. Gentle waves began to ripple at the sides of the ledge where they sat. Lia remained deep within her thoughts. Suddenly she realised the boys were near and turned to look up, her hand shielding her eyes from the light of the winter sky. She waved, and then stood up. As she turned back towards Ormus she noticed a large swell appearing way out upon the water, followed by two fins emerging from beneath the waves as Millie and Max swam towards them. Lia could see the mermaid swimming beside them, her translucent body shimmering in the light of the pale morning sun as she dipped and flipped, somersaulting in and out of the calm water. The journey was to be a passage of magical enlightenment for the three visitors.

Tanithe, the Mer angel sent to guide them through the underworld to the City of Five Pathways, had almost reached the ledge when Ormus stepped onto the water to greet her, his translucent form reflected in a sudden burst of sunlight that fell upon his flowing cerise cloak untouched by the ocean beneath his feet. Tanithe raised herself onto the ledge and let her long tail swish gently in and out of the water, her body moving gently back and forth to the motion of the sea. Lia met the gaze of hypnotic blue eyes that dominated a face surrounded by long pale hair the colour of sea spray and as straight as a horse's mane, thick and lustrous, cascading down about her waist; a subtle shade of amethyst glowed about her silhouette as she raised herself upon the ledge.

Ormus and Lia welcomed Tanithe and the dolphins.

Tanithe's wings of translucent white, shaped like dove tails, fluttered above her head. When she spoke her voice was melodic and soothing. 'You are the one called Ormus from the other-worlds, and you are Lia?'

Lia's face was full of joy as she said, 'And you have come to take us to the City of Five Pathways?'

Tanithe answered, 'Yes, and my name is Tanithe, Lia.'

Lia thanked her warmly; she had remained standing by the water's edge as Tanithe approached. Now she felt drawn to the angel and sought to embrace her. Moving forward she touched Tanithe; immediately spectacular images of the City of Five Pathways passed through her mind. Lia realised that the journey she was about to take would be unforgettable, a link to the world of healing, to which the Otom race aspired.

Deron and Paul reached the ledge and stood observing the Mer angel, Tanithe. They were fascinated by her appearance and that of her escort, the dolphins, Millie and Max; the dolphins were transforming into Mer beings as they looked on. When the transformation was complete, they raised themselves upon the ledge to sit beside Tanithe. Ormus introduced Deron and Paul to the Mers, Millie and Max, and the angel Tanithe, who reached out to greet them. Immediately, Deron and Paul received the same magnificent images of the City of Five Pathways that Lia had seen.

Millie and Max re-entered the water and resumed their dolphin shape. Deron and Paul, now at ease with the creatures, dived into the water beside the dolphins. Soon they were swimming and diving together, and moving further out into the bay. The water was icy but the men had become used to swimming within the deep ocean and were naturally acclimatised to the cold of the underworld. Tanithe joined them as they swam and dived in the ocean, the men holding on to the dolphins as they leapt and plunged in the foaming spray. Tanithe swam ahead, her body arcing rainbows of colour as she leapt from the water and then plunged downward in twisting spirals, the translucent colour of her body flashing like a shooting star as she appeared and then was gone again in a cloud of ocean spray.

Ormus' thoughts began calling them back; it was time to start their journey. Wrapping his cloak around Lia's shoulders, he lifted her gently down into the water. Lia felt no shock as she dipped down into the icy ocean, just a gentle falling and a feeling of buoyancy, then she was far out into the bay with the others. Ormus began to chuckle as the dolphins rose from the water to skim the surface. Faster and faster they sped across the water, circling Deron and Paul who looked on with amusement. Finally, Ormus and Lia came to rest beside them in the water. Tanithe's laughter could be heard above the rolling ocean as she beckoned them to dive deeply and follow her back towards the cliff face.

The water turned murky as they swam near to a bank that led down to the caves on the ocean floor. The caves they were about to enter had been Ormus' undisclosed home within the binary world, where he had spent much of his time when living on Earth. Lia, once inside, would also recognise the caves above the Causeway, for it was there her transformation from Earthling to Holocene had taken place.

Tanithe swam towards a rocky outline that was the cliff edge and entrance to the caves. The water began to get clearer as they approached, revealing the mouth of a large cave ahead. Tanithe headed for the cave, her tail sending a current of water out towards those swimming behind her. They entered the submerged caves and continued a while; suddenly Tanithe stopped. Turning towards Millie and Max, she brought her hands across her chest and bowed her head, then opened her arms as though to release them. Tanithe was saying goodbye. Millie and Max had to return to the ocean; it would be unwise for them to go any further. Their work was done. Ormus thanked them, and said goodbye. Lia, Deron and Paul watched as the dolphins turned back, their large tails disappearing into the shadowy distance. It was time to move on.

Tanithe and Ormus were now well ahead, but the caves before the three were strangely luminous and the water clearer with their approach. They had been travelling through the cave-like tunnels for some time when Tanithe and Ormus stopped to wait for them to catch up. The three companions following behind were unaware of how far they had travelled or their location, their sense of direction and time having diminished as they swam.

As Lia, Deron and Paul approached, Tanithe sat perched upon a crystal plinth that rose centrally from within a water-filled cathedral of vast scale. From a distance, they had seen her mount the plinth with one flip of her long slender tail. Now she sat there waiting patiently for them with Ormus by her side. They neared the end of the tunnel and entered the cavern. Immediately their attention was drawn to the ceiling. Elaborately carved figures of every species of life that had existed upon the planet Earth gazed down at them. The white crystal walls of the monument were inscribed with every language spoken upon Earth; man, animal, bird, insect and plant life. The crystal edifice held the chronicles of life on planet Earth. Beyond where Tanithe stood, a raised portal adorned the front of the cathedral where steps led down to the chamber floor. It was here that a white unicorn, hewn from the crystal wall, stood guard before the portal door.

Ormus approached the three companions, while Tanithe asked the silence for permission to bring her companions to the Mer angels' world. Ormus motioned for his friends to make a half circle in front of her. They did so and sat down.

'Prepare yourselves,' Ormus said quietly.

Chapter 30

The Twelve Celestial Spirals

Tanithe waited for the three companions to reach a meditative state, then, motioning to Ormus, she slid from the rock plinth and entered the water with a gentle splash. Moving into the centre of the half circle, she linked the hands of the three companions together with Ormus and closed the circle around her. The core of the plinth began to glow with the subtle hues of a rainbow, drawing those within the circle up into the core of intensifying light. The rock plinth disappeared within the single ray of light and then re-emerged in the likeness of the pristine white cathedral walls surrounding it, the plinth's transformation revealing the secreted chronicles of the Mers.

The ray of light surrounding the plinth began to spiral downwards as those held within began their journey; the vortex of light travelled down through the void of the binary world, circling the inner layers of the Earth to reach their destination. At their journey's end, they had entered the underworld and were standing on the summit of a mountain. A waterfall cascaded down between twelve plateaus that led to the valley below. At its highest point, the philosopher Pythagoras held out his arms to greet them, his beautiful butterfly-shaped wings extending out behind his body, which was clad in flowing white robes. In his hands he held his works of mathematical genius. He motioned to them to look downwards. Below them, where the waterfall joined the river, a mermaid waited to welcome them to the City of Five Pathways. The mermaid sat upon the bough of an ancient tree, its gnarled branches hanging low over the river. Her long golden hair fell below her waist, touching the swift running current beneath her. The mermaid waiting there was the guardian of the underworld; she guarded the gate to the City of Five Pathways, and her name was Simlify.

Lia was taken back in time to when she had crossed the world's gateway between life and death to journey with the guardian of Earthly souls; there, she had met the spirit granddaughter who was soon to be born to her daughter, Carlen. The Hermit, as he had made himself known to her, guarded the souls entering the Earth world, as Simlify guarded the souls entering the underworld. Simlify had miraculous powers, observing both the astral and the physical world, and yet she was not a Mer angel but a mermaid. The trust of guardianship forbade it, and required her to be conscious of all five senses of the flesh, aware of all feelings and desires that might pass by her and on through the gate. Turning towards them, she beckoned them through.

Tanithe was the first to enter the gate, followed by Deron and Paul.

Before Ormus passed through, he turned and smiled wistfully at Lia. Then he said, 'Hold tight, Lia. We have a journey that reaches into the past before we arrive on the other side of the gate and enter the City of Five Pathways.' A moment later they re-entered the void of zero energy, their consciousness silenced by the loop of nothingness.

Deron and Paul sat with Tanithe in a time long past; they were waiting for Lia and Ormus to become visible upon the landscape. When Lia appeared, Deron gasped with shock. What had happened to his mother, and where had they travelled to? Lia's appearance had changed to that of a young woman in her early twenties. The lifetime that Deron was witnessing was not the one he now shared with her but one many thousands of years ago. Lia had experienced life as a Mer when the City of Memories had been cast into the ocean's depths. She had held the same position as did Senithe now, as custodian of the cave of divine magic, and had served her kind well.

Lia sat upon a half submerged rock watching the waves roll in towards the beach, the light breeze catching her long golden hair and tossing it into the ocean spray that billowed about her. Her face implied that a warm and beautiful creature existed within the surreal body coloured gold. Her dark green tail mirrored the colour of her eyes, but her features were unmistakable; the mermaid was Lia. Lia's extended hand was holding out a pearl, and above her hovered a small red dragon: a natural dweller of the Earth at that time. The dragon's tiny hovering form appeared to be fashioned from fire as it reached out and took hold of the pearl between its front claws, and then settled on the palm of Lia's hand. Immediately they became deeply immersed in conversation. Deron and Paul watched in wonder as Lia and the tiny dragon laughed together and the dragon struggled to keep hold of the pearl.

Deron studied the dragon, sensing that it was female. The dragon, feeling the concentration of Deron's gaze, turned towards him and then flew from the hand that held her. The blazing dragon grew rapidly in size, her shadow blocking out the light above those who watched her. Then, lowering her majestic body to the earth, she waded onto land, her body now towering over the sandy beach where Deron and Paul stood. With Tanithe by their side, and unafraid, they waited to see what would happen, but the dragon remained still.

Ormus appeared beside them. 'The dragon is a being from the planet Mars. The Martian race has known from this lifetime that the human race would come amongst them in the future, and that time is almost upon them. Within the next fifty Earth years the Otom will arrive upon their planet, and that is the reason why your race is returning to the Earth's surface at this time to face the Cunmen: to bring mankind's conflict to an end.'

With Ormus' explanation, the dragon disappeared.

Paul wanted to know about his past, of which he understood so little. His life had been one of contentment, where he had grown up surrounded by love, and mysterious and magical happenings, in the world of the Mers. Now the Otom were returning to the land above the oceans, he sought answers to many things, including the beginning of his present lifetime, of which he had few memories.

Ormus read his thoughts; the time was right for him to revisit his past.

Ormus continued. 'In the Earth's ancient past, everyone played, as you observed Lia playing with the dragon. It was considered most necessary for man, and all living creatures, to revisit their childhood, for that is where happiness lies ... within the child. The ancient civilisations had their rituals and pageantry for this, when all would dress up and gather to sing and to dance, to be happy, be free from the mundane toil of daily life, and bring forth the child element from within. But then, as civilisation blundered on relentlessly, modern man turned these customs into material and extremely stressful affairs that had lost the joy experienced by their forefathers. Both you and Deron have had other lives with Lia, and with me, and all with joyful experiences. We are a group of souls that are evolving together, and have evolved together in the past. Our souls weave in and out of the various phases of the otherworlds, including the planet Earth. Sometimes we have had closely shared lives together, and other times not, but the soul family that we are part of will always play a role in each existence, and somewhere there will always be a thread.'

Deron and Paul nodded in acceptance of Ormus' explanation, and Paul asked if he might see part of the past for himself. Ormus gave a command, pointing out beyond where Lia now sat alone upon the rock. Two creatures appeared from far out in the ocean and began to swim towards her. Deron could just make out their shapes as both moved effortlessly in the rolling waves. As they came nearer, Deron realised it was a merman with a small male infant. The child was swimming excitedly towards Lia, his little arms waving above the foam as he swam by his father's side. Deron thought the child's features held a likeness to his own, while the man looked remarkably like Paul. As they came alongside the rock, the tiny dragon reappeared and alighted on the child's head. Lia, the merman and the infant began to laugh at the dragon's attempt to keep hold of the pearl. The merman held Lia to him as she drew the infant into her arms and kissed his forehead; lovingly they cuddled up together.

Deron and Paul remained silent as the past reality became tangible; they had been Mers. The life they had experienced then was parallel to the life they now lived, only now they lived in the Mer world as immigrants, forced below the oceans while the Earth healed from mankind's destructive forces. They were messengers from the past, reincarnated to help the future mankind in his battle to survive. The vision of their past began to fade as a sphere of multi-coloured energy began to enclose them.

Tanithe explained to her companions, 'The sphere that encloses you is the core to all existence, and is created from the twelve spirals of celestial energy. From the twelve spirals, Hafnium, the grand master of Universe Four, created all within his realm, and it still remains so, except for humankind who exist with only two spirals of the sphere's knowledge in place.'

As Tanithe spoke, they were overwhelmed by the energy of the spirals, a force so divine that all were absorbed by the total pureness surrounding them.

Tanithe continued, 'Humankind now lives in an age of limitation, with only two spirals of knowledge intact. He absorbs energy into his physical and spiritual bodies from above and below, as a column of continuous power from the Earth planet and the universe. The column of energy that sustains his being is constantly forced towards the Earth by gravity; it is his connection to the column of energy from above that heals, supports and sustains his body's Earthbound duality. Without an awareness of this energy, the column of mass and energy is weakened, and the spiritual strength within is diminished, which causes the body of mass to disintegrate. But the truth that mankind does not clearly see is that to harness that energy, he must call upon the god power within, for he will never find his way back to the One by the belief that his power lies beyond himself. This you see in the appearance of the Cunmen, whose bodies, without the protection of the spiritual rays, have disintegrated rapidly. Their original DNA blueprint is all but destroyed and can no longer replicate those beings as humankind, only as badly mutated forms of their former likeness. The Otom, however, have mutated only to adapt to their new habitat, and their human appearance has barely aged while they have lived within the spiritual harmony of the Mer world, because they have come to know they are manifest as godlike creatures: they are a fragment of Hafnium, of Universe Four. When the Otom return to the surface, they will again return to their former likeness, and will be empowered with the knowledge that they are godlike creatures.'

Deron was reminded of the anger that coming into contact with the Cunmen had evoked. The thought came to him that one could quickly grow old under such extremes of emotion.

Tanithe picked up his thoughts and continued, 'Surrounding the columns of energy are gateways from which humankind draws his experiences of the past, present and future, both good and evil. It is his choice which door he chooses to enter and experience, or depart at his will.' Then she added quietly, 'However, the final destination can never be changed by mortal man, though his mortal will may desire it. Mankind's vision of his life purpose is limited to a moment by moment awareness of the destination, which is unknown. Only when he loses the physical body will the picture be revealed to him. Humankind is on the brink of evolutionary change, and he was meant to experience wickedness in order to vanquish its hold forever. Mankind's future is dependent on his embracing a new chapter that will be the foundation for man to become perfect. The Earthly battle is almost over. Man has accommodated himself with evil until he can no longer find a reason for it to continue. The Otom are hoping for a peaceful end to the ensuing battle with the Cunmen, not war, and so it shall be. But for the Cunmen, who are bound to Aspheseuos, death must take them from the Earth.'

Simlify appeared within the sphere's energy. 'Hafnium is taking his children, the Otom, on a journey that will eventually lead them to the sixth universe. Once there, he will leave them to flourish as the new tribe of man, to experience life as non-physical beings, where their souls will continue to aspire to the ongoing evolutionary light of Good. But not in your lifetimes, for that journey is an aeon away for both the Otom and the Mers, who will make the journey together.'

Chapter 31

The City of Five Pathways

As Simlify sat waiting, her thoughts were taken up with Ormus and his companions; she had heard many stories of the people that lived among her kind but she had never spoken to any of these beings.

Simlify's lifetime of fifty years had been spent within the walls of the City of Five Pathways; it was all that she knew. As guardian of the gateway, she had been trained from childhood for the day when she would protect all from those that might enter the city. When Simlify's lifetime as guardian was over she would become a Mer angel and guard the infant souls held within the Cradling; that was the destiny of all guardians to the city's gateway.

The garden of all colours, held within the twelve celestial spirals, contained all life that had been, was and would be within the Mer world. Simlify experienced all knowledge of the Mers' physical senses from within the gateway's hologram. She had seen the City of Memories and walked within its boundaries, but only from within the hologram. Today she would meet and speak to the ones called the Otom for the first time.

Mikell had become accomplished in all that Ormus had taught him, and had shown a particular interest in all subjects associated with the disciplines of meditation, especially travel beyond the physical body: an art in which he was now adept. When making their first journey to the surface of the Earth, Ormus and the council of elders had observed Mikell following their ascent. They knew that his curiosity lay well beyond any interest in helping the Otom back to the surface, and that his treachery would soon be under way.

When plans had been made for Lia, Deron and Paul to visit the City of Five Pathways, Mikell, undetected as he thought, had followed Ormus and his companions into the void of zero energy in order to enter the city where the Cradling was held. Ormus, having been aware of this, made sure that Mikell did not follow them into the past, and then onward to enter beyond the gateway. Ormus watched his companions enter the firewall of the twelve spirals, unaware that Mikell had accessed the garden where Simlify waited. Mikell had entered the garden through the hologram whilst it had remained open for a brief moment, and as Ormus and his companions travelled back into the past, Mikell was approaching Simlify.

Mikell stood before Simlify, his dark eyes smiling at her, his manner charming.

Simlify listened to the soft deep voice that cloaked his malevolent intentions. 'Have you come with the one called Ormus?'

Mikell smiled again and answered, 'Yes, but I have been separated from them and have missed the journey into the past. May I sit with you and wait for them? We are going into the city to see the young infants and the one called Senithe, a friend.'

Simlify smiled and beckoned him to come and sit beside her; she liked the one called Mikell. If he was typical of his kind, then she felt sure that she would like all that were allowed to come to the garden and pass into the City of Five Pathways.

Ormus, having realised his perilous mistake, listened as Simlify's instinct for deceit was blinded by Mikell's gentle charm. Ormus sighed, realising this was just as it was meant to be; Simlify's first encounter with Mikell had left her innocently blind to the danger that now surrounded her and the City of Five Pathways.

Mikell made his move. 'May I walk about the gardens, Simlify? They are the most beautiful gardens I have ever seen.' He leaned towards her and touched her hand. Simlify's heart quickened and she felt herself being drawn towards him. Mikell kissed her gently. At first she responded, but then a shadow of warning passed over her; *were these feelings hers, or his will affecting her mind?* Simlify moved away as she felt the alarm quicken within. Mikell stopped, his calculating mind knowing every step of the way. He held her from him and smiled into her eyes, a smile that made her feel ashamed.

'May I go and walk in the gardens now, Simlify?'

She nodded, evading his gaze, realising that he had been playing with her and that she had been unaware of his deception; she began to feel another emotion, one that she had experienced at times within the hologram, regret. With Simlify's permission, Mikell got up to go, kissing her on the cheek as he did so.

Ormus watched them, his anger stirring. Mikell's treachery had been foretold and yet Ormus' heart was pained for Simlify, for her naivety. Trust was all she had ever known until this moment. Ormus gathered his cloak around Lia; it was time to follow Tanithe back to the hologram where they could enter the garden.

Simlify sat upon the ancient tree where they had left her, her head bowed as she sat weeping. Ormus went to sit by her, while the others looked on in bewilderment questioning what had happened since they had last been with her. They all sensed the evil that had passed through but were unable to identify its source.

Ormus gathered the weeping Simlify into his arms and spoke to her comfortingly. 'Simlify, please do not blame yourself. Your meeting Mikell was inevitable, preordained, and you responded as was your destiny to respond. Mikell has now passed into the city. From there he will begin his ascent to the world above, but not before he has brought about the terrible act he intends to perpetrate, and taken charge of that which he intends to take with him.'

Simlify stopped crying and looked at Ormus in alarm, the guilt in her eyes now evident.

Ormus said gently, 'This is your first and last experience of the deceit that man is capable of. Now be at peace, and remember that we can all be blind to evil when it appears, and when packaged in such a goodly fashion.'

Ormus put his hands upon Simlify's head to soothe her; she began to settle into a sleep that would heal her heart and her pain, but not before she and those about her had pondered on the secreted truth of Ormus' warning.

Mikell found his way to the road beyond the gardens and headed towards the City of Five Pathways until he reached a crossroads; to his left, he could see the ocean filling every space above, in front of and below him. Dolphins swam to and fro, engaging playfully with the Mer pilgrims on a visit to the Cradling. He turned and faced the road opposite the one from which he had come, and there was the city that he searched for, its towering walls of white and emerald coral gleaming in the distance. Mikell made his way forward without further thought to the two pathways leading off to the right; he had found the one he was seeking.

A white unicorn guarded the city entrance, his manner welcoming and gentle. Nearby, a mermaid sat upon the rocks of an ocean inlet; both appeared absorbed in their conversation with each other though neither expressed movement or sound. A Holocene 'wise one' listened to their conversation while resting in the waterway beside the mermaid, his body floating peacefully within the tidal current that washed gently over his silhouette; the merman Burah was strong and supple and his short-cropped icy tresses and fierce amber gaze presented to others an unyielding character, although that was not his nature. Burah, like many Holocenes, had been called upon to support the emerging one tribe of man as he faced the desire to step back into the darker emotions of his past.

Mikell felt confident; it appeared he not been seen and he held back in the shadow to watch them. The unicorn's magical horn touched the ground as he stooped to reach the mermaid Sharis' hand, which she held up to him in a gesture of love and friendship. Burah looked on. No one appeared to notice Mikell, but all were watching his every movement, as was Ormus. Burah knew that Mikell would make his way forward to enter the city, and onward to where the infant Mers were cradled.

Mikell moved forward quickly with only one thing in mind, his destination: the amethyst cave below Uluru Mountain. Hoping not to be noticed, he walked forward beneath the shadow of hanging foliage. Mikell, the tension mounting in his chest, breathed deeply. If he were caught, his chances of returning to the underworld would be gone forever. Under the cover of his invisible cloak, he stepped out into the light and walked towards the entrance. As he moved forward his mind remained centred on his goal, to reach the Cradling. Mikell reached the entrance and once hidden waited for a moment; the unicorn and his companions had not noticed his brief appearance as he passed to the other side of the gate, but Mikell felt uneasy. Quickly he walked on through the tunnelled entrance. Once inside the city, he moved stealthily into the shadows and made his way towards a small passageway to his right, following the pathway until he came out from the darkness into semi-light. There it was; Mikell almost wept; the amethyst cave of the Cradling, its entirety lit by the light of the violet crystal from within.

Mikell stepped in and looked about him; he realised that the cave stretched for miles, which might hamper his plans. The ground beneath his feet ran with water that trickled from the ceiling of the cave, its colour of pale turquoise reminding him of the paleness of an infant Mer's skin. As he moved deeper into the cave, crystal formations of all shapes and sizes began to hinder his pace, and the water became much deeper. The surrounding ferns and flowers grew in all shades of violet, the most pure of healing colours. This, he was certain, was the nurturing bed for all infant Mers, those who would grow to be of a spiritual and giving nature, as were their kind: a legacy from the Earth's past that the Mers would protect at all costs, now and in the future. Mikell was astounded that this place of sacredness was not guarded. The crystal organisms surrounding him listened to his thoughts; he did not know that they observed his every move. Held within their crystal form was all that was needed to nurture the Cradling infants and instil within them the wisdom of the Mers.

Mikell moved silently among the crystal rocks surrounding him, each with its precious charge. He had come to steal an infant and then make his way to the surface. The Cunmen were waiting to use the infant's power to heal their ravaged bodies, and having regained their health, they would then make war on the Otom as they emerged from the underworld…

As Mikell tried to focus his thoughts he saw her; Senithe lay asleep with an infant cradled in her arms. Mikell's heart jumped; he had not realised that he might meet her here, one that could recognise him. Mikell crept closer to where Senithe lay. As he approached her, his chest was pounding heavily and he clenched his fists. He knew what he would have to do should she wake. Stealthily he picked up an infant from the crystal nest that it lay sleeping upon. The infant opened his eyes but remained quiet; the knowing in his eyes suggested betrayal to the vigilant gaze of Mikell.

Senithe woke up; something was wrong. In the dimness, she looked about her then laid the infant down in the cradle by her side. The infant picked up the hostile charged atmosphere that had shattered the peace of the cave; it began to cry. The noise startled Mikell and he moved; as soon as Senithe saw him she began to swim towards him, her face filled with anger. Mikell's mind began to function in a way that it had never done before, and he knew that Senithe and the crying infant must be silenced…

When all was done, he remembered nothing of the deed that took her life as he towered over her fragile frame, his fist coming down to meet her head, and then her body disappearing beneath the deep water. Senithe lay submerged below the waterline, death having come within an instant. Mikell held her there in silence for what seemed an age, and then he let her go. Senithe's body stayed submerged at the bottom of the cave, nothing stirring; only the gentle movement of her tail could be seen in the softly flowing current of water. Mikell looked for any movement around him, his body tensing to every sound. The infant had stopped crying; all was silent. Momentarily, he felt remorse, and then in one swift movement he gathered the infant of his choice into his arms and made his way to the entrance of the cave. The moment Mikell had the infant in his arms he drew his cloak about them and their bodies became invisible. The infant and Mikell were now entwined in a bond that was not of the infant's choice; he was now vulnerable and in danger as he lay in Mikell's arms. The tiny Mer lay silent; unable to resist or reason, the infant found his only escape from his helpless situation was to go to sleep.

Ormus had watched with grief as Senithe's life slipped away; having made their way to the crossroads and stayed a while with the unicorn and Burah, they were now approaching the entrance to the infant Cradling. Ormus let Paul lead the way; he knew it was Paul who must find Senithe, the Mer that he loved.

Paul pushed against the gently moving water towards the entrance of the inner cave. On the last part of the journey he had felt a deep grief within. At first it had worried him, but now he felt a deep foreboding and wanted to turn back. Ormus remained close behind him, urging him to go on. Paul entered the cave and drew in a deep breath, his gaze beholding the peace and stillness of the amethyst Cradling and the infants being nurtured there.

Paul said softly, 'This is an amazing place.' He stood motionless, taking in the tranquil landscape that stretched far beyond his vision. The cave was vast, and so far removed from anything he had seen before. In the turquoise pools of water, the infants lay on crystal mounds submerged in the gentle flow.

Ormus came and stood by Paul and put his hand upon his arm. It was then Paul saw her, his beloved Senithe, her tiny silhouette floating in the water, her tail caught between the crystal rocks. They held her fast, preventing her body from floating further down into the cave. Ormus' hand slipped free as Paul jerked forward and waded through the water towards her. Paul could not believe what he was seeing, not wanting to believe it, it was a dream, a horrible dream. *Please let it be a dream.* Paul's arms thrust into the water and pulled her body towards him, and he buried his face in hers, calling her name gently.

'Please wake up, Senithe. Please wake up.'

Ormus stood close by, waiting. Senithe was dead, and Ormus knew it was meant to be. Paul and Senithe had been parted.

Lifting the infant that had survived Mikell's visit, he handed him to Lia. As she held him she felt the surge of love that had such a little time ago been Senithe's support through her time of transition.

The unicorn stood outside the cave with his head bowed in sadness; mankind's evil had struck the Mers a double blow. With the Otom's return to the Earth's surface, the Cunmen would try to destroy both the Otom and the Mers; the final age of mankind's iniquity, and the death of the innocents had begun.

Ormus bade Paul to lay Senithe down beside the unicorn, whose radiance now flowed out towards her, the white flames of light enveloping her still body until she disappeared beneath the ethereal shroud that encircled her. Tamelia appeared beside the unicorn, the pale hue surrounding them becoming stronger as her long silvery tail entwined with the unicorn's flowing mane. As their mystic powers united, Senithe's body became substance again, and with her spirit released, her body was ready for the journey back to Subterrania, where all mortal Mers were taken after death. As the Mer angels accompanied Senithe's body to the city gate, they began their songs of mourning for those that would be lost without her. From the gate, she would be escorted by Deron and Tanithe to her final resting place in the valley of Lacofpartin.

Paul's anger moved him beyond his grief as Mikell came to his mind, his body grew strong with rage, and a roar of pain tore from his chest like the howl of a wounded animal. 'It was Mikell. He has taken Senithe from this world. I will hunt him down. I will have revenge for his brutality!'

Deron held his friend, whose cries were now so muted that those around could hear the distant sound of thunder as it rolled out over the ocean and beyond.

'I will have my revenge,' Paul repeated softly.

Ormus bade Deron release his friend. Deron would have to return to the City of Memories with Tanithe as escort to Senithe's body.

Burah appeared beside Paul; there was much Paul needed to

learn before facing the Cunmen. The anger he felt for Mikell could turn his soul towards hate. Burah must try to persuade him otherwise. 'Man is a sum of energy, like all manifestations that dwell in this universe and beyond. We, the Holocene race, also lived in man's image a very long time ago, while evolving upon another planet in this universe. The Holocenes have existed for trillions of years, and so, having reached Universe Nine, it seems that we will soon cease to exist. That is because we know universes one to nine exist, but not what lies beyond the ninth universe, other than the Globe of Living Energy to which all form returns. That is our belief. Perhaps we have much to learn? We initiated mankind's separation from the animal kingdom to one of spiritual awareness, and with our knowledge the Earth man has been transformed. All species created live in various stages of evolvement, and each one plays a part in the others' progress. It is a puzzle, and a curious and delightful one to the aspiring mind. Man, animal, vegetation, they are all tears in the vast cosmos we call Universe Four. When first Hafnium began to create, he made all light; the creator then began to experiment, and what man perceives as the explosive beginning of the universe was actually a reversal of that belief. As Hafnium streaked the colours of life, in all forms, across the universe's canvas, vast areas of blackness appeared. The light had been scattered and the canvas torn by the dense areas that formed within. We, the Holocenes, know that Universe Four does not appear to humankind in its true dimensional form, nor does man know the truth concerning the unseen spatial void that surrounds all objects. Mankind is part of the dark area of the canvas. He belongs to the dense substance, matter, and will do so until he evolves to the sixth universe. Man is not separate from other men; he is a thread of life woven into the universe, of which every thought, every action becomes part. The Otom act as a whole, even though there are still some who regard their actions as independent of others. Those actions, both major and minor: all are locked into a continuum of life experiences that add to the canvas as does a rolling scene within a hologram, and whatever is in your mind will manifest to become part of the canvas.' Burah gazed compassionately at Paul.

Within the brief moment of quiet that followed, Ormus wondered, *Perhaps somewhere out there is life that we have absolutely no knowledge of, which sees us as embryos, not yet born into a real existence, and still incubating, still asleep.*

Glancing at Ormus, Burah acknowledged his thoughts. 'We must strive towards the light, Paul, not entrench ourselves deeper into the blanket of darkness with emotions of hate. We must open our minds to faraway horizons. I see so much more than you, and yet I, and my race, know little of our future other than the belief that our existence is nearing the end. We have accepted this, and now embrace it. Because of this, I believe that we will soon awaken to a new reality, another universe perhaps, which at this moment we do not know exists.'

Ormus had long felt that the universes one to nine, each with its own creator, and in which he had lived out his multi-existences, were presided over by a higher force way beyond the Globe of Living Energy. Ormus pictured the human brain and wondered if the nine universes were the brainchild of another mortal life far beyond his comprehension. The feeling that the Holocene race would exist elsewhere was growing stronger. Turning his thoughts to Paul, he said, 'Find peace within, Paul; there cannot be any other way.'

Chapter 32

Madagascar – Makot

Mikell found his way to the surface. The Mer infant lay fast asleep in his arms without stirring; it was as though his spirit had withdrawn from physical life. Mikell looked down at the infant, his concern growing. It was essential that the infant reach Makot while still in good health.

Makot was Mikell's contact on the surface, and like him, he was an outwardly pleasant-mannered man, with badly scarred dark skin and deep set eyes, the Asian continent having been his place of origin. Makot's temperament, however, did not reflect his manner; his hidden nature was sinister and his moods unpredictable. In this Makot and Mikell were like-minded.

Mikell stood among the undergrowth of densely rich flora that covered the island of Madagascar. In the southern hemisphere the atomic fallout had not been as devastating as it had been in Europe and the east, the point of multiple detonations, from where the Cunmen were emerging from the underground sites to make their way south to a continent that would sustain them.

Mikell started to walk, making his way down a steep course that led to a clearing. Once there, he would stop and get his bearings. No need; as he appeared upon the pathway a jeep came into view. As it approached, Mikell could see Makot sitting in the driver's seat, a rifle slung across his shoulder. The approaching vehicle came to a halt and Mikell got in carefully, not wanting to disturb the sleeping infant.

'Is the infant in good health?' Makot asked.

'Yes, I think so,' replied Mikell, deciding not to speak of his concerns.

'Good. Then we must get him to the mother who will be nursing him; she is waiting at a house along the main beach road. It is close to water and the infant can be bathed frequently.'

Mikell did not answer; he felt weary. What he had done in the past few hours was flooding back and he was feeling uneasy; Senithe was dead. The infant was now Makot's prisoner, no more than a valuable fish that would spend his days in an aquarium at the beck and call of the Cunmen, who would use him to heal and empower their wasted bodies. They would then be strong enough to wage war on the emerging Otom. Mikell pushed the thought from his mind; this was the day he had been waiting for, the day he had dreamed of for years, to be free of the Otom where he knew he did not belong, away from the watchful gaze of his Aunt Mary, and Ormus. Mikell settled back in the seat, his mind now eased. He looked down at the infant; his face was hot and red. The infant when healthy would have a bluish tinge to his skin.

'Get a move on, the infant needs to be immersed in the ocean. Hurry up.'

Makot gunned the jeep with little thought for the infant in Mikell's arms. He did not like Mikell giving him orders.

The jeep devoured the landscape as it raced towards their destination, a small airfield beyond what looked like a plantation. Green shoots could be seen breaking ground in the surrounding acres, all of which looked healthy. *The Cunmen must be getting things together.*

Mikell's thoughts were interrupted by the sighting of another vehicle, which appeared to be chasing them. Makot gunned the jeep and they gathered speed. A crop that had grown to maturity lay ahead and the jeep was heading for it. As if sensing the imminent destruction of the crop, the vehicle chasing them lessened its speed and came to a halt. Makot continued towards the crop, then suddenly turned sharply right.

'Always works! They'd rather lose me than the crops.'

'Who are they?' Mikell asked.

'Your kind, who else? They have been working on many sites all over the southern continents for a number of years. Soon this place will be populated with Otom; the perimeter of the site starts just beyond the line of the horizon. It has been up since they first came, and the living quarters have almost filled the complex. Some Otom families have already moved in.'

Mikell realised that the Otom elders had advanced the resurfacing further than he had thought. The Otom were on the threshold of re-inhabiting the surface of the Earth. He should have listened more closely.

The jeep was now climbing at speed. Beyond the hill top, in the dip that followed, a small airfield came into view. A small aircraft waited for them. Mikell could see the pilot pacing up and down. The noise of the jeep made him look up, and then he turned and climbed into the aircraft.

No introductions then? Mikell thought sardonically.

The jeep came to an abrupt stop. Getting out, Mikell placed the infant in the back of the jeep. 'You have your instructions. Get the infant to the nursing mother. And remember, do not touch the flesh of the infant; he must be covered at all times unless immersed in the tank.'

Mikell started to walk towards the aircraft. The jeep turned and headed towards the coast and the woman waiting to care for the infant.

The small aircraft was a mid-twentieth century design that had been patented and then stolen from the inventor, to become a top secret government project. The design bore no resemblance to any other aircraft at that time. The project had taken decades to perfect; saucer shaped and streamlined, it had been the subject of many UFO sightings around the world for many years, the sightings perceived as proof of alien life. The final model was named Meridian, because of its circular perimeter. It moved at lightning speed, while navigating in all directions. But most importantly it was powered by laser light and faster than the human eye, and low in cost to the planet. If the holocaust had not intervened, the Meridian would have become mankind's twenty-first century means of travel.

The first aircraft to be produced had been distributed among the secret underground sites as a precautionary measure against the threat of a nuclear war. When that had come, most of the scientists working on the Meridian project had not made it to a safe site. One scientist had survived to become one of the three leaders among the Cunmen. Now he sat waiting to pilot the Meridian back to Belsize Creek with his passenger, Mikell.

Mikell looked in wonder at the spherical aircraft that would take him to his destination near the Mexican border: a destination that it would take but a few minutes to reach. Steeling his mind, Mikell decided there was no going back; he had no regrets about his decision. Climbing on board, he remained silent, facing the pilot's contempt with equal disdain.

Chapter 33

The White Unicorn

Tamelia, having helped the unicorn prepare Senithe for her final resting place, prepared for her next task, that of telling the Mer infant's parents that their son was missing. For the first time in the history of their race, an infant had gone missing from the Cradling. Tamelia wondered how she would bring such news to them. In the lifetime of a mating couple only one infant was born to them, and if the infant did not survive the couple remained childless. They would then be encouraged to help with the rearing of another couple's infant.

Ormus stood before Tamelia, her thoughts having called him to her side. 'If you wish it, I will speak to the parents of the Mer infant.' As Tamelia made her decision Ormus added, 'At least let me come with you?'

Tamelia was comforted by Ormus' suggestion. 'Thank you, Ormus. I will be glad of your company when facing them with this terrible news. I do not know what I am going to say. Never has the trust of the Mer angels been questioned before; I feel it will send a wave of panic throughout the kingdom to all parenting Mers.'

Ormus remained silent, knowing this incident was part of destiny's plan, and that Tamelia, the primary Mer angel, was unable to see beyond the veil of despair that had descended upon her kind; she was lost, but the light would come again and the sorrow would lift. Ormus said gently, 'Come, let us find the parents. They must be told.'

Paul sat down beneath the tree where the unicorn stood

motionless, as if asleep. Deron had left with Tanithe to accompany Senithe's body back to the City of Memories. Paul felt desolate, so deep in grief that he cared little as to where he was; all he wanted to do was sleep, as if in doing so, he could turn back time and change events. Ormus approached him and sat down. The unicorn stirred slightly, knowing that Ormus needed his help to arouse Paul from the living death in which he was immersed. Paul was needed; there would be time enough for mourning Senithe when the infant was found.

There was strength in Ormus' words, as he told Paul that he had to put his grief aside, in order to deal with the situation they now faced. 'Paul, Senithe is at peace, and she would want you to help her people; they have need of you. The Mer infant is in terrible danger. His fragile life could be terminated at any moment if he is not cared for properly. Please, you must help. Tamelia and I must go to the parents of the infant who is missing. The outcome of that meeting is important to the Mer angels. While I am gone, you must return to the City of Memories where Deron waits for you before journeying to the surface. I want you to go with him. We must retrieve the infant; if his healing powers are accessed the Cunmen will gain full health and descend upon the underworld, and the Mers' peaceful existence will be lost to them forever. The Mer world will be violated beyond recognition, as was the Earth. Mikell has many powers that he has learned from me, but he is unable to travel through the void of zero energy alone; he must first find a party of Otom returning to and from the surface and accompany them unnoticed beneath his cloak of invisibility.'

Paul looked up at Ormus, whose flowing robes of cerise coloured the transparency of his being. 'Before I follow Deron, I would like to come with you to the parents of the missing infant. Senithe has been taken from this world, and although I knew our love could never be, I feel the pain of her death as though it was the death of part of me. The parents of the infant will feel the same pain. For them, there is still hope that the infant will be found. I wish to speak to them, to tell them that we, the Otom, feel responsible for Mikell's actions; Mikell was raised among us. I want to promise them that we will do everything in our power to bring the infant back to them.'

The unicorn lowered his head, his mane billowing out around Paul's shoulders, the energy that passed between them giving Paul the strength to stand.

'We must find the infant, Ormus. Let us be on our way.'

The unicorn opened his eyes to look upon the one called Paul. 'You are of the Otom, a "wise one" in the making. May you and those that work to bring the Otom to the Earth's surface be victorious. And remember, failure of any kind is a transitory illusion, for all will continue to exist.' The unicorn bowed his head. 'Peace, my friends.'

Ormus returned the Holocene sign of peace, crossing his arms across his chest, his thumbs entwined, his fingers spread like a dove in flight. 'Peace.'

Once back in the City of Memories, Deron went before the council of elders. Both he and Tanithe gave their accounts of Senithe's death and the loss of the Mer infant. Deron told his story, his heart pounding within; he wanted to follow Mikell. The doubts that had been stifled for years were now unleashed; he was ready to do battle with the traitor who threatened the future of the Otom and the Mers.

Tanithe had spoken quietly as she was asked of Senithe, telling the elders that all had been dealt with. 'Now we await news of the infant, and I wish to accompany those chosen to find him. It is important that they have someone with them who can care for the infant.'

Deron stepped in, his impatience to be after Mikell palpable. 'We shall be escorted by a small task force of Millans to keep us safe, and one other, Paul, who will join us soon. When he returns, we can ascend to the surface and begin the rescue of the Mer infant.'

The Millans were the Otom military; an army trained to protect those working upon the surface. Their task was to defend, not to encourage conflict.

Lia appeared at her place with the council of elders. 'This conflict could turn the tide for our peaceful task force, even forcing them to act with aggression …' Thoughts of Ormus distracted her; he was returning to the city.

Lia turned to Tanithe, the Mer angel, and asked, 'Tanithe, how will you fare upon the surface among such evil?'

'Thank you, Lia, for your concern, but the spirit of the Mer angels will shield me. Alas, not all Mers will be so protected.'

Lia nodded, 'Of course!' she replied.

Ormus entered the great hall with Paul by his side. Acknowledging those present, he spoke on behalf of the White Unicorn. He wanted to assure them that mankind's evolvement must turn retrograde, as was the planet Uranus returning on her pathway to pursue her progeny, Aquarius. Mikell, with the help of Aquarius, was about to turn the Otom's peaceful existence to one of fear. Yet again, the lessons of remorse had to be learned. 'The White Unicorn has returned to the crystal cathedral where he waits for the keepers of the gates through which all Earthly and underworld life enters and departs. Together, they will wait for Chiron, the consciousness of the universe. When assembled, they will discuss the elements of the new war upon the Earth, for only the Keepers of the Gates can know whose time it is to pass unto death, and only Chiron knows Hafnium's final decision … and we know that whatever the outcome of this war, all must remain balanced in his universe. Uranus' progeny, Aquarius, has abandoned the star tribe to help Mikell. That is his rightful choice.'

The White Unicorn was the bridge between the Earth world and the universe. He spoke the language of sound and colour that all non-physical beings communicated by, a language that Lia had understood the moment she had stepped upon the Heavenly Mountain, so long ago, with Ormus and Raphiel.

Ormus ended, 'The Mer world must not be breached. We must find a way.'

Chapter 34

The Prophecy

The Mer infant lay motionless inside the flimsy beach house as the walls moved back and forth at the will of the wind blowing across the open beach. Makot had laid him at the water's edge for over an hour until gradually his colour had returned to normal. The nursing mother had stood in the water nearby, keeping a watchful eye over him in case he was able to slip away in the waves of the oncoming tide. Makot had warned her that her life depended on the Mer infant remaining with them. The infant's captors had little knowledge of the Mer race, or that a Mer infant was incapable of survival without help, believing they were the same as all large fish and as such survived without assistance.

Mikell had left the infant without seeing signs of recovery in him, telling his charges they must not touch his flesh; this had concerned him greatly, but the leaders of the Cunmen were waiting for him. Another situation also worried him; he would have to return to the underworld as soon as the meeting was over, before his absence was discovered.

Ormus listened to Mikell's thoughts, having been aware of his movements all along.

Mikell sat beside the pilot in silence, his mind focusing on the flight before him. The concerns he had were giving way to his interest in the aircraft and its capacity for speed; within seconds they were airborne and way above the Earth. Mikell drew in a sharp breath which forced its way to the surface as a shrill screaming sound of euphoria, then darkness as they hurtled towards their destination. Looking down at the luminous shape below him, Mikell marvelled at the vastness of the Earth's surface. On impulse he leaned forward excitedly; now he realised why he had wanted to leave the underworld and never, ever, return. *Not much longer now.*

The jeep carrying Mikell plunged up and down along the long winding pathway, speeding onwards to negotiations with the group of Cunman leaders that wanted to use the infant's powers to destroy the Otom. All that Mikell could think about was the journey he had made before this one, and the Earth that held so many secrets within the unopened underground sites, enough to spend a lifetime building another world empire.

Pisces, progeny of Neptune, looked down from the heavens to observe the one called Mikell. It was her time to help the Otom overcome the Cunmen, those whom Pisces knew had for centuries before the holocaust built their empires on deceit and control of humankind. After forty-five years, the Otom were emerging from the underworld, and the Cunmen still survived, but their premature emergence from their underground sites had left them mentally and physically scarred from radiation sickness; they had reaped that which they had inflicted upon the Earth. Their ailing minds were submerged in evil and their bodies racked with pain. The ulcers that covered them from head to foot were hidden by the long robes and head scarves they wore, leaving only their pale reddened eyes exposed to the light.

Mikell was unaware of the danger he was in; the fallout's destructive power to the flesh was known to him, but its destructive power upon the mind had made an already immoral race completely evil. The biological changes to the Cunmen that had made the journey across the wasted continents had stripped them of all bodily hair, their skin was thin and parched, their bodies frail and wasted, their weakened digestive tracts unable to properly utilise the nutrients from the food stockpiled in the opened underground sites; only the evil in their minds drove them on.

Following the atomic holocaust, one half of the Earth's crust had been unable to support any vegetation, though the seeds of all plant life lay dormant deep beneath the ground to await the future. Global storms had raged for nearly four decades, after which the southern hemisphere began to flourish again.

Makot's family had been wealthy bankers, which had earned them a place in the underground site on the island of Madagascar where his family had lived for three generations before the holocaust. Mikell and Makot were the same age; beyond that their childhoods had been very different. The evil culture of the Cunmen had remained, and each site held many factions of equally devious individuals. Within the sites, these groups fought for supremacy, and among the few thousands living in this confinement, leadership was contested constantly and hostility often turned to savage aggression. Mikell's upbringing had been the opposite, but his feelings and behaviour had been the same as those he now chose to be with.

The Cunmen were suffering, many were dying. Just a few million worldwide had survived as the Eastern and European continents were laid to waste. By the fourth decade after the holocaust, half of those emerging from the underground sites had died while trying to reach the southern hemisphere. Like the Otom, there had been few newborn infants and those that had survived birth eventually died. Only a few thousand now remained upon the Earth. Mikell was the dark one's progeny, the new god who was to heal them; he was the future that Aspheseuos had promised. For this reason, the Cunmen struggled on towards the southern hemisphere where it was rumoured that the progeny of Aspheseuos had arisen, bringing with him the power to heal all.

Pisces called across the heavens to Capricorn, 'Greetings, dear sister. Before you pull the mantle of sleep over your winter cloak, I would like to speak with you and our sister, Scorpio.'

Scorpio on hearing her name roused herself. As part of the star tribe, and with her knowledge of the underworld, the secrets of the seasons and their guardians were rarely kept from her. 'Pisces, dear sister, what do you want of me and Capricorn? We are at rest. It is time for you to demonstrate your strength, and tenacity of course.'

Pisces hesitated; here were two stars with great powers that, when necessary, could bring forth the powers of the shadow-worlds. Pisces' manner was light and bright and generous, even though she could just as quickly manifest a dark and wicked nature that was capable of great cunning. However, the situation that she now faced was different. Pisces needed to know the mind of a far more cunning opponent; she must ask her sisters of their 'godfather' Aspheseuos, although heaven knew why they should have been burdened with such a travesty. Pisces had decided to put her request to Capricorn, with whom she felt on safer ground. 'Capricorn, I wish to know of your godfather, Aspheseuos. It seems to me that knowing of him will help me in my quest. Scorpio and you have knowledge of his darkest secrets, and I hoped that together we may share ... some of his weaknesses?'

Capricorn and Scorpio remained silent, both pondering the consequences should they dishonour the one who had taught them all they knew of the darker forces, all they knew of the magic of life and the inevitability of physical death. For Capricorn, queen of the winter, who returned to life the death-veiled seedlings that rested in the ground, and life to the wombs of women and beast, how could she dishonour the bringer of death by breaking her silence? Scorpio was also perturbed, and suspicious of Pisces' request. Both Scorpio and Capricorn understood the dark mysteries of the universe, secrets that were as fathomless as the void itself: secrets kept safe within their silence. Only their gaze gave a whisper of what they knew; deep within those centres of blazing light could be seen eternity.

Scorpio was first to speak, for Capricorn would never be hurried on her decisions. 'Pisces, what you ask is beyond us to give. To ask us to tell you Aspheseuos' weaknesses is to ask us to shut down the light of the heavens. We could not say, even if we considered him to have weaknesses, for as soon as we tell you his secrets then we give you ours, and that will never do. However, remember that Mikell demonstrates his father's cunning and his mother's weakness. With all the powers that Aspheseuos bestows upon him, Mikell was born to succeed. Our brother Aquarius also takes his side, so be vigilant as you pit your wits against him. Aspheseuos and Aquarius' favours will be a powerful force for Mikell, as he challenges the Otom's return to the surface. For this reason it is imperative that the infant is returned to the Mers; the Cunmen must not be returned to health and become Mikell's army.'

Capricorn nodded in agreement, and then, pulling her mantle of ice about her, she lay back down to sleep. Capricorn would not awaken until it was time for her to cloak the Earth in winter's mantle of death again. Scorpio also drew herself into the shadow of sleep, there to wait her turn to reappear with the changing seasons of the world.

Chapter 35

Belsize Creek

The continent of the Americas was habitable and showing signs of healthy growth. The Cunmen leaders, a self-appointed group of four, had chosen areas of land near the Gulf of Mexico to become the new states of America; these four men ruled over their territory with an iron fist that was merciless to those challenging their authority. Migrants heading south to find habitable land were rounded up and put to work. Of the many that were captured, few survived the initial ordeal of plundering, after which the strongest were put to work and the weakest killed. The four leaders' combined raids had kept uneasy peace between their territories. Now they gathered together at Belsize Creek to meet Aspheseuos' progeny, Mikell.

The Cunmen rarely set foot outside their territories other than to attack groups of wandering migrants, or to plunder the open levels of the nearby underground site at Belsize Creek. Occasionally groups would go north to Canada, hunting for human labour and supplies of oil. They would be gone for months, scavenging for anything that was still useable: medicines and equipment to support their meagre existence. Life after the fateful holocaust had changed beyond recognition. Those that had survived now lived in an America that was run down and dangerous. Saved from the worst fallout that had devastated Asia and Europe, they lived without the amenities that they had taken for granted, and oil, food and fresh water were precious commodities.

The underground site at Belsize Creek had a source of power; the Cunmen could hear the generators switching on and off deep within the lower levels of the site. There were abundant stockpiles of food, utilities and equipment held in the deeper levels of the site, but those with the knowledge of the access codes were not to be found, and as yet the Cunmen had not found a way to break in. All hope rested on gaining access, as records showed that there was seed and agricultural vehicles with which to grow crops again. Most of the natural sources of fresh water were still contaminated by the flooding of forty-five years past, and the few fresh water springs found were constantly fought over.

The Cunmen were dying; they had hoped the medicines stockpiled at the site would help with the radiation sickness, but none had helped their plight. Now they awaited the arrival of the one called Mikell; he was their last hope to destroy the Otom and build a new world and a powerful nation, but only if they could be healed of the radiation sickness. The Cunmen, the master race of mankind, would be powerful again. These were the thoughts that kept them alive.

During the last era of mankind's history, an elite society of men and women had ruled the world as an unseen authority. Europe had produced most of these prophets of power, their ancestors having long established empires across the globe, which had almost destroyed the Earth's ecosystems before the final days. Most had vanished in the holocaust, but their legacy had remained strong in the small band of people that had survived and were regrouping; the Cunmen were about to mould a new world order, and the four states of America were the beginning.

The early twentieth century inventions that would have saved the world from oil pollution and constant wars were held in the deepest levels of the underground sites across the world, including Belsize Creek: innovative ecological energy sources procured from warned-off inventors, whose lives had been threatened should they reveal their inventions to the world. The Cunmen now looked to these inventions as the new source of power to restart their empires, and with a labour force held in slavery, they would again rule the Earth.

Mikell was to be their leader; the three Cunmen waiting mulled this over in silence. Their armed guards looked on from close by, waiting for any suggestion of betrayal. All knew that this meeting was their only chance of survival, and they would not give up their power easily. However, Mikell held the key to life or death for them and must take his place as leader of the Cunmen, as prophesied.

Belsize Creek was named after a waterless gully that ran for miles across one of the driest of deserts, where the constant dust storms made it virtually uninhabitable. The landscape surrounding the underground site was the perfect place for the meeting. Its far-reaching vantage point allowed all movement to be seen for miles in all directions. Before the holocaust, Belsize Creek had been one of the biggest top secret intelligence posts in America: a secret underground site where just about anything that would be needed in the event of an atomic war was stored.

Mikell and the pilot entered the debris-strewn unit where the Cunmen stood waiting. All turned to look at the one who was to be their supreme leader; his face looked strangely pale but unblemished by the ravages of radiation, and his body appeared physically powerful but not muscular, while his hands were curiously webbed. Immediately the three leaders hated him; their eyes, shielded by heavy robes, were similarly full of loathing and envy. Mikell sensed their aggression towards him and felt momentarily anxious. The fourth leader, the pilot who had brought him, joined the other three.

Mikell stood alone. Should he have remained faithful to the Otom, Ormus would have prepared him to become a 'wise one'. *But why waste my genius on the Otom?*

He made an attempt to humour them, but this was not how he had intended to deal with the situation. 'I have the infant at a safe location, and we can start the healing process as soon as possible. Who among you wants to become part of my army?' Mikell held out his arms. 'The healing of others will come later as I assess their qualities and usefulness. Last will be the women. We need to raise further generations as soon as possible, and for this purpose I intend to include the Otom women, as soon as the war is won.'

The four leaders listened to what he had to say with interest. They started to relax and feel that perhaps giving up some of their authority might be worth the sacrifice, given the plans that were spoken of by the one called Mikell.

The first to raise his voice asked, 'Who will be the first to take the healing, and where is this to take place?'

'Here,' said Mikell, 'all healings will take place here in the underground site. But first, to bring the Mer infant here, we must work to secure his survival. I will need you to build a large aquarium that will be filled with seawater. This will be achieved by converting one of the water tankers. Another will transport a continual supply of fresh seawater, until the job is done. By the time you are fully restored to health, I will have found a way for us to enter the underworld to secure more infants from the Cradling, to use their powers as we wish. For now, you must keep your part of the bargain and hand leadership to me, and I will return with the infant.'

Mikell waited anxiously for the agreement; the Otom were crossing from this world to the underworld constantly, and from many points. Travelling with them while invisible would be easy, but before he left, he had to know the four leaders would agree.

Mikell noted the interest and greed hidden beneath the questioning of his knowledge from the four leaders. He realised that once they had their health, and access to the underworld, they would attempt to eliminate him without hesitation, but he was not concerned. Mikell's plans were not of his making, and Aspheseuos protected him with a force far more powerful than they were capable of. When his army was ready to invade the underworld, it would be with one leader only. His army! He liked the sound of that, and intended that the four leaders would not survive to fight the battles ahead.

Mikell got up to leave, his concern now growing; he must return to the Philippine trench and await access through the loop to the underworld. His thoughts grew more anxious lest his absence be noticed and his return to the Mer world barred forever. 'I bid you farewell, gentlemen…' Mikell gave a smirk and nodded to the pilot. 'It's time to go, and your answer is?'

With the agreement settled, Mikell left the remaining three leaders to discuss how best they might complete the work.

The pilot returned Mikell to where he had picked him up. Makot was waiting; the pilot watched them as they moved off into the distance. Like him, the three leaders back at Belsize Creek had no intention of relinquishing their leadership, each one knowing they intended to slaughter the one called Mikell as soon as his usefulness was over. The pilot smiled. *He might think he is going to ascend from the ocean and rule us, but we have other plans.*

A bottle of fine malt whisky sat upon the table with three glasses. 'A drink to our future health!' said one of the leaders. They began to laugh, the sound like the howl of a dark storm emerging from Satan's abode.

Chapter 36

The Beginning of the Final Days – Pisces

A black hawk-eagle circled above the jeep as it sped across the landscape, the unseen bird of prey watching the two men below. Humankind and wildlife still shared the surface of the planet, though man was unable to see beyond the Earthly veil to where the world's other inhabitants had been sited at the time of the holocaust.

Makot knew the terrain like the back of his hand, having made the journey many times in the hunt for supplies. Only a sighting of the Millans made the mundane journey interesting to him now. Makot glanced at Mikell, who seemed a little anxious. 'You'll catch your crossing; relax. An agreement has been reached. A good day's work is done.'

'Don't fool yourself, Makot. They will most certainly try to kill us both when the time is right.' Mikell looked deeply at Makot. 'But that's not the reason for my concern. I am late returning. A good day's work may have been done, but three days will have passed when I return to the Mer world. Ormus will be certain to find out that I have been missing. On my return, the reason for my absence will have to be convincing.'

Makot remained silent. Mikell's revelation about the threat of death had gone deep. He had assumed his closeness to Mikell made that scenario impossible.

'And you'd be right. Don't worry.' Mikell began to laugh.

Makot gunned the jeep, while keeping his thoughts tightly under control.

Mikell's thoughts returned to his recent flight. Many times, when entering the hologram of the past, he had experienced the realism of flying. It had given him a buzz that had become addictive. The flight had only added to his wanting to pilot an aircraft. His thoughts idled on the meeting with the leaders of the Cunmen, and then came again to the flight: the thrill of seeing the landscape below him, the Chihuahuan desert flashing by as they headed for the Mexican border, and then the descent into Belsize Creek. The flight across land and water had taken away any apprehension of the meeting that followed, as he immersed his thoughts in the wonder of the Earth from above. He returned to the present. *I must get back to the City of Memories before Ormus returns.* He was sure he had outwitted the old fool. Mikell laughed while thinking of the years in which he had grown to adulthood, years when he had been the perfect pupil for all that Ormus could teach him. Now he would become a worthy opponent to Ormus, the one from the other-worlds, and was determined to win the oncoming battle. Mikell sat back in his seat to reflect on the world of the Cunmen, those who were going to be part of a new world in which he would rule over all three races.

Makot was promised rich rewards for his loyalty to Mikell, and the first gift was to be the healing of his wasted body. Mikell knew he had no worries with Makot, his obedient servant. He held all the cards, and Makot knew this emphatically.

Mikell turned to look at his companion. 'Yes, a good day's work, Makot.'

They both laughed together. Mikell for his freedom from the underworld and the promise of a powerful future, and Makot for the one thing he desired above all things, a body that was free of pain and cancerous tumours, a body that was strong and healthy again. Makot laughed with joy at this thought. His other needs could be met later.

Mary sat in the sanctuary, an area within all Otom homes where one might find personal space. There was no longer the need for communal gatherings of healing and prayer; these had been replaced with a private part of the day in which the Otom took time to meditate.

Mikell had been gone for three days but Mary had not reported his absence. The advisory circle to the elders, of which Mikell was part, had been notified of the missing infant, and the murder of Senithe. In the morning they were to convene with the council of elders, and Mikell had been sent word to attend. With Ormus and Lia away, Mary had decided to say nothing until the appointment was due, hoping Mikell would return. Mikell had often gone off for days at a time, moving between the oceans' continents while absorbing his enquiring mind in something new.

During these times of absence, Mikell would use his gift from Ormus, an invisible cloak, to find his way to the Earth's surface. It had been during the first of these expeditions that his association with Makot had begun. For Makot, the meeting had been by chance, while Mikell was aware of the reasons for their meeting, and of the being responsible. Aquarius, the immortal life form that had arranged their first meeting, entered Mikell's thoughts: he had warned him that Ormus was aware of his challenge to the Otom and would try to hold him in the world below . . .

Mikell reached the point and looked down at the coastline below him. Anxiously he waited; then at last he saw a boat, one of the small fleet that transported the Otom to and from the Mer world through the void of zero energy. Mikell waited until it was alongside the cliff edge, then, climbing down the thickly foliaged rock face, he slid into the water. Quickly he made his way along the side of the boat and climbed aboard. With his cloak of invisibility pulled tightly about him, he made his way down to the hold unnoticed by the boarding passengers. Mikell pulled the cloak further about him and sat quietly on an empty bench, his heart racing. The passengers were a crew from the new Madagascan site, the City of the Sixth Happiness, which had been built in a pass they had named Libertine. The boarding crewmen were on leave, a replacement team having been installed at the site. The crew were in great spirits and sat laughing and joking with each other; they had missed their families while on land for six months, but knew that if everything went as planned, their families would accompany them on their return. Perhaps then they would know whether it was living on the surface or missing their loved ones that had made them languish for the Mer world.

Mikell began to relax a little; their excited chatter made him feel safe. Mikell bent his head forward, his breath coming slow and deep. Immediately, he noticed the water on the floor. Slowly it dripped from his wet but invisible body. Mikell froze with shock as above him a crew member got up and started to walk towards the hold. Mikell needed to stop the water that was dripping from him onto the floor. Quickly he slipped a coat that was lying on the bench onto the floor to cover his feet where the water was spreading. The crewman now stood facing him, looking directly into his eyes. Mikell held his breath, blood pounding in his temple. The crewman's face almost touched his before he turned and bent down to pick up the coat that lay on the floor.

Shaking it out, he muttered to himself, 'How did that get soaking wet?' Looking closely about the hold, he turned and climbed back out again. Mikell heard him walk back to his seat.

'Stop worrying and sit down,' said one of the crew. 'You've checked out the noise, and there's nothing there. You're going home, so relax.'

The other crewmembers laughed and continued with their joking. Mikell let out a sigh of relief and sat quietly waiting for the boat to dock at the loop where they would disembark. Soon after they would pass through the void of zero energy and be back in the world of the Mers, where he would have to face Aunt Mary, and Ormus.

Ormus had watched over Mikell's progress as he returned to Mer, Mikell not feeling his presence, or that Ormus had been sitting in front of him as he reached out for the crewman's coat.

Mary stood outside Mikell's room; she could hear him moving about as he prepared to shower. Pushing open the door she entered. Mikell emerged from the shower room and asked her curtly, 'Don't you knock any more, Aunt?'

Ignoring his comment, she asked, 'Where have you been, Mikell?'

Mikell immediately took a softer approach, knowing it was important that she be satisfied with his answer. 'Now what's all the fuss about? I've been away before,' he said, putting his arm around her shoulder and giving her a squeeze. 'I have been on the other side of the city. I have a friend there, one I would like you to meet, if you behave yourself,' he said with a grin: 'a woman whom I am very fond of.'

'Mikell, while you have been gone a Mer infant has been snatched from the Cradling, and...' Mary stopped abruptly, the tears welling in her eyes. She continued with a sob, 'and Senithe has been murdered. Never have we, or the Mers, since they welcomed us to their world, had to bear such a travesty ... Mikell, where in the city were you? You will be asked this by the council of elders, as will every Otom. The council of advisors convenes before the council of elders tomorrow, and you are to be there. Everyone must now account for their actions at the time of the kidnapping and murder.'

Mikell thought fast; where was he to get his alibi from, if not from his Aunt Mary? He spoke softly to her. 'Aunt, you must help me. The one I love is a Mer, and if this comes to light, she will have to answer for her actions, for you know it is forbidden for the two races to combine. You are our only hope of not being found out. I feel such pain for the loss of our dear friend, Senithe, but if you do not help us, then there will be even more pain for me to endure. Will you help us and say I was with you? If you will do this, I promise, I will end the relationship in respect for Senithe.' Mikell paused, willing her to respond in his favour.

Mary thought about what he had said; she was shocked at his outburst, although not surprised. If anyone would go against the laws of Mer and Otom, she knew it would be her nephew. But for the sake of her dead sister's memory, she wanted to believe that there was some good in him, and he truly seemed full of remorse for the loss of Senithe ... 'Very well, I will tell Ormus that you were here, but you must promise me that you will never break the laws of nature here ever again.'

Mikell turned his face towards his aunt's, his eyes looking deeply into hers. 'I promise. I truly promise, I will never look at a Mer woman again'

Mary looked into his eyes and was almost satisfied with his answer.

Mikell kissed her lightly on the forehead and released her; his part had been easy. He had told her the truth in his promise; he smiled, knowing that he would never be tempted to enter into any kind of bond with a fish, however intelligent. He hated each and every one of them, and looked forward to the day when their world would be in tatters, while he reigned supreme upon the surface of the Earth.

The immortal being Pisces appeared before Ormus. 'Have faith, we have much work to do. You are disappointed with Mary, but you knew that it could go either way. A family bond most often proves the strongest. Mikell would have found a proven alibi; that was foretold. He will get to where he needs to be, prophecy requires it. Do not be ruffled by his success. Look back upon your time upon Earth when the discharge of your powers encumbered you so. That time of change was also preordained. If not, your time with Lia to teach her the ways of a "wise one" would never have happened. Remember, all experiences encapsulate mankind's way forward. Mikell's existence is also part of this. Hafnium's dream is a grand one, and he loves mankind dearly, as does he love all life in Universe Four. Return to Mary, and accept what she has to tell you. It will be the only time that she deceives you, the Otom or Mers. When she realises her mistake, she will be prepared to lay down her life to make amends.'

Ormus felt remorse for his reluctance to allow Mary and Mikell their experiences, so much so that his ease was diminished by the remembrance of them.

'Play your music, my friend,' said Pisces. 'Manifest your hearty goodness. Come, release these old shadows and become your wise self again. You are a "wise one" and must take good care of your soul, Ormus. Your wisdom will be needed to support the Otom when their journey to the surface becomes a battleground, and the Mer world endangered.'

Ormus listened to the words that Pisces spoke. She was from the first moment of the universe: a star that had experienced every age, and who expressed amusement at the games of universal life; she could be gay and charming, as well as spiteful and vitriolic to those that ruffled her. Pisces could be anything, for she was the wisest of them all; caring not for protocol she reigned supreme, and would not be told otherwise.

The following morning, Ormus waited with the circle of elders for Mikell to appear. All were now aware of his treachery, and as the council of advisors assembled before the elders, Lia could not bear to meet Mikell's calm gaze as Senithe's death was spoken of. For the first time she saw him as he truly was. The child that she had always managed to forgive now stood before her as a man who was the most loathsome of men. Mikell had become a murderer and a militant, fanatical enough to destroy a world that nurtured two races of people who were gentle and loving towards one another; they had lived in harmony throughout very difficult years, and Mikell now wanted to destroy them in his bid to be king of kings among the Cunmen. Lia felt nothing except a calm that felt as cold as the snow she had encountered on her last visit to the surface. This reaction was not one of vengeance, but a knowing that all things have their reason, good or bad.

'Welcome to you, advisors to the council. As you know, there has been a great travesty played out here in the Mer world, and though we have yet to find those guilty, we can say without doubt that this sorrowful crime was committed by our kind. Never before in the history of the Mers have crimes of these natures been committed.'

There was silence as the force of the words hung about the chamber like a dense cloud of darkness.

'Each one of you is accountable to those living in your sector of the city. Have any of your people been missed? If any of you have information on this happening ... have any of you anything to say?'

Silence returned as the words died in the stillness.

'Very well then; if those in your quarter are accounted for, then it rests with you to give an account of yourselves.'

Each one came in turn to answer before the elders until only Mikell was left.

Looking straight at Ormus, he began. 'I can say with the deepest sorrow that the crime that has been committed fills me with anger for the one who perpetrated it. I myself felt deeply for Senithe who was like one of my family. My aunt will miss her grievously, so close were they, and I promise you this, I will not stop until the one that committed this crime is found … For myself, my Aunt Mary will tell you that I have spent the last few days in her company.' Mikell paused, his performance of grief extraordinary in the light of his evilness.

'Thank you, Mikell,' said Ormus. 'We have no doubt that you will be fully involved in the search for Senithe's murderer.'

The elders spoke quietly together and then called for a closure to the proceedings. There could be no doubt now, the battle between the Otom and the Cunmen was under way; nothing could stop the oncoming war.

Hafnium, the grand master of Universe Four, cast his thoughts upon the elders of the Otom. 'The Cunmen will suffer grievously if they make war with you before they enter the other-worlds.'

Ormus smiled on hearing these words from the grand master; he felt reassured, his old self again, as he prepared for the battle about to take place.

The Mer infant lay in a large container overflowing with seawater, with a plentiful supply of fresh seaweed; contentedly he sucked on the nourishment floating about him. The nursing mother sat nearby, watchful for any changes to her precious charge.

Chapter 37

The Crystalline Kingdom

The Piscean phase in the heavens was almost over for another Earth year. It was time for Aries to rise from his slumber. Aries was the progeny of Mars, the bringer of revelation through conflict.

Pisces contemplated how she might soften the expansive energy that Aries would bring upon the Otom. She would ask for help from those that were gentle and giving, those that would prepare the way for him. The crystal elders came to mind; they alone could set a precedent that would leave her work in a perfect condition for Aries to follow.

Pisces was renowned for her way of gathering help; she would busy herself communing with other heavenly bodies to see what they would make of her plans, asking for help in such a way that they always gave in to her flustered and helpless plea for assistance, her performance having one goal in mind: to come out on top. The Otom land sites were up and running but she could see from her vantage point that Aquarius had the edge. Aquarius believed that the challenge being played out on the universal chequerboard was flawed; the Otom were not fighters. Those that had initially made the migration to the world of the Mers were a people of peace, and their children were the same, having been reared in a temperate and loving environment. Now they were to face the barbaric nature of the Cunmen to compete for the surface of the Earth. Pisces realised that in war they were no match; however, with help from the planetary and other-worldly forces, they could gain a victory in the oncoming battle. Pisces felt confident that as she withdrew from the universal chequerboard, the game in progress remained balanced. There remained only one more task; Pisces wrapped herself in the cloak of a human to call upon the elders of the Crystalline Kingdom, a vast nation of supernatural beings that spanned the Earth's underworld.

For thousands of years before the holocaust, crystal beings had been removed from their place of origin by humans who mined them for profit. Those who bought the crystals to look at and admire were unaware that within the crystal's beauty resided a transcendental being that gave the crystal its unique healing energy; a feeling of peacefulness that could rarely be found elsewhere upon the Earth plane would enter the environment in which the crystals were placed. There had been many stories told among the indigenous people of the world of thirteen crystal skulls that wielded immense power, which would one day bring unprecedented change upon the Earth. It was this power that Pisces would ask the Crystalline Kingdom to unleash.

Pisces had a plan wherein the Crystalline Kingdom would bring peace and security to the new cities of the one tribe of man: an arc of energy that would span the Otom sites across the world, one that the Cunmen would not be able to penetrate. Pisces needed the help of the crystal elders in order to leave the stage set for Aries, and then she could return to her mantle of sleep. Sleep, how she loved her mantle of slumber, and soon it would be time again to rest within its comfort. Pisces sighed. 'Best I get on with the work in hand, then.'

When giving an audience to those from outside their kingdom, the crystal elders considered it respectful to take the form of their guests. As Pisces appeared before the crystal elders in human form, they too appeared as humankind formed from pure crystal. Pisces looked upon the crystal elders with a deep admiration; a thing of beauty was always a pleasure to behold, and the human creatures in crystalline form standing before her were indeed exquisite.

Pisces' mane of golden hair, dressed with the flowers of spring, flowed about her. Her small form was wrapped in billowing shades of pink, and a crimson robe flowed out behind her. The energy of spring surrounded those gathered about her as Pisces drew the crystal elders into her mantle of colour. Their skull-like faces glowed back, their sapphire gaze undiminished by her presence.

Pisces broke the silence that embraced them; her words, ideas, all flowing at once amidst an air of chaos, as everything came together with a bump. Planning was not part of her nature, but instant arrival with a fanfare of trumpets was. Pisces, her voice warm and encouraging, had begun by warmly wishing for the health, wealth and happiness of all within her presence. Then she got down to business, giving the reason why she had come, the need for their help, and the outcome for the Otom if they should decline her request. And, finally, that she felt certain she could rely on them to accept her plan and make it a success. Pisces knew she had put her case well; now all that was to be done was to let them decide how they would go about the task. They would not refuse; she was sure of that. Pisces stood back, her part having been easy; she was an excellent mediator, and this she believed without a doubt.

The crystal elders thanked her for her faith in them to help and procure an arc of safety for the Otom cities. They bid Pisces farewell, amid her bright and warm thank you to them all. Pisces departed, her work now done. Now to sleep until once more she needed to ponder upon another Earthly season.

Ormus, on feeling Pisces' withdrawal, made his presence known to the crystal elders. He must wait for an answer, and would listen while the thirteen elders considered the strengths and weaknesses of Pisces' arc, which would have to be impenetrable and endure all tests. The crystal elders knew much with regard to endurance, their lives having spanned billions of years, their secret powers having lain hidden beneath the Earth's surface during each epoch in the story of mankind, which had been born and then, as suddenly, ended.

Ormus listened intently to the ideas they debated until a plan began to form. Then, sitting back, he waited for the final plan to emerge.

When the elders were finished and the plan complete, Ormus was satisfied that nothing would penetrate the new sites that spanned the world, all ready and waiting for the Otom to begin life anew upon the Earth's surface.

The Otom people had waited patiently for the time when they would feel sunlight upon their faces and the earth beneath their feet. For some it would be again, and for others a first-time experience, with vague memories from their infant beginnings; they were now, as had been their ancestors, in search of a new life. Their forefathers had travelled the world, conquering the native people of every continent they invaded, and destroying many civilisations, thus giving birth to a way of life that would eventually bring about the destruction of mankind. It was these beleaguered civilisations that had told modern man of the crystal legends, and warned them of the destruction their way of life would bring.

The coming age would be different; the Otom wanted peace, a life in which they would live in awareness of their spirituality and be thankful for the life experiences that graced them each day. They did not know how this would come about, but they trusted, had faith enough to believe they would not have to raise a hand against the Cunmen … but if they had to fight to survive, then they would.

In the City of Memories, Ormus assembled the councillors, those chosen by the people, of each new site. Ormus was to outline the plan for the arc of rainbows, laid down by the crystal elders, and one other matter of importance to the Otom. On completion of the first task, he said, 'You have much to thank the Mers for; as a race, you have taken many of their ways, their beliefs and nature. Your bodies have altered in appearance since first you entered the Mer world; the webbing between your toes, the paleness of flesh and lack of muscle that covers your underdeveloped bodies, these changes have enabled you to adapt to the world that you live in. When you return to the surface permanently, these changes will rapidly disappear and you will return to your natural human state. However, your ability to dive within the deep ocean will remain for many years…' Ormus waited for a moment before announcing what to him was the most important part of all he had to tell them. 'To protect you from the radiation that still threatens some sites, and for your bodies to live safely beneath the crystal rainbows, the ten lost strands of DNA that unite mankind with the knowledge of Universe Four are to be returned to you. These ten strands of energy will merge with the arc of crystal rainbows. Together they will keep all safe beneath its shield. Within five decades the Otom will leave the Earth, having acquired sufficient knowledge from the ten strands of DNA to venture out safely into the cosmos.'

In front of those assembled, a hologram appeared from which thirteen skulls with sapphire orbs for eyes looked out at them; the crystal elders began to speak as one voice. 'It has been decided that the crystal communities to take charge of protecting the new cities will be Zoisite, to serve Australia and New Zealand … Axinite, to serve New Britain, New Guinea and New Caledonia … Epidote, to serve the Siberian taiga, Lake Baikal and the Taymyr Peninsula … Iolite, to serve the Tennessee Cumberland Watershed … Tanzinite, to serve Madagascar and the Cape Floristic Region … Spodumene, to serve the Varzea and Igapo forest of Amazonia, the Andean forests, the Antarctic Peninsula, the Northern Rockies and boreal forest areas, and the marine life in the Bering Sea that is now under threat from the Cunmen. The community of pure quartz will join with those we have spoken of to protect the British Isles. The seven named will absorb the main force of light that will form a global shield to protect the Otom cities. But there will be many more crystal communities adding their light forces to the rainbow project. Each area has been chosen for its former abundance of wildlife species, rainforests, unique flora and fauna, and the ability to provide food for mankind, but this you already know.'

Those gathered understood the elder's words for their education had included all they would need to know for the future.

The hologram expanded to show the crystals that had been chosen for each site. First to appear was a dazzling display of crystal beings that were presently supporting the Earth in her healing process from the holocaust.

The elders began to call forth the crystals by name so that all gathered could recognise those protecting them with their powerful rays of healing light, so powerful that should the Cunmen approach and bathe in the rainbow's energy, they would be consumed by the rays.

A small army of crystalline beings filled the hologram, their long slim translucent bodies marching in perfect time. The more aged they appeared, the more radiant their being, their beautiful long faces intersecting the multitude of crystalline formations that made whole their structure.

Zoisite came forward, the colour of sapphire blue, to serve Australia and New Zealand; Axinite, her colour amber and brown, to serve New Britain, New Guinea and New Caledonia. Epidote came next, her colours of yellow, green and dark brown, to serve the Siberian taiga, Lake Baikal and the Taymyr Peninsula. Iolite, her colour a deep violet, came next to serve the Tennessee Cumberland Watershed. Tanzinite came forward, her colour of rich blue violet, to serve Madagascar and the Cape Floristic Region, and then Spodumene, her colours of yellow, lilac and emerald, to serve the Varzea and Igapo forests of Amazonia, the Andean forests, the Antarctic Peninsula, the Northern Rockies, the boreal forest areas and the Bering sea. And last of all the pure quartz crystal that would serve the British Isles, and close the sphere protecting the surface of the Earth.

With the help of Pisces and the planetary forces, the crystals were gathered into place. Shortly afterwards, the Cunmen watched in fear as giant cascades of light dropped from the heavens, as the star tribe guided the crystals to where they must lay. When all was in place, a multitude of giant rainbows hung suspended over each new city of the Otom, while the unseen rays of the crystal nations' total force began to slowly spread to the remaining land where the Cunmen lived and roamed.

The Otom, knowing they would be safe beneath the giant rainbows, prepared to leave the Mer world to occupy the sites. As they gathered together to leave they could feel each other's excitement. The ever-increasing fear that had shadowed their trust as the time for the migration had loomed had now disappeared.

They began to talk jubilantly among themselves. 'It was prophesied that all would be well,' they said, each one now feeling a little guilty for doubting, and all feeling joy at being proved wrong.

Ormus had made sure that Mikell had been unable to attend the gathering when the plan was first revealed. Now Mikell would know of the rainbows, they were there for all to see, and he would be seething to think that Ormus had outwitted him. Mikell would now know without question that Ormus had known he planned to bring war upon his own kind.

Chapter 38

The Mer Infant

Mikell's hatred reached unknown depths as he watched the arc materialise. Ormus had made a fool of him. The Cunmen would be as angry as he was, and his survival was becoming increasingly questionable. It was time to leave the Mer world, time to be gone from the miserable watery land with its fish people and the timid, spineless 'one tribe of man'. The only humans of use in the underworld were the women, who would bear the Cunmen's offspring. The Mer infants' powers were also useful, and for these to continue, the Mers would be left to bring their offspring into the world, but Zrsiofour, the king of fish – Mikell smiled – he would become fish bait for the dogs.

Ormus listened to Mikell's ramblings and his heart became heavy with sorrow for the kind and gentle Mers, should Hafnium decide their world would be taken. Ormus prayed it was not part of the plan; suffering that would be unleashed upon a race that had no true understanding of evil . . . Ormus turned his thoughts to the missing infant; it was time to rescue him. Mikell wanted to use his powers to prepare an army of healthy Cunmen, but to do so quickly he would need many more infants. Ormus knew he would attempt another assault on the Cradling. There was no time to waste; he had contacted the nursing mother's consciousness during her dreamtime and knew the location where she concealed the infant. For long periods during sleep, Makot was able to close his mind to Ormus' probing, but the nursing mother was not as strong, and while she slept he had found her. The nursing mother's dreams were filled with her fear of Mikell and Makot, while the infant appeared there nightly to remind her of the wrong she was doing. Each night as the infant had entered her dreams, Ormus had searched until he found them.

'Ormus, relax!' Lia came to stand before him.

The gathering had dispersed quickly as all present were eager to take the news of the arc of rainbows back to their families and friends.

Ormus turned to her and smiled. 'I know I should, but I am most concerned. We must retrieve the Mer infant before it is too late, Lia.'

Lia listened, while watching her friend closely. 'Perhaps I can help? Let me enter the nursing mother's dreamtime and talk to her. She may speak to me, whereas she may be afraid of you. I will appear dressed as one of her kind, and then she might unburden her heart to me. I feel she is full of regret for her role in this capture. That she worries for her soul. Leave it with me, Ormus. In the morning we will see what has come to light.'

Ormus made the sign of peace, and thanked her. 'I will return in the morning, Lia.' Ormus faded from view, leaving Lia to ponder her night in the dreamtime.

Simlify sat beneath the waterfall at the entrance to the City of Five Pathways. She had healed from the pain that Mikell's deceit had caused her; her concern now was for the infant that had been stolen, and must be found. Ormus had visited her soon after Lia had offered to speak with the nursing mother, asking her to accompany Lia on her journey into the dreamtime. Now Simlify sat waiting, her intuitive mind listening for Lia's body to release her spirit into the dreamtime; then she would join her to find the spirit they were seeking. Together, they had to persuade the nursing mother that the continuation of her Earthly life was not as precious as her soul's wish to continue evolving within the light of the universe. Simlify stirred as she listened to Lia's last waking thoughts; she had retired to bed after many hours of meditation, making clear in her mind that she wished to visit the infant and the nursing mother, and that she would remember all that had taken place when waking. Lia's spirit drifted into the dreamtime where Simlify waited.

Lia lifted from her physical cloak to find Simlify waiting, her pain now healed and her energy flowing positively about her. She held out a hand to Lia who took hold of it, their spirits becoming one as they concentrated on finding the location of the infant. The colours gathering about them began to shift, at first circling slowly and then their bodies were spinning within a web of colour that flowed back and forth in the form of a figure eight; the vortex of colour began to slow and then disperse. Simlify, having shed her tail, stood with Lia upon the long stretch of beach where the infant was held captive; both were heavily shrouded, the garments feeling strange and oppressive to them. A woman robed from head to toe emerged from a shabby wooden hut and came towards them; her eyes were clear and bright, expressing fear as she approached. Simlify let go of Lia's hand as she moved forward to speak with the woman. The woman made no sound but gestured to the hut further along the beach, and the three women walked the short distance together in silence.

Inside the hut the infant lay sleeping in a container of seawater covered with palm leaves to keep out the light. To his visitors' relief the infant looked comfortable and peaceful. The nursing mother bent down and held his tiny head. Silently she cried; the infant on contact had made her whole, and she knew what she was doing was wrong and wanted to make amends. Each time she went into the dreamtime she heard the cries of the infant's mother and her remorse was now unbearable. Her own body had been racked with pain and lesions, and she would never have held a child of her own. Now all she wished for was to enter the other-worlds and be at peace, but first she must save the infant. The nursing mother had always believed in the afterlife, but she had also believed in the Cunmen's way of life and the easy living it had brought, without ever thinking of the consequences to the Earth and humanity. The Cunmen had suffered, hoping only for an early release from their pointless life. The infant would be their salvation, but for her it was too big a price to pay. When the infant had first been brought to her she had thought that she might gain her health and something of the old life, for wasn't their saviour coming? But when she had seen Mikell, so cruel and cold, she knew he was the devil's disciple and wanted no part of his world.

'I want my soul to live on in the light of the master of good, and have prayed for the rescue of this beautiful infant. With your arrival, my prayers have been answered. The infant's return will be my salvation. Thank you,' she whispered, 'thank you.'

Odelia and Glashadou appeared before the nursing mother as she cried out in her sleep, her anguish now in full flood. 'Come, my dear, your work is done. Do not fear for the infant, his guardian angels now watch over him.'

As the nursing mother began to leave the dreamtime, the location was revealed to Lia and Simlify; they were no more than a few miles from the Otom site on the island of Madagascar. Lia felt her withdrawal from the dreamtime as this last image faded and she began to wake. Quickly she recalled all that had happened, trying not to forget any detail as she struggled from her bed to gather pen and paper, repeating it to herself until everything she could remember was written down and the pages of script lay in front of her. Lia sat back and relaxed; her work was done and the evidence down. 'Three minutes' came into her mind; she wrote it down, repeating it to herself: three minutes, three minutes, what did it mean? The infant was on the island of Madagascar, but what of three minutes, and how did it fit in? Lia stood up and left the room, still pondering the three minutes. She made her morning drink and turned towards the table; Ormus sat there waiting for her to recall the night's events.

'What news have you of the infant, Lia?' he asked with a smile, knowing that her tale would collaborate that of Simlify.

Lia read from the sheets of paper in front of her while Ormus listened carefully. Their recollections of the previous night were much the same, except that Simlify had been able to tell him that the three minutes Lia spoke of was the distance between the Otom site and the place where the infant was being kept.

However, with the distance and denseness of undergrowth between the site and the ocean, the location they sought could be in any direction.

Lia pondered on what Ormus was saying, part listening and thinking. Then she said, 'But the hut is only partially covered by the fringe of dense jungle, it would be seen on the beach straight away. They must search along the beach around the island until they find him.'

'Good thinking, my dear.' Ormus stood up and made to leave.

Lia asked, 'Ormus, what has happened to the nursing mother?'

Ormus reached out to touch the centre of Lia's forehead; her eyes closed, and she was shown what she wished to know. As Lia closed her eyes, a picture began to materialise; she could see the infant, who seemed uncomfortable and was crying softly. Lia immediately became alarmed as beside him lay the body of the nursing mother; she had passed to the other-worlds in her sleep. With the help of Odelia and Glashadou she had passed beyond the psychic plane to the other-worlds.

'Do not worry, Lia. Mikell is on his way to collect the infant, and once he has him I can follow. There is no way he can deceive me now. I will know every step he takes. It is the other one, Makot, that is the problem. I must take my leave, and will see you at the meeting of the elders later today.' Ormus left Lia to prepare her address to the meeting of the elders, concerning the night's events and the whereabouts of the infant.

Ormus stood beneath a crop of palms, their long shadows falling across the silver white sand to gently touch the ripples at the water's edge. Ormus waited, knowing that Makot would return shortly, drawn there by the Mer infant's power to heal. While Mikell was out of sight he intended to take a look for himself. Makot had no fear of the nursing mother telling Mikell; she would do as he said.

Making his way down to the beach, Makot forced his way through the thick undergrowth that hid him from view. Soon enough he was out in the open and walking along the white silvery trail of sand towards the hut, unaware that Ormus watched him as he passed by. Makot felt edgy but he put it down to his risky mission; he was told that just to cradle the naked infant would bring instant healing to his sick and ravaged body, he was also aware that each healing would drain the infant's energy. His people were so sick that even the healing of one Cunman could be fatal for the infant. Mikell had told the leaders that after each healing there must be at least a few days' interval for the infant to recover its healing powers. The infant was now in good health and Makot had been promised the first healing, so it should not make any difference whether Mikell was present or not. Makot was convinced that what he was about to do was right as he headed for the hut. But he was beginning to sense that something was wrong; he quickened his pace; the infant was crying, and his voice sounded feeble and lost.

Makot reached the doorway to find the nursing mother lying there, her body already starting to decompose in the heat. Insects and flies came to rest upon her body, the sound of their droning loud and irritating. Makot moved across to the infant and looked in; the water tank was almost empty and the infant looked hot and ill. Makot remembered what Mikell had said, '*the infant must be kept immersed in seawater at all times.*' Quickly, he took hold of the infant and hurried outside, running down to the water's edge. Holding tight to his charge he plunged into the waves, walking as fast as he could against the water until he was immersed up to his chest.

The infant's body lay submerged beneath the water line, his head resting on Makot's arm. Makot took his free hand and, holding the infant's body tightly, he wiped the infant's face. The infant stopped whimpering and lay peacefully in his arms, his pale green eyes looking up at the one who had made him comfortable. Makot looked back at him in fascination; it was as if his eyes were drawing him downwards. Suddenly a large swell rolled towards them and Makot lost his footing. Panicking, he yelled out as he toppled backwards clutching the infant tightly in his arms. Scrabbling for a foothold Makot pushed backwards towards the shore, the fear of what would happen to him if he lost the infant giving him strength, spluttering as he swallowed the foul salty water.

Makot pulled himself from the water, fear filling his mind. *Mikell would have killed me for sure.* After making his way back to the hut, he laid the infant on the ground, then, making sure that he was safe, he made his way back down the beach for supplies of water. With the infant safe in the tank of seawater, he began to relax. It was time to get rid of the foul-smelling corpse; otherwise the infant would become ill. With his thoughts on these things, Makot had not noticed the ease with which he was walking. His sopping wet clothes hung about him, and he knew he had to undress. He hesitated. Makot rarely undressed; his body frightened him and he hated the lesions that grew ever larger upon the small patches of remaining healthy skin, patches that were becoming less and less noticeable.

With the nursing mother removed from the hut and the infant asleep, Makot began to undress. Slowly he began to strip the partially dry garments from his body, his eyes closed tight, trying not to glimpse the sores that he hated so much. As he struggled with the layers he was forced to open his eyes; it was then that he noticed the smooth and healthy bareness of his arm. Makot drew back the final robe to reveal a body that was strong and healthy. Quickly he examined every part, looking for sores but there were none, his skin was smooth and clear. Makot stood still, hardly believing what he saw ... He began to cry like a baby. He realised he had been healed when he had cradled the infant. Many times he had seen pictures of mankind before the holocaust and had longed to be the same. Then thinking of his face he ran from the hut down to the water edge, his naked body experiencing light for the first time. Running into the waves, he waited for the water to clear so that he could see his face. A pale but strong face with dark brown eyes and hair looked back at him; he was handsome. Smiling broadly at his reflection, he revealed teeth that were strong and healthy, and not, as before, a mouthful of teeth that had started to rot whilst he was still in his mother's womb; it was a miracle that he had survived and grown to adulthood.

Ormus looked on at what was taking place. Makot was transformed; his body was strong and healthy, but not his mind. The infant did not have the power to heal his mind that was evil beyond redemption; only his physical death would begin the journey to accomplish that. Ormus turned his thoughts to the infant, and while Makot was busy he entered the hut. The infant lay fast asleep, his face a little pale, even for a Mer, but seemingly none the worse for the healing given to Makot. Ormus was satisfied that the infant was safe, and decided to leave things as they were; the Mer angels were watching over the infant, and he would not intervene. Unseen, Ormus made his way back to where Makot was still playing in the water. Mikell's arrival was imminent, and he would sense Ormus' presence; it was time to leave, although he would have appreciated being present to witness Mikell's fury when he realised the nursing mother was dead, and that Makot had disobeyed him.

Ormus entered the void and made his way back to the City of Memories, satisfied that the news of the infant's health and whereabouts would be well received by those attending the meeting of the elders.

Chapter 39

The Healing

The jeep lurched over the final distance of rough terrain towards the beach hut. Mikell's thoughts were on Makot and the infant; he sensed that they were not in danger, but that something had changed. When he had left the council of elders, he had been in no doubt that Ormus knew of his deception. Making his way back to the transport section, he had entered the void and returned to the surface. Now he was back on Madagascan soil to take charge of the infant's future. Makot was meant to have met him but was nowhere to be seen. Having found the jeep waiting with another driver, Mikell had asked where Makot was. An answer had not been forthcoming, only a shrug of the shoulders. This had made him furious; he didn't like ambiguity, *especially when dealing with this barbarian.* Soon after the driver lay unconscious and Mikell had taken the jeep and gone on alone. Mikell's mind was racing; did Makot have others with him now? What was going on?

Mikell drove across the rough terrain, his thoughts on the one who had masterminded this venture and nurtured him through his growing years. The being who would come at night to tell him of his future, that he was not like his people and had a destiny to fulfil away from the Otom with another race! The jeep stopped at the end of the track and Mikell jumped out and headed through the undergrowth to the beach. Once there he ran across the sand, his feet dragging beneath the tiny crystal forms that slowed his pace.

Makot heard the noise as Mikell, his breath coming sharply,

raced towards the hut. Makot stepped out to meet him, his eyes shining with pride for his new physique.

Mikell stopped and stared at the young dark-skinned man before him. Makot was completely naked. 'Are you mad? Get inside and find some garments to wear. How long have you been standing in the light?' Mikell realised what had happened, that Makot had not been able to wait, and he began to worry afresh. If the others began to fight for the infant's healing powers, the infant would not survive very long. It would be better to keep the infant here and bring the leaders one at a time for their healing. The infant must be hidden to stand a chance of survival. 'You idiot, Makot, can't you feel your skin burning? The sunlight will harm you if you stand in its light without protection.'

Makot looked down at his body; it had taken on a deep red glow and was beginning to feel sore.

'How long have you been like this, how long have you been exposed to the sunlight?'

Makot on seeing the concern on Mikell's face began to panic. 'Not long, an hour, maybe two. Why, what's the matter, what's wrong with that?'

'The sunlight will burn you, has burnt you, and you are going to feel mighty sore for a day or two.'

'Will I go back as I was?' Makot asked with fear in his voice.

'No, that won't happen,' Mikell answered calmly, realising the euphoria that Makot must be experiencing. 'Where is the nursing mother, Makot?'

'She's dead,' said Makot flatly, the fear of returning to how he was having quietened him.

Mikell looked at him searchingly to see if he was lying. 'Where is the body?'

Makot took him to the edge of the beach where she lay in the undergrowth; her body covered by Makot's cast-off robes. Mikell uncovered the body, and holding his hand over his mouth he gingerly made an inspection; no signs of violence, and how peaceful she looked. Mikell had noticed at once that the rapidly decaying body had been healed, and he was satisfied that Makot was telling the truth. He covered her over again. Mikell wanted to make Makot suffer for disobeying him, but then decided he would use the situation to his advantage. 'Makot, get some garments on, and then we can talk.'

With Makot clothed, they went to sit outside in the shadows to discuss where the infant would be kept.

'The infant cannot stay here, it is not safe. The leaders may have been following you, and if they find the infant they will surely kill him as they fight to regain their health. Each healing must be a few days apart.'

Makot nodded, the infant had given him a new life and he did not want to see it harmed.

'Remember, Makot, there will be many more gifts if you do as I say.'

Makot thought for a moment and then said, 'We can take him to the other side of the island. There are caves beneath the point where the sea rises highest upon the rocks; he can be safely hidden, and there will be water, lots of it.'

Mikell having agreed said, 'We must go now. I don't feel easy here.'

They fetched the tank and lifted it onto the back of the jeep. Then, having taken the infant down to the water, Makot gave him one last dip before the journey.

As they set off for the other side of the island, Mikell's thoughts spun chaotically between his options. Makot would take charge of the infant and he would bring the leaders one by one, but how would he accomplish this without giving the infant's location away? He needed an accomplice, one he could trust.

On the shadowy horizon, Aquarius loomed over, his Earthly cloak looking so fine. 'I will be your trusted accomplice,' he laughed; 'it will be fun to take on a mortal mantle for a while.'

As the apparition disappeared, Mikell knew his immediate problem was over. Aquarius would not let him down; he was supporting the success of the Cunmen in order to prosper himself, and the premature death of the infant would only hinder the plan. When they reached their destination, Mikell was more than satisfied with Makot's choice; the water level reached into the caves, leaving deep pools of water for the Mer infant to rest in.

Makot and the infant lay in the deepest of the pools, one easing his burning skin, the other bonding with his environment.

Mikell gave instructions for feeding the infant and keeping him comfortable. 'I will be back in a few days with the first of the leaders. Guard the infant with your life, Makot.'

Makot did not reply; he was singing to the infant softly and deeply, a tune that had entered his head from the past. Right now it seemed appropriate to sing as a feeling of contentment welled up inside him.

Ormus watched Mikell leave, knowing he would return to the City of Memories to keep up the pretence with his aunt Mary, even though he knew that Ormus was aware of his treachery. Ormus followed him, satisfied that Makot would guard the infant with his life. Makot's healing had formed a bond with the infant and a little warmth had penetrated his heart. The infant was safe with Makot; now that he was healed he would not want to do him harm.

Chapter 40

Aries – Progeny of Mars

Mary lay in bed unable to sleep, she had lied to Ormus and it lay heavily upon her conscience; her nephew had not returned and she blamed herself for the crimes he had committed against the Mers.

Mikell had been devastated when his mother had died and as he grew older he blamed his aunt for her death. Mary had been a nurse working in one of London's busiest hospitals when the United States of Europe had opened their borders; migrants swarmed across Europe searching for work, bringing chaos, old diseases and resentment to every nation involved.

As she lay there, she recalled the events that led to her sister's death. They had been nursing a young migrant with acute tuberculosis who had entered the country a few weeks earlier. Because of his state of health he had been brought to the secure ward where she worked. At that time, Mary had been supporting her sister through one of her worse periods of alcohol dependency, and would visit her each evening, unaware that she was carrying a disease that would bring about her death; within six months her sister, Lucille, had passed away, a victim of tuberculosis.

As Mikell grew old enough to understand he blamed Mary for the loss of his mother, and blamed her more for delivering him to the world beneath the oceans, a place that he hated and where he felt he had been dealt the same fate as his mother, entombed beneath the ground.

Aries came before Ormus in a clap of thunder; the storm clouds were gathering and there was no one better to deliver them than

Aries. Each of the star tribe was gifted with both positive and negative qualities that were also inherent in man. At this time in mankind's evolution only the negative side of the Cunmen's nature was obvious, and the Otom's gentle nature was required to regain balance upon Earth.

Aries was the progeny of Mars, whose truism was to act first and consider the result afterwards. This reasoning had been exacted during the final days on Earth; time and again one act of vengeance had been followed by another until finally the holocaust had become a reality, and mankind had destroyed his world. This time Ormus would be responsible for seeing that Aries was kept from having everything his own way and that his powers were restricted. The Otom had no experience of aggression or revenge; these instincts had been eliminated in their quest to live peaceably among the Mers, and it was hoped they would remain so when they returned to the surface.

The plan had been carefully thought through; the Cunmen would be kept at bay by the strategic choices of Aries, the planner and visionary, and the protection of the arc of crystal rainbows. Aries was able to plan and stand alone, but from that point on his vision of what was good for the whole became shrouded.

Ormus held Aries' steady gaze, the star's thick body and large head giving an overwhelming feeling of strength. His dark thick hair tumbled about his shoulders like the mane of a stallion, while his small dark eyes gazed out from a face with a swarthy complexion; this was the star Aries in the flesh, exuding confidence to all who observed him.

Ormus greeted him. 'Aries, you have awakened to take the place of Pisces who has prepared the ground most expertly for you. The crystal arc is in place and the Otom are ready to return to the surface. They are in need of all your good qualities to help them survive the next fifty years: your will and courage, your ambition and brilliance to aspire to great thoughts, and your creativeness.' Ormus knew that flattering Aries would bring about his best results.

Aries smiled broadly; he loved to be told that he was appreciated.

Ormus took a deep breath; Aries was all these things that he spoke of, but the disadvantage was that he needed to be flattered, and frequently, otherwise he could become uninterested and deceitful. Ormus had paused just long enough for Aries to indulge in the flattery offered. 'In order to raise a healthy army, Mikell, our challenger, who is protected by Aquarius, plans to raid the Cradling for more Mer infants. This must not happen, and I am relying on you to stop him. Mikell is Aspheseuos' chosen assassin, the grim reaper, spawned in the belly of the new tribe of man. Mikell has the knowledge that the ancients have, and his darker side is strong; believe me, I know, for it was I who educated him through his years from childhood to adult. Mikell was born to challenge the Otom and was born within your time of awakening upon the Earth; he is of your nature, Aries.'

Aries tossed aside this last remark and began to talk of his plan. 'It seems to me that first we need to attack, to clear the Cunmen from the place they most value for its valuable provisions, Belsize Creek. Whatever they plan, it will be situated there to begin with.' Aries straightened himself, knowing his directive was extremely valuable to Ormus. 'The Cunmen have built an aquarium at Belsize Creek to hold the Mer infants they intend to steal.' Aries waited for Ormus to acknowledge his statement.

'That is correct. That much we know. But how will we do this without engaging the Otom in warfare? If we were to disable the leaders that are there, others would swarm in to protect them.'

Aries' face opened out into a huge grin and he started to chuckle. 'I have a plan!'

Chapter 41

The Assault on the Cradling

Simlify waited by the entrance to the City of Five Pathways, her tail stirring the flowing water in the river below; she was so absorbed in the loss of the infant Mer, wondering how she could help Ormus to free him, that she failed to realise the danger that was looming upon her.

Simlify looked up from her thoughts to find Mikell looking down upon her, his dark eyes shining with malice. Her heart froze as she saw within his veil of invisibility the ones that were with him, men who looked sinister and unclean and were robed from head to toe; the stench of rotting flesh entered her nostrils. *These creatures are the unwholesome Cunmen that the Otom fear.* Fear of their touch engulfed her and she drew breath sharply. *The Mers are being invaded by the beasts that roam the surface, those without heart and mercy, and having only violent intentions.*

Mikell smiled down at her. 'Simlify, so deep in your thoughts that your devotion to guarding the gate has gone somewhat astray, let me introduce you to my friends.'

The others laughed at his suggestion of politeness and menace, uttered in the same breath.

Mikell moved forward and lifted Simlify from her place at the water's edge. 'We are going to the Cradling where, if you remain silent, we will leave you unharmed.'

Mikell moved ahead of his band of renegades as they made their way along the route that Mikell had taken when first searching for the Cradling. They found the crossroads and a while later were within sight of the unicorn. The beautiful white animal reared as they came into view and the Cunmen stepped back; their sharp intake of breath could be heard in the silence around them. Then they rushed forward wanting to touch the beautiful beast, an animal they had only heard of in fairytales. They crowded onto the river bank, surrounding the unicorn that stood alone. Soon their rough hands were upon him, pulling at his mane; at first the unicorn looked fearful, his nostrils flaring, his eyes looking wildly at the grotesquely distorted humans, their misshapen form clearly visible beneath their robes. All was not well. These poor wretches were dying. The unicorn stood still and focused on the light above his head, willing it to flow into his body and emanate from within. Soon the healing powers bestowed upon him were his to give and he began reflecting the light into the bodies of the throng that surrounded him. One by one they began to heal, and as the transformation took place so each one became aware of the miracle that was taking place. The light was absorbing the disease and banishing it from their bodies. Their hands, which held the unicorn so tightly, became unblemished, while their bodies began to feel healthy and strong.

One caught his reflection in the stillness of the river and dropped to his knees, looking at the reflection of his healthy body, which he had never experienced before. 'Look,' he said to the others, 'look, I am healed. My face, look at my face. I am like Mikell, my face is beautiful,' he cried.

The others let go of the unicorn and knelt beside the water, each one now silenced by the miracle that had just taken place. The unicorn stood motionless, his energy now drained from the evil and disease that had entered his energy field. In the silence that followed, Tamelia appeared above him and soon her rays were flowing down upon the animal. The greyness of his mantle began to whiten again until he stood as strong and vibrant as before, then, as she placed her cloak of invisibility around him, he disappeared from their sight.

Simlify had been tossed to the ground as Mikell realised what was happening. Without success he tried to keep the Cunmen away from the unicorn, as one by one they were restored to good health. Mikell saw his future falling to pieces as the unicorn's power foiled his plan; the band of Cunmen no longer needed to kidnap the Mer infants; they had been given their healing as promised.

The now robust throng of renegades stood naked on the river bank looking at their bodies, each one admiring himself and looking at the others for any differences to their stature and colouring, each one totally fascinated by their uniqueness, which they had never acknowledged before. They had been alike, robed figures all as one, thoughts all as one, and futures all as one. This reasoning had been their culture, their religion, and now they could see a future for each that would be independent of one another, a future that showed promise. The Cunmen had been given a new lease of life, hope, as their new theology – but their minds still remained dark and evil, and now they were a threat to each other; the unicorn could not change that. Tamelia, knowing this, had protected the unicorn with her cloak of invisibility, aware that they would shackle the noble beast and take him with them, bringing about the unicorn's final days on Earth.

Mikell need not have worried for soon the men were ready to move.

'If this is what the power of the unicorn can do, Mikell, then the Mer infants will do so much more to improve our way of life.' The leader who had spoken stood upon the river bank and drew the unicorn's discarded mantle of white and gold silk about him; looking at Mikell with a newfound respect, he said, 'Mikell, lead the way to the Cradling, we're ready to follow you.'

The others on hearing this stood behind the first, their naked bodies in contrast to their finely robed spokesman. 'Lead the way,' they uttered, as two of them hauled Simlify into their now strong arms, one holding her body the other her tail in a rough and undignified way. Simlify was too frightened to struggle, her mind now frozen with fear at what would happen next, and so they began their journey to the Cradling.

Ormus could not contact Simlify after her initial plea for help;

she had been so frightened by the trauma she was experiencing that her mind had shut down to any telepathic communication. Ormus tried again and again but without success, and then a breakthrough; Tamelia engaged her mind with his and immediately he was informed of all that was happening. For the moment he knew that Simlify was safe, but as soon as they reached the Cradling Mikell would take her life. Simlify would be of no use to him once there, and he would extinguish her life and leave her to be found later along with the loss of the Mer infants. That was the only reason Simlify was alive; Mikell had not wanted her to be found murdered at the gate, where they would need to return to exit the city. Ormus knew he was playing a dangerous game by waiting; the Cradling was now a stone's throw away for Mikell.

The council of elders and Zrsiofour called their people to the City of Memories; the assembly was the most significant gathering since the time when Zrsiofour had announced to his race that the future race of mankind was to live among them. Many Otom were now leaving and eventually the rest would follow, then the Mers would be as they were before, but there was still much to be done before the migration to the surface was completed. The Mers would still support the Otom with the food supplies needed for them to remain healthy; they had become accustomed to the food that nourished the Mer people, and it would take a while for them to reintroduce a land diet to their systems, and many more years before the Earth could wholly support them again.

All were now gathering in the great hall of the temple palace, the centre for all knowledge and learning in the City of Memories. The great city was now brimming with the two races, its white buildings full to capacity as everyone waited for the great teachings that would be given over the next few days. All who gathered in the city would receive the teachings however far they were positioned from the temple palace, the teachings being received by the mind and not by the ear. Everyone gathered began to still their minds for the long hours of meditation that would precede the great teachings.

Lia sat in the centre circle of the great hall; she had come before the appointed time to tell the elders and the missing infant's parents all that had taken place in the last few hours, and that she had every hope that Ormus would return the infant to them. The elders listened to Lia with every confidence, for this misfortune had been prophesied. All nodded their approval when she ended her story with the nursing mother's exchange of worlds. Everything was happening just as they had been told it would.

'Trust is such a fragile thing but it has its rewards,' the elders said, turning to the parents of the missing infant; the elders searched deep within their minds, concerned that they might find them troubled and without trust, but they found no such feelings and were satisfied. Returning their attention to Lia, they said, 'We are gladdened by your news, Lia, and have every confidence that all will be well.'

Turning back to the parents, the elders gently dismissed them. 'Ormus will be with us soon, and the teachings can begin. We bid you farewell for now.' The elders bowed their heads graciously and faded from the great hall as a dream fades from the mind on waking.

Lia was left wondering how Ormus would establish Simlify's release from the evil that held her without putting himself in danger; Mikell despised Ormus, who had taught him all he knew, and would delight in attempting to darken Ormus' soul. Ormus must stay focused on Hafnium's plan, not his own settling of scores. Lia's thoughts went to Simlify.

As she accepted her situation, Simlify's fear vanished and the true evilness of Mikell's soul was revealed to her. Her thoughts returned to Ormus and immediately they made contact, his intent becoming crystal clear to her: he would not let Mikell harm her. Simlify felt renewed sadness as she heard Ormus say, *There will be darkness turned upon the Mer world today, but it will not begin with your death.*

Mikell entered the Cradling with the Cunmen following close behind. They were afraid; their healthy bodies had become uncomfortably cold as they walked among the living crystal of which they had never seen the like. The peace and tranquillity made them fretful, an emotion they found hard to understand. The two leaders who had unceremoniously dragged Simlify to the Cradling suddenly dropped her lest she be the reason for their unease. Simlify hit the ground heavily, the pain pulling her from her thoughts. She lay there as the Cunmen continued on without her, then as the last one passed her she pulled her body into a water pool nearby. The Cunmen had barely noticed her as they looked into the water pools filled with Mer infants. A trailing mist began to move amongst the water pools; Simlify turned to greet it, her body making contact, and as she embraced it the mist engulfed her and pulled her down into deeper water. Simlify was safe, secured deep within the chamber of the Cradling from where she could make her way back to Tamelia and the unicorn for a healing. Ormus had done what was needed, and so easy was it that he sighed a deep sigh of relief, a sigh that echoed around the outer chamber like a chill wind that suddenly comes upon you to kiss your cheek.

The Cunmen huddled together for courage, but Mikell barely noticed the events that had just unfolded; he was too busy looking at the infants' gender, as only male infants would be taken. The male infant was the stronger and would survive the journey, whereas the female infants were fragile and needed considerable nurturing prior to adulthood; they were fragile and precious, revered by the Mers as the bearers of future generations.

Mikell had heard Simlify's body crash to the ground but had felt no remorse; he intended to kill her, and so where she lay, hurt or otherwise, was of no interest to him at this moment. Mikell quickly made his decision and gave his orders pointing each of the Cunmen in a certain direction. This time there was no careful Mer angel to lovingly pick the young Mers up, only the rough and disorderly without any concept of how to handle a Mer infant. The infants began to whimper as they sensed the danger that was threatening them.

Mikell lifted the sack that he had carried on the journey, and opening it he began turning out the contents. As the rolls of linen cloth dropped down into the water, he ordered each

Cunman to take a cloth and wrap it around his charge. 'Hurry, we need to be out of here!' Mikell said edgily, having sensed Ormus' presence.

Ormus was indeed in his presence and not far from the entrance to the cave. Ormus waited as the guards from the City of Five Pathways came quietly to stand behind him.

Mikell looked around for Simlify. 'Where is she?'

The two who had been charged with her looked around in panic; if she had escaped there would be a price to pay for both of them.

Mikell sensed Ormus' presence was responsible for Simlify's disappearance. The feeling grew stronger; *Ormus is definitely here.* Mikell waited only long enough for the last of the Cunmen to make safe their charges, and then he stood to his full height and called out to Ormus. 'Ormus, I know you are here and that you have brought help for the infants, but you see you have not been as clever as you thought. You gave me access to the void of zero energy with the cloak of invisibility, but what you are not aware of is that I have learned to throw the cloak much further than you would ever have thought safe to teach me.' Mikell laughed. 'Goodbye, Ormus, you will not stop me, you can never stop me. I am the progeny of Aspheseuos.'

An empty silence remained in the Cradling, and Ormus realised that in the time it had taken him to understand what was happening, Mikell had transported his cargo of Cunmen and Mer infants back to the gate and beyond the City of Five Pathways, afterwards to enter the void and return to the surface to claim the leadership he longed for. Ormus felt the heaviness of another defeat cast its shadow upon his soul, but it was not to dishearten him for long. As he stood beside an empty water pool, Simlify appeared. Placing her hands upon his feet she wept; it was then he remembered how torturous life in mortal flesh could be. Ormus looked down at the tortured soul who was blaming herself for all that had passed. Ormus' spirit stirred.

Smiling, he knelt to take hold of her hands. 'Do not fret so, Simlify, this challenge is not over yet. Make your way back to Tamelia and the unicorn to receive healing to your soul.'

Chapter 42

The Void of Zero Energy

Unseen, Mikell had watched in fury as Ormus initiated Deron and Paul into the knowledge of the void of zero energy. They had been chosen to follow in Lia's footsteps, allowing them to travel unaccompanied between the underworld and the land sites … and in the future to other-worlds. *Key to the void!* Ormus had not sensed the strength of Mikell's fury; Aspheseuos had made sure of it.

As Deron and Paul prepared to return to the surface in search of the infant, they were again summoned before the elders. They were to go to the Halls of Learning where the elders were waiting. Ormus had disappeared again, and Lia was preoccupied with the loss of the Mer infant, the abduction having been made possible while they travelled back in time to the early civilisation of the Mers. Since then everything had been turned upside down. Deron knew that at such times he should leave things well alone; in the brief time that he had seen his mother on their return he had not pressed her on the crisis that had arisen, knowing that her response would reveal little to him, other than that she felt they were partially to blame for having drawn Ormus' attention away from Mikell.

The central hall of learning appeared empty as Deron and Paul waited at the main entrance. Ormus and three elders appeared and took up their places in the centre of the hall, motioning them to come forward and sit with them. A hologram came into view filled with millions of coloured numerals that moved like a swarm of butterflies, and in no particular sequence. Suddenly the movement within the hologram stopped and the numerals hung suspended, as if waiting to be activated again. Deron and Paul looked on expectantly, their minds filled with questions and possibilities.

Pythagoras, the ancient Greek scholar, came into view and the numerals began to move again, forming a spiral above him. Welcoming Deron and Paul, he motioned them forward to sit upon the white stone plinth set before the hologram. Ormus and the three elders came forward and sat on the opposite side of the hologram to face them. Both now realised why they had been called.

Lia had mentioned in passing that Deron and Paul were to receive a special gift but when that would be was dependent upon a change of circumstances. No more had been added to the vague account, which Deron had accepted, having been raised to respect his mother's giving and withholding, and sometimes her taking away.

The hologram widened out as the numerals within began to whirr in a circular motion above Pythagoras' head, and he began to explain the key. 'The key is a mathematical mystery that unlocks the void of zero energy; access to the universe. The key will be required for the Otom to travel within the binary world that connects the underworld with the surface of the Earth. It is extremely simple, as are most things of great importance,' Pythagoras remarked as two triangles appeared with the symbols one to nine and nought upon them; one triangle standing base up, the other base down to form a diamond. Next within the hologram appeared a circle divided into four. In each section were two numerals; the top left contained the numerals one and eight, the top right, seven and two, the bottom left, five and four and the bottom right, six and three, each section adding up to nine. 'Nine is the symbol of unconditional love, from which creation flourished, and Universe Four's duality remains balanced.' Pythagoras smiled in pleasure; he loved to see the students' awareness blossom. 'The division of the circle represents the universal building symbol, four ... and the circle represents zero, the space between all that is created. These numerals, entered as a sequence of codes into the mind of the chosen key holder, will connect them to the spatial energy of the universe. A thought is all that is needed to direct them where they wish to be within Universe Four.'

Pythagoras motioned Deron forward and into the hologram, and as Paul looked on he was asked to key in the first two symbols in the circle, one and eight. Deron did so and the section moved upwards and the quarter circle became a triangle. The triangle decreased in size, moving as it did so towards the centre of Deron's forehead, absorbing into the third eye. The same process was repeated with the second section, seven and two, the triangle vanishing into the centre of Deron's forehead, there to be contained within his DNA. The final two sections changed shape as Deron was asked to repeat the numerals within, each code becoming part of his subliminal memory. As the stages were repeated with the last two quarter circles, the four triangles slid together to form a pyramid; the key was complete; the sides of the pyramid opened to expose the centre square, the void of zero energy, connection to the 'all'. Pythagoras remained vigilant while the simple codes that had been passed on began to play out trillions of mathematical sequences that Deron was unaware of, only his soul would understand and use these codes.

Mikell had not remained to see Paul bestowed with his gift; he was away with the sequence of the codes planted firmly in his mind. Aspheseuos had made sure he would never forget the equation; his use of its knowledge was to bring him too much power for that to happen.

Mikell was back among the Cunmen at Belsize Creek and Ormus wanted to observe the events that were being played out. The band of Cunmen that had entered the City of Five Pathways were now physically healthy, and the stolen Mer infants would soon be used to bring a waiting army back to physical health. As Ormus observed this injustice he wondered if Hafnium's conscience ever wavered from balance. His thoughts were that if he were the grand master he would be tempted to side with the innocent, but then he was a fragment of Hafnium's consciousness, and it was Hafnium's remembering him that allowed him to be. Never would he have vision enough to see true balance, only his part of it.

Chapter 43

Mikell's Return to Belsize Creek

Aries had grown impatient. *What is Hafnium thinking of? To allow Mikell this knowledge will only lead to catastrophe.*

Aries may at times have been rash, but he had a finely tuned sense of fair play, and was not willing to overlook this injustice which would hamper his plans to help the Otom.

Ormus appeared before him. 'Aries, try to be patient. Not one of those helping the Otom is happy with this turn of events.'

'It is as if Hafnium is playing into the hands of Aspheseuos,' Aries replied hotly. 'What is happening?' Lightning streaks of scarlet rolled out across the cosmos, waking the being, Mars.

'Rein in your displeasure, Aries. Why are you so angry? Surely this will make the challenge more interesting and your victory the better for it.'

'I want to get on with the challenge,' he answered, his manner improving with the counsel given by Mars, 'then I can get on with the many other things I have planned.' He shrugged. 'At this pace I shall be beyond my time to help before we've begun.'

'Very well, Aries,' Ormus said wearily. His way was that of calmness and thinking things through, and then digesting matters, and then finally making a decision. Ormus was a true Leo. 'What have you planned?'

Aries laughed eagerly; he had Ormus' attention. Aries liked nothing better than to lead his opponent around in circles, sending them along the wrong pathway while he looked on with satisfaction and great amusement. Aries' plan for the Cunmen would be just that. 'I have a plan that will send the Cunmen flying in all directions and the Otom will not have to raise a finger to them.'

'Well, go on; I'm all ears,' said Ormus quietly, interested in the fact that Aries' plan was without bloodshed for the new tribe of man.

'My idea is to use those of your worlds.'

'And how do you mean to use us?'

'Sit a while, my friend, and I will tell you,' Aries said laughing, keenness exuding from his mortal likeness; he ran his hand through his hair, pushing it back from his face and tossing his head to one side as he did so. 'Now then, Ormus, pay attention, for this is the plan.'

Mikell and the Cunmen were back at Belsize Creek. Those who were healed were in awe of the mastery of the one called Mikell; he was without doubt the one to be their leader. They could talk of nothing else; all thoughts of treachery towards him had been wiped from their minds. Without him to lead them, they felt they would be doomed. Mikell was the prophet they had waited for, the one whose coming was foretold.

Mikell, amid this sudden and overwhelming support, realised with great pleasure that he was back in control. Suddenly things were escalating at a tremendous speed; he had not bargained for the Cunmen being healed, but there was now no need to get the leaders to the first infant. The Cunmen had kidnapped enough infants to raise an army to health in a few short weeks, and if needed, they would go back for more infants. Things were not exactly going to plan, but he was in a better position than he had hoped for.

While Mikell had been attending to the kidnapping, the Cunmen had been busy building an aquarium that would support the life of the Mer infants, or at least for long enough for the healing of an army. Mikell was not concerned that the tank would not be built for long-term survival; there were plenty more infants if needed. The Cradling was unique, the only one on Earth of its kind, and it would always hold Mer infants. Mikell's present concern was that while he was away, Aquarius, under orders from Aspheseuos, had done a good job of getting the Cunmen organised and had altered his plans.

Aquarius was feeling confident; Mikell's existence as leader of the Cunmen would be short-lived, and he would be needed. Having lived all his life in surroundings of stability and peace, a seemingly suffocating existence to Aquarius, Mikell was now drawn into a life of tension and fear, whereupon a dangerous hormone was being released throughout his body. Mikell had little knowledge of just how deadly the hormone adrenaline could be to the human body, especially in large and constant doses. There would be no need for Aspheseuos to terminate their contract; Mikell would oblige with his early death. Aquarius sat back to reflect on his lack of compassion for the Otom defector.

Glashadou and Odelia Cavil had been roaming the other-worlds when the word had come from Ormus that Aries was now in place and understood his task. Aries' plan was to ask for support from the other-worlds, from those that had departed from the physical world and now continued to expand their knowledge in other ways. Within a moment of the thought leaving his consciousness, Ormus' old companions were beside him.

Aries greeted Odelia with affection for she was of his nature; they understood one another perfectly. With Glashadou he was more formal. Glashadou's nature was that of Scorpio, one that was too complex and far too deep for Aries to fathom. However, Odelia was a true companion to Glashadou, and they were inseparable.

Aries stood before them with his plan; he wanted to waste nothing of this opportunity to show himself as a true leader. Aries beckoned them closer as though to foil any attempt to overhear.

'My plan is this,' he said excitedly. 'We know that from the beginning of time man has always feared the nature of spirit, which only the gifted could see and most definitely could not touch.' Aries roared with laughter as one by one he saw the manifestations of his mischief. 'I want you and your kind to go among the Cunmen and show yourselves in such ways that will send them scurrying back into their robes to shake until they are exhausted from fear. That will keep them occupied while the Otom emerge and gather themselves into the new cities, and once started it will then be up to each emerging star to use their special ways to keep the Cunmen in hand. Meanwhile I can begin the attack in such a subtle and ingenious way as to make the Otom feel confident with those that they are dealing with, the Cunmen. The Mers from the underworld will be the first to help.' Aries finished without explaining his last comment, pleased with himself and his campaign speech.

'Sounds good to me!' said Glashadou, raising an eyebrow as he looked tongue in cheek across at Odelia.

'I see,' said Odelia, who could be as blunt and insensitive as any Aries. 'You want our kind to materialise upon the Earth's continents to do this to the Cunmen?' Odelia put her hands to her head and waggled her fingers while exposing a nice pink tongue and making noises like a lofty night owl. Glashadou fell back into the cosmos and roared with laughter, whilst Ormus put his hand to his face trying to hide the smile that had planted itself there. Aries was clearly offended and gave a short sniff and then another, a sign that he was truly vexed.

'No! I did not mean that exactly,' he said coolly, not looking at Odelia while addressing her. 'I thought your kind might be able to come up with something a little more extraordinary.' The word 'kind' was said with light contempt and everyone understood his meaning perfectly.

Glashadou and Odelia were under no misapprehensions; they could see that Aries was about to take off and Ormus would be left without his help. Quickly they gathered their thoughts together and began to placate Aries.

'Aries, I must apologise.' said Odelia. 'You know I have the greatest respect for your ingenuity and I think your plan is brilliant, and to protect the Otom from violence and bloodshed, yes, brilliant, my dear, brilliant.'

Aries smiled. Most definitely he held grudges very deeply but at this moment it would appear that he had forgiven them.

'That is fine then. I have done my work and the plan is there for you to act upon, and if you follow it to the letter you will not go wrong.'

The three answered together. 'I am sure you are right.'

'Let us have the coordinates of what is to happen where and with whom,' said Ormus, 'and then we will leave you to return to your planning of other things, Aries, for it is nearing the time for Taurus to awaken. Thank you.'

'Yes, thank you once again, Aries,' said Glashadou and Odelia as they settled back to receive the finer details of Aries' plan.

The Cunmen, with Aquarius' inspiration, had built the aquarium for the Mer infants, not as Mikell had instructed at Belsize Creek but in an area known as the Tennessee Cumberland Watershed. There would arise many flaws in Mikell's powers of leadership, flaws that were already manifesting in his efforts to take power. As each step was taken he was losing his hold. The things that had gone wrong had not been detrimental to the plan, but now that Aquarius had stepped in and changed the location of the aquarium, his anxiety had increased and with it his ability to think clearly.

Although the Mers could live in the ocean and survive for long periods of time, the nature of their world was that of fresh water. For that reason Aquarius had opposed Mikell's plan and chosen the Tennessee Watershed where the Mer infants would be in an environment not unlike the one they were used to. Aquarius had known that the infants' chance of survival in an aquarium was nonexistent. Cramped and stagnant, it would have killed them within days, and this lack of knowledge was where Mikell's leadership fell foul. Mikell because of his contempt for the fish people had learned nothing of their race, their culture and their fragility. Mikell was a leader without wisdom or compassion, and it was these deficiencies that would be his downfall.

Chapter 44

The Teachings of the Ancients

The Otom elders and King Zrsiofour were calling their races together; the meditation that preceded the teachings had begun. All gathered had created a place of serenity within, a space that was their own. This preparation was a time of great dedication to one's inner spirit, to cast aside the awareness of the flesh and allow the spirit freedom to explore the veiled unconsciousness. In the few days prior to the teachings neither race had consumed solid food, only drinking water to cleanse the body and clear the mind for the long meditation to follow; a once in a lifetime change was coming to the Earth that would affect both races, and it was important that they be of one mind during the teachings.

An eerie silence settled over the City of Memories, a city taken down into the kingdom of Zrsiofour when man could no longer be trusted to walk in the midst of the mystical citadel and learn the wisdom of its ancient teachings. The Holocene "wise ones" had been cast aside and man had reverted to the ways of the beast, and Aspheseuos had become master of the Earth again.

Lia sat beside Mary; she had come to be with her at this important time. Mary had no trouble with fasting; she had not eaten since the death of Senithe, but that was not Lia's concern. She knew that Mary was in turmoil over her nephew Mikell and the disgrace he had brought upon their race, but mostly over the lie she had told to Ormus to protect him; this grieved her most and she was unable to find forgiveness in her heart for the one who needed her forgiveness most, herself.

Lia leaned towards Mary and placed her hands upon her head, one palm to her forehead and one to the base of her skull. 'Mary dear, you must let go. Forgive yourself, release your mind and listen to the teachings of the future. If you do not fill your heart with forgiveness then you will not receive the teachings. You are a part of our destiny that has made the future possible. Hafnium, the grand master, chose you to give Mikell to the world. It was you that cradled the seed of Aspheseuos without malice and with all the love your heart could give. Everyone, everything, has its rightful place in destiny's plan, Mary, you know that; it is in the teachings of the ancients. One of the reasons our soul enters bodily life is to experience physical emotion. Life must have struggle, without it what would be the point?' Lia became quiet; what else could she say? She knew that only those who connected this day to receive the future teachings would be migrating to the Earth's surface in the next few days. Those left behind would face the teachings again at some point, and would then be allowed to join the Otom on the surface. When first the Holocenes had arrived on Earth, Hafnium, the grand master, had spoken in his teachings of a time when man would move out into the universe. That time would not come until strong negative emotions were a thing of the past for the whole of the Otom race.

Mary sensed Lia's concern; heaven forgive her if she was to stop Lia from receiving the teachings.

Lia attempted to calm her thoughts. 'That is not so, Mary. I am ready to receive the teachings. I have waited for this day when the Otom would return to the surface, where his physical body would become strong again beneath the sun's light.'

A light filtered into the room and Tamelia, ruler of the Mer angels stood before them and behind her followed more of her kind, their dappled colours merging into one another as gossamer flames of sapphire, amethyst and emerald.

Such peacefulness, thought Mary. Suddenly her mind began to open like the petals of a rose and her heavy heart to lighten; Mary thought of Mikell and murmured a remembered teaching. 'However black a person's heart may seem, when they are ready for transformation then the light will pierce the darkness and light will enter. They say that Moses experienced the taking of life at one time in his life. I love you, Mikell; I will always love you,' whispered Mary as she slipped into the blissful realms of deep meditation.

Lia was waiting for her where nothing experienced in life can be similar, a timeless place when you are truly at one with the sacred oneness of the universe.

Ormus entered the peaceful manifestation of the two races' combined thoughts; he wanted to find a way to win Mikell back, if there was a way. The unexplainable love that surrounded him was the answer, but he had never been able to make Mikell understand this, just as Mary had never been able to reach him. Ormus had taught Mikell most of what he knew, although sometimes a little distorted from the truth in order to protect the Otom and the Mers. Ormus realised there was only one thing left to do; when they met in the dreamtime he would show him the truth. Ormus had taught him that a meeting with someone familiar in the dreamtime was a gift of pure truth from which to unravel vital information regarding the self.

Mikell had never recognised the shadow personalities within himself; there was too much anger, too much distortion of his character to access the true self successfully. Ego ruled his subconscious mind, and while in the dream state his higher self would try to reach him, his shadow personalities would play a game of charades in which a maze of unintelligible information would keep him restless by night and anxious by day. Now at this most important time it was the same scenario being shown to him; the warning was there, if only he was able to decipher the message hidden in his dreams.

On waking Mikell took only the factual information being given and not the underlying message. Now the leaders were in place at the Tennessee Watershed and awaiting the throng of the blemished. The infants were in the substitute Cradling awaiting the onslaught of Cunmen for healing, an undertaking that would diminish their life expectancy to that of death in infancy. This was his dream, and for him the right way forward. Mikell had failed to see the warning that the slaughter of the infants was wrong, or that that warning was given with so much love from Ormus and Mary, whom his dream had changed to Aquarius and Aspheseuos, to make him think he was right.

The Tennessee Watershed had flourished despite the ravages of the holocaust; the winds towards the Americas had been favourable after the moment of devastation, and for many years to follow in that part of the world nature had been saved from the worst of the fallout. The lush undergrowth and temperate freshwater ecosystem meant it was one of the first sites chosen by the Otom to acclimatise once more to life on the Earth's surface.

Makot made the journey to the Tennessee Watershed; having entrusted him with the Mer infant, Mikell knew he would protect the infant from the Cunmen. Makot was now deeply bonded with the infant and had already decided that his infant, as he now looked upon him, would not be used for the healing of others in his tribe.

The Cunmen were dragging their pitiless bodies from all corners of the Earth where they roamed, scavenging anything of use to them and their survival. Thousands were coming from the dead regions of Europe and Asia, and the upper regions of Africa, all now desert and waste scrubland, and still deeply scarred by the ending of days in the holy land. Soon things were to change, they felt it, and they felt hopeful as they made their journey across the barren landscape and the frozen wastes of Siberia, their journey taking them across the frozen ocean and on to the destination that was to change their lives forever. The Cunmen kept on going, the evil in their minds keeping them alive; alive for the rewards that surviving the journey would bring.

Taurus reared his bullish head, the warmth of a golden orange hue surrounding him; he was doing what he liked doing best, indulging himself. Taurus, like Capricorn, was symbolic of the earth and like her bestowed growth upon the earth. Taurus was to continue the challenge for the Otom's survival, and like her, he would protect the Earth's chosen people come what may. Taurus liked the plan that Aries had set up; it sounded possible, first-rate. He liked everything to work well, and if it was working for him, then it was working for everyone, no argument about that. His nature was loud and hearty and he loved to have fun. Slowly his eyes moved from side to side as he visualised the events taking place; the Cunmen were dragging their weary bodies halfway round the world on the promise of a great victory and many spoils. Taurus gave a mighty bellow of laughter. 'Only to be sent fleeing by some crazy spirits from the other-worlds.' Taurus let out another bellow and the heavens shook. He had just awakened and began to indulge himself in some favourite foods of the gods; he loved to be busy at work or at play when it was his time in the cosmos. April and May had been the Earth's time to blossom and he wanted her to be happy and content again as any waiting mother should be, dreaming of the life that was about to be renewed from within her. As far as Taurus was concerned, nothing in the way of strife was going to upset her healing body, he would make sure of that, and at the same time he could have some fun while helping the Otom emerge from the underworld. Taurus leaned back to bathe in the glow of the cosmos. 'It will be a bountiful season. I've no doubt about that.'

Chapter 45

The Invisible Cloak of Dictatorship

Odelia Cavil listened to Aries' plans carefully. She had her doubts but heard him through; the change must arrive peacefully. She did not want to see the Otom pass into the other-worlds after another futile human battle; the Otom were precious to the restocking of the Earth with humans of a peaceful nature. The animal kingdom was beginning to reappear from behind Hafnium's cloak of invisibility, and as promised its inhabitants would remain unharmed if the Cunmen were returned to spirit in as peaceable a way as could be managed.

Odelia's thoughts went back to when she had first taken charge of the young Lia after her awakening. Lia, who in her own world, Holocene, was held in high esteem by her people, as she was by the Otom now. The transformation bestowed upon Lia by the Mer angels had taken place just before the end of Ormus' final lifetime upon Earth, and it had not been many years after his death that public unrest worldwide had escalated to catastrophic proportions of iniquity and mayhem. A cloak of invisible dictatorship had swallowed up the whole of Europe, intimidating any country that opposed its monetary rulings, and leaving many European countries financially ruined and their people up in arms. With their allies the French, Germany had finally won a peaceful war of European supremacy; it was again a dark time for England. England by the unanimous agreement of her populace had voted to leave Europe behind. In a profound statement from the newly elected government, it was announced to the world that what had been an extremely bad marriage of minds and purpose was over; England would be withdrawing, along with five other countries, from Europe's rule; divorce was the only way forward. The future appeared set as the six reinstated their borders. In the months that followed a powerful game of illusion was played out by both sides, with the withdrawing governments believing they stood alone, or so it seemed. Wars had been raging in the Middle East for many years and with each day they grew worse; violence, bloodshed and death had become an everyday occurrence. England, the United States of Europe and America, having intervened in the rule of the tyrannical dictators in the Middle East, finally yielded to the newly formed governments' demands for a return to self-rule. Hell broke loose from that day as tribal leaders were handed back power to continue taking the lives of those who were not of their thinking. The end of days was approaching its time.

Odelia remembered how panicked the lightworkers had been; those who were to survive were not making 'the journey', uncertain, wanting to stay, thinking that all would be well if they remained. Lia and her family had left immediately after the birth of her daughter, leaving their much loved home, the Causeway, empty. Odelia could have gone with them but had stayed in her London home with her only family, her cousins Lilly and Joseph. They knew they were to journey to another place and had waited for the light of the atom bomb as it made the journey high above Europe before falling back to Earth to take them in its wake; no pain as she remembered, just light, and then Ormus and her family welcoming her to a new life in the other-worlds.

Odelia's passion for a new era of peace to begin upon Earth spilled over; she stood up and with resolve she said loudly, 'It is time for the Otom to move forward. The Cunmen must leave this world without one drop of the new tribe of man's blood being spilt; yes indeed, and the Mer infants will survive and be returned to their world.'

The Cunmen had been trying to infiltrate the Causeway for some time; the building of the new site had made them uneasy and aggressive and wanting a battle. With the first of the perimeter walls going up and the old house showing signs of life again, strange-looking humans, similar to those seen in old books and pictures, began to appear. The Cunmen had become fearful, sensing their territory was being invaded by people from the past. Within a short time the site had become a city and the extended perimeter defences impenetrable. More strangers had come to the new city, and with all that they needed to survive comfortably. The arc of light from the crystal rainbow had turned the darkness surrounding the new city to a glowing radiance, keeping them at bay. Exposure to the source of light caused extreme pain for the Cunmen that tried to group nearby, and had caused death for those that ignored it. They knew the danger yet were drawn to these people and their apparent abundance of comfort and supplies.

Odelia entered the house to find Dorri alone in the kitchen. Dorri sat motionless; she had sensed the deep meditative pull that was vibrating from the world of the Mers below. The time was gathering when the city would be brimming with life, young and old alike, yet this time was one of loneliness for her. Lia was busy with the coming migration and the boys were down in the underworld, safe until all was accomplished and the Cunmen were no longer a threat to them.

Dorri often sat in the kitchen when she was on her own; it was comforting to dream of the family at breakfast or the boys in the garden. Often she would hear their voices even though they were not there.

Odelia entered and stood before her. At first Dorri could not see her but Odelia concentrated her image upon Dorri's mind; suddenly she jumped from her daydreaming as the image of the stout lady with a sprouting head of green hair came into view.

'Hello, I'm Odelia, Odelia Cavil?' she said in her lively manner. Glashadou appeared beside her as if for support, not that Odelia needed any. Being reticent was not part of her nature.

The apparition took Dorri by surprise, but did not frighten her.

Dorri had become accustomed to strange things happening when Lia was in residence, but never when she was left alone in the house.

'This is Glashadou,' said Odelia. 'We are Lia's friends and have come to put your mind at rest, to tell you what will be happening over the next few days. The house will be full, but not with those you love and care for so expertly. It will be filled with our kind, from the other-worlds, who will help the Otom relocate to the land.' Odelia smiled. 'I am sure, Dorri, you will find the whole sequence of events very entertaining.' Odelia continued on without a pause, as was her way.

'Yes, very entertaining,' Glashadou said in his quick and energetic way.

'So let us entertain you. I'm sure you have some time to spare?' Odelia sat down at the table to tell Dorri what she might expect.

Chapter 46

The Chosen Ones

Lia and Mary sat quietly together waiting for the teachings to begin. Mary had made her peace with Mikell's betrayal and the unconditional love she felt for her nephew had returned; a pure love for the spirit that resided within Mikell's mortal body, which had engaged every evil human emotion, and what it might accomplish.

In the great hall, Ormus and the Otom elders had assembled before the spirit form of Zrsiofour. The Mers had also gathered in spirit form; they were ocean people and the City of Memories was built for the footsteps of man.

Pythagoras came forward to give the teachings of Hafnium, the grand master; the Greek mathematician and philosopher standing high upon a marble plinth before those gathered. Above him the Mer angels began to assemble, bringing with them a blaze of colour that reflected across the pristine white walls of the great hall. The air was still as all gathered waited upon the words to be spoken; in the gardens beyond the great hall, peace and solitude surrounded the temple halls as those gathered became silent, the silence swelling outward between the serene white buildings as far as the eye could see, out to the perimeter of the great city that housed all the knowledge of Universe Four, knowledge lost to mankind long before the holocaust.

Pythagoras began by speaking of a time before man came to the world of the Mers. 'This was a time when the United States of America was a source of doubt in the world, its force being seen as bullish and violent, the nation cushioned from the outside world by its apparent wealth and lack-for-nothing culture. Like the Roman Empire before it, it cast a powerful shadow over the world, its economy always ten years ahead of the rest of humanity. The scriptures had foretold that America would become the spiritual anchor of the future, the American race having integrated the customs of all races. No other world continent had been as successful at merging many races into one ideology. They were the blueprint for the Otom.' Pythagoras felt the pulse of minds that were attuned to his teachings; he sensed their feelings of puzzlement at this part of history that now seemed to have very little relevance to their future. They were of one mind, and ready to embrace the knowledge to be found in the outer reaches of the universe, ready to meet those whose lives were based on these teachings. Why would they need to know of an America that was?

Pythagoras continued aware of the thoughts that hung over the gathering, reminding them of the nature of America, how it had evolved through much bloodshed and the near extinction of the original American race. 'But time changes all, and as all races poured onto the American continent, so they merged into one. The American race was born from the good and bad of all races. They were the ones chosen to begin mankind's final chapter upon Earth. The United States of America was a world superpower that was the envy of the world. They were the chosen multicultural race.' Pythagoras stopped for a moment to allow these thoughts to absorb into the single consciousness of the two races present. 'And so it was that long ago many of the chosen ones from all races migrated to America because it was written that when the last days of that time came they would survive and be returned to a land of abundance, the American continent. Others have joined them and integrated into one, from which the Otom race has evolved to become as the Mers, with one philosophy, one belief in Hafnium, creator of Universe Four. Many of you who are ready for the migration will be returning to the Americas. You will take with you a feeling of hope as did the first immigrants, and like them you will face challenges, but this time without bloodshed. To the continents of the north and east only a few will be resettled because the Earth has yet to heal.' Pythagoras turned his thoughts to the Mer race. 'Tomorrow you will take back your stolen infants, be assured of this. They must be returned to the Cradling, and for this to happen the Mermen must challenge the Cunmen. Those chosen to go will make their way to the Tennessee Watershed where the infants are being held and return them to the City of Five Pathways. You will go alone, without the help of the Otom.'

The people of both races remained in the consciousness of the whole to give strength to the Mers who were to make the perilous journey. Pythagoras sensed the bond of love that united the two races, the breaking down of all resistance that the flesh gives to the spirit, washing away all thoughts of self, leaving the spirit free to be as one thought, this thought being of victory and the safe return of the infants.

Ormus' spirit and soul entered the whole; he must be sure they would not waver, and yet still, with some, he could feel fear of facing the unknown. If any were to falter and the whole to break apart, then the Mermen chosen would be in danger of losing their lives. Ormus felt a deepening dread for the chosen Mermen, followed by an appalling vision. The Cunmen were darkness itself and would show no mercy to the Mers. The only thing that would keep them at bay would be the light consciousness of the whole; Ormus prayed they would hold together. There was promise of a wonderful future, man would be free of his confinement below the earth, yet still some had not the faith to see the challenges through. *Is man ready?* Quickly Ormus pushed the thought from his mind, but it was too late. In that moment of doubt his thoughts had mingled with the masses; he now felt the surge of shame within the whole as they received his doubting them. Swiftly their thoughts cleared to become strong, courageous and full of faith. Ormus' gaze embraced them; *Thank you*, he said. If Ormus had been in front of his army giving the final words of command, it could not have gone better. *You intended that I should forget their bond of love. You are so wise in the chance mistakes that move us back and forth across the universe to bring balance, Hafnium. Thank you, again*, he whispered.

Hafnium listened with sadness; Ormus had not heeded the vision but instead had chosen to believe what he wanted to hear. Suddenly Ormus was jolted from his peaceful state …

Lia began to stir; she was aware of Mary's sudden pulling from the whole. Ormus' gentle voice came to her. 'Leave us and follow Mary.' Lia did as Ormus asked; instantly she was fully conscious and sitting beside Mary, who was now crying softly to herself.

'It will be me, I will be the one, I will be the Judas that causes the death of the Mermen; I feel it and know it in my heart.' Mary's voiced trailed off in disbelief. Disillusionment and bitterness had enveloped her as she delved into her deepest consciousness; *I will never keep the whole intact; my thoughts are not pure enough.* Mikell entered her thoughts constantly, and she felt compelled to listen. What had she done to have this heartbreak thrust upon her?

Lia took her hand. 'Mary, you have been tested deeply in your life, and always for someone else's needs, never your own. Find peace within yourself for you cannot change destiny. You must take heart and recognise that with each twist of fate you will do the right thing with good intent, whatever the outcome.'

Mary stopped crying, reassured by the words that Lia spoke to reconcile her with the future; she began to relax as a feeling of tenderness encircled her. Gently she drifted back into the consciousness of the whole, leaving behind the struggle with her conscious thoughts, the place where Mikell always sought her. Idly the worries floated through Mary's mind without her wanting to control them. This time she would trust, whatever the outcome.

As the City of Memories lay still in quiet reflection, the Mers that were to free the infants were awakening from the whole; they gathered to fight under the command of Zrsiofour.

Chapter 47

The Tennessee Watershed

Zrsiofour was ready to leave. The Mermen under his command had never been drawn into conflict before, their race having known only a peaceful way of life. Now they were to fight because of a human who had brought conflict to their world, one who had killed an innocent and stolen their infants. Together, they tried to gather courage in the face of the unknown. The small army of Mers gathered in the Indian Ocean from where they would begin their journey across the seas. Passing Madagascar, Zrsiofour's fleet moved on around the African continent into the Atlantic Ocean and northward towards the Tennessee Cumberland Watershed.

As the Mers came into view of the area they were looking for, Zrsiofour gave his orders and the Mermen began to split up. Some were to find the infants, and after the rescue they were to return them to the City of Five Pathways without waiting for the others. Zrsiofour's vessel was to be used for this purpose, it being the most powerful and swift in the fleet. Zrsiofour would return with his men when all that Hafnium had commanded was accomplished; those that had taken the infants were to be slain; the Mers were to experience the taking of life. Zrsiofour held this in his heart with anguish; he did not understand why Hafnium commanded this. Why, when the Mers were beyond such things, would there be a need for this experience? Perhaps they had been left in a 'Garden of Eden' for too long, and it was time for the Mers to evolve into something else, but what? The only thing he understood was that there was no going back. He must obey Hafnium.

Word had come from the Otom site nearest to the Tennessee Cumberland Watershed that Mikell intended to pollute the area surrounding the infants once the work was completed, leaving them and the ecosystem to die a slow death; such was his careless and barbaric misuse of nature and life.

Makot looked down at the infant in his safe keeping; he felt uneasy and knew that something was wrong. Makot's premonition was sound, for deep beneath where the infant was cradled, Zrsiofour's army was ready to move and waiting only for the word of their king. Among the Mermen was the father of the stolen infant, whose thoughts were constantly searching for him. The infant stirred, he felt the presence of his own kind and the bonding that comes only with one's father; in his tiny consciousness recognition stirred and he murmured as if to make his presence known to the one who was seeking him. Makot picked the infant up and cradled him knowing that something had disturbed him. As if his thoughts were answered there came a shout from the perimeter of the wetland where the infants were being held; one of the men patrolling the bank had disappeared into the murky waters, then just as silently another. In the panic that followed, the line of Cunmen entering the water to be healed broke ranks, each one determined to touch an infant and get out of the water as quickly as possible.

Makot clasped his charge tightly in his arms while trying to fight off the Cunmen who came rushing towards him from all directions. The infants were seized from the nursing mothers' arms, women who were now whole and, like Makot, were reluctant to hand over their charges. The women screamed in pain as multiple fists rained down upon them in order that they might relinquish their charges. The infants were tossed among the men, all wanting to touch them, all wanting to be healed. As the Cunmen regained their health they became aware that something else was going on; more men were disappearing beneath the water and their ranks were thinning rapidly. Panic ensued as they bellowed out too late a warning: the Mermen appeared from below the water like airborne dolphins, hurling their bodies at the Cunmen and drowning them with one thrust of their powerful tails, while others seized the infants before disappearing beneath the foaming water. For the first time the Mers were taking life. It was an easy victory; strong tails lashed out at the struggling men whose natural habitat was land, not water.

In the night air a loud bang rang out followed by another. The infant in Makot's arms shuddered as a moment in time left its mark upon the tiny infant's memory; he heard a cry ring out from his father.

The bullet tore through his chest, the force flipping him over onto his back. The stunned Merman lay still, looking up at the velvet blue sky wherein the stars shone brightly. The noise of the battle began to dim and the pain to subside. The soft whimper of his precious infant surrounded him; pain filled his heart and then began to fade, his thoughts becoming peaceful. The stars dulled in the velvet blue sky as he slipped beyond the Earthly life to the other-worlds where his ancestors were waiting to welcome him.

The Merman lay half submerged in the water. Around him Mermen hurriedly gathered the infants, unaware that he was dead, while others fought desperately to keep the Cunmen at bay, holding them beneath the water until near death and then raising them up again, still finding the taking of life abominable. Moments later the infants were free of their captors and the Mermen had disappeared. Swimming down beneath the bank of the temporary cradling they moved silently along the water passages that would lead them out into the open sea and to Zrsiofour's waiting vessel.

Makot, still clutching his charge, had hidden beneath the dense vegetation; he would not give up 'his' infant. Now he watched in horror those that the Mers had spared as they screamed in fury because of the empty cradling, their chance of renewed health now a fruitless dream. Makot's body froze; *they must not find my infant.* Crouching motionless on the ground, he watched as the next horrific event was played out before his eyes. The Cunmen were looking for revenge. They began to fight viciously among themselves, each one blaming the others for their loss. With Mikell and the leaders at Belsize Creek, they would have killed each other had one not noticed the limp body of the half submerged Mer. Within an instant a murderous cry had gone up and the Merman was dragged from the water; within seconds they had all set upon the lifeless form lest any life or feeling could be found within. They took his body and shackled his tail and then they hauled him high, Makot watched in horror as they hacked his torso from his tail, the cradled infant now wide-eyed and still.

As Makot opened his eyes he thanked the heavens for daylight; the previous night he had watched the rabble feast upon the tail of the Mer. Did he really belong in this world of nightmares? The infant lay still; he had not moved since the night before. Makot feared he might be dead. Not wanting the infant to cry but wanting him to move, he gently submerged him in the water; the infant opened his eyes but did not murmur. *The Earth has such a fragile diversity of life.* Makot realised that something within him had changed; he had realised love. The infant had lost his healing power; Makot sensed this as he looked down at him. *I love him, and will keep him as my own.*

As Makot looked up from his revelation he noticed a purple mist beginning to form and rise high above the surface of the cradling. The mist moved across the surface of the water towards the sleeping Cunmen on the bank; having gorged upon the Merman's flesh, they were now sound asleep. Makot watched as the purple mist began to take on form, and the Mer warriors from the City of Five Pathways began to emerge. They swept forward in the morning mist towards the sleeping Cunmen. Rapidly the mist became a watery grave as the Cunmen, on waking from their sleep, began to choke upon the cloak of water. They writhed and fought the invisible enemy as their lungs filled with water; some stood up and tried to run, wanting to leave the mist behind, but wherever they went so it followed, until all was silent again. Makot held his breath as the Mer warriors disappeared beneath the still waters, leaving the lifeless bodies of the Cunmen strewn upon the water-logged bank. Makot staggered to his feet, wondering why he was still alive.

The infant began to cry, the sound one of helplessness. The infant was without the use of language to express his pain, without the strength to defend himself, and those that had protected him were gone, leaving him without the love that he had known from birth, and his father, a loved one who could never be replaced.

The mist began to return; Makot stared with unbelieving eyes as the Cunmen's ethereal bodies lifted from their gruesome cloaks of flesh. 'No more,' Makot screamed, burying his face in the infant's covers; had they come back for him? Dropping to his knees, he opened his eyes. A light was fast approaching, its radiance pure white. Quickly he placed the infant in the thicket and scrambled away, terrified by what he had seen. The infant sensed the omnipresent love that the light brought with it, and a vision of his father's soul entered his innocent mind; a language formed in music, soothing and strong, that he could understand, told him his time of suffering would soon be over. The smell of his mother's nearness enveloped him, reassuring him that he was to be returned to her. The melody continued to play, dancing upon rainbows of colour, as the infant's father told him that this was the beginning of their relationship, not the end. The future would embrace an alliance between the worlds of man and spirit, preparing both the Mers and the Otom for the time when they would leave their physical cloak behind, and he would return many times in his son's lifetime, and each would see the other clearly. The infant began to sleep; a sleep that would protect him through the last part of his ordeal.

Makot was now in the throes of madness after seeing the bringers of death take his kind, and his sanity. Later, Mikell found Makot near the empty cradling, rambling about angels and demons.

'You will pay, Ormus,' Mikell cursed. 'You will pay!' All appeared lost; the infants were gone and there was more bad news at Belsize Creek. There had been an attack on the depot, and Mikell had recognised the leader of the attack as Deron. Mikell stood looking down into the empty cradling. 'So Deron is now a commander of legions; the whimpering infant of Lia, who is always compliant to the words of the elders and the Otom laws. I will have my revenge, Deron, and your mother will know my wrath as well.'

Mary stirred within her peaceful slumber, her forehead creasing into a frown; both she and Lia had received Mikell's thoughts as they came through like an arrow of vengeance. Lia's voice drew close to quiet her fear.

'Be still, Mary, all will be well.'

Mary's troubled thoughts drifted back into nothingness, the frown disappearing from her face.

Chapter 48

The Light of Hafnium – Taurus

The Cunmen hovered over the bodies that lay strewn upon the ground, wondering what they should do and why they could see themselves asleep on the bank. Then they recalled the scenes of nightmarish proportion that had floated through their unconscious minds, remembering in the depth of a troubled sleep, their bodies heavy with gorging on the Merman, their death from drowning in a wall of water. They had awakened fearing that something was wrong; had they fallen into the water? They were drowning, each one gasping for breath, the pain in their lungs excruciating. The choking sensation seemed to go on endlessly, and then peace. Now they remembered. They were dead! A light appeared before them that at first glowed dimly but then gathered strength, its boundary extending to enclose them. From within the light, idiom without structure spoke to them, a feeling, a voice as deep as thunder, or as silent as the wind, or as soft as the rain, all of these things they sensed within the light that encircled them. Hafnium, the grand master, had come to release their spirits back to the void of zero energy. Having grown tired of the violence of these men, his decision was made; Hafnium began his forgetting of them, watching as their souls dissolved back into the nothingness of the globe of living energy, out of which he continually created the universe. These souls, fragments of his being, would no longer continue along the path of evolution, and in time would become a new form of creation. The task was complete. Hafnium had erased them from his mind and his universe; they had ceased to exist.

*

Within the heavens, Taurus, the progeny of Venus, blazed magnificently among the stars: he waited impatiently for his turn to influence mankind. Venus, the planet associated with all aspects of love, remained close by. Taurus adored her even though she demanded that he accept her choices, and most times he would not refuse. But then Taurus was in love with love; he was enthused by the ideal of a peaceful universe, one that was full of pleasurable amusement that included a little mischief now and then. Venus sensed a challenge of enticement was on the horizon for Taurus, who could so easily be persuaded from the path of sound judgement: another's grazing rights would always look enticing to Taurus. Venus understood his weaknesses only too well.

Venus gathered Taurus beneath her icy white mantle. 'Taurus, listen carefully to what I have to tell you. You will be given an opportunity which I am sure you will be tempted to partake of . . .'

Taurus looked at Venus questioningly, his small bright eyes suddenly alert to her serious manner. Venus' judgement was always compassionate to a poignant story, a breaking heart, and she would always bend the rules for Taurus where she could. Taurus was aware that he was given as much freedom as was possible, but there was a warning in her voice that made him attentive to her every word.

'Aquarius' co-conspirator, the one called Mikell, is not gaining the victory that Asphescuos had hoped for. Because of this, Aquarius will come to you with a proposal from his master offering you great rewards if you do his bidding. I implore you, Taurus, do not be tempted by Aspheseuos. There has been a change in Hafnium's strategy, and he is cleansing his memory in a discerning way; I do not want you to become part of his amnesia. Hafnium is releasing the memories of countless souls back to the void, where they have ceased to exist. Taurus, remember: erased from Hafnium's mind forever, be it human life or otherwise.'

Taurus' interest was beginning to wane as he failed to recognise the warning in her meaning of 'otherwise'. 'What does this human tragedy have to do with me?' he asked.

Venus replied, 'Long before the Otom's migration to the Mer world, mankind was struck by an invasive disease that erased his memory: the human souls that Hafnium recalled were sometimes without memory of all past existence, all memory having been lost before death. Souls were returning to the other-worlds without any history of humankind to influence the future, and it was not only humankind that was affected. Within our universe, there were planets and whole constellations of stars, such as yours, Taurus, that were forgotten.'

Taurus became anxious as he listened to Venus' warning. He was most certainly listening to her now. In the distance the Pleiades' radiance reassured him that his constellation was sound.

'There is one other thing, Taurus. You must agree to Aquarius' demands. It should not be hard for you to make him think you are persuaded by his promises, for they are indeed tempting.'

'I understand, Venus. I will do as you advise,' said Taurus without questioning her on the inducement he would be offered.

'Make sure you do, Taurus, for you know what effect temptation has brought you in the past: a bitter pill that you have found hard to swallow.'

Venus continued her silent vigil in the heavens while Taurus pondered on his future.

The Mer infants had been returned to the Cradling, and their eager parents gathered outside waiting to see them. Never had the Mers questioned the safety of the Cradling or the need for the infants to spend the first two years of their life away from them, but now they felt the infants were at risk and wanted answers to their fears. Zrsiofour was to find his people changed as the Otom began their return to the surface. There was to be a gathering in the City of Five Pathways. The Mer angels who cared for the infants were to announce that the infants would no longer be weaned beneath the crystal mountain; they were to remain with their parents while receiving the Mer teachings. The time for change had come, and the crystal mountain was to have a new employ.

Makot had left the infant on the bank; he had run in fear of his life as the mist had enveloped the dead Cunmen. Now, as he left his hiding place, he worried about the infant; had the Mers taken him with them? Swiftly he made his way along the bank where Mikell had stood cursing Ormus and thirsting for revenge. Scrabbling among the dense foliage Makot prayed that he would find the infant, and that he would be alive; thinking he heard whimpering, he moved towards the sound. Among the foliage he saw a glimpse of the soiled linen that the infant was wrapped in. Makot's heart first jumped for joy until he looked closer; the infant was flushed from dehydration and a deathly red colour. Makot lifted the infant into his arms and plunged from the bank into the water. Quickly he lowered the infant into the cool flowing tide, submerging him completely. The infant responded by drinking eagerly, holding on to life as only an infant can. Makot remembered where the nursing mothers had kept the infants' nourishment, and speaking softly to the infant he told him to be still. Placing the infant on the bank he crawled away to where the food was stored. Moments later he was back and the infant was feeding hungrily. Makot wept with relief that the infant had been spared, his body shuddering with his sobs as he realised the hopelessness of the situation. The infant would not survive if he did not take him back to his kind. Makot realised that for the first time in his dark and rotten existence he did not want to live; he must give up this infant who bestowed love and wholeness to those who touched him. If Makot could not be part of the infant's world then he did not want to be part of his own. 'I must find a way to return him and then...' Makot's voice trailed off; he no longer cared for his own safety. There was only one purpose for him now and that was to return the infant safely to his kind.

Across the landscape Makot could make out the Otom city; he had witnessed the moment it had been surrounded by a coloured arc that he now knew was impenetrable. The arc had flooded the sky, summoning the Cunmen nearby who had gazed in wonder at the fulfilling of a prophecy, that of the return of mankind from the ocean to the Earth's surface. The Otom were the enemy of the Cunmen and had to be annihilated if they were to survive. Makot wanted no part of this plan; he was healed and his body healthy as never before. The arc had already killed the Cunmen who had been drawn towards its light. It meant death to the Cunmen, who simply perished beneath its presence.

Makot looked down at the infant. 'I will take you to the city and I will stand beneath the arc. I am changed. I am healed. I will go among them and ask to be accepted, to be one of them. Yes, that is what I must do.' Makot could hear Mikell calling him again; quickly he held his hand to the infant's mouth. 'Be quiet, little one. I do not want that barbarian to find you. Be quiet and I will come for you later. You will be safe here.' Makot pulled the dense foliage around the infant and sprinkled water over his linen cloth. Gently he laid a hand on him for a moment before moving away and swimming silently downstream. A while later he emerged on the other side of the bank, where Mikell was still calling him, far enough away from the infant not to bring attention to him.

'Why did you run from me?' Mikell's voice was hostile.

Makot knew it would take very little for him to lash out; Mikell was losing the battle against the Otom, an outcome that had seemed impossible a short time ago.

The Mermen sent to rescue the infants were deeply troubled; by their own folly they had missed the infant upon the bank. Such had been the ordeal to take the life of the Cunmen that their usual sense of awareness had eluded them. They had left the infant alone and in danger, returning to the City of Five Pathways to find he was not among those rescued; this would have to be explained.

The Mer race was in turmoil. They had assumed that peace would prevail forever in their subterranean world, and yet a Merman had been lost to violent circumstances, and his mourning soul mate was still without her infant. For the Mers this was unprecedented; not even in troubled sleep could they have dreamed of such a travesty. The Mers were being called to the City of Five Pathways as they had been called to the City of Memories for the teachings and reassurance that the Otom's hopes of victory were high. Now they would have to use their oneness of strength to bring about their own victory.

'Be assured we will retrieve the infant.' Ormus was addressing the gathering of Mers, his profile shadowing the plinth hewn from the centre of the vast subterranean cave. The crystal cave emitted a luminous radiance that was born from millions of perfect diamonds; this was the abode of the Mer angels, which until now had been inaccessible to all mortal Mers. Zrsiofour had broken the written law for the first time and allowed his race to enter. Zrsiofour's people were in the full flood of change, this being necessary for them to move on, to evolve alongside the Otom.

As Ormus began to speak, those gathered slapped their tails in disapproval. The throng was not happy. Why had this spirit come to speak? Why not Zrsiofour? It was Zrsiofour and the Mer angels they wanted to hear, and they wanted answers.

Ormus spoke above the noise. 'Soon there will be a gathering of goodbye for your lost one. Usually this is a joyous occasion when a Mer passes from the life of flesh into the other-worlds. But not this time, this time the death was brought about by violence, a little-known experience for your race.' Ormus sensed their grief; they were beginning to understand the emotions of anger and resentment as though a disease had come among them. Ormus, holding up his hands to them, continued. 'Today your world has changed, never to be the same again. For many years you have opened your hearts to the one race of man and all has been well, but now their presence has brought death and the loss of an infant. These experiences can never be erased from your memories; they have changed your lives forever. You have been made aware of whence came the Otom and this has brought fear to your hearts, for you shall never see them in the same light again. You have been reminded of what man is capable of . . . but you must forgive. Soon the Otom will have completed their return to the surface where they will continue to live peaceably, as they have done in the years spent with you, for you have shown them the way. Man will once again live alongside the animal kingdom, which is also re-emerging, and the animals are as fearful as you, for they have suffered dearly at the merciless hand of man. This present time will begin the last epoch in mankind's evolution upon Earth, and when he is ready he will move beyond Universe Four to the sixth universe. But before he does, he must experience life on other planets, the first being Mars. When he has experienced all there is to know in Universe Four, and is ready to evolve further, he will do so accompanied by the Mer race, which will join him to experience life in another universe. Do not be afraid to continue your journey through evolution with the Otom. Help him; lead him away from temptation, and the eating of flesh. You must continue to help him harvest his food until the time when the Earth is rich in nutrients for man to feed upon.' Ormus paused, and then said, 'The infant Mer is alive. There has been an error of judgement, and the infant's life has been but a breath away from death, but there is still hope for his return.' A rustling of tails passed around the cave. 'We will do all we can to retrieve him, but we must all be of one mind and believe in a positive outcome.' Ormus looked down upon the throng, the radiance of the glittering walls mirroring the many colours of the Mer bodies that reclined in the rock pools beneath him.

This time there was no thrashing of tails; they had listened to the one called Ormus and they knew he spoke the truth. They would help those who had come among them, those of mankind who were gentle and kind. The Mers' resentment was passing and the light of Hafnium was bringing clarity back to their unreasonable judgement of the present circumstances.

Chapter 43

The Healing Mers – Gods of the Universe

The healing angels, the first race of Mers, were untouched by the desire body. They were gods of the universe living only in a body of light, a visible body without flesh and the physical emotions that created a continual cycle of birth and death within the Mer people, and their purpose was to continually create beauty and wisdom to enable the Mer world to exist as part of Universe Four. The same purpose was inclusive of all life, including mortal man, but his ego had been drawn to the shadow source that continually diminished the creation of beauty upon Earth's surface. Hafnium was now erasing most of mankind's past creation from his universe.

In the safety of the evening twilight Makot returned to the bank where the infant lay sleeping. It would soon be nightfall and he could be on his way. Makot had convinced Mikell he was no longer of any use to him with his ramblings of the Cunmen's mysterious death at the cradling. Mikell could not understand how the Cunmen had drowned. Ormus' intervention had proven damaging to his plans, yet Mikell had sensed that Ormus was not accountable for their death. Ormus could not be held responsible this time; Makot had known this to be true as he had answered Mikell unintelligibly, continuing the deceit that he was now in a state of madness.

Mikell felt uneasy about his situation; the leaders of the Cunmen were now fit and healthy and he felt threatened by their strength, even though he sensed they needed him for what he could achieve and were ready to accept him as their leader. He felt alone. Mikell thought about his aunt Mary and a feeling of remorse ran through him. Why had she turned against him? He could have given her everything when his plans had been fulfilled: King of the Cunmen. Mikell shifted his thoughts away from her and on to what to do next.

Aquarius stood before him, smiling arrogantly. 'Well, Mikell, you made a right hash of that, did you not? Did you think that Ormus would let you off that lightly? Going back to Belsize Creek and leaving this rabble unsupervised?' Aquarius goaded Mikell. 'Only a fool, only a fool ... and you have lost your position at the creek. You have lost the infants and the cradling has been totally destroyed. The Cunmen, at this moment, are no longer a threat to the Otom. That's bad luck, Mikell, especially as I went to so much trouble getting that rabble to prepare the cradling so expertly.' Aquarius paused; there was nothing he liked better than to be proven right. 'I have some information for you. I will not tell you how the Mer infants were taken, and I will tell you that the infant that Makot adores so much is still with him, and that right now he is journeying towards the nearest city of the Otom to return him to them. Makot believes, insanely, that they will open their gates to him when he returns the infant and that he will live happily ever after among them, the fool.'

Mikell seethed with anger as he listened to Aquarius. The infant was still at large; then perhaps he could use him as a bargaining power with Ormus. Ignoring Aquarius, Mikell turned on his heel. There was no time to be lost; he must alert the Cunmen and let them deal with the fool Makot before it was too late. Aquarius looked somewhat deflated as Mikell turned, no longer listening to the egocentric ramblings of his co-conspirator.

Makot made his way across the rough terrain. The infant, although small, was heavy and each step on the rough track was becoming an effort; Makot panted as he hauled himself to the top of the ridge. Below him the valley stretched away to the horizon; he knew it could not be much further, but his lightly clad feet were caked in mud from the moist undergrowth and he cursed at the soreness of his swollen feet. Makot breathed a sigh of relief; he could see the arc of rainbows on the horizon and the city that lay beneath it. Not far to go now. Soon he would be starting a new life. He could feel the promise of a new life within his rapidly beating heart. For the first time in his life he said a small prayer. It reminded him of the lullaby he had sung to the infant, which had come from somewhere in the depths of his mind, as did the prayer that now came from his lips. 'Please, creator of all that is good, deliver me from all evil.'

Makot made his way down the steep gully, his toes pressing down painfully inside the rough damp material on his feet. He could see the brightness of the arc and with the bundle in his arms urging him forward he made for the city.

Mikell was hot on Makot's trail. If one of the infants was still free then he was going to have him. Makot had betrayed him, but if he could find him before he drew near to the city he was sure he could persuade him otherwise. Mikell knew that the light of the arc would kill him. Makot would never reach the city; he would be dead long before he reached the gates. Mikell was joined by the four Cunmen leaders to stop Makot; they wanted to be sure that Makot did not hand the infant over. What happened to him after that was up to Mikell.

In the distance Makot heard the whine of a jeep as it slammed against the rough terrain, its engine revving hard to mount the peak. The noise became louder as the jeep came tearing over the top and down the other side. Mikell saw Makot in the distance and let out a yell. The jeep began heading straight towards him. One last effort: Makot started to run, his breath grunting from his chest as he tried to pick up speed with the infant who had suddenly become a dead weight. Makot steeled his mind as though he were hanging onto a precipice for his life, and then the jeep was alongside him.

Makot kept running knowing they would not run him down for fear of harming the infant. The arc was drawing near and the jeep slowed a little, the driver sensing the impending danger. Mikell shouted for him to go faster, then lunging forward he pushed his foot hard down on top of the driver's; the accelerator pedal was driven hard against the floor and the jeep lurched forward, moving between Makot and the arc. Suddenly it was all over. Makot ran beyond the speeding jeep towards the arc of light. From behind the gates the sound of shouting could be heard as the Otom, alerted by the sound of the jeep, came out to watch.

Deron stood watching as Makot lunged under the arc and ran towards the open gate. Mikell on seeing Deron brought the jeep to a halt; now they had all passed under the arc and Mikell knew the consequence of that for the Cunmen. Mikell's gaze met Deron's and he knew he had lost. Within his focus he could see Makot running with his arms outstretched as if holding up his gift of entry to the city. Deron moved forward and the gates partially closed behind him. In his hand a stun gun for protection; he would need nothing more.

Makot was almost there; he began to slow as Deron moved to meet him. Makot felt the hot tears of joy run down his cheeks, his prayers were answered. Deron held out his arms to take the infant, his gaze unwavering and calm; Makot sensed no hostility, just a wistful compassion as he handed the infant to his new carer. Makot felt so strange, he felt so light now, and the dreadful heavy weariness that had held him down upon the journey was lifted, and he felt so full of joy. There in the distance he could see a mist; his thoughts darkened, *what trickery is this?*, and then he began to feel at ease again. This was different, and not as before when the Cunmen had been taken; the mist was inviting him to enter, compelling him to do so; then the gentle peace of sleep.

Deron held the tiny form that was now so still; he sensed the infant's grief as once again he felt the loss of one who had cared for him. An Otom named Rebecca came and gently took the infant. Soon he would be back in the Cradling where he belonged; back in a world that he was familiar with, where creating beauty through the power of love was the only way.

Mikell stood by the jeep; he had alighted when the Cunmen began to die as their bodies slowly changed back, the cancerous tumours returning as before until they lay dead in front of him. Makot had disappeared, his body no longer part of the Earth; his prayer had been answered and he was safe in the other-worlds where the healing of his spirit and soul would begin: his reward for saving the infant. The Cunmen that lay dead at Mikell's feet were to be forgotten by Hafnium, the grand master, for he was creating a new universe in which they had no part.

Upon the universal chequerboard, Aspheseuos' dark being was at odds with Aquarius. The game was not going as he had planned; he had skilfully nurtured the one called Mikell in the ways of isolation and resentment, turning out a perfect flower of human hate that the loss of those close to you and abandonment can manufacture. Aspheseuos' voice thundered across the cosmos. 'Why is my progeny turning out to be useless against Ormus and the Otom? And Aquarius, he could have saved the day had he not allowed his arrogance to blind him to the seriousness of the challenge. I must use my next strategy: I must entice Taurus to do my bidding, but not by the messenger, Aquarius.'

Aquarius realised too late the shroud of isolation that Aspheseuos had placed about him for his vanity and overzealous ego.

Chapter 50

Taurus

Taurus spanned the planetary system; he was expecting a visit from Aquarius and was surprised when the sun darkened and Aspheseuos appeared before him.

'Why, Taurus, I have been searching for you, and here you are, my fine young friend.'

Taurus acknowledged Aspheseuos jovially, unconcerned by the darkened sky and the presence of Satan, the grand master's brother.

From the remoteness of her planetary orbit, Venus could be heard to express a word of warning. 'Be careful, Taurus. I assumed it would be Aquarius you should be wary of, but the master of darkness has come before you. Be alert! Be careful, or he will entrap you.' Venus' words appeared to fall on deaf ears; the unexpected appearance had enthralled him and any awareness of danger had faded with the light.

'Let him speak, Venus. It can do no harm to hear him out.'

Aspheseuos began his account, embarking on a woeful story of how the challenge for the Earth was becoming so unfair. 'Hafnium is taking my challengers from the game and forgetting they ever existed. How fair is that?'

Taurus answered high-spiritedly, 'Well, mortal life's a bitch and then they die.'

Aspheseuos' force grew darker at this flippancy, whilst Taurus was now roaring with laughter at his own remark. Aspheseuos, for once, was forced to agree with those in the planetary tribe that considered the radiant luminary Taurus insensitive to the tribulations of others. He waited until Taurus had quietened and then continued.

'Taurus, I have a proposal for you. One that will leave you feeling well rewarded and in a universe of your own where all you want to attain will be yours for the asking.'

Taurus listened attentively to the shadowy figure before him, his wariness apparently dulled by the promise offered.

Venus, sensing the danger, implored Taurus to ignore him.

Taurus replied, 'If Aspheseuos can blot all light from the solar system, then his authority must be supreme. Hafnium rarely changes anything within our transitory existence. And, Venus, you tell me that Hafnium is with me always, but I can never feel his presence, especially when I desire change, which is most of the time.

'I will do it. I will help you, Aspheseuos. But first you must swear to keep your promise.'

'I will,' said Aspheseuos solemnly. 'I will give you a dark universe all of your own!'

The heavens lightened as Aspheseuos disappeared, believing that his work was done. It was now up to Taurus to complete the plan he had given him, and help Mikell to win the battle with the Otom. Together they would destroy the one tribe of man and any future plans that Hafnium had for them. But Taurus was to redeem himself; he was to show a wonderful side of his nature that always manifested in times of crisis when courage and steadfastness were needed. Taurus was determined the Otom would be reminded of his strength; he had listened to Aspheseuos but also to Venus. To rule a dark universe was not one of his desires.

Taurus remembered the holocaust as though it had been only a moment past. It had been at this time of year upon Earth, May, when he looked forward to the time when he was part of its nature, when all was in bloom and the world, although ravaged by mankind's misuse of her resources, would still produce a mantle of growth that was indescribably beautiful, a beauty that had since been absent for many Earth cycles. Taurus had sought for mankind to experience only the best of mortal life; now he understood that there needed to be both sacrifice and giving in order to create a stable and balanced universe, which both he and mankind had ignored.

Taurus had felt deeply saddened to see the wildlife leave the Earth and return to spirit, and mankind in the remaining days following the holocaust, watching as their lives ended in the billions from the radiation fallout that rode upon the blackened storm clouds obscuring the sky. Then liberation, death, for those remaining on the Earth's surface as the oceans swept overland to heal the Earth's scorched body. Taurus hated any form of pain inflicted upon others; he was a quick-tempered soul but also quick to forgive and move on, and at the time of mankind's fall he had felt great sorrow, wishing it had not been in his time of awakening. Now he had made a choice not to help Aspheseuos and be rewarded with his own universe, in which he was sure he would never see light. Taurus tried to imagine this and his radiance faded; he loved the solar flares that illuminated his magnificence, he loved his tribe. He would help the Otom. They had earned their reward for the courage and self-sacrifice they had shown when accepting their new life in the underworld. Taurus' mind was made up; Venus would not have to persuade him to do the right thing this time.

Over the Bering Sea, Taurus could still be seen clearly in the early morning sky. Below, the Cunmen were preparing to set out to sea at first light; for days they had been plundering the ocean for the recently awakened sea mammals, slaughtering the dolphins and injuring the whales. At first it had been for food, something fresh, a taste of that which they had never experienced, but now it had turned into sport, a lust for blood, a need that always stayed fresh in their minds, for their favourite pastime had been to hunt and kill each other. What other living creature had there been to eat upon the Earth?

The Bering Sea was the gathering ocean, a playground for the Mers of the seven oceans. The ocean dwellers would gather there to communicate and dance. They gathered to celebrate times of joy.

It was a place for recreation, a communal place of spiritual togetherness. When the Otom had come among the Mers the ocean wildlife had vanished. Now, to the Mers' great joy, they were returning to fill the oceans with their colour and sound. For the Mers, the Earth's oceans had been a ghostly place without them, for the species had primordial family ties.

The Mers were beginning to understand that they now lived in a world that must be fought for. Already the ocean dwellers were being harmed, for as soon as the whales and dolphins had been sighted the Cunmen had launched their boats and put to sea for a killing.

Ormus had brought the news to Zrsiofour of the impending danger, and advised him that he would have to summon an army of Mers to fight the Cunmen and stop the slaughter of the mammals that were so precious to the future. The sounds of the injured whales had been heard throughout the seven oceans, their pitiful cries travelling afar. The Mers had grown angry at this new revulsion. They must find the courage to fight! With an army summoned, Zrsiofour set out for the Bering Sea.

In the dim morning light, Taurus was barely visible as he watched the army of Mermen draw near; now was his moment.

The sky lit up as a flash of light thrust downward towards the ocean. The Bering Sea split apart as the blaze of light hit the water and plunged downward, reaching for the sea bed. In the darkness of the ocean, the light manifested horns and a head, and finally a body. On the ocean bed stood a mighty bull, so large that its nostrils rose to the level of the rolling waves in the deep ocean. Taurus the mortal giant, mighty in size and strength, stood before Zrsiofour and his Mermen, his radiance casting a silvery light beneath the ocean that equalled the pale morning sun.

'You are valiant, my friends,' said Taurus sincerely, 'and true to your spiritual nature. Today you will see the Cunmen that have slaughtered the sea dwellers returned to spirit; be assured these shores will not see them again. Take heart now; follow your courage, for you must fight Aspheseuos' soldiers if we are to save the Earth and our universe from his darkness.'

Zrsiofour turned to his army and gave the command. 'Not one of their ships will remain upon the ocean surface. Let not one of the Cunmen be left to breathe air. Leave their bodies to rest in a watery grave forever.' Zrsiofour's army began to beat their tails upon the surface as he held his arms aloft, causing a squall to rise up from the ocean.

The Cunmen had been slaughtering the sea dwellers for days and the mutilated bodies could be seen floating near to the shore. They had put to sea in any shipping vessels left intact that they found strewn about the coastline, for although not perfect in their seaworthiness they were still sailable. The hunt had been exhilarating, and it would be a while before they longed for another frenzied kill. After feasting upon their catch they lay in their boats unable to move, drifting in the calm sea.

The band of Cunmen that had travelled further north, to the Northern Rockies and the boreal forests, had been drawn to the new city of the Otom after seeing the great arc of rainbows suddenly appear in the sky. They had followed the rainbow until they had found the city hidden amongst the icy landscape of coniferous forest. Immediately they had sent word to Belsize Creek. The Cunmen were eager to fight but feared to go near the arc of light that protected the city as it was rumoured that to do so would mean instant death for them. The fear of death had kept them away, but they were bored with fishing and needed a new sport to occupy their minds. They talked of plundering the city and dividing the spoils, which they knew would become a reality as soon as the new leader, Mikell, devised a way.

More Cunmen had set sail at first light to join the small fleet of boats, and now the crew lay idly upon the decks waiting for a sighting. In the middle of the fleet a sudden mass of water rose up before their unbelieving eyes and Zrsiofour towered above them. As the water ebbed away Taurus appeared, a bull so big that his head rose above the decks upon which they now cowered. Beneath the turbulent ocean, Taurus had found a mountainous ridge upon which to rest his forelegs; his head and muscle-bound shoulders rising from the water in terrifying proportions. But he was still no match for Zrsiofour whose head and shoulders, drawn up upon the crest of a wave, towered ten heads above him. Taurus' great head turned to eye the boats surrounding him, then, bellowing as only bulls can do, he thrust his head forward and drove his large horns into the water; one by one the Cunmen's vessels began to capsize beneath his mighty force. The ocean swell that had raised Zrsiofour aloft held firm as he joined Taurus in capsizing the boats that encircled them. The screams of the Cunmen could be heard from the shore as their vessels were driven beneath the water and they were tossed into the deep ocean where the Mermen were waiting for them. The Cunmen fought like wild animals as the Mermen held them beneath the ocean, pulling them down to the sea bed without mercy, their tails thrashing to retain them until they ceased to move.

The calm upon the ocean gave no indication of the battle that had taken place or the mortal remains of the Cunmen that lay in a watery grave. They swam to the surface believing they had cheated death. As they struggled in the water, Hafnium, the grand master, began to forget their souls, which he no longer wanted in his universe.

In the early evening shadow, Taurus' physical body began to fade as his star began to glow against the heavens. The Mers watched from their watery playground as the celestial radiance that was Taurus returned to its place in the sky.

'Well done, Taurus,' said Venus, 'you have put aside temptation and saved the day; for that I commend you.'

Taurus turned to gaze at Venus' beautiful face; it was such a pleasure to look upon her beauty. 'It was nothing, Venus. There was only one possible outcome ... to stay with my tribe basking in the solar flares of the sun.'

'Is that so, Taurus? It is time for you to sleep. Gemini is awakening and it is her turn to take up the Otom's challenge.'

Chapter 51

Rebecca

Rebecca sat waiting with the Mer infant cradled in her arms; she was to travel with an escort to the City of Five Pathways where the infant would be reunited with his grieving mother, Lazuli, whose soul mate had been lost to such a cruel and evil death.

Rebecca was now in her seventies and had witnessed the birth of the one tribe of man, after experiencing the breakdown of the old world. It would not be long before her return to the surface became permanent, even though she did not want to leave the sanctuary of the Mer world. But trouble had finally come to the peace-loving Mers, forcing her to see that change was inevitable. Allowing her thoughts to amble back to the past was a thing she very rarely did these days, for the past was like a horror story that she had no wish to revisit time and again. She was healed of the past and looked only to the future now.

Rebecca, like Lia, had been a young woman when the holocaust had wiped mankind from the Earth's surface; she had known for many years that her life was to change but had not been prepared for the devastation that had taken place on the surface, or the early years living in the underworld. For many years before the change she had been committed to a spiritual way of life and the conservation of all things natural, although these values had become a losing battle against mankind's need for progress and wealth. Rebecca had seen within her own community the disappearance of the grass verges and trees. Private gardens turned to stone as home owners concreted over every space they could for more parking area. Towns and cities became larger and greyer, and the precious green belt areas smaller. Mankind was in serious trouble; his desire to make life as easy as possible was about to rob him of his extraordinary existence. Spring had come with scarce the joy of nature's blossoms, or the guarantee that summer would follow.

Rebecca was reminded of that springtime as she passed by it down the tunnel of time to her childhood. Her early days came with vivid memories, a time when she had been able to play; when the adults in her family world took responsibility for her, and she had been happy and secure. Then just before she was old enough to go to school her father had died, changing her life forever. For the first time she experienced grief, and with it the loss of her childhood security. But still she remembered the good times, the happy memories of holidays, playing on sandy beaches, dressing up in seaweed skirts and eating tall ice creams from long stem glasses. The fireworks in November and the family singing around the piano at Christmas time with their friends. She was happy then and unaware of what life's experiences were to bring her. These memories were her core foundation, good memories, built on love that had carried her through life. All too soon she was an adult and living in the world beyond her family's caring, a world where she learned the rules of an uncaring society that no longer listened or noticed others. Rebecca saw in front of her a hospital room where she lay in a deep and intensely anxious state; the ovarian cancer that had been removed had left her infertile. Rebecca's thoughts moved on; unable to have children she became a health counsellor, the desire to help others helping to push the grief from her mind. Rebecca looked down at the infant in her arms; she was glad she had not brought children of her own into the world.

'Such a sad thought, Rebecca. Life, the fragment of Hafnium which is driven to incarnate in matter, is both a joyous and a sad experience.' The Gemini twins stood before Rebecca, the golden hue behind them casting a brilliance about her that made her feel completely at peace with her memories. Both came forward to touch the infant and immediately his healing powers returned.

Rebecca felt the coolness returning to his body and he began to show signs of waking. The infant would always carry the knowledge of his father's death, and this would bring uncertainty to many decisions that he made in adulthood; there would remain for always a hidden loneliness, and uncertainty when in the company of men. The experience was etched upon his soul to become a future challenge, but for now, he would go home to bond with his mother and help her through her grief and the loss of her soul mate.

In the world of the Mers, Lazuli sensed the change; her infant was safe and would soon be returned to her; she would go to the Cradling and wait for him.

Forty-five years after the holocaust, the mass of darkness that had congested the psychic plane above the Earth was finally clearing as the souls of those trapped there were forgotten by Hafnium, the grand master. Change was under way; the psychic sphere could no longer contain the heavy negative energy that the returning spirits of darkness had created there. With them gone, the Earth would continue to heal at a much faster rate.

The planetary tribe moved into alignment to consider the position, now that the star tribe's plans had been set in motion.

Neptune spoke out, unhappy that the ocean-dwelling Mers were experiencing slaughter. 'The star tribe's plan to help the Otom appears to be going well; the tragedy is that the Mers are witnessing horrific loss among their kind. Something of a new experience for this gentle race, is it not?'

Saturn replied impassively, 'But they are experienced in mankind's history of violence. Remember, Neptune, they are the descendents of the lost Atlanteans that became half fish, lost to the Earth world for the same reason as the Otom. If they are to live among the Otom in the future, here upon Earth or upon another planet, they must revisit their ancestral history, and experience the same ordeals. That they know of mankind's past, and their own, surely means that they will watch for signs of a revival of any abhorrent acts. It is time for mankind to evolve, move on.

Hafnium is weary of the challenge for Earth that is taking place on the universal chequerboard and wants the challenge with Aspheseuos over; he wants to reach checkmate!'

The planets Mercury, Venus, Mars, Jupiter and Saturn resumed their positions in space orbiting the sun, while the triad of the subtle spheres Uranus, Neptune and Pluto argued that the fight for the Otom's continuing existence was not to be accomplished easily, and so, as brilliant as the stars' strategy was so far, they should continue to listen to the wisdom of the planets in order to accomplish much more. It was now time for the Gemini twins to take up the challenge, and with them came the opportunity to apply past experience in order to make good the future.

It was nearing the summer solstice, and halfway through the Earth's cycle; the planetary progeny who had given their services to the challenge, Aries progeny of Mars, Pisces progeny of Neptune and Taurus progeny of Venus, were to be followed by the Gemini twins, the progeny of Mercury, who inspired mankind's intellect.

Mercury wanted to separate those who had been misled from the remaining imprisoned souls of the Cunmen and return them to the other-worlds; he reasoned that they could still be of service to the universe. The Cunmen whose souls could be redeemed contained important historical facts that would be lost forever should Hafnium, the grand master, forget them. But how could those that had been misled by the truly evil be separated from the souls to be forgotten? Hafnium no longer wanted the psychic sphere to shroud the Earth with darkness; it had taken ten thousand years for the Holocenes to mould mankind into one enlightened race, the Otom. Mercury's thoughts lay heavy upon him; his suggestion had not been received well by the planetary forces. Their argument had been that Hafnium wanted to start again with a new race of men for the Earth that his thoughts had already created, complete with new species of animals to exist alongside those already in existence. Hafnium wanted a new beginning for Earth, but most of all – Mercury restrained his thoughts lest others be listening – Hafnium wanted to forget his brother, Aspheseuos.

Aspheseuos had always been an inquisitive angel, which was the reason why Hafnium had chosen him as his challenger, but now Hafnium wanted a spirit of light to return to his universe; he had tired of delving into his own obscurity. Hafnium felt weary from all that he had fashioned, and at times did not want Universe Four, himself, to exist. If Hafnium decided to forget everything, then every soul fragment that he had created would be lost forever. Hafnium needed to enjoy his own existence again, or Universe Four would cease to exist. His thoughts now wretched, Mercury looked around Universe Four; *would it have been better if it had never existed?*

Rebecca entered the boat that would take her to the void of zero energy and back to the world of the Mers. She was still a beautiful woman, serene, and with a figure that was faultless in its slenderness; her hair, now silky white, hung below her waist. Her skin was pale and her hands were long and delicate, the fingers thinly webbed from living so long in the ocean world.

Rebecca's thoughts turned to the abandoned homes that were left after the fallout, which now lay buried beneath layers upon layers of dust; exactly like the historic ruins that had filled the history archives in museums and libraries. Her thoughts wondered some more. Lia's home in England: *was it as it used to be, and were there porcelain cups to drink from?* Rebecca smiled at her wishful and comforting thoughts.

Lia had sometimes spoken of the Causeway, and of Dorri, the housekeeper. Rebecca had loved to hear her stories and had decided that if she were to survive the next challenge to her race, then she would live in England again, *where the roses will bloom in time;* she was sure they would. The infant opened his eyes as if he knew what she was thinking; she smiled down at him, assuring him, telling him that soon he would be back in his home, *the only place that an infant should be.* Rebecca's thoughts drifted on.

Life in the fifty years before the holocaust had seen a massive separation in family ties as children moved away from their roots. Travel was easy, but once kin moved on the ties were broken and families and friends lost touch. Within a half-century the damage of family separation had begun to show. Parents lacking family guidance became disadvantaged parents without the knowledge of the previous generations to help them see where they were going wrong. A surge of human beings without any social graces began to dominate the Earth, people without any thought for the rest of mankind, their constancy being to the money in their pockets and the spending power of their credit cards. *How I hated those last years.* Rebecca looked down at the infant and restrained her thoughts. 'You don't want to enter the dreamtime, do you, little one? You know who is waiting for you.'

A while later they were docking. Rebecca held the infant close as she prepared herself for the final step of her journey and the handing over of her precious bundle. It had been an honour to be chosen to bring the infant home, and she had made a decision that she wanted to remain in the Mer world until the migration was over, and then she would go home to England, and perhaps the roses. Rebecca closed her eyes, her arms held snugly around the little one, and then the gentle lifting as she drifted into the nothingness of the void, where she would be happy to stay forever.

The boatman watched the loop as he had done so many times: first the light coming towards the travellers, expanding out like a great explosion of light and then falling back in on itself, taking with it those who were engulfed in its wake until only a dot remained, and then only the darkness of the ocean. He watched it every day, and yet never grew tired of doing so, for he knew that its energy source was the cause of his existence, light in all its brilliance, and then nothing, nothing except everything, for when you were at the centre of nothing you were everything in existence.

Chapter 52

Gemini

Above the Earth the psychic plane, the first other-world, was still spatially condensed with the departed souls of the holocaust, some of those souls having been received without memory. Hafnium had planned to have these souls pass through the psychic plane and on to the first level of the seven heavens where they belonged, but the psychic plane was choked with the souls of Aspheseuos' army, and those whose lives had come to an end without memory were lost within the mass that had accumulated there.

The twins, Gemini, listened to Mercury's thoughts; he was the communicator, the intellect that powered mankind's evolution, his soul. Mercury drew their attention down upon the darkness of the psychic plane, a shroud that still partially obscured the Earth. What of those who had chosen to forget mankind's transgressions before leaving their Earthly existence, and were trapped there? The disease of forgetfulness was to have helped mankind, but first he had to grow old enough to forget, and there had been little time left; the original Earth race had carried within them the code for extinction, which had led the world towards the last holocaust.

Mercury, having drawn this to the twins' attention, decided that he must first talk to them before their influence was used to help the Otom. The twins were eager to begin. Their energy thrived at the thought of fast-moving ideas that would be turned to positive outcomes. Gemini was the thinker, and would motivate the doer. Aries' ideas of using the other-worlds to help with the challenges had fascinated them. The Gemini twins wanted to continue with his plan by calling on the one called Odelia Cavil and her companion Glashadou, to leave their world with others of their kind, and have some fun with the Cunmen. The twins embodied the youthful mind, and would not provoke the loathsomeness of slaughter; they would rather enjoy their encounter with the Cunmen.

Mercury called upon them to listen, while they, still talking loudly of their plans, continued to argue contrarily. Mercury waited for them to settle. 'Such youthful enthusiasm is to be applauded, Gemini. Although I would like you to take a long look at your sister, Virgo. She is as you, young and bright, but she is of the forces of the earth, as are Capricorn and Taurus, and for that reason they have a great respect for all things of matter, while you are of the element air, light and without the denseness of the earth. You, Gemini, are like the breezes that caress the Earth, light and free. Because of this, you must think through your plans for they will change in substance. Your free-thinking plans must be tempered by responsibility to the physical change your choices will make, especially with so much at risk. Remember, sensitive, home-loving Cancer, from the element of water, will come after you, and she will bear your mistakes, if there are any. She will feel them deep within her heart, for she is the spirit of the Earth mother and will weep for her.'

The twins sat listening intently; they had no wish to disappoint Mercury, or leave a trail of chaos in the path of those to follow.

Mercury, now certain that he had the twins' full attention, continued. 'Gemini, your influence comes halfway through the Earth's year, and at the time of summer when all aspects of spirit that are locked in matter become fertile, and give forth physical birth. The purpose is for spirit to experience, and the will to remain alive is powerfully strong in the young, then as the physical body gets old so does the will to remain diminish. Each one of those lives, whatever the species, is incarnate of your tribe, the twelve stars. So you see, you have a vested interest; within the psychic plane your progeny awaits Hafnium's decision; will they be remembered, or forgotten? Your have existed within the multi-dimensional rainbow of the star tribe, where all non-physical worlds exist. Now you must make your decisions with a physical world, the Earth, in mind. When a physical being relinquishes purpose, it relinquishes all need to exist; the need to engage in emotional challenges, which can lead to negative actions, or indeed positive ones, ceases. The human holds on to purpose because without it, the flesh will give up living and the soul will return to a non-physical existence. Everything that exists within Universe Four has duality, therefore the human spirit encased in the flesh will have been born in duality; somewhere the soul mate will play a role in that physical lifetime upon Earth. When one is separated, both are lost. Purpose is never whole, and both will feel a strong urge to return to non-existence, in order to find peace, love of being within the whole.'

Mercury pointed down towards the Earth, and further, to where a woman and her charge were journeying through the void to the world of the Mers. 'Below us we see Rebecca as she takes her precious charge back to the world of the Mers. She is joyful, but on the Earth's surface her soul mate, a Cunman, who is unknown to her, will soon return to the whole, as you, Gemini, bring your plans to bear. When you return him to Hafnium, the grand master, who wishes to forget this soul, then you also send Rebecca to the same fate, for without her soul mate somewhere in existence within the whole, she cannot continue to exist. If Hafnium is to forget her duality then she must also cease to exist, and all her beauty, her good nature, the history of her forefathers' spirit will cease to exist also; do you understand what I am saying to you? Be careful whom you choose to vanquish, for many in the world of the Mers have their duality in the beasts upon the earth, the Cunmen. I will say that the one called Lia is in the most grievous of danger even though Ormus watches over her with great care, for her duality is the one called Mikell, the most hunted of men, and now the leader of the Cunmen, and will become their king should they defeat the Otom. Much is at risk, Gemini; Hafnium is unstable in his thinking, and we must act with care and must save as many souls as possible, for I am the soul keeper and you are my seed.'

Mercury became silent, and the Gemini twins thoughtful; their task now would be to step carefully in whom they judged, lest they be forgotten by Hafnium, grand master of Universe Four, and an innocent pay the price of non-existence.

The wearied Cunmen were crossing the North American Rockies in whatever transport they could muster. Before them the boreal forests rose lush and green, a spectacle some had not seen in years. It had been a long trip for those travelling across Asia and Europe, but worth it. They had heard of the Mer infants and their promise of renewed health, and of Mikell the chosen leader whose coming had been prophesied for years, and now he was among them. The thoughts of a better future, a future with purpose, kept them heading towards Belsize Creek, where they were told all healing would take place. Among them was an old man who had defied all of life's pitfalls to remain alive. Thomas was seventy-three years, and a living skeleton of emaciated flesh in flowing dirty rags; only his vibrant turquoise eyes, strange and deep, stared out from the shroud to verify that he existed. Thomas had held onto the hope that he would see the transformation of his race back to health and vigour before he departed this world for the hereafter, *whatever that is.* Thomas was a believer that this life was it, and he had made hay while the sun shone! Take all that you could and live life without conscience; that had been his god, his religion, until the holocaust, which he had thought would never happen. *Lord knows, the cranks had been warning mankind.* He would not have played it any differently; as far as he was concerned those who had disappeared over the years had been silenced of their breath in one way or another. There was no promised land, and the rumours of a tribe of man returning from under the ocean was preposterous; no, they were from another planet, and that he thought was good, for they had brought the new leader, Mikell, and with him the power to heal us all. Thomas smiled. *Perhaps the healing will give me back some of my youth; that would be what I'd wish for if I had a choice.* He thought about all the women that had passed through his life; *yes, that is what I'd wish for!*

Thomas was pulled sharply from his thoughts; the vehicle in front had turned into a ravine. Pulling up, he jumped out and looked down into the ravine to see a mess of pieces, some human flesh and the rest metal; he stood looking down for a moment longer without feeling any concern, and then turned to continue his journey. There had never been any emotion within Thomas, and that was why he had been so good at living: no emotion, no guilt; his only aim was to get to the top of his profession and have as much pleasure as he possibly could, regardless of who got hurt in either category. Thomas had been a solicitor, as evil as the criminals he had served in the courtroom, defending their rights. Thomas could not believe his luck when the United States of Europe opened their borders to all within; suddenly anyone who had heard of England wanted to be where the promise of housing, benefits and healthcare was most times free. England's domestic stability was doomed, but not those who were able to make a fortune in the process of her decline, and there were many like Thomas who were quite happy to turn their brilliance to helping these people get everything they wanted, at the taxpayer's expense. Thomas was paid handsomely by the taxpayer for stealing the money from their pockets. Thomas had many homes and many lovers, and friends in government whom he paid to turn a blind eye to his many unlawful dealings; his life was fantastic. Thomas was on the way up, a wealthy solicitor with a title, bought for the price of a holiday home in the Balearic islands for a friend in the government; yes, life was idyllic. Who cared what the papers were saying? Who cared about the moaning masses? When the country was spent he would move elsewhere. And then it came ... the closure to everything he had manipulated and strived for, gone within a flash of light. Thomas had reaped his reward as had many; now there was only this shadow left, a shadow that clung to life in the hope of past glories returning. This Cunman must surely be forgotten.

Mercury looked down from the heavens and pointed to Thomas as he spoke to Gemini. 'You see the one called Thomas? If you were to extinguish his life, then as Hafnium, the grand master, gladly ceases to remember this loathsome creature, we will lose the divineness of Rebecca. For as beautiful a creature as her physical being is, so her duality is equally as loathsome, and if the spirit of Thomas is forgotten, then so too will Rebecca be forgotten. Now do you understand that your task, and that of those who follow you, will not be simple? Remember when Hafnium thought first to give mankind the knowledge of the computer; he was giving mankind the first reality of what he is: a numerical equation that only understands balance, logic. Remember how mankind failed to see that if you did not use logic in equal terms to the processes of the computer then it would cease to work, important work would be lost; man could not delete matter as he pleased, for all is connected in some way or another, and by pure logic of course. Hafnium thought that when man was allowed to invent the computer his intellect, his soul, would move forward and he would begin to understand Hafnium, the grand master, and how the universe truly exists. However, the logic of the computer did not open the window to clarity for mankind; his emotions still fogged his pathway forward. Now, only the Otom is as Hafnium intended; his logic is to balance; he creates like the computer that was intended to enlighten mankind. For the Cunmen, it developed into the most powerful weapon of all, greed.'

Chapter 53

Lazuli

Rebecca's feet trod the familiar whiteness of marble floors in the City of Memories; she had been summoned to the elders who were now in council with Zrsiofour. Lazuli lay in the ceremonial canal that bordered the east wall; the water canal stretched out along the perimeter wall of the great temple where it met with the vast connection of waterways that ran throughout the city. The waterways allowed those from the world of the Mers to enter the city and attend the meetings of the council of elders and Zrsiofour. Few ever came; there was normally hardly any occasion that warranted it, except now when the Mers were engaging in the war of the Otom against the Cunmen. The clear running water dispersed shadows of blue upon the pristine whiteness of the marble walls. Lazuli was a mermaid of the golden yellow species with hair of burnished copper that complemented the prisms of light reflected around the great hall, reminding all present of the sun that rested in the heaven above the oceans; all was calm in the awaiting of Rebecca and her charge, all were at peace now the infant was returned to Mer.

Rebecca entered the temple, her long robe of aquamarine flowing away from her slender body, perfecting the paleness of her skin and flowing silver hair. Standing beneath the entrance to the great hallway, she realised the moment for returning the infant had come. She had grown to love the infant, her longing to be a mother suddenly coming to life: a desire that had lain dormant, stifled by a lack of faith in the continuance of man, but now she felt the maternal desire that so many had felt many times before. The yearning was so strong that she felt she could not pass the infant over, but give him she must.

Ormus appeared by her side; he had felt her longing from far out within the universe and knew that she would need help to relinquish the precious infant, just as Makot had found it hard to do. The infant was special, as his mother was to find out. Lazuli had been summoned to the temple instead of receiving her son back at the Cradling: a place he would not return to, for his time with the Mer angels was now complete. The infant would remain with his mother to grow into adulthood under Ormus' care until it was time for him to leave the Mer world and live among the Otom. Within a half-century the infant, Wootwul, would join the Otom on their journey to Mars.

Lazuli felt Rebecca's desire, and rustled her tail in defensive fear. Ormus lifted the infant from Rebecca's arms; she made no protest, and he moved towards the waiting mother. Lazuli held out her arms longingly, and the infant cooed with joy as he felt the familiar arms come about him. At once Lazuli felt a healing in her heart for her soul mate, for he had left her with the most precious of gifts, a joy in body that was part he and she.

'Lazuli.' The first elder spoke her name and then all spoke with one voice. 'It gives us great joy to see you reunited with your son, and he will give you great joy in the years to come, helping you to forget the pain you have suffered. The infant that you hold within your arms is the one who will lead the Mers to a world where you and the Otom will continue to live together, a world where your races will begin the preparation that will take your descendants on a journey to many worlds and, eventually, to Universe Six. In his lifetime both races will journey to Mars where already the climatic changes are taking place to accommodate both your kind and man. When your infant has grown to manhood and you are still young enough to give him guidance, the journey will take place. Those who will lead mankind are yet to be born, for the lifespan of man is far shorter than that of the Mer. The preparation for the journey we speak of will be the last challenge for the Otom, and the Mers, before they leave the Earth for Mars, which is a blip in time to those of spirit, but fifty years hence for man.'

Lazuli tried to pay attention as she looked down adoringly at her son; most of what was being said she hardly heard, except for the reference to his growing up and becoming a shining example of all that was good within the heart of a Mer.

The elders turned to Rebecca. 'Rebecca, we know of your heart's awakening to motherhood, and you know that it is far too late for this to be, and that is why we feel that you should return to English soil again, as soon as possible. For it is there that you will look back at your life and realise the good that you have done, all the children you have nurtured, alongside their parents, and know your life has been truly worthwhile. We have decided at Ormus' request that you go to the home of Lia, there to be with the one called Dorri, to walk in the gardens among the roses that are beginning to bloom. It is summer, and you will find joy as you walk by the ocean and feel the sand beneath your feet again. Only then does Ormus feel that you will find peace within your heart as you realise that your life has been full of purpose and fulfilment; it will give you liberty, and a time to look within yourself before the completed migration quickens life's pace again.'

The images of the elders dappled, and the sphere at which the council had convened became silent; only Zrsiofour, Ormus and the two women remained in the great hall. Zrsiofour, his ethereal body as spectacular as the Mer angels' beauty, left the sphere; his silhouette moved effortlessly over the marble floor before coming to stand by the water's edge. Zrsiofour slid beneath the water; soon afterwards his body had taken on the flesh of the Mer king and, taking the infant from Lazuli, he acknowledged Ormus with a bow of his noble head before disappearing beneath the water with Lazuli swimming effortlessly behind him, her large golden fantail dipping in and out of the crystalline water. Ormus watched until they were out of sight and then he too merged with the whiteness of the great hall, leaving only the silent walls to contemplate the Otom and Mers' next challenge. Rebecca did not see their going; she was blissfully unaware of her surroundings as she re-entered the void to begin her journey to the surface, and a future that would this time have a happy ending.

Rebecca returned to England as companion to Dorri while they awaited the return of Lia's family to the Causeway. For the first time in many years, Rebecca felt a real sense of being. She and Dorri were both earth element people, good and solid. They became good friends and spent the long summer days talking of the past and a future that was now certain.

Rebecca had her wish come true; on the second week of her stay at the Causeway, she awoke to the sun rising and the first cuckoo song to be heard upon the Earth again, and as she looked out from her bedroom window towards the ocean she felt an impulse to look down; in the garden below her the first rose had bloomed, a white rose, the colour of purity, its powerfully scented head nodding in the morning breeze.

Those who had waited upon the shore as the Cunmen set out for a whaling massacre had witnessed the two great beasts rising from the ocean and capsizing the boats surrounding them, breaking them apart as easily as if they were matchwood. Unbelieving eyes had watched in terror as those in the water drowned amidst the terrifying vision of a bull and a being half-man, half-fish rising from the waves, their mighty tails beating the helpless Cunmen beneath the water.

In the aftermath, those who remained on land questioned what to do; thousands had grouped there waiting for a leader.

Deron and Paul returned to the City of Memories; the Cunmen were amassing around the Otom city in the boreal forest, and thousands more had been seen along the west coast. Before long they would return north to join those already gathered to attack the city. They needed reinforcements for the city; otherwise all they had achieved would be lost.

'Mikell's army is gathering force . . .'

The elders listened to Deron's account, while Paul added that although the Cunmen were hampered by their infirmity, their strength lay in their purpose; the Cunmen had travelled far in the hope of being healed. They believed the healing infants were still in the hands of Mikell, and that when they had vanquished the city in the boreal forest, the City of Boreal, a return to health would be their reward.

In the City of Memories, Ormus appeared before the elders assembled in the great temple. With their consent, he began to speak; his mind was full of many things, but the thought uppermost was that of Mikell and his modest knowledge of the void of zero energy. Mikell knew how to access the void to travel back and forth from the underworld of the Mers to the surface, but only if hidden beneath his cloak of invisibility. What he did not know was that there was a binary world consisting of many loops that linked the new cities around the world's continents, the binary world that Ormus had used during his Earthly lives to travel freely and unseen. Deron and Paul were to have access to the binary loops to keep their army, the Millans, on the move and give safe passage to the Otom.

'It is time to pass this knowledge to the next generation of Otom. The Cunmen must be vanquished in order that the children of the Otom can walk upon the Earth in safety. Deron and Paul are to be entrusted with this information.' Ormus continued, 'Mikell is waiting with his army of Cunmen less than three miles from the City of Boreal, and has sent word to the thousands amassed by the west coast to join him. When they arrive, he will begin the onslaught.' Ormus was sure that Aspheseuos had the power, if only temporarily, to shadow the arc of crystal rainbows surrounding the city, allowing Mikell and his army to vanquish the City of Boreal.

Ormus, having been reminded of life's duality of existence by Mercury's warning to Gemini, was concerned for Lia; he must make sure no harm came to Mikell, her Earthly duality, lest she be forgotten by Hafnium.

'Deron and Paul,' Ormus spoke directly, his thoughts having reinforced his intention. 'You must return to the University of the Third Eye, and tomorrow, with the knowledge that you will acquire there, you will face Mikell on the battlefield. The Otom must complete their return to the surface; otherwise their future will be at stake. And, as you shall learn when you leave here, your mother's future also, Deron.'

Deron looked at Ormus with concern; how could the conflict on the surface involve his mother? She was safe here in the world of the Mers, safe with his wife Mariana and his sons.

The elders moved the proceedings on by interjecting a thought that Ormus had not considered. Mikell was supposedly with the army camped near the City of Boreal, but was he? Ormus had only his thoughts to go on; what if Mikell was not at Boreal but wanted Ormus to think he was?

The elders believed their vision to be sound. 'Ormus, has your concern for Lia clouded your awareness, and is Mikell planning another onslaught elsewhere, whilst the leaders of the Cunmen and their men do battle at Boreal?'

Ormus felt stunned; ice cold energy passed through his ethereal body as he realised that Lia was already in danger, and he had been blinded to it. Words from the past, his final Earthly life, came back to haunt him. *That which is meant for you never passes you by ... Destiny!*

The infant Wootwul, future hope of the Mers, had been returned to Lazuli, his mother, to grow into adulthood. Zrsiofour's warriors sounded the great horns throughout the ocean world to rejoice, for one who was prophesied to lead them into the future was safe.

The infant Wootwul lay cradled in his mother's arms, unaware of the hope that was laid at his tiny tail.

Chapter 54

The Grand Master's Plan

Upon Earth, the voices of the East, South, West, and North walls assembled in the Hall of Chequers: a grey, battle-scarred monolithic building that rose from the wreckage of central London, most of which had been under water for almost half a century. Mercury and Ormus entered the great hall; they had come to speak of Hafnium's plan for Earth.

Not since Lia's initiation ceremony had Ormus entered this place. Some fifty years since had elapsed, but still the bitter memories remained clear in his mind. Before Ormus had time to lapse into the past, a thousand voices rang out.

'Welcome back, Ormus.' The voices of the four directions were applauding Ormus' return.

Ormus mounted the last step and strode through the great black and white doors that stood open before him; the vast space within was known as the Inner Hall, which held the memory of all masters and craftsmen of supernatural wisdom, the unexplained, that which had always existed upon Earth. The ethereal beings of the four directions rested in one form or another upon the walls and ceiling, but not on the floor of silver and blue squares, for this was the sacred space where the games of the universe were played out.

Mercury stood resplendent in the centre of the great hall awaiting silence from the voices of the four directions, custodians of the Earth.

As silence fell, Ormus spoke before Mercury. 'Rumours have

proliferated since Hafnium's plan for Universe Four reached your ears . . .'

The multitude of voices rang out again. 'Where do we, the voices of the four directions, keepers of the four elements of the Earth, fit in?'

Ormus listened in silence to the ocean of self-interest that abounded back and forth. Only the voices of the North, who had promised to protect Lia when first she had stood before them, some fifty years before, remained quiet. Again, Ormus hoped they would keep her safe by protecting Mikell. The voices of the East spoke with the quickness and the babbling of innocent youth, welcoming this most honourable master back within their midst. Ormus thanked them for their kind thoughts. The voices of the South spoke next with quick satirical arrogance, their witticisms unwelcoming and somewhat false. Ormus, remembering their treachery, replied courteously; this was not the time to revive past acrimony. The voices of the West cut in with the guttural sounds of an old witch, welcoming Ormus back, but this time there was no laughter to deride him as before in the Inner Hall. Ormus had proved to be a worthy adversary during the present phase of mankind's evolution.

Ormus turned to address the voices of the North, while they in turn welcomed his presence with great favour. 'My lords, when I last stood before you, I asked your support for the one named Lia; she has proved to be a true "wise one", and all the challenges that have been put before her have indeed been met with true courage.'

The voices of the four directions murmured their approval.

'Today, I bring with me one of the planetary forces, Mercury, who expresses true attentiveness in the twins, Gemini. Mercury is here to tell you what you need to know of Hafnium, the grand master's, plan for Universe Four.'

A deep murmur of interest and speculation swept around the Inner Hall, and when all was quiet again, Mercury came to stand before them, ready to give his address.

*

Rebecca lay upon the big soft bed in the guest room of Lia's home at the Causeway; she had awoken early, her mind full of the dream that had awakened her with a racing heartbeat. Rebecca knew only too well that Lia was important to the future of the Otom; she did not appear to take a major role, and yet she and her generation were the backbone of that which her race hoped for in the future. Lia was an elder for the Otom to exemplify; the elders were the foundation stone upon which their nation was built, the "wise ones", each one bestowed with the Holocene knowledge before man's migration to the world of the Mers. Without their presence among the Otom, the hope of many would waver, and Lia, especially, would need to remain for a while longer while man made this next step forward, beyond the Earth. Lia, and many others of her generation, had been the unseen strength that had brought the younger generations through the difficulties of life in the underworld, with their quiet acceptance of what was to be. For Lia to be taken away now as man was about to surface again would be devastating. Rebecca's mind held the dream again; before her eyes the pictures were vivid, as was the realisation that if what she had seen was prophetic, then there was to be great sorrow ahead for many, and that somehow she was included in this sorrow; she did not know how, but she sensed it.

From the other side of the house Rebecca heard Dorri calling her, or so she thought. Rebecca slid from the cosiness of the pure white sheets and donned her dressing gown; in an instant she was out of the door and moving swiftly down the corridor towards Dorri's bedroom. Again, she thought she heard her call out for help. Rebecca entered the room and went to stand at Dorri's side; Dorri woke up, her eyes wide with fear, and on seeing Rebecca she began to cry softly. Rebecca knew why Dorri was crying; she had seen her own death as she looked into Dorri's waking eyes.

'But you don't understand,' said Dorri. 'The grand master is going to forget you!'

Rebecca seated herself at the kitchen table, leaving Dorri to make tea; in a while they would talk about the situation, in a while …

Rebecca felt numb. She had accepted that she would return to the other-worlds, but this was something new to explore; never to exist again? Rebecca's mind felt like ice; she needed time to understand, and Dorri needed her to explain the dream. Why had she been chosen? And her dream of Lia; now she understood; Lia was to be forgotten.

Dorri poured the tea and sat down at the table; both began to sip the hot tea in front of them, each one silent, holding back the time for discussion while they collected their thoughts, each one trying to make sense of it all. Rebecca thought of Ormus, and her hopes lifted.

'Ormus will make sense of it.'

Dorri looked up, hoping she was right.

Chapter 55

The Binary World

Deron and Paul stood alone in the great hall, the elders having left them to wait for Lia, who was to accompany them to the University of the Third Eye. Ormus had told them that they were to be given access to the binary world that would allow them safe, and unseen, passage to the Otom cities on all continents.

Deron's thoughts were occupied with the reasons why the elders were bestowing this privileged information on his generation. He idled with the thought that perhaps one or more than one of the elders were to leave this world for higher things, and if so, who was that to be? A vision of his mother came close; Deron dismissed the possibility of it being her. With the bestowing of this privilege had come another surprise: both he and Paul were to sit with the elders in the first council, thus according them a primary position concerning the future of their race.

Deron felt troubled by this turn of events; he loved his life working among the ocean dwellers, and the freedom that his work gave him, a privilege that was not given to many. And now the surface was beckoning, waiting for his race to emerge from the underworld and explore the continents above. If he were to become part of the council of elders, then his choices, he imagined, might become very restricted.

Paul sensed Deron's concern, for he was of the same reasoning.

Lia entered the great hall; her thoughts filled with those of her son, Deron. 'Both your lives will be restricted by more responsibility, but you will still enjoy the new life upon the Earth's surface, a life of unfolding beauty that will fulfil your need to wander in open spaces. A new life is opening up for your generation, one that you could only imagine before. And access to the binary world will give you unlimited freedom to explore the world above.'

Deron smiled at his mother and, moving towards her, he embraced her lovingly. Her words had focused his mind. 'Have no worries about my thoughts, Mother, they are already in the past.'

Lia relinquished hold of her son to embrace Paul warmly. 'Then I will accompany you both, and we can enjoy the experience together.' Lia linked arms with them and together they crossed the hall to the circle of great marble pillars in the centre of the temple. They entered the circle and passed beyond the Earth's dimension, their bodies disappearing beyond familiar landscape to the second dimension beyond the psychic plane. Deron and Paul drifted in the amazing spectacle of colour that sped swiftly across the alien landscape in a continual kaleidoscope of yellow, gold and orange hues. For what seemed only a moment, they remained held within the healing light, and then the colour began to change, moving them into a new vibration of yellow and silver, but again, a trillion hues of the same. On they drifted, ever upward, experiencing the unforgettable: the third other-world of learning that was created from the first thought of Hafnium. Deron and Paul gazed about themselves, their minds beginning to take in the steady flow of green that was flooded in a silvery light of unearthly beauty, a vibration only of the celestial, the colour changing in a never ending cycle that healed impurity in all things of physical matter; because of this, both men sensed they would never fear infirmity again, that all Earthly disease had been washed from their minds forever. Suddenly the sea of colour surrounding them vanished and their journey was at an end; before them rose the familiar vastness of the great learning temples within a city of pristine whiteness that disappeared into the far distant horizon.

Upon the landscape, a small speck of colour appeared and began to move rapidly towards them, the dot of blue growing ever larger to reveal the figure of a man encircled by an aura of dazzling blue that to Lia was reminiscent of a Mediterranean sky in the fullness of summer. Raphiel's otherworldly figure came into view: a striking figure, and quite unlike the portly gentleman whom Lia had known and trusted as her mentor upon Earth.

'Lia, I have been sent to welcome you.' Raphiel moved towards her with his arms extended and they embraced, then, extending his greeting to Deron and Paul, Raphiel invited them to follow him.

As Lia walked behind the graceful figure, her thoughts returned to their first meeting upon the Heavenly Mountain that arcs the world, and later, her second time upon the mountain at Ormus' death. Raphiel had taken his place as her guardian, protecting her until the day when she and her family had journeyed to the underworld, and Raphiel had returned to the other-worlds; here lay many memories of the past, fond memories of a true friendship.

Lia focused her thoughts on her charges and the reason they were here.

Raphiel had led them through the entrance of the courtyard and into a small assembly hall, where the initiates, Deron and Paul, were asked to wait. Taking hold of Lia's hand, Raphiel turned and left the hall, leaving Deron and Paul alone with their thoughts.

The courtyard and hall were simple and without ornament; the bare white marble walls towered above them, while the floor space in comparison appeared quite small. Both men, having noticed this, began to study the square hall that they stood in.

'I have never seen space as confined as this, have you, Deron? Look at the walls,' said Paul.

Deron did not answer, but with a slow movement of his hand he touched the wall in front of him; the wall began to move away.

They are ready. Raphiel reappeared as the walls began to fall outwards and a larger space encircled them. The sides of the walls changed to form four triangles, and the memory of the open pyramid entered their minds as they stood within the void. The space around them began to fill with geometric shapes, symbols of ancient law relating to the Earth's construction.

Speaking to Deron and Paul, in a voice as soft as a lullaby, Raphiel began his preparation beneath the melodic influence of the celestial choir's chant, his voice penetrating deeply into their ethereal bodies; their thoughts were now floating upon a cloud of perpetual unconsciousness, as the ten primordial DNA spirals of knowledge were re-awakened within. The preparation for Deron and Paul's awakening had begun. Raphiel asked them to kneel with him.

'The ten primordial spirals of knowledge lost to mankind – knowledge that Hafnium, the grand master, had created and secreted in the womb of the Earth mother, Gaia …'

As the men knelt with Raphiel in the celestial corridor of the void, a gathering of figures appeared around the pyramidal dais where they knelt: old scholars, past mathematicians, philosophers and spiritual leaders of all time. They had drawn near to witness, and be part of, mankind's evolution.

Raphiel continued with the second phase of awakening: activating the ten dormant spirals of knowledge to unite with the two that functioned as man, observing as the spirals located their place at intersections down the structure of the human spine. He continued, 'The desire body is given to man in order that he may use it. It is not to be shrouded or suppressed; it was given for the purpose of experiencing its nature. Religion upon Earth destroyed man's belief in himself, and because of this ten spirals of knowledge were lost to him. Man became the slave of man; he came to believe that a few should control the masses, thus oppressing and supplanting the will that Hafnium, the grand master, had bestowed upon man, in order that he might experience autonomy. This does not mean that all may go unchecked; indeed that was why the Master created the cycle of aging and mortal death, to create generations in all species. The distinction in years allowed the wisdom gained by the elders to be handed down to the younger generations, in order that their young souls should have guidance with the desire body. And I stipulate most strongly, *should have guidance*, for only a fool would allow the desire body of the young to go unchallenged, unchecked by the wisdom of the elders: the wisdom gained from their own mistakes. The Master's plan for mankind's evolution was that the genetic code for each generation would become finer, aspiring to a higher intellect, and the desire body would eventually diminish and become unnecessary. However, the Master allowed his brother, Aspheseuos, an unfair and unchallenged hand. The Master was too generous, his reasoning clouded – not normally his way. The Master now wants an end to this challenge with Aspheseuos; it has polluted and almost destroyed the Earth.

'Before the holocaust, Hafnium's new gift had brought knowledge to man throughout the Earth, but again it was misused as a second dependency. The computer age flourished unchecked, spreading dangerously outwards across the world: man had enslaved man, but not as successfully as the computer had enslaved him.

'The Master has decided there will be sacrifices made in order to heal the wounds of the Earth mother. The source of man's power will not be his intellect; the crystal community, a natural source of power, will provide all that is needed in the new era of the world.'

Deron and Paul listened without understanding the reality of a world where man created his own source of energy; only the elders of their race would have recollection of this. As they knelt with Raphiel, they began to understand that man stood balanced between good and evil, and that their own actions, when making choices for their race, must find a balance between the two.

'Witches and demons are figments of the imagination, conjured into existence by the evolving souls of Universe Four. Aspheseuos is the symbol of imagined fear, and is set apart from the totality of Universe Four, which personifies the Master's creation where enlightened thought exists, "lives". Aspheseuos was created from one thought of doubt: what if? That doubt invoked the illusion of "evil" within Hafnium's universe at its conception. Hafnium deluded himself into thinking that he needed to be challenged, when in truth, he was unsure of his ability to control Universe Four alone. The Master's creation would have been infinitely more enlightened had he not allowed that one fragment of doubt to manifest fear throughout the whole of Universe Four, and it will take aeons of time to eradicate that misconception from the Master's consciousness. But the Master is making a start.

Aspheseuos has become a master at his sorcery, and like Hafnium, he now wishes to bring the challenges to a close. Aspheseuos wishes the Earth and all of Universe Four to become fragments of his darkness forever, and the consciousness of Hafnium to be forgotten. Unless we help the Otom to win this battle against the darkness, then it is possible it shall be so. If the universe does not show signs of recovery, the Master will continue to forget and the first fragment of darkness, born before the light of consciousness, will win the game being played upon the universal chequerboard; checkmate will be reached in Aspheseuos' favour. All will become darkness again if the Master forgets that Universe Four ever existed. There will be sacrifices, as I have said, but they will be given gladly by those chosen; of this I am in no doubt. And we have also much to rejoice about; the Otom and the Mers will fight the Master's battle, and hopefully continue as he planned. Man will evolve and move on, leaving the Earth liberated, for the Master intends to create again, and this time without the influence of Aspheseuos.'

Twelve otherworldly standing stones, resting high upon a plinth, appeared within the pyramidal space of the void. Raphiel and his two initiates entered the circle of monoliths, and the two men knelt before him. Placing his hands upon their heads, Raphiel began to recite an ancient invocation in a language unfamiliar to them, while the song of unseen angels filled the sacred sphere. The circle of monoliths, symbols of healing, began to emit rays of light that moved along each initiate's spine in an upward direction, increasing in radiance as they reached the crown of their heads. Raphiel sensed their joy as each point along the spine was activated by the beams of light flowing through them, the light of unconditional love. Reaching the crown, the beam of light entered the third eye temple of the initiates, transmitting a ray of energy that emptied their consciousness of all thought; twelve coloured symbols appeared, moving into focus and then away, each one assigning a virtue that enhanced the one before and sanctioning their ability to judge wisely and compassionately. The twelve symbols together with the one symbol of darkness, Aspheseuos, were revealed within a cosmos of infinite symbols, Hafnium's fragments of light energy, his perfection and the truth of his being.

The twelve archangels of Hafnium appeared and, encircling the initiates, they bestowed upon them the knowledge of the binary world. As before, the twelve symbols passed through their ethereal bodies, this time causing a sense of mortal barrenness, of desolation, that resurrected the final symbol, the sacred symbol that connected the void of zero energy to the binary world existing upon Earth. This was the most important initiation of their lives; they had gained mastery of the Earth's binary world, and were as Lia and the elders of the Otom, leaders of their race, a great accolade to bestow upon the two men of such tender Earth years. The twelve symbols having been blessed and sanctioned, the two men could exist in the two worlds of matter and the etheric: from this time forward they would be as the elders, able to move freely between the physical and other-worldly planes of the Earth world, and the third heaven of learning. They were gifted ones who would serve mankind, as did Lia and the elders.

Before the Otom and Mers were able to leave Universe Four, the knowledge held within the twelve symbols would have to be accessed and understood by all, as one light-bodied race. This awakening would be realised as they journeyed from the Earth to experience life upon other planets in Universe Four.

Lia looked at her son, a physical being with the knowledge of a Holocene, and the sanction of the archangels. Her thoughts turned to her daughter; at the age of forty-five, she was about to give birth to her first child, late in life, perhaps, but the Otom were living longer and the infant would be one of those to lead the Otom from Earth to a new life upon Mars. Lia felt at peace. 'My work is almost done.' She spoke the words softly.

Deron looked across at his mother; the thought of her leaving their world shadowed the joy he was feeling.

Ormus appeared before him, his words drifting past like a wisp of cloud upon a peaceful sky. 'Your mother is destined for great things, Deron. Do not confine her to the Earth by dreading her physical death. Be at peace, for you will learn as time evolves that you will always be with her. Be at peace.' Ormus hoped he was telling the truth, and Lia would not be forgotten.

In the University of the Third Eye, Hafnium's twelve archangels observed Raphiel and his charges with interest. The two Otom men were now ready to guide their race through the next fifty years, after which the new generations of Otom would make their way across the galaxy to continue life upon the planet Mars. Deron and Paul's first task, however, was to bring the Otom safely upon the surface of the Earth again, there to live in peace with the animal kingdom, and to demonstrate that they were ready for the next phase of mankind's evolution.

With the gathering of the archangels, the spiritual thoughts of all were directed towards the heavenly choir; the symbolic language could be seen and heard above the citadel of the third heaven, music that celebrated the initiation of Deron and Paul, and heralded in the new phase of their lives.

Chapter 56

Thomas

They called him the cannon, Thomas the unbeliever, the profane and breaker of every rule. The untrustworthy one, whose words were a symphony of lies, and those who had the misfortune to cross paths with him hated him to the day they passed into the other-worlds. His word was gathering strength among the Cunmen, and his power as one of the leaders from the north made him an excellent choice of collaborator for the ever watchful Mikell.

Upon the psychic plane, Thomas and Mikell's future was under scrutiny. Aspheseuos was in no doubt of Hafnium's plan to forget him, but if he played his hand right he would become the master of Universe Four. Hafnium had become apathetic to the challenges that faced his universe, he had lost his enthusiasm for the game, and as he became less interested so his power waned and the force of darkness became stronger. Aspheseuos was winning, devouring the light from Universe Four, as Hafnium continued to misjudge the situation.

The twelve archangels were Hafnium's sentinels, his evolving intellect and soul, and their concern for him was growing ever stronger. Was Hafnium, the grand master, really so sightless in his love? 'We may well see the imminent danger but must remain cautious, for advice spoken to one that has lost reasoning could tip the balance erroneously; Aspheseuos could become the Master, the Cunmen remaining free to roam upon the ravished Earth, while the Master becomes the servant of Aspheseuos. The shrouded angel of darkness has played the winning side of the game for too long. Aspheseuos no longer sees himself in the role of Satan; he truly believes that role belongs to Hafnium.'

'Let the one called Mikell be stoned, and let the one called Thomas be drowned,' Aspheseuos spoke with majesty, 'for when they die, the ones called Lia and Rebecca will also be forgotten by Hafnium, and when that happens his future plans will be weakened further.' Aspheseuos laughed aloud, his dark tones rumbling within the cosmos, turning creation's sanctuary to ice.

Ormus and Lia listened to the dark rumblings of the psychic plane, and their souls grew weary.

Lia turned to Ormus and spoke his name softly. 'Ormus, where do I fit into the plan of evolution?'

Ormus held her gaze for a moment, his eyes searching for the faith that she would need. 'Lia, the Master wishes to forget you; it is the only way he can rid himself of Mikell, your duality. And the one named Thomas, he must also be forgotten, and with him Rebecca, his duality.'

Lia held his gaze steadily; she knew what this meant: her past, present and future would cease to exist, and she would be erased from mankind's evolution. All memory of her lifetime would be gone, and like her, her children would not have existed. Lia grew pale at this prophecy, but Ormus could see within her eyes that she did not flinch from the sacrifice.

'Remember,' Ormus said, 'remember when I was leaving the Earth, leaving you behind? I was cynical in my mistrust of the future. But you, Lia, you do not turn away, and all that I can say is that your sacrifice and that of Rebecca will be immortalised. I can say no more.' Ormus felt his sorrow grow as he spoke these words of truth. Lia would not come back to Holocene after her Earthly death; she was not destined to return to him.

Lia changed the subject. 'My granddaughter is born, Ormus, and I hope to see her grow for some years.'

Ormus smiled. 'Yes, Lia, this you will do. You will watch her grow strong and tall and gather great wisdom for one so young.' He held her arm and then drew her close to comfort her, both realising this might not be the truth.

Both knew that if destiny changed circumstance, then the memory of her granddaughter would also cease to exist.

'Universe Four's infinite creation is full of surprises, twists and turns: that is what makes it so priceless, Lia, so perfect in the imperfection of it all. And remember, Lia, there is not one thought created that cannot be recreated in order to serve a new destiny.'

The Cunman Thomas! How could one so unworthy be the reason why Rebecca will be forgotten? Lia sat in her home beneath the ocean, the wall of water that served as a window to her leisure room flowing restfully before her eyes; a moving picture of marine life passed slowly by, the colours magnificent, the shapes and sizes of the life forms fascinating in their weightlessness, and yet right now she longed for the garden of the Causeway, she longed for the air to caress her face. Lia felt confined, and almost desperate, a feeling she had not known for more than forty years. *To be forgotten!* Her thoughts of Rebecca were really thoughts of herself and her family, and as yet, she could not admit to herself that it was real.

During the years from childhood to adulthood, Lia had held the belief that there were other-worlds. The proof of their existence was to come when Ormus entered her life, changing it forever: after that she had lived between the two dimensions of physical and non-physical life, her belief having become a reality for her.

Not many could truly say that, but now she was to be forgotten. Lia realised she needed her faith now more than ever, for without it she felt like a caged animal waiting for slaughter. Lia jumped to her feet and paced the floor. 'I must remain hopeful. If I give in to this feeling of panic, everything will be lost. The future of the Otom will remain, but may move on in a different direction, perhaps into darkness? No ... I must retain my belief in the solid foundation that we have built our hopes upon.' Lia's thoughts returned to her family, and the panic returned. Sinking to her knees she began to pray, 'Master, please help me.'

The light that came was not that of Hafnium, the grand master, but of the archangel Uriel. Laying his hands upon her bowed head, his celestial spirit washed over her fearful body…

When the light had gone, Lia was again looking at the window of ocean and colour, her mind now at peace, for in the light of Uriel's healing he had revealed to her what her purpose was to be, that she and Rebecca had a far greater purpose to fulfil, and in the radiance of his light upon her body, he had filled her mind with the knowledge of her destiny, a future so magnificent, so serene and very much a part of her family's future that she was transformed; she could now face the future and whatever that might bring.

Thomas and Mikell would bring mayhem to the world of the Otom if they were not stopped, but the Master had shown compassion when sending Uriel to do his bidding.

Chapter 57

The City of Boreal

The Otom were unique as human beings in that they could think as one race. The difference in their cultures and status in society had been gradually eliminated while they lived among the peaceable Mers, until their attitude towards each other was one of complete tolerance. This however was not true of the Cunmen whose virtues only merited the self, and as in the past, this would again be their downfall.

Deron and Paul stood beside the military leaders as they gave their instructions to the Millans, priming them for the onslaught as the Cunmen commenced their assault. They had swarmed in their thousands towards the north, looking for the great arc of rainbows that protected the City of Boreal. As the Cunmen amassed at the gates, the unseen army of the planetary forces waited for the Gemini twins to initiate their plan; as Deron watched from the city limits his mind became fused with one thought, that the blood of the Otom would not be spilled.

Paul stood beside him, his face relaxed and without concern. Turning to Deron, Paul questioned his thoughts: 'Will it be so, a bloodless battle?'

Before Deron could answer, their vision was blinded by a radiance they had seen before in the third dimension. The light penetrated the crown of their heads and continued downwards through their spines, revealing a sphere of energy around them. The light continued to disperse outwards until some fifty metres of light could be seen to shimmer about them, and within the surrounding arc of light they saw the binary world, a hologram of loops that connected the Otom cities across the world's continents. They watched as from each city there appeared an army of angels, marching, flowing across the lands, across the surface of the Earth towards the City of Boreal. Deron and Paul watched the army advance, as did the Otom, the race of one thought, one mind; all were seeing the same vision as their elders, Deron and Paul.

The planetary forces moved swiftly across the landscape, releasing the Cunmen's souls from the physical world, liberating the Otom cities upon each continent as they passed on their way to Boreal. The cities began to fill with the sound of chanting; the Otom were chanting: words from the past, words of unity and love that had kept them strong in the dark days before the holocaust. The sound rose to meet the wildlife that had returned to physical life. 'From the point of light within the mind of God...' The Otom cities flowed with angels, and many more were on their way to Boreal.

The Cunmen gathering at Boreal could hear the voices from afar; they stopped their marching to stand and listen to the words, each word chanted driving fear deeper inside their hearts, sapping their courage and making them want to turn and run. Some turned and started back the way they had come, and many of those around the city's boundary dropped their weapons and made to flee. The remaining Cunmen drew closer together, too terrified to break rank and run from the other-worldly army that advanced towards them.

They appeared over the landscape, floating above the city like a flock upon the wing: then swiftly they were upon them. Beyond the first throng of angels, waiting to advance, Odelia and Glashadou appeared upon the unicorn from the world of the Mers. The throng of angels parted as the unicorn passed through, followed by an illusory army of other-worldly creatures that had manifested from the shadows of the Cunmen's minds. Gargoyles carved by stonemasons upon church walls, raised unto life: cherubim and angels, held prisoner on sanctified earth; winged horses white as snow, and with them came the spirits of the dead now residing in the other-worlds.

The unicorn's presence heralded the changing evolution of mankind, with the promise that should the Otom remain a peace-loving race, they would continue to evolve beyond Universe Four to the sixth universe, where physical life was non-existent. The battle was of the gods, the planets and the stars, and with the help of the beings of the other-worlds, a glorious battle would be won.

In the City of Boreal, the Otom watched in awe as their battle became that of the angels, and they prayed that this would end the conflict with the Cunmen. Quietly, they recited the invocation of the Lord. This was no victory; part of mankind was dying; only his past intellect remained from a world of spectacular material progress.

Mikell had never intended to take part in the battle at Boreal, nor indeed had Thomas, who had witnessed the beginning of the battle before abandoning his men. Mikell was safe from death and under the watchful gaze of Ormus, lest any harm should befall him. Lia deserved to see her newborn granddaughter grow to adulthood. Whatever the Master's plan, whilst he remained volatile, as antimatter to matter, then Ormus would use what little power and skill he had to buy Lia time, and Thomas; Rebecca was also deserving of time.

Ormus watched from the plane of the third heaven as Thomas sneaked away to lick his mental wounds, watching fearfully as those about him, their minds dark with insanity, were released from their bodies to be lifted into the unknown and forgotten by the Master. Thomas, helped by Ormus, would be given time, in order for Rebecca to see the Otom live openly upon the Earth's surface once more.

Hafnium, the grand master, listened with a half closed mind. 'Ormus, my friend,' he whispered into the celestial cosmos, 'you are so noble a beast. Why did I not model more upon you? The irony is, my friend, that everything is developing just as it should. The archangels believe I am falling from grace; let them assume it, it is all part of the plan.'

The archangels dwelling in the seventh heaven, where none other than the twelve most perfect can reside, felt whole again; Hafnium believed in himself, and they knew that all would be well. Hafnium, the grand master, was again perfect in his 'wholeness' and in his plan for mankind's evolution and that of Universe Four.

Hafnium turned his attention to Lia: a lighted candle burnt upon a coffin floating in a lake; blinded by the light against a darkened sky, Lia failed to see the giant wave that rose up from the stillness and began to roll towards her. As she gazed into the light upon the coffin her thoughts were full of death. Suddenly she heard the sound of water, and felt coldness rushing towards her before the wave loomed up in front of her from out of the darkness; she realised in that moment that she had surrendered herself to be sacrificed. The wave drove down upon her with a deafening surge; she opened her arms to accept the full force of its power, but it rolled over her and away; Mikell and Thomas stood before her, but she sensed only peace throughout her being. Rebecca appeared by her side.

As Lia observed her duality and that of Rebecca, every sacrifice they had experienced during their present lifetime seemed to gather as one memory in her mind: a force of energy that filled the centre of her forehead, waiting to be released. The images of Mikell and Thomas began to be erased as the amassed energy flowed from her eyes out towards them as a laser burns out disease. Mikell and Thomas began to disappear as the power of Hafnium flowed through Lia, allowing the universe to forget Mikell and Thomas, for eternity . . .

Chapter 58

The Final Challenge

The Causeway: Ormus entered the familiar surroundings of the kitchen, where Rebecca sat drinking tea; he had heard her calls for help as her mind filled with the vision of a stranger, one who had brought to her a dark foreboding. It was time for her to understand the duality that she had shared with Thomas, and that the dream of herself and Lia being forgotten by the Master was no longer a probability; a choice had been made: Thomas and Mikell had ceased to exist, while they remained as part of Hafnium's memory.

'But all things must have a duality, Rebecca, and from this time forward Lia will become your worldly duality.' Ormus gave her his promise that the Master still held them within his future plans, and that they would experience many more years among the Otom.

Rebecca quietly accepted what was expected of her. Only one thing remained an enigma in her mind. 'Ormus, my duality with Lia will be immersed in the feminine experience. If duality exists as one or none, then surely it must be a duality of both the feminine and masculine. I am perplexed by the Master's choice.'

'There have been many who have been released from their duality during the evolution of mankind, and indeed, many other species of life that fill Universe Four have experienced the same. And some, when experiencing a new duality of the same gender, find themselves falling deeply in love with their own sex, which advocates their desire to live as man and wife. There is room for all of the Master's creations, Rebecca.'

Rebecca's life had been filled with selflessness, as Thomas' had been selfish, always putting others' needs first: this had earned her the future she was destined for, but right now Ormus wanted her to live in joy, not in acceptance of whatever the future might bring, and for this reason he called upon the archangel Uriel. Ormus called upon him most earnestly, asking him to present himself to Rebecca as he had done to Lia, and as the celestial light of archangel Uriel presented itself to her, Ormus left them.

Inside the Halls of Chequers, Mercury stood before the four directions with Ormus by his side. And, in a voice as clear as crystal that made those listening recoil with disgust, he began to address the unearthly figures that still squabbled for a position upon the four walls of the Inner Hall.

'The evil burdening the souls that inhabit the psychic plane has left me in no doubt as to why the Master plans to forget them; their needy thoughts and callous attitude have disfigured the beauty of our sister, Earth, and will continue to cast a shadow upon her until the Master acts. Yet still you fail to understand her need to be freed of their mortal bodies, and desire the world to continue as before.'

The voices of the four directions ceased their squabbling, and they turned to looked upon Mercury; this lord of the heavens, so beautiful in all his celestial finery, was as different to them as night is to day.

The creatures resting upon the walls continued to gaze out from the void of mankind's imperfect history, that which had found creation in the darkness of his evil thoughts.

It is time for them to be forgotten, thought Mercury, and he ceased his address. There came a silence as though nothing more would be said, but Ormus knew better, and Mercury cared not.

It was the voices of the North that eventually spoke. In hindsight, they regretted the choices that had rendered the Earth mother barren. In their reticent wisdom, they had deprived mankind of Hafnium's twelve spirals of consciousness, diminishing mankind's knowledge of the universe from twelve celestial spirals unto two. Mercury's presence suffused their shadowy world with light, illuminating their lowly place of abode and reminding them that Hafnium was omnipresent in his glory. Yet still within their own thoughts they could hear the thoughts that Mercury conveyed to Ormus, thoughts that favoured Hafnium forgetting them. *The chains that bind mankind to the voices of the four directions must surely be broken if he is to re-awaken the knowledge of all twelve spirals. Only then can he begin his journey to the sixth universe.* Ormus agreed, while sensing the response of those who listened in. The voices of the North had become like dusty old books, and of very little use in the evolution of mankind; their knowledge was now obsolete to Hafnium's new plan for the Earth; it was time for a new world to begin.

The voices of the East came in excitedly. 'But we are just beginning, why must we be forgotten?'

The voices of the North answered for Lord Mercury. 'We have been brought to justice because we have nothing to offer you young souls, except to be like us, and that will never do, now. The future will see great changes, and we cannot be part of it, our feeling is that the psychic plane of mankind's dark thoughts will be no more…'

The voices of the South and West directions remained silent; if the voices of the North, in their wisdom, accepted defeat, then it was surely the end. There was nothing more to teach the East; mankind's future had passed from their hands. They had reached the final sleep; the walls of Chequers had held them for so long, *so long*; perhaps it was time to embrace the void of nothingness. After all, they had been a part of Earth's history from the beginning of time.

The voices of the four directions became united in their silence as the chequered floor, upon which the universe's games were challenged, began to fade beneath Mercury and Ormus' feet; the walls fell away to reveal the surrounding cosmos, and the creatures of the four directions crossed the threshold into oblivion, the Master eager to forget them. In a vast empty space of the cosmos, Chiron stood before Mercury and Ormus. 'Checkmate!' he said quietly, and he disappeared.

Upon the Earth, in what remained of London, England, the Hall of Chequers that had withstood so many of mankind's challenges began to crumble to the ground.

Ormus' form came into view, his silhouette still rippling from the speed at which he had made his journey across the universe; he had waited a long time to see Chequers fall. Mercury stood beside him.

'Ormus my friend, you do well for the Otom; you must love them very much.' His voice was genuine and compassionate for one who knew nothing of Earthly emotion. 'The voices of the four directions have returned to the globe of healing, to the void, and man has yet to get himself through the next fifty years, before he can leave the Earth for Mars. There will be dark thoughts still to challenge the Otom, but the remaining six star forces that are to work with them will lead the way.'

Ormus answered, 'The dark thoughts being those misguided souls that you have asked Hafnium to spare, Mercury, who will be reborn into the Otom race with great karma to work through; they have left their shadow upon the psychic plane.'

'Hafnium will watch them closely, Ormus, and deal with them swiftly should they upset his plans.' Mercury gave a thoughtful sigh. 'The transition to Mars, with the resistance of the Lord of Mars, will be an interesting time to follow.'

Ormus nodded his head in agreement. 'Indeed mankind's struggles are far from over. The Otom's journey to Universe Six will be fraught with the possibility of extinction. How much time Hafnium allows them to remain in his universe is yet to be seen. They must connect to all twelve spirals of knowledge before moving on; much is at stake.'

Both stood silently observing the vast hole of nothingness that had been Chequers; the earth about them began to heal, and like the mending of a hole upon a torn garment the Earth's familiar greenery began to restore the tear in the landscape.

The star Cancer awoke, her thoughts already on the work at hand. Like the watchful mother that she was, she wanted nothing to go wrong for the Otom and her first thought on awakening was of the two triangles that formed the six-sided star in the gates of the City of Memories. Here was her challenge; her time with them would be exciting, and all the more because it would be through a time of peace. Cancer's energy blazed down upon the Earth; summer was her epiphany, when the world was full of vigour and teeming with new life. The Otom were to establish a new era upon the Earth, and her thoughts were full of joy that she and the five star forces to follow had yet to become part of that blueprint.

As they slept, Cancer guided Deron and Paul to a place in the cosmos where she waited to speak with them. The information they were to receive would rebuild their civilisation to magnificence far beyond the last. The Otom and Mers would begin to merge as one tribe as the Mers left the ocean worlds to live upon the land. Cancer, having told them these facts, continued, 'The six-sided star gate can create an infinite amount of energy when connected with the power of Uluru's crystal caves, the Cradling. The two races will build a star ship that will remain hidden in the underworld of the Mers, until the prophesied time of their departure from the Earth. The void within the two opposing triangles will provide a natural source of crystal energy that will unite with the crystal arcs of each Otom city, providing an abundance of energy, far more than will be needed for the Otom era of the next fifty years.' Cancer returned them to a healing slumber; tomorrow they would wake knowing what was to be done.

The Otom had much to work through. Man's desire body, always torn between the excesses of the four directions, power, ardour, intellect and emotion: this was to vanish from the Earth as all twelve spirals of knowledge began to flourish.

The Great Halls of Chequers stood no longer, and with its fall, the four directions had dissolved into nothingness; only Aspheseuos remained to unseat the Otom's fair play. The darker elements of man's desire body were beginning to fade; he had experienced primary desire in the physical, and now he was to experience desire on a higher level, learning to love in all dimensions of his spiritual and physical life. Mankind would move forward in the next fifty years, never to return to his dark carnal desires; his love would be filled with respect for all, the family, the soul mate, and the civilization that he was part of. These disciplines were to be experienced and perfected before spiritual enlightenment was attained at a level at which they would move on to the sixth universe.

Cancer's thoughts transferred to the sleeping forms of Deron and Paul. Mankind's need for religion was based on thwarting this natural progression, and they must experience spiritual independence in order to relinquish desire without conflict. Cancer's energy flowed about them as she left them with her thoughts to remember when they awakened. *To know a path is wrong one must have no desire to tread it, for then the soul has learned that it is no longer desirable.* This would be the Otom's final challenge, before the planet Mars summoned them from the Earth.

Had Hafnium changed the plan? Ormus smiled. 'The Otom are to draw upon the crystalline energy that is held beneath Uluru to power the new era, and what of the infants, my friend?'

In the great hall of the City of Memories, Zrsiofour balanced upon the edge of the dais, his tail moving gently in the flow of water surrounding him. The two of them had remained together after the assembly of elders had left, both enjoying the heightened sense of peace that flowed throughout the city. For a long time the question of where to find an instrument of power that would take the Otom from the Earth had remained a mystery; the Mers would again provide the means, and would help the Otom build a civilisation far greater than the one before. 'The Mers are to have the same life as the Otom, raising their offspring from cradle to adulthood. Both races will be guided by the power of Hafnium's light, and I will cease my Earthly life and return to the ninth universe, to our world, Holocene. From there I will watch over the Mer infants, who will need my guidance when the angels of the Cradling are gone.'

Ormus' thoughts continued to focus on the future; the crystal rainbows that had protected the Otom cities would become the source of energy to power the star ships on the journey to Mars. The Otom had much to thank the Mers for, and indeed the crystal people, for their gift of a future. 'A crystal's heart is as courageous as it is clear.'

'Blessed are they, Ormus.'

Zrsiofour and Ormus poured out their prayers unto the universe in the hope that all would be well.

Chapter 59

Destiny – Ormus' Gift to Mankind

Lia received a call that morning from the Oceanic data website, requesting an interview; normal life was resuming at the Causeway, and in the Otom cities across the world, people were busy communicating again. Lia played back the message requesting an interview; the voice sounded eager to make contact, but destiny had stepped in and denied the caller access. *Destiny!* Lia recalled the learning process by which destiny delineates our future responses … and for the optimistic caller, well, it was a lesson in patience for them.

Lia remembered the gift that Ormus had left with her, and to the world: unbeknown to him, in the despair of his Earthly death, he had seen and spoken the truth, that destiny was our only pathway and mankind's true salvation. Mankind had been given one purpose, which was to find his way through physical life from birth to death, as was mapped out for him, with only one obstruction, the illusion of self-will, to sabotage his progress. Returning to the beginning of her life, she was reminded of her first lesson, the loss of a parent, and that all experiences needed to be reasoned with and finally understood, for there was no guarantee of constancy; that was an illusion. Man's fear of loneliness, his dependency upon others, was part of the illusion that blinded him to his true course.

'Destiny always leads us, Lia, opening our minds to the right decisions and commitments, inviting us to listen to the spirit within.' Ormus sat down beside her and took her hand.

'When things went wrong, it was because I had remained in a situation for too long, or gone against my true judgement; then destiny would step in, first with a warning tap, and sometimes with a sledgehammer.' They both laughed at the personal revelation that had taken her many years to understand and accept.

'Remember how you felt when first going through the void of zero energy? It seems so natural to you now, Lia. Destiny gives us an intuitive shove as we begin each new cycle of life, which is most times accompanied by a sense of loss as the last cycle completes itself, and we begin to connect with a new purpose, or the purpose of others, those who will help us manifest our new beginning ... Both you and I are feeling this loss.' Ormus sighed. 'Destiny will have its way. We must accept that.'

Lia remembered how long she had sometimes waited for the new connections to be made; how the doubts had been quickly sown, and lack of faith would follow, then she would use self-will to open other doors. She smiled; *all in vain!* 'Will life remain upon Earth when the Otom and the Mers are gone, Ormus?' she asked.

'The Master's plan for the Earth has changed again, Lia.' Ormus suddenly felt weary of all the changes that filled his thoughts. 'The Master's first thought was to fill the Earth with the spirit forms of the wildlife created there. His second thought was to bring them back to physical life; that he has done. And his thoughts now are to create another human hybrid to replace the Otom. The answer is yet to be created. In the absence of the soul's immortal knowledge in the ten missing DNA codes, the desire body, created from two spirals, was to teach humanity to become masters of the physical journey, while searching for the ten missing spirals, their soul ... and I feel that Hafnium has yet to abandon this game.' Ormus had been shown the game in progress: he was a god, who by his own free will had entered the game being played out upon the Earth. But the Otom's challenge upon Earth was drawing to an end, and Hafnium had at last told him of his plans for Lia. Ormus would return to his own world, Holocene; to his people who, with the blessing of Hafnium, had awakened mankind to the presence of his soul. Ormus visualised the game before him, the rules, the defaults; it was hard to believe that the Earth and humanity might all be unreal. With the two realities before him, he began to study the rules of the game. Was Lia, whom he loved so dearly, an imaginary figure in a virtual reality world, the Earth? Ormus had remained hopeful that Lia would return to their world, Holocene, but now sadly it would not come to pass. Hafnium, the grand master, had created a future for her that even he would not deny her . . . but then, if this world of matter was unreal, how could he know the truth?

Lia was woken by a gentle tugging on her arm. Her small son stood by her bed in the darkness of early morning. In the distance the muffled sounds of a baby's cry sounded. Lia focused on her son.

'The baby's crying, Mummy.'

Quickly Lia pushed back the covers and took her three-year-old son by the hand. They padded silently out of the room and down the hallway, the floor cosily warm beneath their feet. Downstairs in the hotel where they lived, Lia's husband and father-in-law had been up for more than an hour organising the staff as breakfast was prepared for the guests. Having put her son to bed, Lia picked up her daughter and went back to bed to feed her. As she sat propped against the pillows she began to recall the dream that had taken her so deeply into the dreamtime that she had not heard her baby's cry.

Her thoughts went to her husband in the hotel below. She smiled, remembering him being an architect in the dream, *as if he would have done anything else than follow in his father's footsteps*; both were mightily proud of their well-known hotel in the city of London. As the tiny form that she held took her nourishment, flashes of the dream came back to her and she pushed them away, not wanting her alarm to be passed on to the infant attached to her.

With the baby fed and changed she put her back in her cot and looked over at her son. Deron was sleeping peacefully again. The clock in the nursery showed a quarter to six. Lia returned to her room and slipped back into bed. The dream returned and she began to panic; the baby in the dream was newly born, and Carlen was three months old. It was just a dream. The thoughts continued and her anxiety worsened; *if our world were to end like that I would rather die.* Twelve spirals of light began to develop around her and Ormus appeared in the sphere of light that enclosed them: Lia returned into her dream to seek the next challenge awaiting mankind.

Other Titles by Barbara Dean

Rattalia's Birthday Stories

Rattalia Rat
and
Musette Mouse

ISBN Hardback 978-0-9572470-4-8
ISBN Paperback 978-0-9572470-5-5

The Progeny of Angels

Hafnium God of Fire
Book 1

ISBN Hardback 978-0-9572470-6-2
ISBN Paperback 978-0-9572470-3-1

The Progeny of Angels

GAMEBOY ♂♀ – THE SPHERE OF HIGHER KNOWLEDGE

BOOK 3

Prologue

The Ten Strands of Lost Knowledge

All life in existence began as fragments, omnipresent beings, of a consciousness known as the family of 'One'.

Nine universes were created within 'One's' consciousness; the ninth, Holocene, held the memory of all life existing within them.

The Earth, in Universe Four, created humanity from the stardust of twelve Zodiac stars in the Milky Way.

The Zodiac forces, having given humanity life in their likeness, directed mankind's evolution under the guidance of Hafnium, master creator of Universe Four.

As time passed men ceased to remember the 'One' consciousness and chose self-rule under the guise of kingship, religion, and other man held beliefs.

The disconnection with the 'One', creator of the nine universes, caused humanity to forget the first ten strands of knowledge that recognised the one omnipresent existence.

Mankind, though intellectually advanced became spiritually sightless.

No longer believing in their spiritual autonomy within the one consciousness, they became bound by fear and insecurities.

Lia's Chronicles

The days of those first dreams awakened me to a bizarre but nevertheless, magnificent future. Like the world of the fast evolving play-station, Gameboy, I witnessed mankind's technology advance to initiate the end of our twenty-first century civilisation.

In the middle of the twenty-first century AD, eight billion people were being subdued by a small but powerful elite group of men and women that ruled the world and called themselves the Cunmen. While scientists dismissed any truth in the rumour, the progress of science had been rapid and secretive for the Cunmen. They discovered that the movement of the planets in our solar system had as much influence over mankind as the moons power over the Earth's tides. Realising the power to be gained, the Cunmen harnessed these forces to subdue or agitate the masses. This gave the Cunmen the power to manipulate an entire nation at will. By inducing panicked migration and mass starvation, they controlled the global population. But the Cunmen had not accounted for the power to be released as the Earth ignited and the oceans rose up as one force over the continents. The Cunmen secreted in their underground sites throughout the world's continents survived; each site giving refuge to five thousand people with enough supplies to sustain them for fifty years.

As the twenty-first century civilisation neared its end, there were those of us that knew and believed we would survive. We developed telepathic skills to communicate with each other. The realisation that we were empowered with the healing energy of the universe drew us together, not in churches, mosques, synagogues, or temples but as one mind – as the 'light workers' of the Earth. We, the first Otom 'the one tribe of man' were to witness the old hierarchical powers die, leaving us upon the Earth to continue mankind's journey.

In my dreams I came upon a life-form that lived below the oceans, a race called the Mer; some years later mankind found their world.

The hidden world of the Mer had been discovered during an exploration of the Marianas Trench, found in the deepest part of the North-West Pacific, which revealed a way into their world beneath the ocean. The site had been considered for the dumping of nuclear waste but the idea was quickly abandoned on finding the riches that lay beneath the Earth's crust. The discovery of the Mer world led to the plundering of its rich natural resources and would have ended in irreversible damage, had not a chain of atomic explosions swept humanity from the Earth's surface. When the end of the last civilisation came the Mers became our rescuers, taking us into their world beneath the Earth's oceans.

The Cunmen remained below the surface for three decades before opening their sites and exposing themselves to the radiation poisoning that still contaminated the Earth's surface. My people, the Otom, remained below the oceans for a further fifteen years before exploring the world above, and stayed free of radiation sickness.

The Otom's final war with the Cunmen saw victory ours, with peace settling upon the Earth for a fifty year period that we named the 'Resting Time'.

During our time in the Mer world a comet passed through our solar system, altering Venus' trajectory and causing chaos in the surrounding cosmos. When Earth and Mars settled into the re-formed curvature of the solar system, life as we knew it had changed. The Earth and Mars were positioned the same distance from the Sun but in opposition to each other. And Venus, when passing near them on her precarious trajectory, caused violent storms to erupt across both worlds.

The shift in the Earth's axis caused great changes in the Northern and Southern hemispheres. The British Isles lost most of her east coastline with five hundred miles of land emerging upon her south-west furthermost point. The scientists among us, when emerging from the Mer world, began their journeys overland to record the changed continents, climate, and weather patterns. Gradually they reformed our knowledge of the world about us. The wildlife returned and we lived peacefully alongside them with the Mers, who joined us in restoring the Earth's badly damaged surface.

Another race we have come to rely on are the spirit people, the Holocenes from Universe Nine. Their spaceships were seen in centuries past, as they monitored mankind's advancing technology. The Holocenes have been life-forms in all nine universes on their evolutionary journey, Universe Nine being the last universe known to them. From there they believe their evolved spirits will return to the void, the final journey of the soul to non-existence. They have re-awakened my people to their 'oneness' with spirit, and now live among us as teachers and philosophers. The Otom call them the giant spirits because of their towering cat-like forms that they change to Man or Mer while living among us. With these giants to guide us we learned about life in the universes beyond our own, Universe Four. Gradually the atmosphere on Mars changed to that of the Earth. This truth we know from our friends the Holocenes – Mars will be a new beginning for our people.

My people now understand that everything in existence is finite. Their minds are open; they accept the stars and planets as living beings of a far more advanced intellect. That humanity is the progeny of these angels of the universe. Because of this, they have regained part of the knowledge lost to them and in time all will be remembered.

The angelic masters of the stars and planets together with the Holocenes have been my people's navigators, guiding us through our final years on Earth.

For the past fifty years we have prepared for the journey that will take us out into the surrounding galaxy to the planet Mars. The years have passed swiftly since my family's return to the South West coast of England; the Causeway, where the supreme council of twelve elders that guide our race reside.

I know that I will not journey to Mars with my family. The time in the Mer world has brought longevity to my people, far beyond the life expectancy of a human. Yet I will not live beyond the one hundred and twenty-one years that I have reached. For in the knowledge that a far more advanced being is manifest in my grandchildren, it will give me pleasure to stand aside as they take their place as elders and lead the Otom to the new world.

I believed in God … later, I could not believe there to be a God in existence … and now all the reasons for mankind's pain are known to me … I believe in a God of Science who adjusts mankind's experiences, and the world about him, accordingly.

The year is AA95 and my people are preparing to leave Earth for Mars. I feel at peace knowing that all is now in place for the Otom to move on … My name is Lia Debarc-Major. We the elders have documented the Otom's journey through the past fifty years for those who will be our future.

www.ingramcontent.com/pod-product-compliance
Lightning Source LLC
Chambersburg PA
CBHW030422310726
48979CB00009B/1572/J

* 9 7 8 0 9 5 7 2 4 7 0 1 7 *